# AN END TO ETERNITY

## A Novel
## Dennis Badeau

APulp Fossil Release

**For the procrastinators, astronauts**

**and hopeless romantics.**

An End To Eternity

**A Note To The Reader:**

While the author has gone to great lengths to ensure a historically accurate portrayal of the era, certain creative liberties have been taken, and as such, there exist several major points of diversion between the timeline of our world and the alternate world of the book circa 1923. The generous reader will hopefully see past these changes as a natural part of the story telling process, and the unwieldy first work of a young writer.    The reader, generous or otherwise, should also be prepared for a book full of lies, half-truths, and page after page of exaggeration, like any good love story.

# PART ONE (SEX)

An End To Eternity

# 1.

# THE ELEPHANT IN THE ROOM

## New York City,    1923

"Any last words, Caulfield?"  New York City Chief of Police, Cody "Fats" Macalister's voice boomed as he watched the executioner in the white coat run his hand down the back of the leather chair, securing some loose end before giving a thumbs up. The prisoner felt the prick of the electrodes up against the back of his shaved head and legs.  Felt the shiver of the restraints at his wrists and ankles.  "If you have a message to give the devil, you'd better make it quick."

Cody almost laughed as he bit down into his sandwich and signaled the all clear to the executioner. The sentence came down with a blast of light and smoke, the prisoner's head reeling back as the electricity coursed through his body.  A crowd of spectators stared grimly as the lights burned out and the smoke faded away, all of them watching as the coroner unstrapped the body and loaded it up onto the gurney. All of them except for Chief of Police Cody Macalister; he was busy with his tuna sandwich, the remains of which he piled clumsily into his mouth.

Speaking of mouths, at that very moment, Betty Macalister, who was pretty, young, blonde and almost shockingly seductive, was using hers to make love to one Jeb Chamberlain. Back and forth, back and forth. Betty moved slowly as she came up for air, crawling on top of him as his hands reached down, fingers slipping beneath clasps, tugging black lace down past her garters. Betty's eyes swam around the dim white walled room as he kissed her breasts, his musk like whisky and cheap perfume. Her fingertips felt at his chin- rough, it needed to be shaved. The room was growing dense, smothering; he traced the ridges down her neck and along the small of her back with practiced hands, their lips meeting, fingertips lingering for a moment before tightening. She let out a long, sweet sigh as he entered. Time slipping by, hands reaching out, groping for the edge of a bed post, grasping for something strong, something-- She screamed as he lifted her up and pressed her against the wall, her legs coming together, tightening around his hips as she moaned. Oh God- A smutty prayer! Oh God- she screamed again. Back down onto the bed, still enveloped in each other, muscles sore. Jeb brushed back a strand of her short, peroxide blonde hair. Her bee stung lips pouted and red, he kissed them again and smiled.

"*C'est le bu, etoiles,*" he whispered into her ear.

"Is that French?" she asked.

"Yeah," he whispered, eyes a brassy, satisfied green as he looked down at her. "It's an old expression.    It means that I think you're more beautiful than all the stars in the sky."

She smiled and kissed him, her heaving breasts pushing up like dusk against his muscular body. "You're so smart."

Jeb buried a grin as he bent down and kissed her stomach.   Smart?   Hell, he didn't even speak French, he just knew women liked to hear it in bed.   *C'est le bu etoiles?*   It could mean anything.   For all he knew it was Swahili for fuck off.

As she flipped him over and climbed on top of him Jeb got that old, nostalgic feeling again.   The smell of her, the touch of her flesh like some flowering consumption, eating away at his self loathing, making him feel alive, even if it was for just a moment.   And then he opened his eyes and saw her smile, and just like that it was gone.

He wondered what was wrong with himself as his fingers danced up and down Betty's bouncing, perfumed breasts.   It certainly wasn't the fact she was married that bothered him.   'Fats' Macalister was a first rate bastard.

*The chump.*   Well into his forties, he'd married Betty, his third wife, after meeting her in a low rent speakeasy in the Bronx where he was collecting bribes. She was only using him of course.   Naive, barely nineteen and all lonesome and alone in the big city, the consummate young flapper decided she needed a sugar daddy.   Rich and influential, Cody fit the bill perfectly.   Betty winced.   *'If only he wasn't so rough with me.'*

At least she had Jeb.

He looked up at her, smiling like the cat who'd swallowed the canary. He was tall, but not too tall. Mean, but not *too* mean. Blonde hair, witty green eyes, and a face that said work.

Not to mention good in bed.

At twenty six he was also nearly two decades closer to her in age than her husband. Sometimes Betty thought she should marry him, but she always thought better of it in the end. She was, after all, a realist, never stupid enough to believe in any illusions of love. Besides, she knew Jeb had other girls...

Across the street in an old cedar rocking chair sat the weathered frame of Martha Masterson. A widow in her eighties, she'd lived in the city all her life. Alone since her husband's death battling the Shawnee more than forty years earlier, she filled her days with cleaning, (Not that her small, fifth floor, one bedroom apartment needed much of it.) and the piecing together of miniature tile mosaics of sailing ships and tortoises. Lately she'd taken to watching the street and her various neighbors through the windows of her apartment. What had started out as hobby, merely a way to make use of the two dollar and forty eight cent telescope she'd sent away for, had quickly become a bona fide obsession. Day after day she watched through the lens, prying and spying and digging deep into the dirty underbelly and goings on of the people of New York.

She'd learned many things these last two months. The paperboy was a queer, for one. She'd realized that more than a month ago, watching as he and another boy held hands soon as they thought no one was watching. *But Martha was watching.* The Tuesday she'd seen the boys kiss she decided enough was enough and threw out the waste from her chamber pot over their heads. She'd telephoned the paper's offices, lambasting them for hiring deviants and mongrels.

It was nice to have someone listen.

Recently though, she'd become more concerned with a gentlemen caller who always seemed to appear at Mr. Macalister's place on Mondays and Wednesdays.

He almost never missed a day, and he came when Mr. Macalister wasn't home. She had been shocked one day, *shocked*, to discover as she peered through the telescope, the form of a naked man who was not Mr. Macalister opening the curtain to the Macalister's bedroom, as what appeared to be the form of Mrs. Macalister lay languidly on the bed behind him. Well, *enough was enough*, she had said after that, and so, on this particular Wednesday, she had gone out to see the Police Chief as he left for work and told him that perhaps he could come home just a few hours early today and there might be something special for him to see. She hadn't told him what exactly. *That*, she thought, *would ruin the surprise*. Martha smirked as she watched Macalister's car pull into its parking space. She was practically gagging on the sheer joy of the fireworks to come.

"Did you hear something?" Jeb asked as he sat up and found the silver, bedside alarm clock. "What?" Betty opened her eyes, unwrapping her arms from around his chest. He looked concerned. "What time is 'Fats' gettin' home?"

"I dunno, babe. Same time as always, I guess," she said hesitantly.

Jeb looked satisfied enough with her answer, and lay back down. It was only five o'clock, and the old man didn't make it back till well after eight.

Betty paused for a moment, a poorly concealed look of concern on her face. "Do you love me?"

Jeb looked back at her, not wanting to lie. Love? Hell, he didn't even know what the word meant anymore. Not since *her*. Not since... Well, it was all just a memory now.

"Well?" she asked again, this time impatient as he stared blankly at her.

He could see the need in her eyes. "No," he whispered awkwardly, looking down. "No, I don't think.... *Sorry.*"

She sighed. "It's okay. I don't love..."

Jeb half smiled and she grinned back at him. She touched the side of his face, her voice coming out like gossip. "I do like you though! I mean, I really, *really* like you."

"I like you too, babe."

"Yeah?" She bit the corner of her bottom lip. "You know you really are the cats pajamas, you just got the cutest smile, an' eyes, an-"

A creaking noise came from the front door down below and the sound of heavy footsteps started up the stairs, thudding drum beats echoing out in slow motion. *"Shhhh!"* Jeb shushed Betty, clasping his hand over her mouth.

*"You have to hide!"* she hissed, a terrified look spreading across her face.

"Where?" Jeb glanced around the small, white room caked in dust and sex. It was furnished sparsely with two white dressers, a couple of ashtrays, alarm clock, an oversized trash can carved from an elephants foot, (it had been given to Cody by the Governor,) and the large, lime green bed on which currently sat the panicked and completely naked forms of Betty Macalister and Jeb Chamberlain, a slow burning cigarette in each of their hands. The pounding footsteps grew louder, like an orchestra building to a violent crescendo as the elephantine figure of Cody Macalister burst through the door, a pistol at each side.

Cody stood motionless, his great hippopotamus mouth agape. A solemn hand pulled off his policeman's cap and it dropped with a dull thud onto the wooden floor. The fat man's cruel eyes squinted, a hint of recognition in the twist of his mouth. "I know you... You work for Jerry, down at the docks."

Betty's hands trembled. "Cody, I..."

Cody shook his head. "You're fucking a bootlegger in our bed?!"

*"NO!"* cried a desperate Betty. "We're just friends! I swear that's all. Jeb tell him!"

"You fucking mook! You disgusting fucking mook!" Cody roared, his piggish face contorted into a grimace as he stared at the half naked Jeb.

Jeb stared back at him awkwardly as he buttoned his pants. "Well I... Look, you two obviously have a lot to talk about so I think I should go..."

"You're not goin' anywhere," said 'Fats.'

"No?" Jeb asked nervously.

'Fats' grunted as he used his index finger to wipe the sweat from his brow. "Don't worry boy, I ain't gonna' hurt ya."

*Yeah right.* Jeb looked over at Betty, nervous, unsure what to do. Could he take on Fats? *Maybe.* But he was so.... Big. Like a bull elephant, like a skyscraper, like a- -Well, like a six foot, three hundred and fifty pound man with all the strength and rage that comes with finding your wife playing hide the hoagie with another man's penis. So *yeah.* Jeb was a little scared. He put his hands up as he walked towards the angry bull. "I don't wanna start a fight here."

Cody's eyes went into angry slits like two dark crescent moons. "Too late."

The bull's fist ricocheted off his jaw. Betty screamed as Jeb careened wildly, smashing into the window behind him, knocking down the curtain and providing the perfect view for the nosy Martha Masterson. Jeb stood up, trying desperately to fight back, but his opponent simply had too much mass and too much rage on him. It was David and Goliath, and he didn't even have a slingshot. A second, more violent punch to the gut startled Jeb, and he collapsed onto the floor. "Shuddup!" Cody bellowed, turning back once again to the now screaming Betty. Martha watched rapturously as Cody slapped Betty again and again, violent red marks covering her delicate face. "Tramp! Filthy fucking whore!" Betty had her back up against the wall, slumped, crying, trying desperately to block her husband's fevered blows.

Out of nowhere, a sudden brutal smash! Echoes of darkest Africa filled the small white room as Jeb hurled the elephant's foot trashcan into the back of Cody's head. The beast released Betty from his grasp, tossing her to the floor as he spun around and stormed towards Jeb, his night stick now in hand. **"Crash!"** The bludgeon splintered the wood of the white washed dresser as it slammed across it. A second hit found its mark, blazing into Jeb's side as he tried to land a right hook and missed. Jeb steadied himself, dodging a third blow from the heavy wooden nightstick before managing to get off a good left cross to 'Fats' face, and knee him in the groin.

The veritable continent of flesh whined like an animal caught in a trap as he collapsed to the floor. Jeb breathed heavily, stumbling back towards the door. **"Click."** He froze at the metallic snap, bloodshot eyes watching the grim figure of Cody Macalister pull himself up off the floor, a gun aimed right at Jeb's head. Jeb stared at him. "Don't do this, you son of a bitch. You'll never get away with it."

Cody snorted. "Don't you know who I am?"

"I mean it. They'll string you up by your neck, 'Fats'. Assuming they can find a rope strong enough."

"Oh that's real clever, kid," he said with a sneer. "You're a known bootlegger who I just caught burglin' my home an' rapin' my wife. Man's got a right to defend himself, don't he?" He laughed. "Hang me? Hell, kid, they'll promote me! Maybe I'll run for mayor on the anti-crime platform."

"Please, Cody, don't do this!" Betty cried through a wall of tears.

"I said shuddup, didn't I, you ungrateful slut?!"

"Don't you talk to her like that!" Jeb shouted.

"I'll talk to her any damn way I please! Now say goodbye, fucko!" Cody said, as he tightened his flabby fingers and began to pull the trigger. Terror gripped Jeb. *True terror*. The kind that can only come from staring down death. Terror deep, and dark, and empty enough to lose your soul in. Sweat dripped off the brow of the bull, his Lilliputian eyes gleaming white with hate. He loved the moment before a kill. Arm muscles flexed, he began to pull the trigger and-

Cody cried out, pain shooting up through his arm like jagged shards of glass from where Betty had sunk her teeth into him. The gun tumbled out of his hand as he shoved her off of him, knocking her to the floor. Jeb saw his chance and dove for the gun, 'Fats' reaching into his second holster with the urgency of life and death. He gripped the handle, pulled it out and began to aim-

**"BOOM!"** The gun erupted in a blaze of fire and death. Time stopped for the briefest of moments as

18

the hot lead slug ripped through Cody Macalister's fat encased skull and dropped onto the floor boards below. He started to gag as he stumbled backwards towards the window, one last cry erupting from Betty's mouth as her husband tumbled through the thin pane glass, the balls of his feet just grazing the edge of the fire escape as he fell. There was a great whoosh of air as the enormous body hurtled down to the ground, before crashing with a sudden, sickening thud.

Jeb leaned over the shattered glass window and peered below. He shuddered, the image of the dead man drudging up faint memories of The War. Splattered with blood, a terrified Jeb looked up to see the frail figure of a women he did not recognize peering at him from the building across the street. He dropped the gun. *"Oh shit."*

Betty ran across the room towards him, shaking and clearly in shock. "You killed him."

Jeb didn't move. The initial shock of what had just occurred was wearing off as he realized what kind of trouble they were in. Self-defense or not, he would never get away with this. He had, after all, just killed the Chief of Police.

He exhaled sharply as he put his hands to his head and tried to think. "Look, just tell em' everything, tell em' what happened. You'll get off clean, and I'll... Well, I'll just have to stay on the lam for a while till things quiet down, that's all."

*"My God."* Her lips quivered as she slumped against the wall. "What have we done, Jeb? What

the fuck have we done?" She began to sob quietly, heavy mascara running down her swollen red cheeks.

"Stop it! Stop it!" Jeb grabbed her shoulders, trying to keep her calm. "We've got to keep our heads here, alright? The bulls are gonna swarm this joint any minute, I've got ta' get outta here, you understand? Now you're gonna be alright... OK? You're gonna be just fine.... as long as you... Just pin the whole God damned thing on me, ok?"

"No, no, no!" she sobbed. "I can't!"

"You have to!"

"Don't leave me, Jeb!" her voice shrieked. "Come on, we'll just tell them what happened. They'll understand, Jeb, they will! You ain't gonna go to the slammer for self-defense!"

He shook her. "Damnit you dumb Dora, of course I will! I didn't just knock off some random shlub, he was the God damned Chief of Police! Now pull yourself together and face this mess we're in." She stopped sobbing as she touched the red swells at her cheeks and looked down with cold, frightened eyes. "Oh... okay."

Quickly, Jeb cleaned himself up with a dishrag and threw on the rest of his clothes. A tight navy undershirt with horizontal white stripes, loose gray pants, and a bluish-gray tweed blazer stained with the smallest drop of blood.

"I could go with you. Run away together," whispered Betty.

He paused in front of the door. "No. You can't." He reached out and put his hand on the knob.

"Fuck!" he yelled as he heard the approaching police sirens, and ran back towards the shattered window pane, jumping onto the fire escape.

"You're really gonna leave me here?" cried Betty.

"I don't have a choice," he said, as he slipped the gun into his back pocket. He pulled her body close to his and kissed her one last time, her lips aching with tears and that mix of longing and sadness that goes along with kissing someone you know you never will again. He lifted her chin. "I'll miss you, doll face."

As his hand left her face, the world weary and tragically young Betty Macalister barely managed a soft "*goodbye*."

# 2.

# SHE WOLF

*"Excuse me, Madame! Coming through! Coming through!"* the exasperated Alan Youngbridge cried as he shuffled through the crowd, moving along the water-worn NYC docks. He could make out his ship, the tramp steamer "She Wolf" about fifty yards ahead. A slight, short British man in his mid-sixties, with heavy rimmed glasses, a long hooked nose, unnaturally thin neck and a noticeably receding hairline, Alan was the penultimate scholar. In his left hand he carried with him a very large, very brown leather suitcase with the initials A.Y inscribed in a cheap gold overlay. "Excuse me," he asked hesitantly, raising a veined, well-worn hand to adjust his glasses. The addressed man spun around to reveal a striking olive face. His eyes beaming, hair slicked back and colored an artificially dark shade of black, he gave a friendly yellow grin. "Evenin' Professor."

"Um," said Alan Youngbridge. "Er, yes, good evening, Captain. How are we coming along then?"

Leonard Virtrolli gazed down at the slight, bespectacled man. "Right on schedule, boss. Should be ready to head out within the hour." A deafening clap of thunder shook him and he looked up.

"Does look quite a bit like it might rain," said the professor.

Virtrolli shrugged in a way that said he was used to shrugging. "Don't worry, a little rain ain't no problem fer' my crew. Sides', what can ya' do about it, amirite?"

A resigned look crossed Professor Youngbridge's face. "At any rate, my niece should have been here by now. You haven't seen her, have you?"

Virtrolli shrugged again. "'Fraid not, pops."

The Professor looked away, cursing under his breath. "Well if you see her first, um, tell her I said to stay onboard the ship, eh? I'm afraid there are a few loose ends need tidying, but I assure you they'll not take long."

Virtrolli nodded. "You's wants us to take care a that bag for ya, Professor? I can have it locked up on board the ship."

Alan Youngbridge looked doubtful. "No. Um, no sir, I.... I wouldn't want to trouble you."

"It'd be no trouble," Virtrolli said with a smile.

"No really," said the Professor. "I assure you captain, um, uh, I promise you, this bag and I will be quite alright together."

\* \* \* \* \* \* \*

Another furious clap of thunder followed the trail of lightning in the evening sky. Sirens blared behind him as Jeb ducked into an ash covered ally on 34th

Street and climbed up onto the overpass. Suddenly a drop of rain. Then another. Then another. Within a minute it had begun to pour.

A long, metallic-silver tram stormed out of the tunnel ahead, banking a hard right as it began to roll down the overpass directly towards Jeb. The train let out a long gust of steam as it whistled, quick Fords and old jalopies scattering about as Jeb hurled the murder weapon into the train's path and jumped off the high wooden platform onto the street below.

The cars honked at him as he pulled his jacket over his head and ran towards the sidewalk, disappearing into the crowd. The gas lights lining the walkway seemed to flicker and moan in the rain, casting thin shadows upon well-dressed people and wet stone streets. Whatever blood had remained on Jeb's cool blue tweed blazer was now washed away, feet dancing in the slippery wet mess as the lone figure turned away from the crowd and ran blindly around the next corner into a dark alley, the howl of sirens nipping at his heels.

A bright electric sign up ahead shown in large pink letters, "The Owl's Trumpet," and below, in much smaller, nearly illegible letters, *"Shoe Repair."* There was a faint air of perfume in the breeze and one could almost hear the muffled sounds of a piano playing. Jeb pounded on the door and a small slider opened to reveal a pair of dark, glimmering eyes. "Good evening, sir. Password please?"

"Open the damn door, Jerry, it's me!" Jeb shouted in an annoyed voice.

The dark eyes didn't blink. "Password?"

Jeb groaned, *"mugumbo,"* and the dark eyed man closed the blind and opened the door.

As Jeb entered the speakeasy the swirling jazz hit him like a ton of bricks. He followed the thumping beats and drunken laughter coming from down the hallway to the padded, red velvet doors. He pushed them open and like a fever he was enveloped by the thick scent of perfume, bourbon and sex. In the left corner there was a beautifully gilded stage on which Effie Proudout stood singing, her shimmering, jet black hair pinned back in a tight bob, skin and lips pale, small patches of rouge on her cheeks. The drunken crowd was howling and dancing wildly as a twelve piece jazz band backed up every smoldering, erotic note of her whiskey stained voice. Her dark eyes lay fixated upon the piano player as she sang out the lyrics to a jazzed up version of *"Ain't Misbehavin'."*

Over to the right side of the wild, raucous room sat the bar. Its cherry and mahogany frame decorated with gold leafed mirrors and turquoise and silver plaques inscribed with clichéd inscriptions like *"Sing!"* and *"Live!"* Three tuxedo wearing old men, two of them bald and one of them nearly so, sat at the bar alongside a regal looking woman in her mid-forties who had evidently refused to turn over her raccoon fur coat to the doorman. Behind the counter stood Jeb's old war buddy, the bartender, Sam Ammatto.

"Sam!" Jeb called, as he sat down next to the giant raccoon.

"Hey old boy, how are ya?" Sam grinned nervously. He was a young man, about the same age as Jeb. Amber eyes, dark brown skin, and a flat, close cropped head of hair. He wore a cost-more-than-it-was-worth silk shirt, and flat ironed gray pants. He was doing well for himself in the booming post prohibition bar business, but Jeb knew him from the war days, the dirt poor days, and at the moment he was the only person he found himself willing to trust.

"So how it goes, man?" Sam asked as he poured from a long, clear bottle.

Jeb grimaced. "Could be better."

Sam put the glass of vodka down in front of him and sighed with the tone of a mother learning her son got in a fight at school, "what happened?"

Jeb downed the vodka in one shot. "Nothing. Just, uh, just you know, bookies, loan sharks."

Sam looked concerned. "Damnit old boy, I keep telling you, you can't mess with people like that. Those guys don't screw around."

"Tell me about it." Jeb sighed.

Sam's face screwed up. "So wadya need, huh? Cause I ain't given you no money. I got my own problems, ya know?"

"No, no, nothing like that," Jeb said quickly. "Just, um, just somewhere to lay low for a week or two. Just let me hide out down here for a bit till things calm down."

"I don't know, man," Sam said reluctantly. "This ain't a hotel. If you need a place to stay, why don't ya go check in at the Ritz."

Jeb searched the room until his eyes found the bar's owner, Harpo Wernheim, an old Hungarian who

Jeb used to know as a bootleggers lawyer before Harpo cashed in and opened up his own place. "The boss ain't gonna mind if I lay low here for a few days."

"He'll mind if you're layin' low has anything to do with Bill Dwyer and his boys. You're not worth a turf war to him, Jeb."

Jeb shook his head. "I told you, none of the bosses are involved, it's just loan sharks."

Sam stared out across the floor until he met Harpo's cool gaze. "I don't know."

"I'm begging you here," Jeb pleaded. "Shit, you do this for me, Sam, I swear to God I'll never ask you for nothing ever again."

Sam rolled his eyes. "And how many times have I heard that one?"

# 3.

# THE OWL AND THE PUSSY CAT

The neon sign for the Owl's Trumpet *"shoe repair"* shone brightly in the evening air as two well to do couples walked arm and arm across the street towards the entrance. The men were dressed smartly in black silk suits. The women, peroxide blonde hair curled loosely around their shoulders, wore short silver skirts revealing blue sequined garters underneath. The girls giggled and clapped as one of the men began to neck with the blonde to the right. The blonde on the left laughed even harder when she saw the powder and rouge smudged onto his mustache as he came up for air.

Meanwhile, a now half drunk, or at the least, very buzzed Jeb was sitting inside at the bar, a half-finished glass of cherry bourbon clutched in his hand, a miserable scowl cast upon his face.

"What is wrong with you, old boy?" asked Sam. "I never seen you act like this before."

Jeb groaned. "It's nothing."

"Applesauce! Now that doll over there's been giving you the look since you come in here, and you ain't made a move." There was an accusatory tone to Sam's voice. "Now either these loan sharks of yours already busted in your nuts, or there's something you're not telling me, cuz' I ain't never known you to pass on a dame before.   Least not one with a caboose like that."

"Firstly, Sam, nobody says *applesauce* anymore, it's passé.   And secondly -wait, secondly?   Is that right?   Never mind.   Secondly, uh, maybe you haven't noticed, but I'm just not in the mood tonight. Ok?"

"Bullshit!"   Since when are you not in the mood?"   Sam laughed.

"Look the truth of it is--" Jeb began.

*"Hey sugar."*

Jeb spun around.   "Ah..... ah, hi, hello there."   He stuttered, trying to smile casually.   It was the women who'd been looking him over.   She wore a short, tight black dress with long, black lace gloves that came up past her elbows, a smoldering cigarette in her right hand.

"I see the way you keep looking at me," she said in a husky voice as she lowered the white cigarette from her lips and blew a ring of smoke into Jeb's face. "You have wonderful eyes."

"Uh, thank you."   Jeb coughed.   He hadn't found her particularly pretty when he'd first seen her, but she was looking better and better with each drink.   She leaned in.   "Listen," now she was speaking in almost a whisper, "I've seen you here before, and I know you've got quite the kisser."   She pouted slightly as she stared down at his mouth.

"Thank you?" managed Jeb.

*"Mmm..."* she purred and tilted her head, angling down as she parted her full, ruby colored lips.

*"Mmm...."* Jeb closed his eyes as he felt her soft tongue in his mouth. His mind was swirling. On the one hand he'd just killed a man and was on the run from the cops. He couldn't be fooling around right now. But on the other hand this women had her tongue in his mouth and her hand at his thigh.... *"Hmmm."* Her kiss was gentle and wet, like soft summer rain. This girl had experience. He moved his hand up the back of her neck. *Ah, hell.* If he was going to spend the rest of his life taking it up the ass in Sing-Sing, he might as well get what tail he could before they took him in.

\* \* \* \* \* \* \* \*

"All aboard!" the First Mate of the She Wolf belted out. The old girl looked beautiful, the reflection of the full moon gleaming off of the black metal portside of the ship. In the distance a short, dark colored figure hobbled towards the ship, an umbrella in one hand, brown leather bag in the other.

"Professor Alan!" rang out the steady voice of Captain Virtrolli. He stood stoically holding an umbrella in front of the wooden gangplank leading up to the ship. "I was beginning to fear you wouldn't make it back!"

"I wouldn't miss this for the world!" The bespectacled man said in a fey British voice. "No sir, I was simply held up by this rather dreadful weather. I say, um, are you still sure we'll even be able to cast off in these conditions?"

"Oh yeah, yeah, doc, absolutely. That ain't gonna be no problem at all," Virtrolli said proudly. "She's a tough old gal."

"And," the Professor began, "I presume Olivia has already arrived?"

"Uh, I'm afraid not, no," said Virtrolli

"Damn that niece of mine!" the Professor exclaimed. "Oh dash it all, we've got to set sail!" He paused for a moment. "We set off the moment she comes aboard, do you understand? I do so hate this dilly dallying!"

"Sure thing, doc. The moment she comes aboard we'll cast off." He smiled his toothy yellow grin.

Professor Alan looked back at him and nodded. "Ah, what would I do without you and your employers, captain? Once again I must thank you for your excellent accommodations on such short notice." He stopped for a moment and frowned. "I do apologize for not being able to reveal more to you about why I must get to Africa but as I told our mutual friends, when this is all said and done it will be well worth your while." The two men shook hands and the Professor started up the gangplank. Virtrolli looked back, a sneer written flatly across his face. "I'm sure it will be, Professor. I'm sure it will be."

* * * * * * * *

*"Ayaba dee doo bop, a deebadoo bop pop pow!"* the piano player sang as he wrapped up his jazz ditty with a bit of scat. Jeb was now lounging on a large,

green leather chair in the back corner of the room, all lit up in sleaze. It had fat brass arms and legs, and big white ivory buttons. There was a tall, gold leafed lamp and an oversized painting of a lion hung on the wall behind him. He sat alone. The trampy dame with the ruby kisser and the gams that wouldn't quit now on the dance floor, petting and stroking some other guy. She'd get bored with him and move on to someone else within a few minutes, just as she'd just done with Jeb. Tramp.

Jeb felt worse than ever now. *Never again, God, I swear. Not with a married dame,* he muttered to himself, as he glanced down at a two day old copy of the '*Post*' someone had left on the chair next to him. "***Lost Tomb of Egyptian King Unearthed***!" screamed the headline. Further down on the page were two murders, a robbery, and a review of the new Buster Keaton picture. At the very bottom lay a blurb concerning the alarming rise of organized crime. Jeb sighed as he saw Sam coming over with a glass of something blue he didn't recognize.

"What is it?" he muttered as the band started up a lively rendition of "*Them There Eyes.*" The air smelled heavily of spilled drinks.

"It's blue," said Sam. "You'll like it."

"Eh." Jeb took the glass. "Cheers!"

Sam looked disquieted as Jeb gulped it down with a bit too much enthusiasm.

Jeb glanced down to see if he had missed any of it. He hadn't. "You were wrong." He grinned. "I didn't like that all."

"You're a lousy liar," said Sam, as he picked the day old paper off the chair next to Jeb, folded it up neatly, and sat down. "Speaking of which, are you gonna tell me what's really goin' on, or what?"

*"What?"* Jeb coughed.

Sam frowned. "Come on. Just tell me not you're not still running liquor for Jerry."

Jeb shook his head and looked down, his hand stroking the brass arm of the chair. "Nah, I stopped running rum for him months ago when the scene got too hot. Picked up a few small jobs since then, but nothing too crazy. Or profitable." He smiled wearily.

Sam shook his head. "Well if it ain't any of the bosses given you trouble, what then?"

Jeb cradled the empty tumbler in his hand. "You remember back in the war. What is was like?"

"Of course I remember. The bombs, the trenches, the constant stink of death. Yeah, it was shit," Sam muttered.

"Mmm." Jeb paused. "The bodies. Everywhere. Sam, I don't like to kill."

"Who does?" Sam sighed. "You been having flashbacks to the war, is that what's bugging you?"

"Something like that," Jeb said dryly.

Sam looked down. He could feel the scar lines in his hands, and the memories of scaling barbed wire fences in the heat of battle. "You know, old boy, what we did... man, you know we didn't have no choice."

"I'm not one for avoiding sin, but look at this place." Jeb stared at the raucous party before him.

"Maybe we're all goin' to Hell, least so says the preacher man."

"Hey, just what are you trying to say about my clientele?" Sam grinned. "I think our souls are ok, old boy, preacher man's seal of approval or not." Jeb forced a smile and said he hoped so. And, for a moment there, not a long moment, but a moment non-the-less, things were alright again. Like he'd forgotten what he'd done. And then it came howling back at him with the shrill pierce of a woman's scream, and a sudden cacophony of police sirens. A dozen cops in blue trench coats blew into the room, shouting in gruff, bombastic voices. Jeb's face went pale. *"Fuck."* The word slid out like paste from a tube, forcing his heart up into in his throat, sending his body tumbling forwards in a cold sweat.

"No way!" Sam shouted, horrified. "This is bullshit!" The cops fired rounds into the ceiling as the terrified party goers scattered out the exits and into the waiting arms of the fuzz. "This don't make any sense!" cried Sam. "Why us?"

Jeb's blood was running cold. "I can't get caught! Listen to me Sam, I cannot get caught." He grabbed his friend's shoulders, a desperate look in his eyes. Sam looked at him almost like he could see what was lying just beneath the surface. "Well no." He pulled away from Jeb's grasp, and the look of understanding was gone. "Come on, I've got another way out."

Jeb winced as he watched a man topple and get trampled under the feet of the hysterical crowd. The bull's bullets ricocheted off the ceiling, breaking off little chunks of plaster and dust as Jeb and Sam slid under the counter and snuck out the back stairwell through the office. Jeb looked back just once, as the cop's pumped tear gas into the crowd and they started clawing their eyes out. "I think we're in the clear!" Sam gasped, completely out of breath as they came out the back door that led from the hidden stairwell behind the bar and stepped out into the still pouring rain. There was a faint redness in Jeb's eyes as he stared up into the rain, trying to wash it out. "I hope we're not takin' off in that tin lizzy a' yers'," he said as they rounded the slick pavement corner, running down the back lot where Sam had stowed his Studebaker Special Six.

"It's a good car!" Sam shouted defensively.

Jeb snorted. "It's a crate, and you know it."

"Well A, asshole, you don't even own a car, and B, you're in no position to be picky right now. Just be glad I didn't feed you to the pigs."

Jeb rubbed the red out his eyes and stared at Sam's third hand, banana yellow rust bucket. There was a sudden crunching of wet autumn leaves under heavy boots. "Hey you, freeze!" shouted an angry, Tommy gun brandishing thug of an officer.

"Horse feathered shit!" cried Jeb. "Come on!" He grabbed Sam's arm and pulled him against the car, just missing an angry flurry of lead.

**"RAT-TA-TAT-TAT-RAT-TA-TAT-TAT!"**
The bullets blew by his head, punching holes into the driver's side door as Jeb jumped through the shattered

window and ducked down.   *"Keys!"* he screamed over
the howl of bullets, and Sam flung open the passenger
side door and slid in next to him.   "You must be outta
your damn mind if you think I'm giving you these
keys!"

"Gimme' the keys!"   Jeb shouted over another
blast of bullets, and the sound of shattering glass.

The Studebaker roared to life with a throaty,
primal groan as it peeled out of the slippery blue lit
back alley, down Park and then out onto East 49th.
The cops sped after them, six or seven of em' cribbed
into every car like sardines.   The city flew by in a gas
lit blur as they soared up over a bump in the road and
sped down the hill.   Sam screamed as Jeb made a hard
screeching right, just barely missing a kid crossing the
street, the car careening so close to him it blew the
moppets hair back.   Jeb flicked the steering wheel
back to the left, turning down a lonely back alley near
the docks.   It was so dark and he was moving so fast
he didn't even notice the broken nail board lying across
the rain soaked road.   Even if he had, there'd have
been no way to avoid it.   *"PIIIISSSSSHHH!"*   The air
streamed out of the popped rubber tires, sending the car
careening sideways into the nearest brownstone.   Jeb
screamed as his face slammed into the dashboard, his
neck nearly snapping with the force of it.   There was
an explosion as the engine ruptured and the car caught
fire.   "Fuck it!"   Jeb cried, his green eyes gone red
with the flames reflection.

"Damn it, this is why I didn't wanna give you my
keys!"   Sam shouted as they jumped out of the car and

into the slick alley. The cops ordered them to stop as they formed a blockade out of their cruisers and came after them on foot. Jeb and Sam bolted, but their running just seemed to make the bulls angrier, some of them going so far as to shoot off their guns as they let loose a particularly bad tempered German Sheppard. With a sudden **KABOOM!** the vehicle exploded, it's metal frame blowing into a hundred rusted pieces, thick smoke choking the air.

"Up! UP!" Jeb shouted at Sam as he scaled the chain link fence. "The dock is just over there. We'll hole up in one of those boats." Sam let out a blood curdling scream as the German Shepherd sank its teeth into his leg. "Good idea, Old Boy!"

# 4.

# BON VOYAGE, NYC

The loud screech of the siren was beginning to get on the nerves of Lt. O'Reilley as he pulled up onto the curb at the corner of Green and Broadway. As such he was happy to be getting out of the car. "Any sight of him?"

"No sir. We lost track of the suspect somewhere around Soho," muttered Detective Umbridge.

"Fuck. He could be anywhere by now." O'Reilley let out a long, disgusted sigh. "Do we at least have a name on this guy?"

"Sure. Girl sold him out soon as they brought her in. Says he goes by the name Jeb Chamberlain, a bootlegger working out of the East Side. Thick headed, arrogant, dangerous. At least that's what the people we talked to said. He was a hero back in the war. Saved twenty men, got the Silver Star. Probably could have made a career out of it if he hadn't been discharged."

O'Reilly stood rubbing his jaw. "What for?"

"Insubordination." The officer answered quickly. "At any rate, the girl says he seduced her, two of um' goin' at it like jack rabbits when the Chief found um' together, went ballistic, opened fire. I guess 'Fats' missed twice before our Valentino wrestled the gun away and blew the Chief ta' kingdom come."

O'Reilley groaned.

"What?"

"Eh, nothin'. Just, you ever feel you're the only one who ain't gettin' laid?" O'Reilley pulled a tin snuff box filled with tobacco from his back pocket and a rolling paper from his trench coat, before making a long brown cigarette in the rain. "You know if the DA wants to prosecute the girl?" he mumbled through clenched teeth, flicking his lighter as he spoke.

"Nah," said Umbridge, "DA ain't gonna touch her. Can you imagine the press?"

"Huh!" O'Reilley smiled as he inhaled the smoke into his lungs. "With what passes for news these days? They'll make the biggest stink in the world outta nuthin."

"They'll rough her up." Umbridge shrugged. "Teach her a lesson..."

"Ha." O'Reilley smiled mirthlessly. "Sure, let the boyfriend hang for it, and she can claim rape." He stood stoic, right hand placed firmly in his pocket as his left dragged up the long cigarette. He exhaled slowly. "Assuming of course... It's a big city." He took another drag.

"Yeah, yeah I know the drill....." Umbridge looked around nervously before pulling a flask from his coat. "Word is the perp spends a' lot a time at a speakeasy down on the West side. They're gonna raid it tonight and see what they turn up. Find out what the owner knows." He took a swig from the flask.

"Oh yeah?" O'Reilley asked with another puff.

"The uh, Golden Owl or somethin'. You know the joint?"

"Can't say it sounds familiar." O'Reilley frowned. "Shame we weren't there to make the bust though. These lowlifes with their hooch and their whores, they don't give a damn about the law. No respect anymore, ya know?"

"Tell me about it." Umbridge raised his flask and took another gulp. "So, *Lieutenant*. Ya gonna miss the Chief or what?" he asked in a hesitant voice.

O'Reilley stopped for a moment to think. *"Pfff."* He took another drag. "That fat prick? Fuck no." He smiled as they both began to laugh.

\* \* \* \* \* \* \* \*

Wave after wave crashed upon the rotting harbor wharf, water rushing up and smacking the feet of the young women as she ran across the silt sand beach. The sound of sirens and thunder shook the girl and she dropped her umbrella onto the ground. Emerald green dress flapping in the rain, short fire red hair blowing across her eyes as she bent down to pick it up. She dropped her overstuffed, hastily packed suitcase into the sand, pulled down at the spokes of the blown back umbrella, and with a flick of her wrist shoved her hair back into place. Her hand cast a black shadow down across her eyes and over her lips as she held it there, shielding herself from the rain as she caught sight of a black ship roaring to life in the distance. She abandoned the umbrella and grabbed her suitcase, her heart going into violent palpitations as she charged forwards, voice screaming out in an English accent, demanding for them to wait.

As she ran up the gang plank of the She Wolf and onto the deck, Olivia swore she could hear the sirens growing louder.

\* \* \* \* \* \* \* \*

"Come on!" Jeb shouted over the roar of thunder as he vaulted the top of the fence. Sam crashed onto the wooden wharf behind him with a scraping thud that sounded like it hurt. "Quick!" Jeb yelled as the two made a mad dash forwards. "That big boat! That one there!" The screaming police, barking dogs and wailing sirens all melted together into a tortuous sonic wall that ran at the two friends. Jeb looked up at the ship ahead, black acrid smoke pouring from its stack and out into the shimmering downpour which seemed to grow more and more violent with each passing moment.

**"Rata-tat-tat!"** One of the bulls fired off his Tommy gun into the rain as Jeb and Sam leapt off the dock onto the moving ship below. They could feel the bullets pass behind them as they crashed onto the deck with a sound like pavement smacking against more pavement. Jeb spun around frantically, looking for any witnesses to their jumping onboard, as he hurried Sam towards a nearby winding staircase and down into the presumed safety and anonymity of the stinking, bilge soaked cargo hold.

Jeb hushed Sam as they tiptoed down two flights of steps and slid across the rusted metal floor, over to their own hidden corner of the cargo hold. Safe behind the towering stack of wooden crates. Safe, at least, *for now.*

# 5.

## HOW THE FUCK SHOULD I KNOW?

The cargo hold of the ship was not a pretty sight. White glazed floors covered in orange welts of rust like cold sores, two undersized port widows with a crumb view into the murky harbor water, and long olive green walls that seemed to stretch on forever with more exposed rivets and bolts than Frankenstein's monster. Big, messy piles of rubbish and debris were strewn across the white and welt floor, along with a few toppled steel cages and a few dozen yards of ragged rope. Large wooden crates and metal barrels cast long shadows across the dimly lit room, as hundreds of gallons of stagnant water seeped out from the boilers at the back of the hold.

"Jesus Christ!" Jeb cried aloud. "It smells like manure in here!" He looked up as he pinched his nose in disgust.

Sam looked over at him. "So where the hell are we now?"

"How the hell should I know?" Jeb shouted.

Sam leaned back against one of the wooden crates as Jeb began to roll a cigarette.

"-I'll tell you Sam, something doesn't smell right, something doesn't smell right at all. We've gotta take stock of the facts here-"

"Uh huh."

"-figure out what we know. And what do we know? Well, we know we're on a boat." Jeb pulled a dry match from his back pocket and scraped it across his thumb.

"Oh, really, a boat? Any other big revelations?" Sam spat as he knocked the unlit tobacco from Jeb's hand and onto the bilge wet floor.

"Hey!" Jeb exclaimed. "What's the meaning of that?"

"Sure, go ahead and get us caught, it's not like it can get any worse than it already has!" Sam threw his hands up as he began to take in quick, shallow breaths, the adrenalin draining from his system.

Jeb stepped towards him cautiously.

"What the fuck happened back there, man?! That bar was my life, Jeb! Workin' there I had security, I had money, I had everything I wanted. It was the first time in my life that I'd got to be a part a something beautiful, something solid and reliable!"

Jeb looked away. "Something illegal…"

"Like you're one to judge!" Sam snapped his fingers. "And now, poof, just like that it's gone. Fucking gone!"

"I know, it's not fair." Jeb mumbled, eyes still avoiding Sam's furious gaze. And he was furious. Hell, Jeb wasn't sure he'd ever seen him like this, at least not since the war.

"Shit, the band?! All the staff? They're stuck in holding pens now, or God knows where, and here I am hiding out in the bottom of a boat. Headed away from everything I worked for!"

"I'm sorry, Sam." Jeb hunched over and began to trace his finger across the rusted steel floor. His eyes dragged themselves across the puke colored walls and up the high, riveted ceiling as he struggled not to look Sam in the eye. He ran his hand back through his hair and took a deep breath. "Why do you think they raided your joint?"

Sam bristled at the question. "The boss probably pissed off a cop. Didn't pay off the right person, how the hell should I know?"

"Yes. Yes, I'm sure that's it," Jeb said confidently.

"…*Yeah*…" Sam looked at him curiously, and Jeb knew then that the thought had indeed crossed his mind. "Jeb if you know anything… If you're being there had anything to do with the cops-"

"Jesus, Sam, you're my best friend, how can you accuse me like that!"

"Just tell me now. Don't let is fester, man, if you had anything to do with it just tell me now."

"How dare you!" Jeb gasped. "How can you even think that I'm behind all this? The nerve!"

Sam eyed him suspiciously.

"Honestly, in all my years, in all the shady, back handed things I've done, you know the one thing I never did was double cross a pal."

Sam didn't speak.

"Look I told you I didn't do anything! It's not like that, ok?" Jeb scratched the back of his neck nervously, his voice strained and beginning to crack. "I mean I suppose there is some small chance…" Jeb coughed into his hand as he shifted his body back towards the wall. "Some tiny, infinitesimal sliver of a chance... I mean, I'm not positive or nothin', but there is a chance that the cops might possibly have been there for me, yes that's true. Maybe. I don't know, all I'm saying is there's a chance that's what happened. That they were there for me."

"Maybe?!"

"*Maybe*. Look, I told you I was in some trouble!"

"Loan sharks, Jeb. You told me you were in trouble with loan sharks!"

Jeb laughed nervously. "Well, yeah, ah, that wasn't exactly, you know, exactly true, *per-se.*"

Sam had stopped sniveling now. He leaned forwards, his face going dark as it moved out from the dim aura of lamp light. "Just what kind of shit have you *maybe* gotten me into?"

Jeb looked back and forth hesitantly as he rung his hands. "I shot a cop."

Sam lurched backwards. "You what!?"

"Not on purpose! Shit, I mean, ya know, like I didn't really shoot him, it was an accident!"

"No, this is not happening. This is not happening!" Sam shook his head.

"Come on, Sam, don't be like that about it. If you were in my position you would have done the exact same thing! Fats had it coming."

"Fats Macalister? You... murdered the *chief* of police?"

"No! No, I didn't murder him. No, that's a very strong word, *murder*; I don't like that kind of terminology. What happened was strictly accidental."

"So is he alive or not?" Sam held his breath. Jeb paused for a moment before shaking his head. Sam covered his face with both hands. "Holy shit you killed a cop!"

"Aw come on," Jeb groaned, "I said I was sorry, didn't I?"

"S-sorry? Sorry?! Y-y-y-you b-bastard!" Sam stuttered, his voice dropping below a whisper. "You have just involved me as an accomplice! I'm as guilty as you are now! They're gonna give me the chair! They're gonna light me up like a Christmas tree!"

"*Shhhh!* Somebodies gonna hear you, ya idiot," Jeb hissed as he got up to face him.

"You're calling me an idiot? Are you kidding me, you damn fool?!" Sam snapped as he made his way towards Jeb. "I ain't lyin', I'll kill you man!"

"Buddy! Pal?" Jeb put his hands out in front of him as Sam grew closer. "Now let's not do anything rash!"

Jeb gasped as Sam wrung two thin hands around his neck, strangling Jeb as he bashed his head against the wall. "You've ruined my life! You've ruined it!" he screamed as he shook Jeb back and forth, his mind a swarming haze of violent thought. "Even if the cops don't catch me, Harpo will blame me for you're being there! That old Hungarian piece of shit is gonna put a price on my head so big I won't be able to come within fifty miles of New York without getting fitted for cement shoes!"

*"Come on, man!"* Jeb gasped as he fought against him. "Come on old buddy, old Sam old pal, you're my best friend, man, my main man, man, the Abbot to my Costello, the tonic to my gin, the cheese to my pizza, the OH FUCK OH GOD THAT HURTS!"

# 6.
# INTERLUDE I

### Summerset, New Hampshire, 1898

*"Push!  PUSH!"*  Cried the old women, as Joan struggled against nature and herself.

It was a cold November morning.  The red-orange and yellow leaves blowing, and billowing around outside of the small, one floor farmhouse of Jim and Joan Chamberlain.  Jim was a farmer.  He grew corn and pumpkins and apples in the rough shod New England soil.

As the old, Parkinson's addled midwife shouted for Joan to push, a cold streak ran through him.  This wasn't right.  *He'd never wanted anything like this.*

Several months ago he'd tried unsuccessfully to talk his wife into a nice, tidy, coat hanger abortion. She'd refused of course, on account a' she'd always been soft.  And so, the next night as she slept, he'd crawled under the covers and done it himself.  She'd screamed and screamed, and of course the damned sheets were still stained a muddy red, but somehow the little bastard had survived.  Jim scowled as he heard his son's first cries.  "It's a boy!" the midwife declared happily.  Jim looked over.  A smile on his wife's pale, pock marked face.  "A boy, huh?" he asked.

"That's right." The midwife smiled. "Misses Chamberlain, would you like to hold your son?"

"I'll take him." Joan was smiling softly as she coddled her baby boy in her arms, a soft blue blanket wrapped around him. She smiled as she gestured for her husband to come closer. A look of something transcendent on her beleaguered face.

"Lemme see him," Jim muttered, lifting the baby up with a rough gesture. "Huh," he grunted, "bit of a runt, ain't he?"

The midwife gasped, and Jim shot her a nasty glace.

"Well," he sighed, "I reckon, if ya' had to have one, might as well be a boy." He looked over at his wife slowly. "One bitch is enough for this house, I spose'. Hey, grandma, how's about you make yerself' useful, and grab me some gin."

The stunned midwife nodded slowly.

"Then you can just get the hell out, ifin, ya' don't mind."

Again, she nodded and complied.

"Goodbye Estelle. Thank you!" Joan said apologetically.

She smiled warily. "Congratulations, Misses Chamberlain."

As the old wooden door slammed shut, little Jeb began to cry.

"Oooh," his mother cooed. "He's so cute. Look at him, Jim. He's got your eyes."

"Yeah." Jim nodded. "I reckon he does."

Joan grabbed her husband's shoulder, squeezing him tightly. "I'm so happy."

"Yeah?"

"Yeah."

"Well, that's good, I guess." He smiled. "Least now we'll have someone else to help out in the fields, 'sides Maurice."

"What are we gonna name him?"

"Dunno." he said with a wide, wild eyed grin. "How's about Ryder?"

"Jim junior."

"Hell no." He scowled. "Even I knows' that one a' me is more than enough."

She smiled back at him, teary eyed. "I love you, Jim."

"Yeah I.... I know."

"Well?"

"Well what?"

"Do you love me too?" she asked, a desperate look in her eyes, the shivering, newborn baby Jeb in her swollen arms.

He smiled. "Sure I do. Course I love you."

# 7.
# CONTINENTAL EXPRESS

First: running footsteps. Then: a loud crashing sound. Then: a deep voice.

Sam dropped the beleaguered Jeb to the ground as he spun around to face two tall sailors wielding pipes. "Aw shit," he muttered.

*"Whuh?"* gasped a blue, oxygen starved Jeb. The sailors hogtied Sam and Jeb and dragged them up to the captain's quarters where they struggled, pleading with their captors. "Sam, old buddy, look, I'm sorry," Jeb pleaded as the sailors tossed them into a brightly lit room.

Sam glared at him. "Can it."

The bright yellow walls of the captain's quarters were decorated sparsely, with only a few select sepia photographs, a nautical map of the earth, thermostat, an Italian flag, and, in the northwest corner of the room, a large oil painting of a black woman dressed in a pink tutu, her eyes staring longingly up at the moon.

The captain's eyes pointed down at Sam and Jeb in a vice like glare, his retinas focused like tiny machine guns. "Where did you find these people?" he asked in a glib voice. His brown leather jacket was balled up on his desk in a way that said he didn't care, and he made an imposing figure in black leather boots, grey pants, and a thin white shirt. His slicked back hair and dark gleaming eyes made him look like a Black Mass fresco. "What are you boys doin', sneakin' yer' way ta' Africa?"

Jeb blinked. *Africa?*

"Look sir," Sam began, speaking in long, drawn out syllables as he looked up and shuddered from the ground. "I am, soo sorry old boy. You see this idiot here is the one that dragged me onto your ship an-"

"Shuddup," the captain cut him off. "These baboons workin' for Sal?"

"Dunno," muttered one of the sailors. "Maybe deys with Dwyer? Maybe Mean Jack Fin?"

"Or Lucky Donnie Dossaronto," mush mouth chimed in.

"Egh." Virtrolli raised his hand to shut them up.

"We're not workin' for nobody!" Sam cried out.

"I said shuddup!" an angry Virtrolli shouted as he kicked Sam in the gut. "We're carryin' some hot shit boys. Who knows who da fuck deez wise guys is workin' for." He started to circle around them. "Frankly," he said as he kicked Sam in the face.

"Oww!"

"I don't give a fuck." He turned, pointing an olive finger at the second sailor. "Macky-- toss 'em overboard. And do it real quiet like, I don't want the professor catchin no wind a dis." He leaned over and whispered in Macky's ear, "We'll deal wit' him when the time comes."

Macky smiled, his bulbous face glowing as he shown his bright, crooked teeth.

"I'm sorry," Jeb whispered, as he lay down on the floor.

"Fuck you," Sam replied, blood trailing past his lip.

Jeb tried to scream as they stuffed the gag into his mouth. The larger of the two sailors threw Sam up and over his shoulder, and the smaller, mush mouthed one dragged Jeb by his feet, letting his head thump across the cold steel floor. Jeb made a vain attempt to escape from the ropes tied around his wrists, his muffled screams clawing at the gag, but it was no use. The second, stupider looking sailor chuckled as Jeb wriggled around like a hooked salmon. *"Heh, heh, heh."* he looked over at Macky and winked.

"What?" Macky asked, a gruffness in his voice.

"Well uh-" he paused for a second, his thick brow beginning to crease as he smiled. "Just like old times, huh?"

"Yeah." Macky smirked with just the corners of his lips. "Just like old times, pally." The two thugs stumbled and slid across the rain soaked deck of the ship, towards the skinny guard rail as Jeb and Sam prepared themselves for the icy embrace of the ocean. Suddenly an excited British voice echoed out across the deck. "I say! "What in blazes is going on here?"

Macky stopped and looked over. "Ah fuck."

"Uh, Professor?" the sailor asked slowly, "is dat you?"

"What the- Put those men down!" Youngbridge gasped, his wrinkled and blue veined hands fidgeting wildly with a small pair of bifocal glasses. He wore a look of disgust on his face. It was a look he'd worn all too often these last few weeks.

Sam was wriggling around wildly as Macky struggled to control him. "This ain't none of yer' concern, Professa', just walk away."

"If you're throwing men overboard to drown, that is most certainly my concern!" an exasperated Youngbridge shouted. "This is a voyage of science, not piracy!"

*"Science?"* As the shadowed figure of the professor came closer, a furious lightning strike in the distance illuminated the old man's face. Something about him seemed familiar to Jeb, but he couldn't say what. Then again, something seemed familiar about all of this.

# 8.
# THE BOTANISTS

*"We're botanists,"* Jeb said confidently.

Sam looked on with a volatile mix of contempt and admiration as a sputtering Jeb convinced the professor that he and Sam were simply two bumbling botanists trying to hitch a free ride to Africa in order to study the local fauna. It was of course total bullshit, but he figured a professor would be more receptive to the pleas of a scientific confederate. Sam nodded convincingly as Jeb told their story, making sure to shrug and apologize in all the right places. Jeb lying his ass off and Sam covering said ass was a routine they'd practiced plenty of times before. The old man smiled, saying that while he couldn't quite condone what they had done, they seemed to be upstanding young men, and he certainly admired their scientific fervor.

"Well there's no time to waste turning back, so I suppose we have no choice then but to keep you aboard," said the professor, as he made arrangements for the two men to stay in the cargo hold while the tramp steamer made its way to the African coast. Virtrolli made it clear they'd be earning their keep, feeding coal into the furnace and swabbing the deck.

It would be hard work and Jeb knew it, but for the moment he could accept that.

The professor yawned as he looked up at the clock. Quarter past two in the morning. "Excuse me, but even the world's foremost scientists need sleep, and I..." he stopped to look out the port window. Jeb followed his eyes and squinted at the moonlit figure as she made her way up the clanging metal steps towards the Captains office. She looked just the way he remembered, with an angsty intelligence, the body of a pin up, and eyes you'd never forget. Jeb had just one question: What in the hell was she doing here?

"You bastard!" she shouted as she entered the room.

"It is rude for a lady to bare her teeth, my dear," the Professor said with a polite smile.

She ran her fingers through short, still wet red hair, her body shaking violently as she pointed at Jeb. "I told you I never wanted to see you again."

The professor motioned towards Jeb. "I'm sorry, do you two--"

"Oh we know each other alright." She rolled her eyes. "Uncle, please tell me you didn't invite him here, did you?"

*"Bonjour mademoiselle,"* said Jeb, a suave, counterfeit French tone to his voice as he kissed her hand. "You look as beautiful as ever."

She pulled her hand back. "Don't think for a minute that I don't remember your tricks, Jeb."

He grinned. "I'm glad they're so memorable."

"How do you two know each other?" The professor asked tepidly.

"We're buttonists," Jeb said with all the confidence in the world.

"BOT! Botanists!" interjected Sam.

"Of course!" Jeb chuckled. "You see Olivia and I went to university together. Studying.... *things*. Isn't that right dear?" He begged her for mercy with his eyes.

"Listen, if this guy's bullshiting us, I'll have him thrown off." Virtrolli sneered.

Olivia's blue eyes held Jeb's gaze, unblinking. "No," she said slowly, "no, he's telling the truth. These two are indeed....."

"Botanists." Jeb finished for her.

She smiled sarcastically. "Of course you are."

"It's like I was telling your friends earlier, we just wanted a ride to Africa so that we could study the local fauna. We really are sorry for any trouble we've caused. I swear it wasn't intentional."

"Oh it never is with you, Jeb." She shook her head.

Jeb looked into her eyes, which were gorgeous and bluer than blue, and made Jeb hope that the shiner around his eye, along with the numerous other bruises he'd acquired over the years, didn't look too bad. As he smiled, a nervous sigh escaped him. The girl stared at Jeb for a long time, her eyes going over him as though she were appraising a particularly bad piece of art. Surely she was having all the same feelings he was, wasn't she?  She had to be.  Her stomach had to be doing just as many somersaults as his.

Or not. She was the one who broke it off, after all.

She grabbed a lit a cigarette from the hand of one of the sailors and took a long drag.  "It's good to see you again, Sam."  She turned and walked away, chin length red hair blowing in the breeze behind her as she opened the heavy steel door and stepped out onto the deck.

Virtrolli waited until everyone else had left the room before calling over Macky.  His voice was low as he spoke, and his dark eyes gleamed in the yellow lamplight.  "I've seen him before.  The white kid.  I don't think he recognized me, but I'm sure I've seen him with Dwyer's gang, bootlegging back up in Montreal. Question is why the girls covering for him."

Macky shook his head.  "The other question is what do you think he wants?  You don't think Dwyer and his boys know about the Professa's plan to--"

"*Shhh.*"  Virtrolli shook his head.  "Not now. Just keep an eye on him, alright?  Any funny business yous lets me know."  He pulled down on the desk lamps hanging chain, and his face was swallowed up by darkness save for a flickering ray of moonlight that cut across his cheek like a scar.  He had a way about him as he passed Macky and left the office.  A sway to his walk like an old jungle cat who'd been pent up in a cage for too long, but never forgot what it meant to have power.

# 9.
# FIRE, BRIMSTONE, ECT.

Jeb heaved yet another shovelful of coal into the ship's mighty furnace, its flames burning hot as a thousand suns. He wiped the soot from his eyes, cool sweat streaming down from his short blonde hair. Another shovelful. He listened to the crumbling, cracking sound it made as it slammed into the roaring flames of the heavy steel furnace. Sam muttered some curse under heavy breath, his lungs filled with black smoke. "She lied for us. For you," said Sam as he choked through a smoke drenched cough. "Why? I thought she hated you?"

"I don't know, judging by the look on her face I think she still does. Maybe she just felt bad for your ass." Jeb grinned.

"Hey don't you dare smile at me, Jeb. You and I ain't done by a long shot."

"Aww, let it go man," Jeb groaned, his hands blistering as he shoveled in another load of coal. "How many times can a man say he's sorry? We all make mistakes sometimes."

Sam scoffed as he scooped in another load. "We don't all sleep with married dames and then murder their husbands."

"Would you stop? Alright? Stop that, it sounds bad when you say it like that!"

"Oh, I'm sorry." Sam mocked him with another gagging breath. "How would you prefer I say it?"

"Like I said, it was self -efense. It could have happened to anyone. Besides, that prick had it coming."

"Yeah. Whatever." Sam scooped up another heaving load of coal and poured it into the furnace.

"You know what I've always admired most about you, Sam?"

"No, and what would that be?" Sam grumbled.

"Your sense of compassion, and what an utterly and completely forgiving person you are."

"Fuck off," said Sam. "And why'd it have to be my bar anyway? Of all the bars in all the world, Jeb, why'd you have to ta' walk into mine?"

He shrugged. "Lack of options? You were the only one I could trust."

Sam shook his head. "I suppose bootlegging ain't exactly conducive to making friends."

Jeb grinned. "Oh you make plenty of friends bootlegging, they're just not the most dependable sort."

Sam rolled his eyes.

"Hey, you know working in any bar under the current political climate is a risky proposition." Jeb shrugged. "Frankly, it was bound to come crashing down around you sooner or later."

"You're an asshole," said Sam.

"Oh I know, Sam old buddy old pal, I know, but just try to look at it all as an adventure!" Jeb said, as he did his best impression of an academic. "After all, this is your chance to pass yourself off as scientist. And thou art always saying you want to travel more."

Sam shook his head. "Scientist's don't say *thou.*"

"No?"

"No, you damn fool, that's Shakespeare."

"Oh." Jeb heaved in another shovelful of coal. "See you're a smart guy, Sam. These are the things they don't teach you in school."

"These are exactly the things they teach you in school!"

Jeb turned to him. "Jesus, I'm *trying* to give you a compliment! Anyhow, we'd better shut up about all this before we get in real trouble. With our luck someone's liable to hear us." He scraped the bottom of the hard metal floor with his shovel before raising it up and dumping it in. Hot sulfur hung in the air, and the fumes brought him back to France, back to Mersei' where he'd nearly died. He closed his eyes as the dry heat washed over him flush with the memory of flame throwers. Back to the sting of mustard gas as it flowed out over the battle blasted trenches and into the eyes, and lungs, and souls of so many men. Corpses falling down into the mud, their death immutable, irreversible, everlasting. Jeb shuddered as a flaming piece of something drifted up and burned his face.

He cried out and grabbed at the seared flesh of his cheek. "You alright?" Sam asked before pausing for a moment. "Not that I care."

"Yeah." Jeb frowned. "Yeah, I'm fine."

Hungry from their work, Jeb and Sam headed up to the mess hall. Jeb ached as he slid open the heaving metal door and walked inside, Sam following a few steps behind. It was an ugly little room, with the cook standing in the back of the kitchen with a soup ladle in his hand, flies buzzing around. In the middle of the room there were three oval shaped wooden tables illuminated by the bright oil lamps that hung overhead. At the first table sat Macky, Louis and Clyde, their oily, leering frames pressed tightly against the wooden tables, Macky's eyes focused tightly on Jeb and Sam. At the second sat the navigator, Percy Piven, along with the radio operator Tyson Biggels, a midget, his tiny hands wrapped tightly around a cup of stale joe'. At the third table Olivia sat alone reading a book, trying hard to ignore the ogling of the sailors. "Well, this is certainly interesting," Jeb said as he nudged Sam, whispering for him to give him a few minutes alone with Olivia. He grabbed a bowl of putrid pea green soup, a chunk of stale bread, a piece of boiled chicken and a foaming mug of grog before making his way towards her. "Two and a half years together, and only now do I finally get to meet your family." He smiled sarcastically.

She looked up reluctantly from her book, a frown on her face. "I was wondering when you'd show your face." She had on a tight pair of white pants, and an itchy looking tan safari jacket with more room for storage than a suitcase.

"It's nice to see you too. Miss me, darling?" He wiped the soot from his face. He smelled like shit.

"Hardly." Olivia sneered, trying hard to make her disgust as obvious as she could. "Look, I'm sure in your mind you're being real charming right now, but I'd really like to be left alone."

"Well I'm sorry, doll, but this is a pretty public place."

She stirred her coffee idly, eyes focused squarely on her book.

Jeb looked down. "Anyhow um... Well you look really..."

"Yes?" She looked up at him, an annoyed look on her face.

"Come on, if you *really* wanted to be alone and read, this probably wasn't the best place to come."

She rolled her eyes. "And where, exactly, would you prefer I eat my lunch? *Hmm?* Would the bathroom, would that work out better for you, Jeb?" She slammed her paperback down, her voice a whisper. "It's been three years! What are you doing, stalking me?"

"God no! It's not like that!"

"And it's bad enough that you followed me here, but did you have to drag Sam along too?"

Jeb reached for her hand but she pulled away. "Woman, there are things in play here that you don't understand. Look, honestly I had no idea you were gonna be on this ship, if I did I wouldn't have fucking come onboard. Believe you me."

She shook her head. "And why did you come onboard?"

"I…." Jeb paused, remembering the way she used to look at him and how differently she did now. "I got in some trouble back home.  Had to skip town."

"Of course you did."  She scowled.  "That's so typical."

"Hey, at least I never disappeared!"  Jeb snapped, a hurt look in his eyes.  "Two and a half years together, and then out of the blue you decided that we were nothing. You killed me when you left!"

"Am I the one who slept with half of New York?" she asked.

Jeb shook his head.  "You pushed me away! You pushed me into doing what I did."

"Aww, you're right," she said, "it is all my fault you're a whore.  Why I practically tied you down and forced you to let all those other women have their rotten way with you."

"You know what I meant.  Emotionally you pushed me into it."

She shook her head, "Jesus, I can't believe I'm listening to this all over again."

"I'm sorry," he began, "things back then were---" He was trying to sort out the words into something coherent as they tumbled out from his mouth.  Before he could finish though, he was cut off.

"Hey baby."  Macky smacked his lips together as he idly unbuttoned and redid the top button on his sleeve.  "What does your man think about you keeping your hair like that?  Most men like a women better with a nice mane.  You know, something to grab onto." His eyes tightened as he finally looked down at her. "If you don't mind me saying."

"Hey you mind, pal, we're trying to have a conversation here," said Jeb.

"Oh yeah?" said Macky.

"Yeah," said Jeb. "Now back the hell off, or you'll have me to deal with."

Macky cracked his knuckles. "Oooh, big man."

Olivia frowned disgustedly. "For God sakes, why don't you two just whip um' out and get it over with?"

Macky's deep sunken eyes shone like flashlights from out of his torpedo shaped head. "You'd like that, wouldn't you darlin.' For me to whip it out."

Olivia leaned forwards, grabbed Jeb's collar, and looked him straight in the eyes, her voice a sharp whisper. *"Don't."* Jeb met her gaze for a moment before taking her hand. His kissed it gently and leaned back.

"This part I did miss," Olivia said sarcastically. "It's like a watching a train plummet off a bridge."

"I'm talkin' to you, boy." The oily haired, oily faced Macky grabbed Jeb's shoulder and spun him around. "Take a hike, why don't you."

Jeb's expression stayed cool as, with as much civility as he could muster, he reached up and lifted the man's hand off of his shoulder. "Last chance."

The bastard smiled crookedly, the sound of a lougie being formed in his mouth.

*Well.*

He'd tried to stay calm, but really, enough was enough. The lougie flew out of his flopping mouth as Jeb's haymaker sent him spinning to the floor. The girl stormed out. Jeb didn't bother to look back at her as he threw his hands up over his head triumphantly. "Who's next?" he called out to the roomful of glaring faces, "which one a' you lazy eyed bitches wants a piece a' this?"

Every warm chair in the room squeaked back and they came at him, pummeling Jeb against the floor till he couldn't breathe.

# 10.
# ATLANTIC OCEAN BLUES

She was standing at the bow of the ship, her sun tan yellow dress flapping faintly in the breeze, a serene expression on her face. Her lips were rough from the salt in the sea mist, and her eyes were accentuated by long, dark black lashes- like soft blue sea glass they shimmered in the midday light.

Jeb walked up behind her, his hair combed, face and hands washed. (Arms still covered in soot, but a plaid, long sleeve shirt stolen off the laundry line covered that up nicely.) "Good afternoon," he said as cheerfully as he could.

She turned around and scowled at him as she ran clear polished fingernails through her hair. Jeb just stood there smiling stupidly. "I don't wanna talk to you," she said.

"Yeah I'm doing just fine, thanks for asking," he replied.

Something warm flashed across her eyes, though she tried to fight it as she turned her face away. "I heard you took quite the beating the other day. Not that it was entirely undeserved."

He sniffed and cracked his half broken nose back into place. "Well nuthin' I couldn't handle."

*"Hmmm."*

"You look nice by the way," he said.

"Thank you."

"The shoes and the dress and the way it all… You know."

"So articulate. What are you running from anyways?"

"Don't change the subject, Olivia. I think you look really pretty."

*"Ugh,"* she groaned. "Save it for those boys in the kitchen. I'll bet they'd love to hear it from you."

"Oh I'm not sure they're the romantic types," said Jeb.

She laughed sarcastically. "What is it you want from me, Jeb? *Hmm?"*

Jeb gave a look of indignation. "Who me?"

"Don't play games," she said, rolling her eyes just the way Jeb remembered.

He couldn't help but smile. "Say! Now how come when those twenty guys-"

"It was three men and a midget."

"Oh come on now, there were at least ten of um. And besides, that midget was jacked."

"What are you getting at?" Olivia asked.

"There I was, defending your honor like a god damn knight in shining armor, and you didn't even care when I got taken down. I mean you just let them come right at me!"

"So it's my fault?" Olivia gasped. "I didn't ask you to stick your neck out for me."

"You didn't have to," Jeb said. "You know that."

"I don't know anything about you, Jeb. Not anymore."

He rubbed his jaw and tried to look away. "Did you tell your uncle that--"

"No," she said flatly, "I didn't tell anyone."

"Thank you," said Jeb.

"Don't thank me," she said, crossing her arms, "I did it for Sam, not you. I heard he got out of the rum running business, anyhow. What'd you do to drag him back in?"

"I didn't!" Jeb reached for her arm as she pulled away. "That kid hasn't made a run in two years. He's out of the game."

She searched his face. "Obviously you're not though."

Jeb threw up his hands. "Jesus, woman, I feel like we're back in Boston going over the same worn out ground all over again! And you, just as self-righteous as ever, judging us all from up in your ivory tower."

"Oh, get over yourself!" Olivia said as she pointed at him, "I'm not gonna do this with you."

"You know that everything I did back then, I did for us. For you!" said Jeb.

"Horseshit!" said Olivia.

"You never cared. Never fucking cared. Jesus, Olivia, I could fall off this boat right now and you wouldn't even care then, would you? You probably wouldn't even so much as throw me a life preserver!"

She pushed her finger into his chest, her voice rising angrily. "And I suppose if I fell in you'd come right in after me, is that it?"

He paused here for a moment. "You know I would."

"Ha!" She shook her head as she turned, walked up to the edge of the ship, and climbed onto the top railing, stretching her arms out like a high wire walker to balance herself. "Say, what are you doing?!" Jeb called out nervously.

"Relax." She smirked. "I know exactly what I'm doing. I dated this amazing acrobat after we broke up, and he taught me all kinds of things. He was a Russian touring with the Ringling show. Incredibly flexible that man. And then of course, speaking of flexible there was Jamie, who, I mean she was just…"

Jeb's voice grew suddenly serious. "Don't do that."

"Don't do what?" she said as she pretended to sway and lose her balance on the black painted metal edge, the mist from the sea coming up, tickling the back of her neck.

"Please. This isn't gonna end well, I promise." Jeb said, his eyes going wide as he watched her step forwards.

"Jeb, you never used to be afraid of heights." Olivia smirked.

"The only thing I'm *afraid* of, is clumsy women with something to prove."

"I have nothing to prove to you!" Her voice grew indignant. "You arrogant son of a--" she screamed as an outsized wave rocked the side of the ship, and she went tumbling forwards. *"Fuck!"* Jeb cried, diving forwards to grab her, his chest pressed against the railing as he pulled her back up and over the side. She sagged into his arms as he lowered her back onto the deck. "You alright?" he asked.

She nodded, the breath gone out of her as she tried to speak. "Let me go."

He groaned. "A thank you would be nice."

"Not on your life."

He shrugged. "Saving damsels in distress. What can I say, I'm kind of a hero."

"You're scoundrel, a womanizer, and a cocky son of a bitch."

He grinned. "Is that all?"

She pulled away from him and he followed her down across the deck, hands in his pockets, thumbs hooked out over the edge. As she made it to the edge of the stairs he put his hand on her shoulder, turning her around as he leaned in towards her lips. For a moment she leaned in to meet him, feeling that old, nostalgic -wait a minute-

She slapped him. Hard. "You animal!"

He ran his thumb across her bottom lip. "I missed you, Olivia."

She pushed him away.

"Baby look, it's gotta be fate or something that we both ended up here, isn't it? I mean what are the odds?"

"Don't," she warned him.

"I see the look in your eyes, you can't tell me you don't still have feelings for me."

"Oh my God. Three years later and you're still in denial!" She pulled away as he came closer, shoving back his hand. "Stop it! You idiot, don't you get it? Do I have to spell it out for you?"

"Spell what out?" he asked.

"My finger." She held up her hand. "The ring, Jeb, look at it!"

He stared at it. "Yeah, it's nice. What is that, an emerald?"

She through her hands up, her voice exasperated. "I'm married, you schmuck!"

Jeb sank back like he'd taken a punch to the gut. "What? To who?"

"Who does it matter?!" she shouted as she shook her head. "You and I, Jeb… I'm a different person now, and whatever there used to be between us is gone. We both accepted that a long time ago."

"You're married?" The words felt heavy and foreign on Jeb's tongue. "I never even got an invitation."

"Jeb, I'm not joking." Her eyes turned away from his.

"How rich is he?" Jeb asked bitterly. "Tell me, dear, which of the ivy leagues did he go to?"

"Don't be an ass."

"Oh, and for the record, woman, I am over you. I've been over you for a long, *long* time."

She shook her head. "Good. I've been over you too. Completely over you. Why wouldn't I be?"

"Good." He scowled. "Because to tell you the truth you're not even as good of a kisser as I remembered. A bit too much tongue for my taste, sweetheart, and you can tell your husband I said that."

She balled her fists as the old, maddening drumming noise pounded inside her head. Drumming she hadn't heard in years. She made her way to her cabin and the bottle of scotch she'd stashed there. God, she needed a drink.

### Boston, 1917

Olivia turned herself slowly within the folds of the peach colored sheets, letting out a warm sound of contentment as he stroked her inner thigh with his fingertips. The moon was just a sliver in the window now, everything in the room dark, black, and that was the way she liked it. Without sight she was only left with the sensation of his touch, the caress of his body against hers. Without sight there was only his smell to grab hold of, that musk and perfume and sweat that she knew so well. "I can't imagine not feeling this way," she said, her lips soft and just barely parted. "Being in love with you."

Jeb brushed away a strand of long red hair from her eyes and kissed her forehead. "Neither can I." He kissed her again, and they wrestled beneath the sheets, feeling the itch of the wool blanket slide against them in the dark.

Even then he knew that it wouldn't last forever.

# 11.

# MOBSTERS UNDER THE BED

### Three Weeks Later

"Oh. Jesus." She slumped against the wall and sank to the floor. Had she really been that drunk last night? The ship rocked back and forth, stirring the nastier aspects of her hangover to life. Her head throbbed as the rain poured down outside, each plunk of water like a hammer against her skull.

Three and a half weeks now she'd been stuck on this God forsaken ship with nothing to do but stave off sea sickness and count the rivets in the wall. There was a deck of cards strewn across the floor from the other night when she'd played poker against him and Sam. She'd been bored and needed company, that was all. There was nothing more to it… There was nothing left between them. Nothing.

Fuck, she hated him. She hated the cruel fate that had them both stuck together like awkward sardines. She hated the way he smiled. She hated the way she kept finding excuses to spend time with him. She hated the looks he gave her, the questions in his eyes that she wasn't prepared to answer. She buried her head in her hands, trying desperately to hide from the world as she remembered just a few weeks earlier when she'd left for this stinking, bilge soaked voyage, and said goodbye to her husband. She wished Colton was with her so badly right now.

Sam motioned towards the ocean as he and Jeb made their way across the deck. Far past the waves he could see the continent in the distance, and only now did he gain a sense of just how dark and mysterious equatorial Africa was, how dangerous and dimly romantic the idea, the whole concept of it felt. "So we'll be landing there, on the Skeleton Coast, eh old boy? Sounds a bit spooky to be honest," he said.

Jeb nodded. "It is actually. You know the professor told me that the Namibians have another name for it?"

"Oh?" Sam asked.

*"Onawungu Gatta."* Jeb gulped. "The land God made in anger."

**"PHOOOM!"** The ships whistle rang out, and Jeb whirled around, staring at it for a moment.

Sam ignored the whistle, his eyes still turned towards the sea. He took a deep breath of the ocean air, and as he did tiny bits of soot, like flotsam, shot out and danced in the breeze. "So, what are we gonna do when we get to port, huh? How in God's green earth are we gonna get back?"

Jeb shrugged. "Ride back with these folks if they'll let us. I dunno. I'm sure we'll figure something out."

Sam could tell Jeb's mind was lingering elsewhere. "Whatsamatter with you, Jeb? Get your head outta the clouds, man, we've gotta figure this out!

Hell, you're the one who got me into this mess in the first place!"

"Don't you think I know that?" Jeb's voice was quiet. "Sam, I'm sorry. You know I am."

"You're sorry?" Sam was exasperated. "What is wrong with you?"

Jeb continued to stare morosely out at the sea. He was motionless. Silent.

\* \* \* \* \* \* \* \*

The galley walls were muted and splotchy, just like the cooks complexion. "Here buddy, try dis one on fer size," he said in a low voice.

"What is it?" Jeb asked as he took the foaming cup and downed it.

"Whale piss," said the cook.

"Same old, same old then, huh?" Jeb grinned as he downed the brown, tasteless liquor. "Gimme another."

Five pints later and Jeb stumbled out of the kitchen in a stupor, trying desperately to get his bearings. After fumbling down two metal flights of stairs he finally managed to make his way back to the cargo hold, only to lie down in a dark corner behind a huge container filled with semi-rotted apples, where he passed out before his head hit the floor…

"Is anybody down here?"
"Nah. Ain't nobody"

*Huh?*

"What about those prick botanists? You sure they ain't down here?"

"Fucking no, Johnny, aight? Don't you wise guys think I already fuckin' checked? Ya fuckin' mooks!"

*What?*

"Sorry Macky."

"Shuhdafuckup."

Jeb rubbed his temples, his head a raging, foggy mess. He groaned. Whose voices were those? He could hear footsteps coming down the stairs. Brooklyn accents, and nasty slurs. Something about gold. *What?* So disoriented. So hung over. *Ugh.* He wanted to go back to sleep.

"….so we trail him, see, and then as soon as that wet blanket unearths the gold and brings it back onboard the ship…." Jeb peered around the corner, his eyes catching sight of a half dozen or so of the sailors huddled in the corner of the room. One of them, a large man with crooked yellow teeth, seemed to be in charge. He drew a long drag from a cigar before finishing. "Then we take him out."

"Two ta da fuckin' chest, huh' Macky?"

"That's right, Biggs."

Jeb crawled on his hands and knees through the darkness, trying to better hear what they were saying. He could see now that it was Macky in charge.

"What about the girl?" muttered a voice that sounded oily and lecherous.

"I think da Boss wants a piece a' that ass first," Macky said, and they all began to laugh. "After that, you boys can pass her around."

"I'm gonna tear that English bitch a new one, baby!" Tyson let out a high pitched squeal.

"I'm gonna heh, uh... I'm uh, I'm gonna squeeze her tits. Heh heh," the mush mouthed Leslie Sacco laughed. "Like uh.... Like a water balloon, or some shit, yeah?"

The murderous mob laughed in agreement.

*I've gotta warn Olivia.* Jeb screamed inside his mind. *I've gotta warn the captain!*

"To Leonard Virtrolli: a toast. May he beat the ever living shit outta any one in his fuckin' path, God bless him," Macky cheered.

"Here, here!" the mob agreed.

Jeb cursed under his breath and decided to scratch that last part.

A pig's squeal rose up over the Mafioso chatter. It was Tyson Biggels. "Hey, what the fuck are we gonna do wit' those two rat fuck biologists, or whatever? Dey gives me da' fuckin creeps."

"I here you man," bemoaned one of the other sailors Jeb had tussled with some weeks earlier, "Those lousy fuckin' pricks, pair a faggot's if I ever saw one."

"Relax." Macky grinned in the darkness. *"Jeb and Sam ain't gettin off this boat alive."*


As soon as the coast was clear Jeb crept up the stairs and grabbed Sam, whispering the details of what had transpired to him as they made their way towards Olivia's cabin. "Forget the girl, Jeb, we need to grab a lifeboat and get off this ship NOW." Sam demanded under his breath. "What do you care what happens to her anyways?"

Jeb shrugged as he knocked on the door before them. "I… I don't. I just want answers." He began to pound on the door more impatiently.

"Jeb? Sam?" she asked in a hushed voice as she cracked opened the door. "What are you doing here in the middle of the night?"

*"Shhh!"* Sam hissed as he pushed past her and came inside, Jeb following behind. Jeb made sure the door was closed tight behind him. "Olivia, what is it your Uncle's carrying around in that briefcase? Why is it you're headed to Africa, the real reason?"

"I'm sure I don't know what you're talking about," she said quickly.

He grabbed her. "Damn it, woman, I want the truth!"

"Get your hands off me! Jeb, what in the world are you talking about, what briefcase?"

"I know this is gonna sound crazy," he said as he nervously rubbed the back of his neck, "and I know things are moving fast right now, but you need to listen to me when I tell you that we are in grave danger."

Olivia raised an eyebrow.

"Haven't you noticed there's something very wrong with this ship?"

She groaned. "Jeb if you're about to try that ridiculous line about the ship being haunted again, and needing to spend the night here-"

"Olivia, would you shut your trap for one minute!" Jeb's voice was deathly serious. "I don't know what back alley dive you picked this crew of yours up at, but I'm telling you, every single one them is an honest to God gangster."

"Gangsters?"

"That's right, and they're planning on killing the whole lot of us, right after they force your uncle to find the gold for them."

Olivia turned away. "Gold? You mean they know about... *Midas?*"

Jeb eyed her suspiciously. "What, like King Midas?"

She looked back at him, her eyes terrified. "Something like that."

\* \* \* \* \* \* \* \*

Jeb's fist clanged against the door of the professor's room. "Yo' doc!" Jeb called out.

*"Yes?"* A fey voice replied from somewhere on the other side.

"Uh, we have something important to discuss."

"Uncle Alan?!" cried Olivia.

*"Olivia darling, is that you?"* He opened the door and stopped, his eyes swimming around slowly, taking their time to size up Jeb. "What the Dickens is

the meaning of this, Mr. Chamberlain? For God's sake, man, it's the middle of the night!"

Jeb did his best to keep his voice down and play it cool, but it wasn't easy considering how he felt. Quick as he could he spun a scandalous tale of double crossing mobsters and Treasure Island conceits that held the professor spellbound. But as Jeb whispered to the old man of how he'd heard every word the gangsters said, little did he know there was someone in the shadows listening to every word *he* said. Little did he know that as he confronted the tired, elderly figure of Professor Alan Youngbridge with his damning accusations, Tyson Biggels lay lurking in the shadows of the hallway, listening.

"Alright, well... Well come here then." The Professor whispered, a panicked look drawn upon his face. "Here," he said as he pulled a book down from its shelf and tossed it to Jeb. "If what you say is true we'll be needing this." He sighed and began to collect his things. "Hurry Olivia, go and gather your materials." Jeb motioned towards Sam and he followed her out of the cabin. Jeb looked down at the small, well-worn book in front of him, its ivy green cover emblazoned with rich black font. "INSANITY DEFENSE?" he read. "What the hell am I supposed to do with this, read it out loud and bore them to death?"

"Open it up, lad," the professor said absent mindedly, as he held up a large brass instrument covered in dials and switches, examining it for a moment before dropping it down into the oversized brown suitcase.

Jeb stared at the old book and lifted up the cover. *It was hollowed out.* Inside the chunk of missing pages lay a small brown revolver which Jeb quickly tucked into the back of his trouser pants. "I had no idea you were so well armed."

The professor frowned. "One never knows what the situation may call for."

"I know, but *this*." Jeb paused. "What is this, Smith and Wesson?"

"Saxon," the professor replied, "9 millimeter."

"Huh." Jeb turned the pistol over in his hand.

"I don't suppose a botanist has any sort of experience with that type of thing," the professor said quietly.

"No more so than an archaeologist, I'm sure," replied Jeb.

The professor opened his mouth as if to say something, before pausing. A frown slid across his face and his posture stiffened. A sudden, angry look about his entire person, he lay down the mechanical instrument he'd been holding and turned to face Jeb.

"What?" Jeb asked.

"Nothing." Professor Youngbridge scowled. "It's just that you come here with this fantastic, wild eyed story about gangsters and gun molls, and how ...and how we need to escape with you. How we need to run away from the safety of this ship, and....and go..." He glared at Jeb, a fiercely suspicious look in his eyes. "Away with you. *You* and that other stowaway, Sam." He snickered callously. "My God. It's been a set up from the beginning, hasn't it?"

"Yeah. Yeah, that's what I've been saying. Somebody must of found out about your work, and set you up with these gangsters."

"Yes, *someone* did know about my work, and undoubtedly I have been set up, but not by a whole ship load of Mafiosi. *By you.*"

"Me?" Jeb asked.

"I can't believe I didn't see it sooner. It's all so obvious. Two stowaways? Botanists? Ha! I think not! I knew there was something wrong with you two from the moment I first laid eyes on you. That time you complimented me on my *rosalias*. A first year botany student would have known they were *zanzabushes*! What kind of a fool do you take me for anyhow? At the time I shrugged it off, but now-"

"Doc', listen to me, you've got this all wrong."

"Oh, no, Mr. Chamberlain, if that is your real name, it is you who's got it wrong." He pulled a sharp, brass letter opener from his back pocket, wielding it like a knife. "How much is my brother paying you two anyhow? To steal my life's work? My fortune? The backstabbing cretin, he'll never take this from me, NEVER!" The professor lunged like something feral. "And neither will *you.*"

"Buster, I didn't even know you had a brother, let alone work for him!" an outraged Jeb protested, as he leapt backwards.

"LIAR!" shouted the angry Alan Youngbridge. "You filthy liar! I'll have you hanged for this treachery!" He swung at Jeb's throat, makeshift dagger in hand. "I'll kill you!" Jeb turned, barley dodging the old mans fevered blow. A shuffle of feet and a quick woosh of air and again Jeb leapt back as the Professor dove for his stomach. Reluctantly he moved his hand back and gripped the cool handle of the revolver. "Don't make me do it," said Jeb.

"Do what? Ya' gonna kill me, you thief?!" the professor screamed.

"I'm your friend, Doc'. I'm tryin' to help you here!"

"That's a laugh!" A wild look in his needy eyes, he arched back his arm, preparing to hurl his weapon when-

**"Ooow!"** A battered figure fell to the floor.

"Olivia!" Jeb rushed to her side.

"Don't nobody move!" Macky ordered them, Tommy gun pointed squarely at Jeb's chest.

*"Oh my."* The dumbstruck old man dropped the letter opener to the ground as a dark shadowed figure walked into the cabin. He was humming an old tune, his voice like black velvet. "Hello Professa'," Virtrolli said, his lips turned up, smiling wickedly. "Pleasure ta see ya'."

# 12.

# HENS IN THE FOX HOUSE

Some time had passed between Professor Youngbridge's rude awakening concerning his travel arrangements and his current dilemma which involved not one, but two gun barrels pressed up against his face. The already heavy fog rising up off the sea was only growing denser as the ship approached land. Monstrous, unforgiving waves rocked the steel mammoth back and forth, as the sound of far off animal roars and jungle drums poured forth from darkest imagination. *They had arrived.* Jeb looked out in awe and terror at the bleak sight of the Skeleton Coast. The Namibians hadn't exaggerated; it was the most desolate thing he had ever seen. Massive black cliffs rose up out of the ocean around it, standing sentinel like gate keepers at the mouth of hell. The coast line, a barren desert, stretched on for miles and miles as far as the eye could see, and the massive rusting hulls of forgotten ship wrecks rose up out of the fog like gravestones.

At least Jeb and Sam were still alive. *For now.* As was the professor and his beguiling niece. Olivia pleaded with their captors, but it was no use. Virtrolli came down the winding stairway from up in his office and stepped onto the exposed deck bellow. His hair a slick black oil stain, jaw strong and wide like a B movie star, he wore a six round pistol in a holster around his waist, a brown leather jacket he'd brought back from South East Asia, and a pair of boots that were just as wet as the waves that crashed over the port side deck.

"Professa'," he said with a smile, "how unfortunate we should find ourselves here."

"You bastard!" Youngbridge cried, still clutching tightly to his large, brown suitcase. "I trusted you! We had a deal!"

*"Oh please."* Virtrolli drew his gun from its holster, turning it over in his hands as he circled around the professor like a vulture. "You trusted me? Really? You trusted me? Hell, you wouldn't even tell me why you were headed to the dark continent."

"The gentleman I found you through said that didn't matter. He said you wouldn't ask questions. Besides, it's quickly becoming apparent to me that you already know *why.*"

"Gentleman, eh? Is that what you call that rat, Donnie Binzwitch? In case you ain't figured it out yet, Doc, he's the one who sold you out. Here's a tip -never let a shadow broker plan your travel arrangements- least, not one who's in debt to the mob."

"No..." said Youngbridge.

"A, yeah, *duh.* God damn it you're stupid, for bein' so smart."

"And you're an animal."

Virtrolli frowned. "Enough with the sweet talk, Doc, truth of it is I know everything. You're not just after some old Brontosaurus bones or an African relic. You two are goin' after something far more profitable."

"We are going after what may be the most important archaeological find of the decade, if not the century!" the professor cried defensively.

"Biggest of the century, huh? I think Carter already beat you to the punch, Alan. Or don't you read the papers?"

"Tutankhamen's tomb may be impressive on its own merits, but it's child's play compared to that of Midas!"

"I'll say. How much of a payday are we expecting to find down there, anyhow?"

"It's not the gold, you fool, it's where it came from. It's all in the map!" The professor was screaming as he strained against his restraints. "The eastern coast of North America navigated over two thousand years ago by the Greeks?! Can you even imagine? Do you realize the implications?"

"The only implication I care about is that this shit is worth enough to the big boss that he sent me half way around the world to get it." Virtrolli sneered as he cocked the barrel of his gun. "Now you're gonna lead a couple of my boy's ashore with you and dig up everything that's down there. You'll bring it all back, see, and if it's worth enough for this whole fucking trip to have been worth my time, *maybe* I'll let yer' pretty little niece here live. *Comprende?"*

The Professor acquiesced with a nod.

"NO!" Olivia cried. "Uncle you can't! You can't just hand over your work to this pack of thieves!"

"My dear, I'm afraid I have no choice," the old man sighed.

"Listen to your uncle, girl. He's a smart man. Unlike these two," Virtrolli said, gesturing towards Sam and Jeb. "I shoulda' tossed you mooks overboard the night I found you."

"Now's your chance," said Jeb.

Virtrolli snapped his fingers and two undersized gorillas in white sailor's suits hauled Jeb and Sam through the thick cloud of fog to the back of the rocking, tumbling boat. Olivia was still shrieking when Macky pistol whipped her across her face, bloodying her cheek. Sam flailed wildly as one of the sailors pushed him up against the railing, another of them holding Jeb's hands tightly behind his back, immobilizing him. The sailor sneered at Jeb as he tightened his grip on the trigger and whispered, "*first you watch*." Jeb thought back to that fateful day, just a few weeks ago at Betty Macalister's apartment. Thought of how it had felt to pull the trigger then. Trace memory of the event stained his muscles. Memories of the men he'd killed. He rocketed his head forwards like a weapon, ramming it into the sailor's chest, knocking him off the slippery deck and into the raging waters bellow.

In the confusion the second thug's grip let loose, and Jeb reached down into the back of his pants and pulled out the concealed revolver, blasting the man twice in the face. **"Pow!"** Another fat nosed slug and the mush mouthed Leslie Sacco got what was coming to him and more, as his wrecked skull fell to the deck like a smashed pumpkin.

"Sounds like it's over, doll face," Leonard Virtrolli snickered, as he stared into the opaque wall of fog crossing the deck.

Tears were running down her face. She knew Sam and Jeb were dead. "I swear to God I'll kill you, Virtrolli!" she hissed. "You're dead -DEAD- do you hear me?!" She shook, struggling to free herself from the thug's embrace.

"Would you stop it?" The thug holding her muttered, barley able to restrain her.

"I hate you!" she screamed at Virtrolli.

"That's alright, baby, I like um feisty," he said as he stepped towards her, running his finger beneath her chin and down her neck. His breath was hot against her ear as he whispered to her how long he'd been waiting for this moment. "We're gonna have some fun, ain't we, sweet cheeks?"

Olivia spat in his face. "Fuck you."

Virtrolli stopped to wipe away the spit. "You'll pay for that," he said, raising his hand. "I'll--" suddenly he looked up, a shocked look upon his face.

"Hands off, mother fucker!" Jeb commanded as he pulled the trigger, the bullet sending Virtrolli to the ground, as Sam's stolen Tommy gun screamed, spraying bullets into the crowd of sailors as he burst out from the fog.

Jeb ducked as he ran forwards, grabbing Olivia's hand and pulling her to her feet. "Come on!" he screamed as a hail of bullets made it clear they were still outnumbered. "Let's get the hell outta' here!"

"And go where?" she said, panicked, as the bullets flew by her head.

Jeb dived behind cover, pulling her close against his chest. "You remember how to swim, right?"

"Sure." Olivia nodded. "Afraid I don't have my bathing suit though."

A burst of gunfire exploded behind them as Sam stumbled through the fog. "You alright?" Jeb asked.

"Peachy." Sam groaned. "Just like the old days."

Olivia grabbed the gun from his hands. "Give me that."

"The hell do you think you're doing?" Jeb gasped, holding her back as she struggled to make her way out from behind cover.

"Let go, I'm getting my uncle! I'm sure as hell not about to leave him here."

**"SCREEEECH!"** The hull of the She Wolf scrapped across one of the huge, jagged rocks jutting out from the sea. Men tumbled and fell as the ship raised up on one side, Jeb, Sam and Olivia sliding across the deck before smashing into the railing. Water flooded the lower decks. *"She"* was sinking.

Jeb tore the gun from out of her hands. "Give me that!"

"Uncle Alan!" she cried.

"I'll get him, I'll get him!" Jeb groaned. "Don't get your panties in a bunch." Water continued to flood the lower decks and the ship rolled the other side, sending half the crew down into the raging seas. "Alright you fish, time to swim!" Jeb screamed, gripping the railing tightly. "Don't let go of him, okay?" Jeb said as he helped Olivia and Sam up and over the railing. He brought his face close to hers, as he brushed back a strand of short, silky red hair from across her brow. "I'll see you on the shore," he said as she and Sam leapt backwards into the raging waters below.

With a sudden, terrible lurch the ship rolled again, this time righting itself flat in the water. "Professor!" Jeb called out wildly, as he scurried across the sopping wet deck. "Where are you?!"

"I'm coming, I'm coming!" a familiar voice cried, as the old man emerged from the dense fog.

"Faster!" said Jeb. "Take my hand!"

"Boy, I'm sorry," he coughed as he said the words, "I'm sorry I didn't believe--."

The professor screamed as the shots rippled through his frail back, popping out like zits through his bloody chest. "Gaugh!" he gurgled something unknowable as a stream of blood leaked out from between his thin, pale lips. His wrinkled face splattered with small drops of crimson, his eyes wide open, he tumbled over the railing. Back stiff, arms outstretched, his corpse fell down into the raging sea like a crucifix. Virtrolli laughed like a mad man as he pulled the trigger back again, sending Jeb screaming as he threw himself over the railing and into the sea below, a monsoon of bullets flying behind him. With rapturous commotion Jeb plunged down into the dark blue sea-- he struggled beneath the currents, coming up for air with a great gasp of breath.

Olivia and Sam floated far off in the distance, their bodies small dots disappearing for minutes at a time into wave, after massive wave. Jeb closed his eyes as he saw the corpse of Allan Youngbridge floating nearby, the octogenarians locked leather briefcase still clutched tightly in his cold, dead hands. Jeb grabbed it, hoping it would float, as he watched the She Wolf disappear beneath black waves.

# 13.
# SHIPWRECKED!

Jeb hacked up sea water as he crawled to shore. *"Olivia!"* he shouted in strained tones as his hand slipped against the sand and he began moving further inland, away from the receding tide. The waterlogged suitcase he'd floated nearly a mile to shore on now lay out by a pair of sun bleached whale bones more than twelve feet high. The coast was lined with the carcasses of sea animals and sailing ships, all brought ashore by the convergence of the whaling industry, and the powerful, fog producing tide.

Shirt ripped off. Pants soaked. Jeb pulled off his drenched boots, tossing them aside as he moved further inland to build a fire. Suddenly a huge wave toppled over him, and in an instant he was drowning again, suddenly dragged back out to sea.

Jeb fought off the waves, exhausted as he struggled to make his way through the waist high tides toward the presumed safety of land.

A weary wreck, he collapsed onto the beach, his stilted breathing echoing in the cool air as he tumbled into a deep, deep sleep. Dreams of lazy Thursday nights spent in Harlem speakeasies where he and Sam could soak themselves in drink and jazz. Eccentric women and wild men, white boys on roller-skates cruising around, jotting down notes in cheap moss back journals, memories of slow burning seduction, of smoky voiced Nairobian queens with lips like red swells, of machine gun trumpets and out of tune pianos. Just beyond recollection. Hazy. Almost there. Like a daydream at dusk. He could almost reach it. Could almost bask in it all over again. But not quite. Not enough. When he awoke it was all gone, and Jeb was staring up at the sky, lying in the sand where he'd passed out, his arms empty of Olivia. Jeb yawned, his unfocused eyes tracing the dark blob shapes of ash rising up into the pinkish dawn of the sky like fuzz on an old film reel.

The suitcase! Hoping it might contain some answers he fished it out of the tide pools and pried it open, breaking the brass lock with a rock. His hands shook as he lifted the cover, shocked at what he saw.

Mountains of papers and maps all waterlogged from the ocean, black and blue ink running down into an indecipherable puddle. Jeb's hands ran through them, eyes pouring over the unreadable texts. Half blurred drawings nearly washed away, images of temples and tombs, maps of Greece, maps of North America. There were newspaper clippings and old photographs. Strange mechanical devices the uses for which he couldn't imagine. There was a photograph of Olivia as a child, now wet and ruined.

He lifted up an ancient, heavy thing from out of the suitcase. It was shimmering gold, about six inches long and shaped like a key.

For those first few hungry days walking along the shore he really thought he might find them, might spy their shadows far off in the distance and run towards them, only to see that they were fat and happy and safe. They'd roast fish on a spit and drink from some oasis they'd found in the middle of the endless beach desert. But after a few days, as his stomach turned in and his legs grew sore, he realized that they really were gone and he was alone.

Dennis Badeau

# 14.
# DEAD/GONE/BURIED

It had been several days worth of hiking since Jeb left the beach where he'd landed and he was, by now, completely emaciated both mentally and physically. He stared up at the massive sand dune before him, the sound of crashing waves still ringing in his ears, a faint stench of blubber hanging in the air. His stomach growled as he clutched his sun burned chest and stumbled through a blinding patch of fog. *"Dammit,"* he whispered, his lips dry and cracked. Things were growing red and smear. Was that a woman in a black dress? Who was she? His throat was so red and dry. Tiny white lumps were beginning to line it. He could feel them. In desperation he ran up to the shore, cupped his hands and brought the water up to his mouth.

*"Phhth!"* he spit it out and began to gag, body convulsing in pain as he wiped the salt from his lips. His body felt like it was dying.

He flashed back to the night a week or so earlier, on the boat, when they were in her cabin and the scotch was gone, the last taste of it still wet in the back of their throats.

"Call."

"It's your funeral."

"I said, call."

"Flip um."

She frowned.  "You first."

"Fine."  He flipped the cheap, red wax coated cards.  "Aces and kings.  Read um' and weep."

She groaned.

"Sorry, dear.  I tried to warn you."  He reached for her chips.

"Wait," she said, "you haven't seen my cards yet."

A look that was almost hesitant.  "Go ahead."

Her shadow reflected brownish red in the wax as her pale, slender fingertips pressed down around the well creased corners and flipped them over.  "Flush. Ace high."

Jeb groaned and shoved the pile of off-blue chips towards her.  "You got lucky."

"Damn!"  Sam exclaimed.  "Old boy, she cleaned you out."

Olivia smirked as he waved her off with a flip of his finger.  "I've just got your number you bastard," she said.  "All these years later, and I can still read you like a book."

Back on the beach Jeb hobbled along the shore, looking for food or water, vultures circling overhead.

*What's this?*

He stopped to stare at the first bit of vegetation he'd seen in miles.  Several small, brown mushrooms stood upon a patch of weeds, stems bending against the breeze.  With shaking hands he reached down, ripped the mushrooms out of the dirt and shoved them into his mouth.  They were bitter to say the least.  They had a nasty, sulfurous taste to them, bad even compared to the slop he'd been served aboard the She Wolf, but still, at least it was food.

The sun was rising higher in the sky, the air getting hotter and hotter, sweat clinging to his face. Gorillas danced in the distance, gold spires rising up out of the sand with a great whirring of gears and machinery. His vision was growing hazy, the horizon a blur.

I love you.

There was a black horse running towards him, its mane flared out, black tendrils reaching for the sky. Hooves pounding across the sand, fire erupting from its eyes and nostrils. *Fire.* I love you. *Fire.* I love you. *Fire.*

The horse kept running, ran right through him, passing through his body like a ghost, cold waves rippling through him. I love you. I know. I love you. *Fire.*

Jeb was standing on the docks in Montreal, gat in his pocket, his fingers itching at its trigger. A cop was walking towards him, his eyes on the men loading the crates of whiskey onto the boat.

*Fire. Fire. Fire.*

I love you.

Olivia was lying in bed laughing, her hands covering her breasts.

Jeb was in Boston. He was ducking behind a park bench. A rival rum-runner was firing at him. There were sirens in the background. There was whiskey spilled on the ground.

*Fire. Fire. Fire.*

The building around him was burning to the ground, liquor gone up in flames. Someone was shooting at him. Sam was telling him to run. He ran.

Olivia was sitting across from him at a table in an Italian restaurant. Talking politics. Talking about the war.

He was crouched in a muddy trench. He couldn't feel his foot. There was blood everywhere. A plane screamed overhead. The sky exploded into a thick smear of orange and red, and he could see a machine the size of a city rising up around him, and a bomb falling on Hiroshima.

Jeb screamed as he woke up. Body drenched in sweat, head throbbing, the taste of sulfur clinging to the back of his throat; he groaned as he realized he was laying atop a fifteen foot rock formation, his legs covered in his own hot piss.

He climbed down the sharp, rocky outcropping and headed towards a patch of green in the distance, as the fire and the memories faded away.

# 15.
# ARABIAN NIGHTS

He waited for a sign from the God he scarcely believed in, but nothing came but guilt.  Guilt for Sam, whom he'd dragged into all this mess.  Guilt for Betty, dealing with God knew what back in New York.  Guilt for Olivia again!  Hadn't he forgotten her all those years ago?  Hadn't he danced this dance before, grown sick of it, and moved on?  He hated himself.  Hated everything.  Hated how it was all so hot and so dry.  He just wanted to run into the ocean and let the waves carry him off.  Just let it all go.  Just let it all...  He dreamt how good it would feel to let the ocean carry him away.  To let the waves burry him, and all that he was, all that he hated about himself...  To be swallowed up in salt.  To be consumed by it…

*A sign?*

Up ahead it appeared out from behind the fog, like a mirage, poking up in golden tents and shimmering minarets.  "Help!"  Jeb shouted hoarsely as he stumbled through the fog, his half-naked, sun burned body startling a short, bearded man sitting in front of the caravan of tents.  He wore loose yellow robes, a black turban, and had a flowing gray beard that twisted out into little paint swirls around his shoulders.  He shouted something in a language Jeb didn't understand.

"What? Please I just... Just need help... Water..."

*"Beni Oldurmec, Sabah?"* the short, bearded man repeated as he pulled a long, silver dagger from his robe.

"No! Please, I'm just trying to get some help!" Jeb cried desperately. "Water. I need water!" He made a poor attempt at sign language with his hands, trying to communicate the idea of water by wiggling his fingers across his hand and making a *"swish...."* sound. Jeb wasn't very good at charades.

A mysterious voice issued a command from somewhere within the caravan of tents, and with a scowl the bearded man put down his dagger. A tall, dark eyed stranger emerged, dressed in magnificent silk robes, all puffed up and decorated in peacock feathers, gold lace and jewels. The thinly pointed black devils beard upon his face was striking, as was the low, dulcet tone of his voice. "You speak English?" the stranger asked.

"Uh, yeh, yes." Jeb coughed, his voice dry. "I'm an American, I was shipwrecked here."

The stranger seemed pleased as he stroked his long devils beard. "American? *Pow! Pow!*" he said as he shot imaginary finger pistols. "Big American cowboy, eh?"

"...something like that," said Jeb.

*"Mmm."* The stranger thought for a moment as he straightened a bejeweled turban. "My name is Salid. This is my footmen, Baggesh. We are... travelers here."

"Oh," said Jeb.

"You think my English is good?" he said with a heavy accent.

"Ah, yes very."

"Yes I know it is." Salid flashed a smile. "I study four years at Oxford University. Do you know of this place?"

"Oxford?"

"Yes."

"Uh, yeah, I've heard of it."

"Yes I know, everyone has. It is very prestigious school. Only top minds," he said as he tapped his head. "Come, you must join me for dinner. I will have Baggesh fetch you some water."

Jeb nearly passed out. "That would be amazing, thank you!"

"And I will tell Baggesh to give you one of my spare robes." A look of discomfort crept across his face. "Your body… You're peeling like a snake"

The intoxicating nature of the smell was the first thing that struck Jeb as he entered the palatial tent. Some foreign spice brought from a far off land; its aroma deeply sumptuous. Dozens of large wax candles burned brightly, illuminating the dark tent with a sensual atmosphere that was only amplified by the exotic chords of a sitar being played with old world mysticism by a dark skinned man in a green toga and turban. "Sit, sit!" Salid commanded, as he motioned towards a luxurious oriental rug on the floor, its deep burgundy backdrop emblazoned in gold and turquoise thread. Sitting at the center of the rug was an ornate wooden table, and upon the table two more candles. They burned slowly, letting off a rich scent of cinnamon and frankincense as sinewy drops of wax dripped down into thin pools around the candle's base. Jeb took his place on the rug, crossing his legs as he made a slight bowing motion towards his host. "Lovely place you got here," Jeb said.

"Yes, I know," said Salid, twirling his long, thin, black beard. "Baggesh!" he yelled as he snapped his fingers. *"El Ashika!"*

As quickly as he had been summoned the bearded man scurried into the room, two gleaming silver trays in his hands. The chords of the sitar seemed to linger in the air as several delicate Middle Eastern girls draped in pink silk veils, and barely there belly dancers costumes entered the candle lit tent. One of the dancers set down a pair of wine glasses before her master and began to pour to each man from a bottle of sweet smelling red wine.

"So. Enjoy," Salid commanded Jeb with a smile, as the girls began to dance to the sounds of the sitar.

"Believe me I will." Jeb said gratefully, as he rushed to move the food into his hungry mouth. Walls of brown couscous mixed with dates, eggs and red olives, lotus shaped dumplings and spice encrusted crawfish, and a big, fat looking piece of rare red meat, dripping in blood juices and foreign dressings.

*"Bismillah!* In the name of Allah," Salid said as he raised his hands and smiled.

"To Allah!"   Jeb said as he set down his fork and raised his glass in a toast.   "Many thanks."

# 16.
# OASIS

Jeb told Salid what had happened and how he'd come to be shipwrecked, during dinner the night before (or at least he'd told the Arab a version of what had happened). At any rate, Salid promised Jeb that he'd help him to find his friends, and as the sun rose the following morning the two of them headed out along the coast.

"You know, you asked me my business last night, but I never got a chance to ask you what it is you're doing out here," Jeb called out to Salid from atop the camel he was now riding along the shore of the desert beach.

Salid looked over at him, his camel moaning and drooling. "I am a... *merchant*. I am here with my many servants surveying trade routes."

"I see." Jeb nodded, his new red robe sailing in the wind.

"Speaking of which, why don't we head back and I'll show you more of what I do."

"But--" Jeb sputtered. "But not now, we have to keep looking for them!"

Salid shook his head. "My friend, it has been miles and there have been no sign of them. Perhaps we should turn back."

"Just a little bit further," Jeb pleaded, a crestfallen look on his face. "There's a small patch of brush up that way, about a mile inland, that I still wanna check out."

As the jungle brush came closer into view, its vivid green palms rising up from the desert below, Jeb began to hope. Hope that maybe Sam and Olivia weren't corpses lying dehydrated in the desert. Hope that maybe they'd reached this oasis. Hope that he wouldn't need to lay another foundation of guilt upon his conscience. He'd already let go of Olivia once, he could do it again, couldn't he? But if Sam... *no*. He couldn't think like that. Couldn't say it, not even to himself.

The jungle foliage grew increasingly dense as Jeb and Salid made their way through the oasis. Jeb ducked as a big blue parrot with zebra stripes took flight from one of the palm tree branches, before perching on top of a vine covered rock that jutted out from the mossy undergrowth. The blue parrot squawked and whistled as it began to clean a raised wing.

"Look at that." Salid pointed towards the bird.

"Beautiful," Jeb said admiringly.

"Yes," said Salid. "I have fifty at home."

"Really?" Jeb asked. "Where is it you're from, anyhow?"

Salid paused, saying nothing. "Somewhere else. It is far from here."

Jeb shook his head. "I figured as much, Salid."

*"Squawk!"* the bird loudly interrupted him. *"Water! Water! Phwee-phwoo!"*

Jeb whipped around to face Salid, a stunned look on his face. "Did you hear that?"

"Yes, he can speak," Salid said, unimpressed.

"No, no, no, no! Well, I mean sure, but that's not the point!" Jeb sputtered out quickly.

"It's not?" Salid asked.

"Didn't you hear him, he said water! He must have picked that up from my friends! They must still be alive!" Jeb fought against the silent, cynical voice in head telling him that it might be one of the murderous sailors. He had to hold onto the hope that it was them.

*"Water!"* the bird squawked again. *"Water! Polly wanna cracker?"* He whistled and squawked before flying off.

Jeb laughed as he watched the bird disappear. "It's them! It has to be."

Salid's eyes gleamed. "Your friend and the girl you spoke of earlier, yes?"

"Yeah. Yeah, that's them. It's got to be them," Jeb said hurriedly, as he whipped at the beast's reins and the camel charged forward through the jungle oasis. "OLIVIA!?" he called loudly as he rode. "SAM!?"

Jeb dismounted as he approached a thicket of bushes and trees too dense to ride through, and Salid followed suit, tying his camel to the trunk of a baobab tree. "So these two friends of yours," Salid asked, "tell me about them."

"What do you wanna know?" Jeb shrugged as he pushed past the brush, making his way deeper into the jungle. "Sam's a friend of mine, and Olivia, well… she's a woman. What is there to tell?"

Salid stroked his beard. "I sense that you are a troubled man, Mister Chamberlain."

Jeb smiled at Salid, blissfully unaware that as he made his way through the jungle, calling out the names of his friends, he was being stalked by a Bugantu hunting party. By the time he realized anything was wrong it was already far too late.

Jeb whipped his head around as he heard a branch snap nearby. "Olivia?" he called out as he shot up. "Sam? Is that you?"

**"PHWEW!"** Jeb screamed as the poisoned blow dart hit his neck and he toppled to the mossy ground with a thud, white foam beginning to gurgle out of his mouth as the poison entered his blood stream. **"PHWEW!"** Another shot from the blow gun and Salid went down just as fast. As they lay on the ground gagging, the band of painted cannibals danced wildly, hooting, hollering, chanting madly. Their hunt had been successful and the isolated village of the Bugantu would eat well tonight.

# 17.

## THE MYSTERIOUS GHOST OF GERTRUDE MALONE

**Kent, England, Four Weeks Earlier**

"You may enter now, Miss Shaw," a deep voice bellowed from inside the dark, fourth story drawing room of the illustrious Von Wauller mansion. Guysbie, the butler, opened the great oak door and Miss Elizabeth Cornelius Shaw sauntered into the richly decorated room. Her sparkling black dress was partially covered by a long white boa, which she promptly set down on an antique oak table, next to a fossilized Pachycephalosaurus skull.

"I pray you are not here to disappoint me," came the deep voice of Sir Richard, his lean, angular frame sitting hunched in a satin and leather chair that was at least two sizes too big for him. In his left hand he held an orb from which emanated a dim, glowing yellow light, partially illuminating the dark drawing room.

"Of course not, m' lord," Elizabeth said as she bowed, a diamond necklace reflecting the light as she bent forward.

"Good." The lean man smiled. He was only fifty six, but already he'd accumulated one of the largest fortunes in the empire. His hair was graying, and his fingernails hadn't been cut in nearly three years, giving him the appearance of having claws. He wore a red smoking jacket with a bright golden watch in the left breast pocket. He set down the ball of light carefully, picked up his favorite ivory pipe, and began to smoke. "My Son arrived from London yesterday."

"Oh?"

"Yes. That's where he got this... thing," he said, gesturing to the glowing ball. "Another of Tesla's toys."

"How is Preston?"

"Fine. Fine. His mother's death was hard on him of course, but I feel he's taken it rather well."

"Strong like his father, I'm sure."

*"Hmm.* You flatter me, Miss Shaw."

"Only with the truth, no doubt." She paused and reached into her purse, producing a small golden box. She lifted the cover, revealing a neatly folded map which she carefully removed and handed over to Sir Richard.

"At last, the Midas map!" He unfolded it quickly and lay it out flat on his desk, next to a softly purring calico cat. "I trust Professor Youngbridge did not part with it easily?"

"He did not."

Richard laughed. "The old fool. When will people learn that my will simply cannot be denied? If he'd only given it to me when I first asked, all of this messy business could have been avoided."

"His loss," she said.

"Indeed." He stared at her. "I trust you took care of him?"

She remained silent, avoiding his gaze.

"What?"

"There was a mix up, sir, I--"

"What?" Von Wauller's face turned a red shade of furious as he stood up.

"I killed his accomplice and recovered the map, but the old man managed to escape before I could--"

"You incompetent fool, you let him go?!" he roared as he went around the desk, and stepped towards her.

"I admit, I made a mistake, but without the map there's nothing he can do. He's not a threat to us!" the girl protested.

He slapped her hard across the face. "You idiot! Don't you think he made copies? That bastard is probably half way to Africa as we speak!"

"I.....I...."

"Assemble your team tonight, I want you on the next ship to the Skeleton Coast! I'll not lose my prize because of your incompetence!"

"I'm sorry, sir," she whispered, nursing the red welt on her cheek.

He sat back down behind his desk, his eyes dark slits. "No- NO! You don't know the meaning of the word! But hear this: should you fail me again, Elizabeth, I promise, I will teach it to you. If I lose my prize because of you, I swear I will make you pay!"

"I promise you, I will not fail," she cried as she felt at the old wounds on her back, from the last time she had failed her father.

"If you thought last time was bad," he sneered, "just try me again, you whimpering sod. It's not enough that I have to worry about Olivia, but now that bumbling old faggot too? Ugh," he groaned, and gestured Elizabeth out of the room. She curtsied quickly and turned towards the heavy wooden door. "OUT!" he bellowed, and she practically broke into a sprint. As the door slammed shut Sir Richard frowned and reached into his desk. Fumbling around for a moment, he pulled out a small metal box, and poured a small amount of its contents upon his desk. With a pen knife he swatted away the cat and sorted the fine white powder into lines, moaning happily as he threw back his head, sucking up the remaining cocaine into his nose. *Sniff... Sniff...* The high was incredible. "Sensational stuff," he muttered, as he wiped at his nose and leaned back.

"Guysbie? I thought I told you not to disturb me," he said violently as the door opened. "What is the meaning of this?"

The dark figure made its way slowly through the shadows, high heels clicking on the wood floor. "Forgot my boa," she said.

"Elizabeth? I told you to go and get out of here, you miserable cunt!"

"Sorry Daddy," she said, raising her pistol.

"What! What are you doing?"

The gun went off with a blast, dropping Sir Richard in his own home. Elizabeth sneered. She was sick of being pushed around by him, was glad she'd done it. Born a bastard child, none of the family fortune would be hers, but that didn't matter, now she would make her own fortune. A chill ran down her spine as she stepped out of the room, the pool of blood creeping silently behind her. It had been a long held legend in the mansion that the previous owner's great, great grandmother, Gertrude Malone, had hung herself, and that her ghost now roamed the long, gilded hallways. Elizabeth had never believed in ghost stories growing up in the old house, but if Gertrude did exist perhaps now she'd have some company.

# 18.
# TO SERVE JEB

Jeb awoke to find himself hog tied to a stake in the ground, his head a confusing, swollen mess. To his left was Salid, also tied up, and laying passed out in a puddle of his own drool, and to his right two of the dark skinned natives were hunched over a fire pit. The puncture mark on his neck where the blow dart went in had puffed up and was beginning to itch. Jeb shook his head, violently trying to scratch his neck up against his shoulder.

The two bushman were busy dumping wood into their fire, and so they didn't notice as Jeb reached the tips of his fingers beneath his robes and pulled out the dinner knife he'd taken from Salid's tent back when he still wasn't sure about him. Quietly as he could he began cutting the ropes.

The first native was incredibly fat, with massive breasts and a great, port belly that made him look pregnant. He was completely naked except for the yellow gourd that covered his dick, and his enormous body was painted with bright stripes and symbols made from ground up berries and ash. The second native was much skinnier, with a hunched over posture and eerily small, childlike hands. His body and face were painted too, and on his head he wore a tremendous head dress made of bones and driftwood. His eyes were an eerie shade of milk white, and his long, angular nose shot out like a bamboo rod, an ornately carved bone running through the septum.

*"Meshet maka ben!"* Salid screamed as he awoke from his drug induced trance. *"Adu halmelas omek, nasil degin!?"*

Jeb tried to hush him, but it was too late. The fat native stomped towards them, a massive club in hand, and beat them both over the head. When Jeb awoke, some indeterminable time later, he had a lump on his skull the size of a pear, his body was covered in grease, and the knife was gone.

"MUSATUKA AL AL! MUSATUKA AL AL!" The natives chanted furiously as they carried Jeb and Salid high above their heads through a sea of hundreds, towards a massive fire pit. The high priest of the natives stepped out of his hut, a stone ax cradled in his hands. He wore a gigantic head dress carved out of skulls, and around his neck he had strung a hideous necklace of dead rats, their tiny tails knotted together in a daisy chain of the devil. The moment Jeb saw it he tossed chunks all over one of the natives backs, who proceeded to scream wildly. The diabolical chieftain lifted the ax over his head, his rat necklace waving in the breeze.

"Al al tuki-tuki!" he screamed to the crowd.

*"Al tuki-tuki ta!"* the crowd replied in unison.

Jeb watched as a half a dozen pale faced strangers were led towards the fire pit ahead of him. They weren't sailors from the She Wolf; Jeb was sure he'd never seen their faces before. They looked scared and desperate and dying for a way out. The crowd roared with a frenzy, licking their lips as Jeb and Salid were pushed into line with them.

As the smoke rose from the fire pit it began to flow outwards, forcing Jeb and the natives into a spastic bout of coughing. Jeb screamed in horror as Salid was thrown head first into the bonfire, wailing as the flames ate him alive. Dizzy from smoke, Jeb wanted desperately to shut out the sight before him and the smell of burning flesh, but he couldn't look away. He had to know what awaited him.

Salid and the other men shrieked as they too were tossed into the flames, leaving Jeb alone as the priest pointed at him, ordering his men to throw him in. "NO! NO!" Jeb screamed desperately, "I don't even taste good, I swear!"

The crowd chanted over and over in some hideous tongue, as jungle drums beat steadily in the background. Two huge, blood soaked natives lifted Jeb up by his shoulders and swung him forwards-

A tall, blonde female figure emerged from the brush, a large riffle in her hands. She stood in tan, skintight riding pants, and wore a loose, low cut top with a shimmering diamond necklace. "Get down," she commanded, and Jeb ducked out of the way as she blasted the men holding him, with pinpoint accuracy.

The high priest screamed, but it was too late for him as a bullet ripped through his skull encrusted head dress and deep into his brain, leaving him spread on the ground, dead as the rodents around his neck.

The cannibals turned and fled back into the jungle, leaving Jeb face down in the dirt. The woman in the riding pants ran towards him and lowered a pale, French tipped hand, which he gladly took.

"On your feet," she said, "quick, they'll regroup soon. When they do I won't be able to hold them off."

Jeb nodded and ran head first after her through the thick foliage ahead. *"Poor Salid,"* he thought to himself, as he caught a glimpse of the slow burning corpses behind him.

For a moment he swore he could still hear one of them screaming.

# 19.
# WELTSCHMERZ

Jeb gasped for breath as he ran stumbling through the thick jungle brush. "Who are you?" he asked through shallow gasps.

"Your new hero," she said in a posh London accent as she pushed past the outlying bush and back onto the sands of the coastal desert. She had Cupid's bow lips, a pointedly feminine nose, slate gray eyes, and a figure that filled out in all the right places.

"Jeb Chamberlain," he said, fumbling through the heavy bush. He put out his hand as he stopped, and she shook it.

"Elizabeth Shaw, at your service."

Jeb looked around. There were two dark figures walking towards them. "They with you?" he asked as he motioned towards them.

"They're with me."

"Lisbeth!" the first figure called out. "You find 'em?"

She nodded. "Oh, I found them alright."

The taller of the two figures came close and looked Jeb over. "And who the fuck is this?"

"Uh, Jeb... Jeb Chamberlain," he said.

"You. Don't talk," Elizabeth said to Jeb as she pulled a cigar from her back pocket. "I found him trapped with the crew, lined up and ready to be eaten by the local welcoming committee."

"Eaten?" asked Arnold.

"You heard me, eaten," Elizabeth said, raising a lighter to the end of her cigar. "This place is loaded with cannibals. Man eaters like the Donner party as far as the eye can see."

"Fuck," Arnold cursed under his breath. "So where is the crew?"

"Split up in several dozen different digestive systems, I'd assume," she said glibly. "By the time I tracked them down it was too late. I barely managed to rescue this... whoever he is."

"I told you, the name's Jeb."

"And I told you not to talk." She glared. "But since you seem to insist on blabbing, why don't you explain to me what is it you're doing out here, serving yourself up to cannibals in this sepulchral jungle?"

"Cannibals..." the second, shorter figure turned the word over slowly.

"I was shipwrecked, along with my entire crew. We were split up, but I'm still looking for two other survivors," Jeb said, still very much out of breath.

"Yes, we too were split up from the rest of our group, and you saw how well that turned out. Chances are if your friends were anywhere near that 'oasis,' they ended up just as barbequed as the rest," she said. "You know my name already. These two are what's left of my team. To your left, amateur leprechaun Seamus O'Bannon, and to your right, hired thug and all around dickless asshole Arnold St. James."

Arnold groaned. "If we're done with the pleasantries then, little lady, I feel it my duty to remind you that we are running on a very tight schedule," he said with a cockney accent.

Elizabeth took a long drag from her cigar. "Don't forget who's in charge here."

Arnold began to say something before thinking better of it and backing down.

"And so..." She pulled the knife from its sheath at her hip, toying with it in her hand as she made her way towards Jeb. "We come back to you, Mr. Chamberhall."

"Chamberlain," Jeb said quickly.

"Whatever," said Elizabeth. "We're down six men, and that leaves us with not nearly enough manpower for our purposes. The way I see it you have two choices: You can either join up with us, or you can stay here alone and look for your friends. Although should you wind up on the menu again, I promise I won't be there to save your arse."

"And, may I ask what said purposes are?" said Jeb.

"You may not," said Elizabeth. "You need only know that your loyalty and discretion will be expected, and that your reward will be handsome."

"So much secrecy," Jeb said, as he stared at the shovels and pickaxes hanging from the backpacks of Seamus and Arnold. "If I didn't know any better I'd say you lot came out here to bury someone. That, or you're treasure hunters. Tell me, what is it you're digging for?"

"Dinosaur bones, Mister Chamberlain. Dinosaur bones."

"Call me Jeb."

She gestured angrily with her cigar. "I'll call you whatever I damn well please, and you'll learn to like it."

Jeb shook his head. He had to believe that Sam and Olivia were still alive out there somewhere, had to believe that if he just gave it more time he would find them. He only had one real play, a huge bluff, and a dangerous one at that. "Don't play me for a fool," he said, hedging his bets that his suspicion was correct, "there's only one reason in the world someone would mount an armed expedition to this God forsaken place. You're here for the Tomb of Midas, aren't you?"

"How do *you* know about that?" Arnold asked, his hand at his knife.

Elizabeth's eyes tightened like screws. "Have you been following us?"

Jeb paused, uncertain whether or not to say more. "The only thing I've been following is the work of professor Alan Youngbridge. I assume you know of him?"

No one answered.

"The truth of the matter is that we were partners headed together for the tomb," Jeb lied. "I know all about the... gold."

Arnold looked questioningly at Elizabeth, but she ignored him. "Did Professor Youngbridge survive the wreck?"

"Hard to say." Jeb shrugged. "Look I'm super grateful for you saving my life an' everything, but that sort of information comes at a price."

"Is that a fact?" Elizabeth said dangerously.

Jeb stood his ground. "You help me find my friends and I'll tell you everything you wanna know, and take you to the tomb myself."

"I don't like the way you do business," she said. "What makes you think I won't eliminate the competition and shoot you right here, just like those cannibals?"

"Because you want what I have. No, scratch that, you NEED the information I have if you're going to get your hands on the treasure, and I need your help to save Sam and Olivia."

"Olivia?" Elizabeth's hand shot to the hilt of her pistol. "Olivia Youngbridge is here?"

Jeb studied her face. "As a matter of fact she goes by Ostrum now that she's married. How do you know her?"

"We go way back," Elizabeth said grimly, as she dropped her cigar to the ground, crushing it into the sand with the heel of her boot. "Spread out. If she's alive, she can't be far. Don't let her escape."

*"Escape?"* Out of the corner of his eye Jeb could see the gun the Arnold was pointing towards his head. "What the hell is going on here?!"

"Can I fuckin' kill 'im?" Arnold asked with a cockney accent, his revolver raised high.

Elizabeth stopped to consider the request, her eyes drifting about from the captive man before her to the cannibal filled jungle behind.

"Well?" Arnold shouted. "Come on, you know they're workin' together."

"Make up your mind, Lizzy," the Irishman muttered.

"I'm thinking!" she said shrilly. Part of her wanted to kill him and part of her wanted to fuck him. She mulled over the decision for a moment before opening her mouth with a twinge of hesitation. She gave the word. "Shoot him."

There an explosion and Jeb toppled to the ground, the bullet ripping through the edge of his shoulder, spraying blood across the sand.

"Oh you *suck!*" she laughed, the smell of gun powder heavy in the air. "What, did a little girl teach you how to shoot? That was awful!"

Seamus began to snicker. "Oooh, big man!"

"Shut up," Arnold groaned, "he moved!"

"Targets tend to do that" She sneered. "Be a dear and aim for his head this time, won't you?"

Arnold grunted as he readied another shot. "Wait!" Jeb cried out, clutching his bloody shoulder as he struggled to get up off the ground. "Don't kill me, I can help you!"

"How's that?" she asked.

"I....I.....I know where Olivia is!"

"No you don't," she said dryly. "How stupid do you think I am? And don't try that shit about you having some sort of secret information either, cause I know for a fact that I already have everything I need."

"Well..." Jeb grasped for any reason to keep him alive. "Let.... Let me join you! I had little loyalty to Youngbridge, and certainly none to Olivia. You should let me join up, I could be a great help to you!"

Elizabeth paused, mulling the proposal over.

"I mean it, let me help you! After all, you wanted me on your team five minutes ago, and it's not like that much has changed. You're still down six men, and I guarantee you I can be more useful to you than that pasty hobbit you've got hauling shovels over there."

"HEY!" Seamus called out in a hurt voice.

"That hobbit can read Aramaic, Egyptian and Phoenician," she said, "what can you do?"

"I can carry a gun," he said with forced bravado. "At least if you patch up this wound, and really, with aim like that, it's safe to say you need all the help you can get!"

She frowned. "Arnold, what do you think?"

"I think we can't trust 'im," the cockney growled. "I think we should kill im'."

"Yes. Yes, my thoughts exactly. How can we possibly trust you, Jeb. After all, you are in cahoots with Olivia."

"Cahoots with her? I barely even knew the girl, you can trust me. You can!" Jeb's hands were shaking. "I swear to God, you can trust me. I don't owe that bitch a thing, so if you wanna hunt her down like a dog and get whatever it is you're after for yourselves, hey, good for you, who am I to judge?   I'm a hired gun, babe, I just work for the highest bidder."

"I'm the one with the gun."

"And that makes you the highest bidder!"   Jeb said smiling, feeling like a two dollar whore with a bad case of the clap, over the way he was selling out Olivia.

"Alright."   She shrugged.   "I think we can trust him."   Arnold groaned as he dropped his gun to his side.   "Arnold," she said with a sneer, as she motioned towards Jeb.   "Keep a close eye on him."   She pointed towards a towering rock formation shaped like a flamingo, about half a mile in the foggy distance. "We meet there in four hours.   And Jeb?"

"Yeah?"

"If you double cross me, or either of my men, I swear to God, I will make you regret it."

"I understand."

"Understand this.   Fuck me out there and I will rip the left eye from your socket, shove it down your goddamn throat with a wooden spoon and then feed whatever I don't finish off to our cannibal friends out there, is that fucking clear?"

Jeb gulped down the lump in his throat. "Crystal."

# 20.

# GRAVE YARD PARADISE

It was nearly sunset now. Cool ocean breeze
wafting over the sand dunes, birds disappearing above
in the quickly darkening sky. Arnold was about
twenty five feet ahead of Jeb, climbing up a sand dune,
a vast expanse of desert surrounding him in all
directions. Briefly, Jeb considered making a run for
it, but there were too many unanswered questions on
his mind. For now, at least, he'd just have to play
along.

"OLIVIA!?" Jeb shouted out across the vast
desert sands.

*"Quiet!"* Arnold shushed him. "Just shut up,
alright?"

Jeb looked at him indifferently and shrugged.
Fine. It was better they didn't find them. He just
hoped Olivia and Sam had made it to safety, and
somehow avoided the cannibals. Jeb shuddered as
Salid's last moments tore across the memories of his
mind. The image of his scorched, slowly peeling
fingers reaching up from the inferno, his eyes turning
yellow, the fear that he'd be next. Jeb had a long
history with fire. The stuff seamed to follow him
around, to hound after him like a curse. The farm, the

war, the factory, and now this cannibal holocaust. It was all too much to bear.

*"Over here,"* Arnold ordered him, motioning towards the edge of a rocky plateau. Jeb nodded and followed him towards it. *"Look at this,"* he whispered as Jeb inched closer. Jeb squinted as the sun glare hit the corner of his eyes, and he tried to make out the white shape. He gasped, jumping back. On the rock was a skeleton, its arms missing, as well as its feet. "Hope that ain't one a yer' friends," Arnold snickered.

Jeb gulped, made his way down the plateau, and knelt beside it. The bones were old and sun bleached. The missing ligaments weren't the worst part about it though. The worst part was the bite marks.

Jeb and Arnold continued through the desert for what felt like miles before coming across a large outcropping of palm trees and a stagnant pool of water. "I gotta take a piss." Arnold said is a deep, grunting voice, the lines that crisscrossed his suntanned face winking in the orange glow of sunset.

"Alright," Jeb said hesitantly, "don't let me stop you."

"Get outta here," Arnold said, as he pointed towards one of the larger rocks. "I ain't gonna have you watchin me, ya' bloody fag."

Jeb snorted, uncertain if he should defend himself against this latest insult.

Arnold hummed loudly as he drained into the desert pool. *"A British tar is a soaring soul, as free as a mountain bird!"* he sang out into the dry desert air.

"I could do with a little less singing!" Jeb said impatiently. Something about this place made him uneasy. The sentinel rocks jutting out of the sand like crosses, their dark, imposing forms seemed to serve as a warning of some kind. "I really wish you'd give me a gun."

*"Ahh...."* Arnold let out a happy sigh as he pulled up his pants. "All done."

"Is it weird that you seem proud about that fact?" Jeb scoffed as he looked back up at the top of the tall rock he was leaning against. "I'm beginning to think that you-" he froze in silent terror as two pale eyes stared back at him from atop the rock. Jeb screamed out to Arnold, but it was too late. The cannibals were already on top of them.

Arnold screamed as one of the men leapt at him from atop his rocky perch, plowing him into the desert ground. Jeb grabbed a dead tree branch from the ground and swung it like a baseball bat, smacking down one of the natives midair. "ARNOLD!" Jeb screamed, as he bolted toward the cockney, smashing a path through the throng of cannibals as he ran. Several gunshots fired off and Arnold stood up, covered in blood both foreign and his own. Frantically, he pointed his gun towards Jeb, pulled the trigger and blew the face off of a long, slack jawed man; a group of flies nestled in his rotten yellow teeth. The bugs fled their nest as the man eater slumped to the ground. "Come on!" Jeb screamed as he motioned towards Arnold and began to run towards the safety of the open desert, a pack of the natives close behind.

"There's too many of them!" Arnold cried out desperately as he ran up alongside Jeb, a Springfield sniper rifle gripped in his tan hands. He pointed it up as he ran, blasting an oncoming native square in the chest.

"At least your aim's improving!" Jeb said as they ran. They dived behind one of the rocks for cover, and Arnold tossed Jeb a pistol and ammo belt.

"Oh, now you trust me?" Jeb said sarcastically. He popped up from behind the rock, fired it into the chest of one of the cannibals, and turned back to Arnold. "We've gotta make it to that clearing. Away from these rocks." As he said the words another cannibal leapt down from one of the podium rocks. Now there were seven racing up behind them. "We'll never outrun 'um!" Arnold screamed as they took off and began again for the clearing. A look, not quite of regret, but something close crossed his face. "Sorry mate, but it's a dog eat dog world out here." A baffled look came across Jeb's face for the briefest of moments, as Arnold reached out his long orange arm, shoved Jeb to ground, and ran off.

Jeb screamed as he tumbled down into the sand, the pounding footsteps growing closer behind him. *"You double crossing fuuuuck!"* he shouted out as he raised his pistol and aimed for Arnold's back. A shot rang out from his barrel, but it missed, leaving Arnold to turn and laugh. Jeb twisted back towards one of the incoming cannibals, blasting her as she lunged at him. **"POW! POW!"** the rounds exploded, striking a second cannibal in the knees, **"POW! POW!"** a violent flurry of shots, and two more cannibals were half decapitated by the .45 magnum rounds. They stumbled across the ground like bloody sprinklers before collapsing. Jeb reloaded and aimed at the remaining man and two women, their blood soaked frames running wildly, clubs in hand towards him. The man leapt up and jumped atop Jeb, wrestling him to the ground, his rusted knife stabbing wildly at Jeb's throat.

Jeb whipped his body back, barely dodging the mans fevered blows. He screamed as the knife slipped into the corner of his neck, blood spraying out into the low tide smelling air like a bad mist. Jeb pushed back with all his strength against the hideous mad man, the knife dropping to the ground as their hands became entangled in a primal struggle.

*"Grrugh!......Grrr.....Greugh!"* Jeb wrestled the man onto his back, slipping his right hand out from the cannibal's fist and slugging him across the face. He continued his attack again and again, as he beat the bastard's face into a bloody pulp. He screamed as one of the women came up behind him and sunk jagged, meticulously filed teeth down into his calf muscle. Picking up the sand covered gun, he pulled the trigger and she collapsed to the ground in a mound of blood and misery. The man eater on the ground came back to life, hissing as he lunged upwards at Jeb's throat, his dinner denied by nothing less than the business end of Jeb's pistol, as he rammed it down the cannibals throat and pulled the trigger, blowing the son of a bitch to kingdom come.

Jeb's eyes were red with rage as he raised his gun and steadied his aim on the last of the natives as they ran away. With a thud he collapsed in a sweaty heap onto the ground, his bloody body and ragged, war torn mind unable or unwilling to pull the trigger.

There were no such hesitations in the minds of the cannibals though, as they climbed up atop the rock pillars like crows nests in hell. Arnold was still running- gasping- out of breath- he could see the end in sight now. Freedom just a few footsteps away. He wailed happily as he approached the clearing, but, alas, it was not to be. He tumbled to the ground as one of the natives dive bombed him from atop his ghostly perch. Ten more of them swarmed around him, leaving Arnold to scream and fire off his Springfield blindly, but it was too late. A few more of the cannibals went down, but the rest crowded around him, tearing him limb from limb. A mass of twenty or so more maniacs rushed in from the desert, clubs, spears, forks and knives in hand. The men and women of the Bugantu tribe devoured him bite by bloody bite, leaving oily flesh strewn about the sand for the vultures to finish off.

And once again, Jeb was alone.

# 21.
# SAND PAPER

Several hours later the sun was just a dim memory, devoured by the moon. Jeb had put a good two miles between himself and the tribe by now, but he still reeked of blood. He was, after all, covered and encrusted in the shit. The dark crimson itched on his skin as it cracked and flaked in the dry desert heat. Jeb shuddered as he peeled off a small, scab like piece of it and flicked it into the sand, a gust of wind quickly taking it away.

Far up ahead he could see two black, ant like figures silhouetted against the massive pale moon. They didn't move like cannibals. Their postures were too formal, too erect. One of the figures made its way towards Jeb. "Elizabeth!?" Jeb called out in the night. "Over here!"

The figure tilted its head, and the dark shape behind it began to move closer. "Jeb?"

"Olivia?!" Jeb could barely believe her voice. "Is that you?" He smiled, opened his mouth wide, and then smiled again. "Olivia!" he shouted it out as loud as he could as he ran towards her.

"Jeb! JEB!" she cried as she ran towards him and they crashed into each others arms, embracing warmly, clutching each other tightly as he pressed her against his chest.

"You're alive!  You're alive!"  Olivia cried in seeming disbelief.  "Oh Jeb!"

"Olivia, Olivia, Olivia!"  He kissed her forehead, clutching her face as he shut his eyes.  "I thought...  I thought I'd lost you."

"Jeb..."  She looked down, a horrified look on her face.  "Jeb, you're covered in blood!"

He paused, letting go of her as he looked down at his chest.  "You wouldn't believe the day I've had."

"We found an oasis we-" she began.

"Oasis?  How did you escape the cannibals?" His eyes darted across her face, only half believing she was actually there.

"Cannibals?"

"Hundreds of um'.  In the jungle.  They didn't find you?"

"No, Jeb.  No, we…"  She looked back at Sam, who was still walking towards them.  She gazed over at him, a strange look on her face.  There was a new bond between them.

Sam smiled as he hugged Jeb.  "You okay, Old Boy?"

Jeb let out a crazed laugh.  "NO! *Not even a little bit!"*  He stuttered for a moment, trying to get across the severity of what he'd been through.  "I've been attacked by cannibals, fought off starvation, dehydration, and death!  I watched a man get eaten alive!  Not to mention the fact that some blonde cunt tried to kill me!"

"What?" Olivia asked, shocked look on her face.

"Yeah, Elizabeth Shaw, that was her name."

"Elizabeth…. How do you know about my sister?" asked Olivia.

Jeb's mouth fell open. "Sister? Sister, you don't have a sister?! You're telling me the woman who held a freaking pistol against my head, that was your sister?"

"Oh, God." She buried her head in her hands. "This is even worse than I thought!"

Jeb's mouth hung open. "We date for three years and that never comes up in conversation? You have a secret, murderous blonde doppelganger running around and you never told me?"

"It's complicated!" Olivia turned away. "Is my father here too?"

"Your father? Jesus, I thought your dad was dead? You definitely told me he was dead!"

"Not dead, just evil," Olivia whispered. "I'm afraid, Jeb, that there are a few things you don't know about me."

"Oh, gee, ya' think?" Jeb cried apoplectically. "How is it I know how you take your coffee, the sound of your snoring, your fears and passions, your favorite places to be, the name of every pet you've ever owned, and that one spot where you love to be touched in just that special way that makes you--"

"JEB!" she cried.

"And yet after all that you never got around to telling me that you had a long lost-"

"Twin sister. Yes." Olivia shook her head. "You… you don't know what happened to my uncle, do you?"

Jeb shifted uncomfortably. "Olivia, he..."

She nodded. "I thought so."

"Olivia I'm sorry. I'm so, so sorry." He touched her hand. "But you've been keeping things from me, *big things*, and I need to know what they are."

Olivia moved slowly, her face turning away from him. "Alright. Alright, I'll tell you everything. But I need to know exactly where it is you've been, and everything Elizabeth knows, and I need to know it now!" She fought against the tears brimming in her eyes. "Alright, well maybe not right now… Let's get a fire going first, it's getting late."

\* \* \* \* \* \* \* \*

"Come on!" Elizabeth shouted at the Irishman as he lagged behind. "The flamingo is just up ahead."

"I'm a' commin'," the tiny man muttered, staring up at the huge flamingo shaped rock not twenty feet ahead of them, his sweat soaked hands gripped tightly around the straps of his rucksack. They hadn't had any luck finding the girl, but perhaps Arnold had. They'd find out soon enough. Assuming, of course, that he'd made it back to the rock. Elizabeth looked around. "Nothing." She scowled. "They're not here."

"Ah fook," the little man said, "fookin' sooks."

"Indeed," said Elizabeth. She leaned up against the rock, her tight, tan riding pants accentuating every curve of her posterior. She rolled a cigarette and lit it, shoving it into her large mouth. Pink lips pursed around the tobacco, she took a long drag of smoke like a man, before blowing it back out. She sighed, lowering the stick to her hip.

Seamus looked away. He didn't smoke. His wife wouldn't let him. He shrugged the bag off of his back, set it down into the sand, walked over towards the rock and sat down with his back pressed against its jagged edge. "Elizabeth?" he said hesitantly.

"Yeah?"

"What do ye' think about Arnold?"

"What do you mean?"

"Can.... can he be trusted?"

"I think so," she said through a puff of smoke. "So long as he gets his money, we can trust him. Why?"

"I dunno," Seamus said quickly. "The man just rubs me the wrong way, that's all."

She shrugged.

Neither one of them spoke for several minutes as they sat in the dark, African night.

"I miss me wife," Seamus whispered into the silence. "I do."

Elizabeth didn't seem to care.

"I do. I miss her." Seamus closed his eyes and thought back to their cottage in Killarney. He opened his mouth and was about to say something when suddenly a part of the stone broke loose from the very top of the flamingo rock and came hurtling down to earth with a surprising rapidity, plunging into Seamus' gut, impaling him in the sand. Elizabeth screamed as the rocks came down in a thunderous crash around her, but for Seamus the time for screaming was over. He lay dead, his eyes open, mouth agape, a bit of drool dangling from his mouth.

* * * * * * * *

"So then," Jeb continued, "they gave me a choice, either join up with them and help hunt you down, or die right there on the spot." He took a sip from Olivia's canteen. "So, it wasn't like I had that many options." Jeb stopped for a moment to examine the canteen. Olivia had told him they'd found it inside the hull of one of the wrecked ships, along with some whiskey, a compass, iodine tablets and a collection of canned foodstuffs. The wreck couldn't have been more than a few weeks old, but they had seen no sign of survivors. The three of them were now camped around a small fire, the flames casting a yellow pall across their faces and chests.

"So, my sister," Olivia said quietly. "How is she looking these days?"

"What do you mean?"

"Is she.....*healthy*?"

"Uh. Yeah." Jeb paused for a moment. "She seemed fine to me. I mean aside from wanting you dead!"

Olivia looked as though she might cry. "Look, I'm sorry I never told you I had a sister."

"Twins? God did I miss out on that." He bit his lip. "I always did wonder back then why I never got to meet any of your family. At the time it seemed convenient not having to ask for anyone's permission, and besides it wasn't like I had anyone either," he admitted. "Did you tell any of this to your husband? I mean, like at the wedding, was he at all suspicious when your side showed up with pitchforks and tried to off you?"

"Don't be jealous, Jeb, it doesn't suit you. And besides, it's not like I'm the only one who's been keeping secrets."

"Oh, and how's that?"

She looked over at Sam, and he turned away sheepishly.

"What?" said Jeb.

"You killed the Chief of Police, my dear ex."

"Jesus, Sam, you told her that?"

"I'm sorry, I thought you was dead! The guilt was eating me away and I had to tell somebody. You know I ain't no good at keepin' secrets," said Sam.

Jeb rolled his eyes. "Well did Libby Loose Lips at least tell you why I shot him?"

"Because you were screwing his wife?" Olivia suggested.

"No!" Jeb said indignantly. "Well... I mean I was, but that's not why I shot him. Obviously. For your information it was self-defense."

"I know all about your self-defense, Jeb," said Olivia. "And then your throwing poor Sam under the bus, too. I mean *really.*"

"Well at least I never lied to you when we were together! Not like you did, obviously."

"You never lied?!" She pressed her finger into his chest. "That's right, you worked for a shipping company didn't you? And then the post office? Right, right, right. Or maybe that's just what you told me while you were running rum. It's hard to remember, what with the details being so foggy."

"I ran rum for you!" he said, throwing his hands in the air. "Everything I did was for you!"

"Even the other girls, Jeb? Did you do them for me too?" she barked.

"You-- that's not--" He bit his tongue. "Fair."

Olivia shrugged. "Enough rehashing. Do you wanna know the truth or not?"

"Yes!" Jeb exclaimed. "I want answers damn it, I want the truth! I wanna know, first of all, why on earth your own twin wants you dead?!"

Sam reached out his hand and touched Olivia gently on the arm. *"It's ok,"* he said with a soft smile, as she turned and smiled back.

Jeb looked from one to the other, a poorly hidden look of jealousy on his face. "I'm sorry, you told Sam already?"

"We thought you were dead, Jeb." Olivia said with a shrug. "Elizabeth and I we were born as... Our father, Sir Richard Von Wauller, was, is one of the most powerful men in England, and my mother was his mistress. He cut my mum off financially as soon as he found out she was pregnant, and she raised us till we were eight."

"I thought your mother died when you were eight," said Jeb.

"She did," Olivia whispered. "Afterwards I was sent to live with my uncle, the only family I had left. And Elizabeth, poor thing... After mum died our father came to meet us for the first time. He took a tragic interest in my sister and brought her back with him to that dreadful house. God knows how he raised her. How he ruined her. I haven't seen her in years."

A sympathetic look crossed Jeb's face as he reached out for her hand, but before he could reach it she pulled back.

"Last I heard she was working for him. My father. And I know that he was after Uncle Alan's work. She's racing us to get to the tomb first. She's dangerous, Jeb. Believe me, she's dangerous." Jeb couldn't bear to see her like this. He just wanted to hold her and tell her everything would be alright. To comfort her and tell her that she was special and brave and strong and that he'd make everything better for her. But he couldn't. She wasn't his anymore, and he knew you couldn't just go around saying things like that to people.

"I'll tell you about Midas now, Jeb." She wiped away the tears from her cheek, a new strength returning to her voice. She looked at him, her bluer than blue eyes still wet. "I'll tell you everything now."

# 22.

## GOLD, GIRLS, AND LIFE ETERNAL

"Shut up." Olivia frowned, that new strength still growing in her voice. "Do you want me to explain things to you or not?"

"By all means. I'm just impressed with how scholarly you can you be when you want to."

She scowled. He'd interrupted her again in the middle of her story. She warned him not to do it again.

Jeb raised his hand. "I'll behave, teach. Promise."

"You better." Olivia scratched an itch just above her breast. "Now, where was I? In ancient Greece there lived a powerful Phoenician King by the name of Midas. Midas was famous throughout the ancient world where wild stories were told of his infinite riches and his palace built of gold. Midas acquired his vast wealth, it was said, thanks in no small part to his alchemist. A man who, supposedly, had unlocked the mysteries of turning lead into gold. Dust into riches. Water into wine. You get the idea.

"In his youth the King was powerful, brilliant and dangerous, but as he grew old and frail his younger brother, Hermes, sensed weakness and started a coup to overthrow him. As his world collapsed around him Midas gathered the last of his loyal soldiers and his treasury of gold, loaded them all onto the deck of a massive trireme, and set sail to find the fabled fountain of youth. It was his hope that if he could regain his strength and youth, he might have revenge against the brother who had betrayed him.

"But Midas never set foot in Greece again, and the history of his life and his kingdom was largely forgotten, and presumably would have remained that way were it not, some six centuries later, for the actions of the poet Philisothocles, who returned from a long voyage at sea claiming to have met Midas alive in his own golden tomb. Philisothocles said that there lay hidden seven clues to the whereabouts of said tomb scattered across the globe. *'Hidden,'* he said, so that only the cleverest and most hearty of travelers might find their way to him, having proved themselves worthy of the gift of an eternal life."

"Naturally not many people believed Philisothocle's story, even in that age of Gods and monsters, thinking him mad or worse. But of those few who did, a handful went searching for the clues themselves. *None ever to return."*

Jeb leaned forwards, the fire casting a yellow pall across his chest. "Now this is gettin' good."

"The memories of Midas' legendary greed and alchemy devolved into the story of the golden touch which survives in the imagination of western folklore to this very day. The whole ridiculous fairy tale would have remained as much, largely written off as mythological nonsense, were it not for the work of one man."

Olivia dabbed at her eyes. "Oh, he was a saintly man, my uncle. Always fascinated by Greek mythology, and more specifically Greek literature, of which he was a professor at Oxford. I remember sometimes he used to read the Odyssey to us at night, my sister and me. One time he bought us each little wooden swords, and we dressed up as Odysseus and the Pirate King and rubbed lipstick along our arms and cheeks for blood. Elizabeth was covered in it. Just... that was her, always the theatrical one. She broke her leg that day, jumping off the balcony. She was walking the plank and I was the rogue pirate sending her off with a knife in her back.

"I think I could have stopped her. I know I... I should of. It wasn't a game anymore, not when the real blood ran down the lipstick stains and spilled onto the ground. I think she liked it more that way, when it was real. Or maybe that just made it more so. Just a game with higher stakes. I'm sorry, I've gone terribly off target. I'm sorry. The point is... the point is that Uncle Alan was a good man. He didn't deserve what happened to him. Didn't deserve to die like that, he..." Jeb reached out and touched her hand.

"Enter Dr. Jay Greenbaum: cartographer, amateur treasure hunter and an old friend of Uncle Alan's. While on assignment for the National Geographic, mapping the area surrounding the Dead Sea, Dr. Greenbaum was paid a visit by fate. It had washed up on the salt beaches of the Holy Land, locked in a box made of half dissolved stone: A small golden cube with a disjointed map inscribed upon it. A map, not only of

North Africa and ancient Greece, but what appeared to be the eastern coast of North America. The pieces of the map shifted and interlocked like a puzzle box: Each square, quarter inch piece of the peculiar cube covered in Phoenician letters, the precursor to the Latin alphabet.

"The scholars and scientists at the National Geographic who Dr. Greenbaum presented it to derided it as a hoax, a petty fake and an obvious one at that. Lacking all credibility he returned to his native England, his old Alma matter, and his good friend Alan Youngbridge. *'Le Carpe Aldous carne aum om' lentriala.'* That's what the map said once the pieces of the puzzle box had been twisted and turned into their proper places. *'Herein lies a signpost on the road to life eternal.'* There was a map hidden inside the sphere. Old, weathered, inked in faded blue onto yellow canvas. And on that map, marked only a few dozen miles away from where we are now, lies whatever it is it leads to. Oh, it's not the tomb, but it's a clue! A signpost on the way there. Inside of it we'll find another clue, another map. And from there another and maybe even another still. But eventually we will find it."

Jeb stared at her, slack jawed. "I hate the very idea of living forever, that sounds terrible to me. But the gold, Olivia. Is that real?"

Olivia frowned. "This isn't about gold, this is about finishing what he started. This was his big break, his once in a lifetime, and I'm gonna see it through. And not because I speak Latin, or

Phoenician, or because I know my Greek history, I'm gonna finish this because he loved me and he wanted me to be here with him on this, and I'm not gonna let him down. When he and Greenbaum realized where the map led, they knew what they had to do. The scientific community which had mocked Greenbaum earlier would have to eat a whole banquet of crow when he returned smiling from Africa, a mountain of gold and a rewritten history book in tow. However, there was one problem. They had no way to get there.

"Any voyage to the dark continent is prohibitively expensive, not to mention dangerous. Compounding this obvious problem, no commercial vessel would ever travel where they needed to go and they needed to get in and out without hitting customs."

*"So?"* Jeb asked.

"So desperation often leads to poor judgment, and having run out of ideas and options, Uncle made the fatal mistake of returning to my father's house," said Olivia. "Negotiations between the two did not go well, and Alan stormed out of the mansion, his map and research in tow, swearing he would never make the mistake of coming to the old man for help again. Two weeks later, as Uncle Alan sat with his friend in a London flat, waiting for the boat that would take them to America and meet with me, an assassin stormed the building, slitting Greenbaum's throat. Uncle bailed out of a third story window, crashing down onto an open canopy below, not too worse for wear. But the map was gone. The first thing he did when he got to safety was draw up a copy from memory.

"It wasn't hard to convince me to join him. He told me that he had found a generous benefactor to fund the expedition, and that we would be leaving under cover of night in just a few days. I should have been more suspicious of the whole thing. I should have known better. He went through the kind of men you work for, Jeb, scoundrels and villains, selling his soul to the devil as he made a bargain with the mob.

"So here we are. And no, I don't know why Elizabeth would want to hurt me, and I don't know if I can forgive you for lying to me about why you came aboard that boat, just as I don't know if you can forgive me for lying to you. But I am glad you're here right now, and even if I don't know who the assassin is who did Greenbaum in, I do know who shot my Uncle. I'm not a violent women. I'm a peaceful person, I'm a pacifist, I'm… *something*. But if I ever catch up with that bastard, Virtrolli, I don't know what I'll do. I don't think I could kill a man. I don't imagine I could ever kill anyone. Not like you, Jeb. I'm not cold blooded enough, I don't have the constitution for it, the veins flowing with ice. I'm more like Sam. Gentle, like Sam is gentle. At least I'm trying to be. I'm trying not to let this eat me up."

Jeb stared at her. "That's a nice story, Olivia. It really gets ya, right here." He put his hand over his heart.

"Is everything a joke to you?" she asked.

"No, it isn't. You know, I'm not as cold blooded as you think I am. I'm not a bad man."

She looked down, drawing her hand from the wisps of her hair down to her stomach. "You must be excited. After all, if you pull this off you'll be the richest man in the world." Jeb looked away. He could buy himself a pardon. Politicians could be greased couldn't they? Of course they could, the lying bunch of pigs.

*The richest man in the world.* He mulled the phrase over and over in his head. It was almost too fantastic to believe. Yachts, and women, and racecars, and champagne. Sam grinned at him and Jeb could see the same gleam of greed in his friend's eyes. The richest men in the world.

# 23.
# BULLET POINTS

### The Next Day

Jeb rubbed his eyes as he sat up, the formerly raging fire now a pile of ash. He looked around, making sure no one had noticed he'd dozed off. It had, after all, been his turn to stand watch. As he stood up and peered at the clear blue sky above him he breathed a sigh of relief. He was excited now. The truth about all this Midas business finally revealed, and the prospect of making a fortune off it all left Jeb in understandably high spirits. There was a faint smell of burning wood in the air, and a little yellow bird was soaring overhead.

Things quickly came crashing back down to earth as he looked over at the sight of Olivia fast asleep with a wedding band around her finger, and remembered that he couldn't forget her. Her head was rested upon a pillow of sand, and there was a sweet, soft look upon her face. Jeb clenched his fists. There was something about her that he'd never been able to fully let go. Or at least, if he had let it go, it had come back to him now.

Olivia yawned as she opened her eyes. "How'd the night watch go?" she asked.

"Couple boring hours counting sand dunes, nothing I couldn't handle," Jeb said as he scratched a bit of crisp, dried blood from behind his ear.

Olivia caught something sour in his voice and reached for his hand. "Are you OK?"

"What do care?" asked Jeb.

She walked up to him and took his hand. "I care about what's happening to you. To all of us."

"Yeah right. You can lie to yourself, but don't try it on me, sister," he said.

"Try what on you? You don't think I care?" she asked.

"No, I don't think you ever cared. You lied to me. You lied to me from day one, and then you had the audacity to turn things around and get mad at me for doing the same thing. The hypocrisy of it all is staggering."

"Really?" she said as she crossed her arms.

"Yeah, really," he said. "I mean, Jesus Christ, it's not like I haven't been through enough out here already, fighting off God damned cannibals and gangsters. And then I've got your sister chasing after me. Do you know she promised to cut out my eye if I turned on her? God damn! You just don't mess around with people who promise things like that!"

"Jeb, would you relax?"

"No, I won't. How can I now that I know everything between us was just one big lie."

"You think we were a lie?" She looked stunned. "Jeb I gave you everything."

"No I gave *you* everything, and you left me with nothing!   Nothing but scars and broken bits of myself that I had to try and scrape back together.   Don't you think it's hard for me to find out about all this family stuff after the fact?"

"Don't you think it's hard for me?!" said Olivia. "Try living with it.   Try keeping it from everyone around you like a chained up monster that keeps trying to escape.   I never even told my husband what I told you last night."

"I'll bet there's a lot of things you never told your husband.   A lot of things about us."

"Shut up."

"No."

"I don't wanna dredge up the past with you," said Olivia.

Jeb shrugged.   "Why not?   Too many secrets you don't want slipping out?"

"You're an immature pig.   You're vile and stupid and you infuriate me!" she cried.

Jeb through up his hands and stormed off. "Good!"

"Did I miss something?"   Sam said sleepily as he sat up.

"Nothing."   Olivia glared at Jeb.

"What happened?   You two talkin' about me?" Sam asked again.

"No one is talking about you, you narcissistic jackass, now go back to bed."   Jeb snapped.

Sam looked hurt.   "But it's morning."

"Well then wake up and eat breakfast, I don't' know!" Jeb said as he picked up a can of red beans from the ratty knapsack Sam and Olivia had been hauling around their newfound foodstuffs in. "How are you opening these up, anyways?"

"We picked up a sharp chunk of steel off the beach," Olivia said coldly, "it takes awhile, but you can use it to make a hole in the lid, and yank it open." She was about to say something else when Jeb dropped the can to the ground, took a few steps back and pulled out his pistol, blowing the lid off the can in one ferocious shot.

"You idiot!" Olivia screamed as Jeb knelt down, pleased with himself as he picked up the shattered can, red beans leaking out from its many cracks. "You're so fucking reckless!"

"Woah, watch the language there, sweetheart," Jeb said with a smirk.

"Don't call me that! First it's doll face, now it's sweetheart?!" she said in an exasperated voice, as she pushed against his chest.

"Don't let him get to you, Old Girl," Sam said calmly.

"Don't call me that either," she snapped.

Sam looked hurt as Olivia trudged down the far side of the shit smelling, moss, sand and rock hill they were currently atop.

"Where are you going?" Sam asked Olivia.

"Getting our bearings," she said. "I need to figure out how to get to Harriramma. It's the nearest town." Olivia paused for a moment as she looked out at the sweeping desert landscape before her. Tiny stones and bushes dotted the landscape, and in the far off distance she thought she could make out the hulking mass of an elephant against the red sun.

**"POW!"** another violent gun blast.

"Damn it, Jeb I thought I told you to stop that?!" A sudden sick look tore across her face as she saw the tall blonde holding the smoking gun.

"Hello sister," said Elizabeth.

"Hello Liz," Olivia replied. The silver pistol pointed at her chest, Olivia made the long climb back up the hill, only to see Jeb had his gun fixed on Sam.

"Nice work," Elizabeth said to Jeb. He nodded, and she looked back at Olivia, who was scowling.

"You're in on this too, Jeb?" Olivia stared at him with knives in her eyes.

"He knows what will happen if he doesn't fall in line," Elizabeth said dryly. "Good job finding these two."

"It was nothing," Jeb replied.

"What happened to Arnold?"

"He was lost," said Jeb. "The cannibals-"

Elizabeth shrugged. "He's replaceable."

Olivia looked over at Jeb again, trying to catch his eye, but he and his pistol were focused on Sam.

"Jeb," Elizabeth shouted to him, her eyes still fixed on Olivia. "Kill that man, we don't need him."

Sam's eyes went wide with fear.

"Sorry, but I don't shoot my best friend for nobody," Jeb said, as he whipped around, turning his gun on Elizabeth.

"What the hell?" Elizabeth cursed.

"And by the way, that man's name is Sam Ammatto, and he's a God damn badass, so drop the gun, cupcake," Jeb commanded, as he cocked his pistol.

"Very well." She paused as she began to lower her gun.

"Easy," said Jeb, his gun still trained on her. Her movements were smooth, almost catlike, and her long, carefully toned legs bent with precision. For a moment Jeb forgot who he was looking at.

That moment was all she needed. In a whirlwind, Elizabeth spun around, her gun pointed up at Jeb's face. It was life or death. In one carefully aimed blast, he shot the gun from her hand just as she was about to fire. He blew the stream of smoke away from the barrel as Elizabeth stood screaming and shaking her hand.

"That's some fancy shootin', Tex," Elizabeth said through clenched teeth.

"Not to sound clichéd, but I *was* aiming for your head."

"Ha. Ha." She forced a bout of sarcastic laughter out her mouth, as she rubbed her shell shocked right hand. "Funny."

"What do you want?" Olivia asked as she came up behind her sister. "Uncle Alan is already dead. I hope you're happy."

"Olivia!" she said in a sinister voice, as she whipped around to face her sister, her gray eyes smiling with madness. "Why of course that doesn't make me happy. How could you even say such a thing?"

Olivia sneered. "So father sent you here to kill me?"

"No darling. I'm afraid, much like Uncle Alan, father has passed on to the next."

A look of shock came across Olivia's face. "He's dead?"

Elizabeth smiled. "He's in the great beyond, the hall of the angels, or perhaps, oh, I don't know, the seventh circle of Hell. At any rate save your tears."

"My eyes are dry enough." Olivia paused. "But you must miss him."

"Yes. Yes, I think I missed him most when I was pulling the trigger," said Elizabeth. "Oh please, don't give me that look, you wanted him off'd just as much as I did! The old bastard had it coming."

Olivia shook her head and looked away.

"Don't worry, Olivia, it's not like I stand to benefit from it. The will was very specific about leaving both of us out, I'm sure. Believe me my motivations were much more personal than financial." She smiled as she reached into her back pocket and retrieved a tattered, ancient map. "Olivia, I didn't come here to kill you, I came here to help you. Besides, with dear Uncle Alan gone, you're the only one who can translate this thing."

"What about Seamus?" asked Jeb.

"Seamus is dead." She gave a small shrug. "He died of a broken heart."

"Yeah right."

"It's true," said Elizabeth. "Swear to God." She pouted her large, pink bow lips. "Olivia. Let's go find the treasure for ourselves. Split it between us." She put her hands on her sister's shoulders and whispered. *"We could be rich!"*

Olivia shrugged her off. "I don't care about the money, I'm in this for nobler reasons. Think of the historical value of this find. Whatever gold may be in Midas' tomb, it belongs in a museum, not a bank."

This last statement concerned Jeb slightly. Were they not going to keep the gold? Was that line about him being the richest man in the world really just a dig? He had no lofty ideals concerning museums or knowledge. He wanted his own mansion, God damn it. Maybe a nice yacht and a sports car. A couple of butlers and maids. Bi-monthly vacations to the Caribbean and a bi-sexual contortionist mistress from the South Sea's with an exotic name like *'Zantara.'* Was that too much to ask for?

"Olivia, you don't have a choice here, you need my help," said Elizabeth. "Not only do I know the way to Harriramma, but I can arrange transportation to the first clue once we get there. Not to mention the boat I've got waiting off the coast for me. We can all get in, get out, and go home rich, no customs, no questions. And donate *most* of the finds to museums, of course."

Olivia looked her over, scanning her twins face.

"Come on, Olivia," said Elizabeth. "We're sisters. Twins for God's sakes! You can trust me."

There was a long, awkward silence as Olivia sized her up. "I don't trust you. Contrary to what you may believe, I am not so naïve as I once was, nor am I that same silly girl who you convinced had ghosts living under her floorboards. Even if I did trust you, it doesn't matter. There's probably no way to get what we came here for without the key."

"Key? What key?" asked Elizabeth.

"It was locked up in the puzzle box along with the map. Uncle Alan had it on him, and so I can only assume it went down with the ship," she said, her voice ragged with melancholy.

"Wait!" Jeb blurted out, as he fished his hand through his back pocket and retrieved the same long, shimmering gold object he'd recovered from the professor's suitcase days ago. "Is this it?"

Olivia's eyes lit up, Sam breaking the group's silence as he cleared his throat and made his way towards Elizabeth. "So I've got a question for you, you toxic, white trash piece a' shit. How far?"

# 24.
# BEHOLDEN

It took days to reach Harriramma. Days of dry desert heat and bickering between Olivia and Elizabeth. Days of suspicion and furrowed brows. Days spent dreaming of a million ways to spend a fortune in gold.

And then, at long last, they had arrived.

"Finally." Elizabeth smiled, her face glowing, drenched in sweat as she looked up at the city walls. Sam raised his hand. "Uh, question. Is this place safe, or what?"

Elizabeth shook her head. "Harriramma is a slum, a colonial German trade post gone sour. You will never find a more wretched hive of scum and villainy."

"So I take it that's a *no*," Jeb said dryly, as he rubbed his jaw.

"We'll head for the city bazaar first thing once we get inside," said Olivia. "Liz has got plenty of money on her, so we'll stock up on supplies, refuel ourselves, and then hole up for the night in a hotel. Assuming we can find one."

"And then-" Elizabeth interjected, "first thing in the morning we'll secure transportation, and head out into the desert. You can follow that map, Olivia, can't you?"

"Of course I can." Olivia snapped.

"Swell." Elizabeth pursed her lips together. "I'll handle the guards."

"You speak German?" asked Jeb.

Elizabeth nodded. "That, French, Spanish and a bit of Japanese."

Clockwork spires and old stucco buildings rose up dimly from behind the massive white wall that surrounded Harriramma. At least sixty feet high and lying in a pale state of disrepair, the wall towered over them, casting black shadows across their faces like spilled ink. Two Germans stood guard at the old passageway through the wall, a great, rusting gate separating the desolation of the rocky desert from the busting metropolis within. Elizabeth slipped them each a folio filled with bank notes and they nodded for the group to move along through the great rusted gates and into the city, where a sand swept stone road led them to a bustling open air bazaar. Hundreds of beautifully dark Africans moved about from left to right, a small band of pale European guards watching like wolves from guard towers overhead. "What was all that about with the bribe?" Jeb whispered to Elizabeth.

"Don't ask," she said dryly. "They're just not used to tourists."

Small stands and tents lined the edges of the bazaar, tall, robin egg blue buildings casting shadows in a crisscross pattern. Olivia's eyes gleamed as she made her way through, stopping to look at wicker baskets filled with live, slithering eels and ivory carved trinkets. There was a man sitting atop a red rug weaved with orange diamonds and silver moon shapes, his head shaved and pupils a pale, milky white. Dozens of black scorpions scurried in the shade, the man snapping them back with a splintered wooden rod as soon as they crawled too close to the edge.

Jeb followed Olivia, passing by vegetables and weapons and everything in between, silently taking note of all the wonders around him before the massive form of a grounded Zeppelin stopped him in his tracks.

"Spooky, ain't it?" Sam said as he walked up behind Jeb, placing a hand on his shoulder. "Don't suppose it brings back any memories?"

* * * * * * * *

The oddly named Hyena Hein Sphincter was a rundown colonial building commissioned and built in 1883. While the modestly sized building had been founded as a civic office and church, it had since changed hands several times, having been used as a schoolhouse, antique shop, bookstore and ultimately a whorehouse before being seized by the colonial government during the War. After the War ended the government ceded control of the building and it was put up for sale, where it was soon bought by the Madame of the former whorehouse, Fraulein Ava Fox, who converted it into what was officially a hotel. However, in a city where the official story was rarely the truth, the Sphincter had become well known as a place where one could find women of accommodating morals.

Jeb found his room, taking his time in the bath before getting dressed in fresh clothes. He dozed off on the bed, waking up a few hours later to find himself late for dinner, and he quickly made his way down the long, strawberry colored hallway and stairs towards the hotels dining hall where he waved at Sam and the girls.

"You started without me?" Jeb asked he sat down.

Sam shrugged. "You was late and we was hungry. Deal with it."

Jeb smiled, poured himself a glass of red wine from a half full bottle, and took a swig. "This is good stuff," he commented. "I mean, you know, for kraut wine that is."

Elizabeth scoffed. "What is it you two have against Germans, anyhow?"

Jeb shrugged. "I was in the war, alright? I saw Europe devastated. What those krauts did too…" he droned off as his mind drifted back towards distant memories of the war. The grotesque images of death and destruction. The invisible chains that bound him there. The way things had changed so much between he and Olivia when he'd returned.

"Jeb, are you ok?" Olivia asked in a whisper, her hand upon his.

"I'm dandy," he muttered as he shook her off. "You folks mind if we change the subject?"

"Please do," said Sam, as he marched his fork across the table, glaring at Elizabeth. "Any more a' this and I might just--"

"Heresn you are," Ava declared loudly, as she sat down their plates.

"Mein thanks, fraulein," Jeb said as he turned towards Olivia. "What'd you order me, anyway?"

"Sour kraut," she said with a smirk.

"Boooo," Jeb frowned as he lifted the cover off of his plate. It was a large casserole served with peas and a biscuit.

"A toast," said Sam, everyone else's face half stuffed with food. "To old friends. New adventures. *And unbelievable riches.*"

"Here, here," Jeb said as he chomped down a slice of chicken casserole.

"Now, admittedly," said Sam, "there are harsh feelings between some of us."

Elizabeth avoided the table's glare.

"Some of us who, it might be said, are crazy. Or dangerous. Or psychotic. Or hey, maybe just tried to kill me or whatever."

Jeb cleared his throat.

"But that's all in the past," said Sam, "and maybe... maybe Jeb and I can put our differences with the Germans in the past too." He grinned. "Though I wouldn't count on it." The promise of vast amounts of gold was helping everyone to get along, as was the wine, all three bottles of it. Sam smiled at Elizabeth and she returned the favor. Had she been a man or ugly he'd probably knock her in the teeth for what she'd done.  But she wasn't, and Sam was easy.  "To Elizabeth."  He smiled.  "The nastiest bitch I know."

She took it as a joke and laughed.

"Now," Jeb interrupted, scratching his chin, his thoughts on Elizabeth much the same as Sam's, "if you all don't mind, I'd like to get a refill."  He held up his glass in the air and called out with liquor wrapped around his tongue.

"Ja?" Ava asked as she walked over.  "More vine?"

"Uh.. Yeah.  Yes please," said Jeb, "and a bottle a champagne too, if it's no trouble."

"Not at all," she said with a smile.  "It vill' just be une minute."

"Gracias."  A blurry eyed Jeb smiled.


An hour and a half later Sam was passed out, Elizabeth was laughing, a chair was broken, and chocolate cake was smeared across Jeb's face.

*"Hey,"* Jeb murmured, as he sat down outside on the front steps of the hotel, squeezing in the middle between Olivia and Elizabeth, the two twins so different from one another.

*"Hey,"* Elizabeth whispered, and touched his hand.

Olivia looked over at him, a glum look on her face.  "Yoouu loook whittled as aaaa penguin."

"Um," said Jeb.

"Talk about penguins, I'm stupid zozzled," Elizabeth said as she began to giggle.  She threw her head back and roared with laughter, her blonde hair ruffled, loose and wild.

Jeb looked over at her and shook his head. He sighed and looked back at Olivia. "I'm gonna go to bed."

*"Ok,"* she whispered.

"No!" Elizabeth cried as she grabbed his arm. "Stay!" She had a wide, bright smile on her face, and her gray eyes were twinkling. "Please Jeb, for me."

"I don't know," Jeb said in a slow, hushed voice. His head was throbbing and he felt like crap.

"Please?" she asked again, clutching his arm tighter.

"Did yoouu get Sam back upta his room aright?" Olivia asked, pushing a finger into Jeb's chest.

He nodded.

"Gooood." Olivia slurred. "I think he was drunk."

Jeb nodded again. "I think so my dear."

"Doo not call me that," she said.

"What?" he asked.

"That."

"Dear?"

*"Ummm...."* Olivia leaned back till her head hit the marble step behind her, and she cried out in pain.

"Olivia?" Jeb turned his head over to her.

"Yes dear?" she said, looking him and Elizabeth over.

"Do you love him?" he asked.

"Who?" asked Olivia.

"Your husband."

Elizabeth looked up, staring carefully into her sisters eyes.

"I...." Olivia stopped and thought for a moment. "I..... I think so." She nodded slowly. "Yes. I love him."

Jeb nodded, a dead feeling in his stomach, and he thought about her husband touching the small of her back and telling her some quaint inside joke, and making her laugh in that way he loved. Her husband.

"Jeb, I thought you were magnificent tonight," Elizabeth said with a smirk.

"Yeah? You thought so, huh?" he asked.

"Oh yes. Yes definitely."

"How about you, Olivia, did you think I was magnificent?" asked Jeb.

Olivia shrugged. "Not particularly."

Jeb frowned and looked back at Elizabeth, who was still smiling as she stared into his emerald eyes. Her warm body pressed up close to him. Gently, she moved her hands up his arms and began to stroke him, her teeth clenching her lower lip. He half smiled and looked down, enjoying the warmth of her body. "You've got something there," she said in a low voice.

"I've what?" Jeb asked.

"On your face. You've got cake. There's cake on your face." she laughed. "Here, I'll help.... I'll help you." She brushed the hair from his face, along with a bit of the chocolate cake. Jeb could feel the heat of her breath as she moved closer, her mouth on his cheek as she let out her smooth, wine soaked tongue and began to lick the chocolate from his face. Her wet kisses inching closer and closer towards his lips and his mouth.

*"Mmmm,"* he moaned as the tip of her tongue stroked his upper lip. She peered down, an unmistakable look of hunger in her eyes, and they began to make out.

"I'm gonna...." a drunken Olivia said as she began to stand up, before gagging and hurling all over the steps in sickening brown splendor. Jeb pulled away and groaned, a sympathetic look in his eyes, before being forcefully pulled back into the recesses of Elizabeth's mouth. Olivia made her way up the stairs and Jeb and Elizabeth soon followed, hand in hand.

# 25.

# THE MORNING AFTER

He woke up naked except for his socks, in a pale pink room. Body covered in a film of sweat, right hand handcuffed to the bed post, and the unmistakable stench of sex, whiskey and cigarettes heavy in the air. Elizabeth was lying next to him in a similar state, her hair a wild, tangled mess. There was dried blood and a bite mark on his lower lip.

Jeb found the key lying near her breast, and wriggled out from the handcuffs to find his right arm numb from sleep. Blood and a taste he assumed was Elizabeth lingered in his mouth. He moved out of the bed slowly, and pulled on his trousers. He turned around, his pants only half way up as Elizabeth made a light murmur of a sound. *"Mmm,"* she sighed as she batted her eyes.

"Hey." He smiled awkwardly as he continued to pull up his pants.

Elizabeth shuffled around within the sheets before sitting up, the white cotton half wrapped around her breasts, her face frowning. "What the hell happened last night?"

*"Well."* Jeb shrugged. "I think that much is obvious."

She looked into his eyes. "You'd better be clean."

"Wugh..." Jeb seemed taken aback. "Yeah... Yeah, of course. You? I mean we did you use some kind of... *protection*. At least I hope so."

"Doesn't matter," she said as she wiped her nose. "I've got an empty oven."

"...what? Oh. Oh!" Jeb paused. "Well uh, I'd better be going then."

She nodded.

"Well. Ok." Again he half smiled as he looked around the pink, sparsely furnished room. "This is a nice place."

She shrugged. "Not really. This whole continent is shit."

He started to say something, before she lifted a hand to stop him. "Look, you're a handsome bastard, I'll give you that. But you talk too much."

"Um," he said.

"I think you'd better be going, Jeb. I've gotta get moving and make final arrangements for our little safari today," she said in a husky, wine weary voice.

"Good bye Liz- Elizabeth," Jeb said awkwardly, as he turned and opened the door.

* * * * * * *

"Hey!" Olivia called out to Jeb as he entered the dining room, a friendly look upon her face.

"Oh, hey," Jeb said in a half cracking voice. His shoulders were slumped as he sat down in the chair next to her. Sam was also sitting down, a half-eaten slice of bread, slathered in purple jam, held precariously in his hand. "Here," Olivia said as she passed him a tall, cool, glass of milk.

"Thanks," Jeb said reluctantly. Olivia stared at him, but he couldn't look her in the eyes. "Have you seen Elizabeth?" she asked.

Jeb choked on his milk, coughing as he put it down. "Who? Elizabeth?"

"Yeah?" said Olivia, a strange look on her face. "Why, what happened?"

"NOTHING!" Jeb said in a voice that was much too loud. "Nothing happened. Uh... I saw her in the hallway, and, um, she said something about going to make travel arrangements."

"Ah," said Olivia. "Good."

"Man!" Sam shouted to no one in particular, as he swallowed his last bite of bread and jam. "What happened last night, huh? Honest ta' God, I have got such a headache!"

"Oh, me too!" Olivia groaned. "I was so bombed, I.... I don't remember anything."

"Huh." Jeb forced a smile as Olivia began to laugh at the situation. "How about you, Jeb, do you remember anything at all?" she asked.

"Not really." Jeb shrugged. "I think you threw up."

Olivia looked away, clearly embarrassed. "Yeah, I could tell this morning."

Jeb groaned as he rubbed at his left eye. "Sam, pass me some a' that toast, will ya'?"

A half an hour or so passed before a proud Elizabeth strode into the room, her hips swaying like a pendulum as she beamed, two large canvas bags held firmly in her hands, Jeb's suit jacket tied around her waist. "What's all this?" asked Olivia, as Jeb looked away, trying ineptly to cover his face.

"Supplies." Elizabeth smiled. "Here Jeb," she said with a smirk, "you forgot your jacket."

"Oh..." Jeb said slowly. "Yeah, I thought I dropped it back in the hallway."

*"Mmm,"* Elizabeth said with a sarcastic nod, as Sam stared at Jeb from across the table. A knowing, and thoroughly disgusted expression covered his face.

"Everything is set," Elizabeth said proudly. We've got camels, porters, food, water, all the supplies we need."

"Wonderful!" Olivia said with a smile. "That's fantastic news."

"If we leave before ten, how long do you think it should take us?" Elizabeth asked Olivia, before shooting a knowing glance at Jeb, who hurriedly looked away.

"Oh, two, three hours maybe," Olivia said. "It shouldn't take too long. According to the map, we're really quite close." She pulled out Elizabeth's neatly folded copy of the map from the breast pocket of her shirt, and laid it out on the table top. "We're here." She pointed at a spot somewhere in the middle of the hastily shaded area meant to represent the desert, and traced her finger towards a large, red X. "Assuming

Uncle Allen's calculations were correct, that's where we need to go.

"Sounds good to me," said Elizabeth. "What do you think, Jeb?"

"Me? Abou- about what?" Jeb stuttered.

"About Olivia, of course. She's just so smart isn't she? Such a good little navigator."

"Yeah." Jeb half smiled as Olivia looked towards him. "Yeah, she's great. She's wonderful."

"Yes. Of course she is," Elizabeth said. "Always has been."

# 26.
# INTERLUDE II

### Summerset, New Hampshire,  May, 1903

Growing up in that creaking, wooden farm house wasn't always easy for five year old Jeb.  He was a frantic, naturally happy child, always running through the corn fields, and wading across the brooks and marshes in the back woods.  He was sitting in a pair of white overalls and a sky blue shirt, a smile on his tiny face.  Jeb looked up at a nearby dragon fly, its wings fluttering madly as it took off from its perch atop a sun flower and landed on his nose.

*"Ah!"* he gasped as the creature buzzed atop him.

"Jeb!" His mother called out as she waked towards him.  "There you are!" she said with a smile, "there's mommy's little boy!"

Jeb laughed as she lifted him up.  "Dragonfly."

"That's right."  She smiled.  "Good job."  She hugged him tightly before setting him back down. She took his small hand and walked towards the flat, sunset bathed farm house.  Short, white puffs of smoke came up through the chimney.

"Here," she said as they entered the house, stepping softly onto the well worn green rug.  "Your daddy came home this afternoon."

"Daddy?"

"That's right."

Jeb frowned. "I don't... But... but he went away, mommy."

"Well now he's back." She smiled, her face scrunched up, drenched in murky shadows. She reached up and lit a candle on the book shelf. "And we're very lucky to have him!"

Jeb fidgeted in his white overalls. "Do I have to?"

"Yes!" she said. "Jeb, your father loves you very much. OK? He wants to see you, don't disappoint him."

"Ok, mommy." Jeb nodded as he made his way down the hallway and through the last door on his left. "Daddy?"

Jack sat in the far corner of the kitchen. A small, red book in his hands, his feet kicked up on the white tablecloth. He had dark emerald eyes, just like Jeb. There was a dim, mildly amused expression on his face as he looked towards his son. At nearly six and a half feet, he towered over the boy.

"Mommy says were not 'sposed to put our feet up there."

Jack frowned as he set down his book. "Is that right?"

"Yup." Young Jeb smiled. "She says that we.. Um... Well, our feet, and dirt, um... and..."

"Come here," he commanded.

Jeb stood there nervously, before taking a few tepid steps, his hands pushed into the white pockets of his overalls.

*"Now,"* Jack said sternly.

Jeb rushed over quickly, his tiny legs carrying him as fast as they could.

"So," Jack said, a smile on his face, as he lowered his large hands down onto Jeb's shoulders, gripping him tightly. "Say that again?"

"Well I mean..." Jeb said, "I mean, mommy said, no feets on the table, and..."

"OW!" Jeb cried as Jack hit him against the head with an open palm.

"You listen to me, boy. You don't tell me what to do. You understand me? You don't ever tell me what to do. I'm the daddy, God damnit, and you will show me respect, do you understand?"

"Ow! That hurt!" Jeb cried.

"That's not what I wanna hear!" he growled. "Tell me you understand."

"Yes daddy..." Jeb said softly.

"Speak up."

"Yes daddy!"

"Why do you make me do this, Jeb, huh? Why do you make me to do this to you? Do you think I enjoy this? You think I enjoy having to punish you?"

"No..."

"Damn it, you little retard, stop making me treat you this way!" he shouted, as he slapped him again. "Say you're sorry like you mean it. Like a man."

"I'm sorry!" he cried.

"Now get outta here!" Jack roared as Jeb scampered out the room, and into his mother's arms.

"Jack, I'm sorry!" she said. "I'm so sorry he's like that. I don't know what the devils gotten into him but-"

"Damn sorry excuse for a mother you are, letting him run around like that." he frowned.

"…Jack, I…."

"Kid ain't got no manners. Ain't got no respect for his own daddy."

"He just-"

"That kid. After everything I done for you. Everything I done for him. The things I've sacrificed!" He scowled as he looked up at a small, green dragonfly hovering up near the ceiling. "Fuckin bugs," he grunted as he grabbed his book and crept up out of the chair.

"Jack I'm sorry I just-"

*"Shut up,"* he hushed her as he slammed the book down atop the dragon fly, crushing it into oblivion.

# 27.
# BLINK OF AN EYE

After a few hot and hazy early morning hours the gang had largely left the desert behind, and were now traveling across the grassy, sun burnt plains of the savannah atop a gaggle of drooling camels. Massive baobab and jackalberry trees rose up from out of the brush, along with thousands of wildflowers and weeds, as vast herds of zebra grazed on the brush. A bright orange sun rose up above the mountainous horizon, and the entire landscape became infused with a warm, slow burning majesty.

The leader of their three porters, Hunjii, was a Masai warrior exiled from his tribe in British Kenya. He wore a brilliant red tunic covered in beads and other ornamentations, and his hair was tightly braided into a long black ponytail. Hunjii's eyes were sharp, hawk like, and so it was only natural that he be the first to notice the massive airship far off in the distance behind them.

"Look over that!" he called out. "Dis' is da' *Zeeeppelin.* Dis' one have bin follow us."

Jeb whipped his head back and choked the reins, causing his camel to groan to a halt. It took him a few seconds of squinted concentration, but eventually he realized what the Masai was talking about. "You're right," he said. "What the hell's it doing out here?"

"Where?" Sam looked out at the vast, blue horizon for a moment. "Oh I see it! Yeah." He turned towards Jeb." Looks like the same one somebody had parked behind the slums yesterday."

"Yeah, I'd imagine so..." Jeb drifted off, as he stared at the massive dirigible hovering out far behind them. After a few moments the oversized balloon disappeared behind a mountain range and Jeb waved it off, continuing onwards. At the time he didn't think much of it. None of them did.

"Up there!" said Olivia, the creased, folded over map in her hands. "Two more miles due east, then we should be able to find the next landmark." She looked down at the map. "We're looking for a small, dormant volcano. Hunjii, do you know of anything like that out here?"

Hunjii nodded gravely, and led they continued onwards, passing by the landmarks foretold on the map. First past an ancient, crumbling red mound buried in glassy, swirling magma, then over a river and up onto a dark plateau: it's pale grass and weeds growing under the constant shadow of the two enormous cliffs which sat on either side of it. The Zeppelin continued to drift in and out of view. Sam suggested that perhaps they were being followed, but the rest of the group shrugged him off as being paranoid. After all, it wasn't like anyone in town had seen the map, or realized what it was they were chasing after in the middle of the Savanna.

The untamed, virgin landscape seemed to roar like the beasts upon it as Jeb studied the setting sun. He tugged at the reins of his camel and rode up alongside Olivia, the marmalade yellow light washing over her, caressing her curves and features with a generous kind of warmth. She turned away from the sun for a moment, her pale face becoming a suntanned brown, like a shadow cast underneath an oak tree, her eyes cold reflections of the sky.

"What's that look, Olivia?" Jeb asked.

She turned to face him. "What look?"

"That look," he said. "That look of *'I'm sitting on a bomb that's about to go off and I'm terrified and don't know what to do'.*"

"Oh, *that* look," she said as she brushed a strand of short red hair from her face. "That's just the casual, everyday way I look when I'm traveling with my murderous sister and ex-boyfriend on my way to a three thousand year old unopened tomb."

"So then you're not feeling stressed out or anything?"

"Who me?" she said, pointing to herself. "No, Jeb, of course not, why would you ever think such a thing."

He wiped his hand across his forehead in mock relief. "Well that's good to hear." Jeb pulled a droëwors from the pack on his camel, and bit down. "So say this all works out, your sister doesn't try to kill us, and we do find the gold," he said through bites, "here is my question to you-"

"I'm listening," she said.

"What are you gonna do with your share of the treasure? Besides, you know, museums and charity and blah, blah, blah, all that other stuff you talked about, which, you know, of course I agree with completely."

Olivia shrugged. "I suppose I'd vacation somewhere nice, drink lots of overpriced wine, and buy something expensive for my husband as a thank you present for being so damn patient with me."

There was a long pause. "Well…" Jeb said impatiently.

"Well, what?" asked Olivia.

"Well, you gonna ask me, or what?"

"Ask you what exactly?"

"What I'm gonna do with my share."

"Oh, that," she said.

"Aren't you curious?"

"Not really." She smiled. "I'll let you think about it for a while though. And then someday I'll ask you and you'll have a really good answer for me, instead of whatever sweetly acerbic comment I'm sure you have on the tip of your tongue."

Jeb blushed. "Me lady, I think you know me too well."

She struggled to hide a smile. "That's just the problem, isn't it?"

\* \* \* \* \* \* \* \*

Wet eyed hyenas laughing in the distance, vultures shrieking overhead, and there, just over the horizon, the resting place of Midas' first clue.

*"It exists!"* Elizabeth whispered. She flashed her sister a smile, and together they rode down towards the massive Grecian arch. Its legs were golden pillars, each one inscribed in small, ancient Phoenician lettering. Upon the top of the arch there were two enormous golden lions, their front legs stretched out towards a sinister looking eye that dominated the entire structure. An orb of blown glass lay at its center, serving as the pupil.

Jeb stared at the ancient structure. *"Had no one else come this far?"*

As soon as they saw the arch the porters began to shout frantically at each other in their native tongue. Hunjii frowned. "De' odah two men, dey say dat dey know dis' place."

One of the porters shouted out in fear, his hands covering his face.

"He say," Hunjii began, "Dey village eldas, where dey grew up. Dey av' heard dem speak a' dis place. Dey say dis' place is cursed ant wicked."

"Cursed?" Jeb asked. "Are you sure that's what they said?"

"I'm sure," Hunjii said solemnly.

"Fuck!" Jeb said as he dismounted his camel. "People have been here before then. The clue could be already pillaged and gone."

"What's going on?" Sam asked. "What do they mean *cursed*?"

"Long dey hear stories from de' elders of the deeevils arch," said Hunjii. "Of de cursed eye."

"The cursed eye?" Sam looked back towards the gargantuan gold structure, and the admittedly eerie looking eye carved into the top of it. Olivia and Elizabeth were both standing directly under it now.

"Dey' say dat' de' eye be det' a de' deeevil. Dat' Satan's eye kill anyone who dare look upon it."

"Enough with the hocus pocus." Elizabeth frowned. "Jeb's right, I'm more concerned with whether whatever artifacts we need have already been looted, then I am with their superstitions."

Hunjii shrugged. "Dey will not stay."

"Make them!" she ordered.

"How?"

*"Ugh."* Elizabeth walked away, leaving Olivia to step in. "Give them whatever supplies and provisions they need to make it back to Harriramma," she said, "but make sure they leave all the excavation equipment. If what we need ends up being buried underneath that thing, I don't wanna dig it out by hand." Hunjii nodded before sending the trembling porters on their way, and as quickly as they could they rode off. Jeb rubbed sand from his eyes. "The Devils Arch. Spooky."

Olivia ran her hand across the base of the structure. "The inscriptions don't say anything about Mephistopheles or a curse."

"Well what do they say?" asked Jeb.

"Roughly translated... *only the eye can see the way.*"

Jeb fumbled around with his backpack, digging his hand in deep until he found the golden key. "So, where do I stick this tomato?"

She raised her eyebrow. "Away from me."

"Ha. Ha."

"Would you two stop sucking each other off? Jesus!" Elizabeth snatched the key away from Jeb, and plunged it deep into a keyhole in the archway. She struggled to turn the key to the right, her efforts eventually rewarded with a soft clicking sound, followed by the great mechanical shifting and whirring of some ancient, unseen machinery housed within. The inscriptions upon it came alive, glowing with orange light as the arch grew taller and taller, rising up from the ground. The eye at the top of the arch burned like fire as it shot out a beam of light, and the ground opened up with a long moan of earth shifting against earth, exposing a small shaft that led down into a tomb below.

# 28.

## BEWARE THE UNHOLY ONE

And there it lay before them; dark and ancient and full of secrets. "So what now?" asked Sam. "Is this it? Is this what we've been looking for, the tomb of Midas?"

"No," Olivia said abruptly. "Definitely not. The legend and the map are quite clear, this is merely a signpost on the way to the actual tomb. Whatever's been hidden down there should only contain the location of the next signpost. The next clue."

"Right, I knew that. And then so on, and so on from there," Sam said in an uneasy voice. "So... Does one of us really have to go down there? I mean come on!" He looked up at the sky, dark clouds forming overhead. "Besides, it looks like it might rain."

"Oh grow a pair, Sam." Jeb scolded him. "Of course someone's gotta go down there! How else are we gonna get the next clue?"

Sam shrugged. "I dunno. But I'll tell you what's for, I sure as hell ain't going down there! Place gives me da' creeps."

Jeb groaned. "Coward."

"Gimme a break!" Sam guffawed, as he looked around the mysterious valley they were now arguing in. There was an ancient, rotting baobab tree about fifty yards away, a small ape crawling atop one of its withered branches. The monkey could hear thunder roaring in the distance, and scurried off. "I don't like this." Sam muttered. "I don't like this one bit."

Again Jeb groaned, and Elizabeth rolled her eyes.

"Wuh, uh-" Sam stammered. "Well if you're so damned tough, you go down there and get it!"

Jeb shot him a cool glance. "I will." He grabbed one end of the gnarled sailing rope and tied it around the right leg of the arch, pulling it as tight as he could. "There," he said, tossing the other end down the shaft. "Olivia, you're with me."

"Why me?" she asked incredulously.

"Because when I get down there I'm gonna need someone to tell me what it is we're looking for. Hunjii, go grab us three lamps."

"Three boss?" Hunjii gulped.

Jeb nodded. "You heard me."

\* \* \* \* \* \* \* \*

The friction of the rope against Jeb's arms and legs made a terrible sound as he slid down into the narrow shaft below. He barely managed to land on his feet after the rope ended several feet before the ground. *"Ooh!"* Olivia cried as she dropped down, making a soft landing in Jeb's waiting arms. She unhitched the fat oil lantern from her belt and held It up, illuminating Jeb's face in soft, yellow light. He set her down slowly, before shouting up to Sam and Elizabeth. "You take good care of him, Elizabeth. If there's any trouble up there, I don't want him getting hurt."

Elizabeth laughed.  "I'll be careful."

"Break a leg, Jeb," said Sam.  "I mean it."

The three of them then made their way down the narrow pathway, their bodies trembling as they stepped into the darkness.  The path carved into the earth was only about five feet tall and two feet wide, and so the three of them were forced to bend over considerably as they squeezed through.  The entire tunnel was silent and odorless, save for the staggered breath of the intrepid explorers, and the thinly veiled smell of death, both ancient and immutable, that hung heavy in the dust choked air.  Olivia was leading the way, with Jeb in the middle and Hunjii at the back.  Save their oil lanterns, there wasn't an ounce of light in the ancient tunnel.  Jeb thought he now knew how Carter must have felt in the Valley of the Kings.  "The walls," Olivia cried, "there are inscriptions on the walls!" She held her lantern up to the small Phoenician letters, long ago set in stone.

*"Caveo nocens unos,"* she whispered as she read the words.  "Beware the unholy one."

Jeb looked concerned.  "Does that mean this place is booby trapped?  Do we need to watch where we step, or what?"

"I don't think so," said Olivia.  "There's no record of a Greek structure ever being booby trapped. That's much more an Egyptian phenomenon."

"Well this ain't exactly your average Greek tomb. I'm mean, we are sixty feet under the surface of South Africa for Christ's sake."

"Just don't-" she began before pausing to think. "You're right Jeb, we don't know what we're dealing with here."

He nodded. *"You're right, Jeb.* Now that's what I like to hear."

She rolled her eyes. "Just... just be careful what you touch."

The passage grew smaller and smaller as they continued down it, and within a few minutes all three of them were crawling on their hands and knees. "How much more of this?" groaned an exacerbated Jeb. "I mean, Jesus, how long does this thing go on for?"

"I don't know," Olivia called back to him. "These walls are all lined with lime stone. Who ever built this, it must have been a massive undertaking. Digging this whole place out."

"Yeah," said Jeb, "they definitely weren't messing around. Although I do wonder, were they dwarves or what? I mean these people they-"

Hunjii let out a blood curdling scream. "My leg! Something touch my leg!"

"What?" Jeb shouted, turning back to face him.

"My leg it... some... wet... some she… brush up again my leg!"

"I didn't feel anything," said Olivia.

"I don't like dis' boss. I go back," said Hunjii.

"You will not!" Jeb shouted. "Relax. It was probably just your imagination."

"No. It was not."

Jeb looked at Olivia, the fat, butter yellow lamp light throwing itself across her face. "There's probably plenty of cracks in this tunnel. Maybe some mud seeped up through one of them." Concern grew across his face. "Come to think of it, this whole place could collapse at any second. Go ahead Hunjii. She'll follow you up." He turned towards Olivia. "You go ahead. I'll find the clue myself."

"Are you nuts?" She sneered. "If you're that scared, Jeb, then just run away."

"This place is dangerous! I'm just trying to protect you."

"I don't need protecting, ok? This place has been here for two thousand years, what could possibly make you think it's gonna collapse in now?"

"Well I..." he stammered.

"Please. I'm far more concerned with whether or not Elizabeth's gonna shoot me in the back once she gets what she wants then I am with the integrity of this place. Look," she said as she knocked on the wall, "solid limestone."

"Well yeah, but..." Jeb was about to say something when she grabbed his shoulder.

"Did you hear that?"

"What?"

Her eyes grew wide and terrified. "That! That sound. Almost like a scream."

"Ah, fuck you!"

She laughed at him. "God Jeb, you're easy."

He muttered under his breath as he followed her down the long, stone tunnel. His knees were seriously starting to bother him. "You really think Elizabeth would shoot you?"

She smiled. "Maybe I'm not quite as naive as I pretend to be."

"And maybe I'm not quite as stupid. And maybe Sam-"

"Hold that thought!" Olivia commanded. She stopped dead in her tracks and held up her lantern. "Look!"

"Come on, I'm not falling for that again," he said.

"I mean it, Jeb," she said. *"Look."*

Jeb squinted through the darkness, smiling as he saw what lay beyond the large opening ahead. They crawled through the last few feet of the tunnel and into a massive chamber, their lanterns casting a hazy yellow glow about the place. Olivia gasped at the treasure before them. The ceiling was at least twelve feet high, and the huge room itself was at least twenty by fifty feet all the way around, all of it solid gold. At the center of the circular room there lay a grand, jewel encrusted sarcophagus of gold. Giant, polished golden statues of the Gods and Goddesses lined the walls, the floor was tiled in emeralds and sapphires, the walls painted in elaborate murals depicting wild orgies, and ritual sacrifice. Perhaps most intriguing of all, two massive, ten foot golden dragons stood at either side of the doorway, enormous matte rubies serving as their eyes. Odd though-- The jewel encrusted floor and painted walls were filled with holes that led down into a series of long, interconnecting tunnels only a few feet across, and just as high, making them too small for any man to do more than crawl through.

"Here!" Olivia blew long settled dust from the sarcophagus, revealing an imposing block of text, as well as several intricate etchings of what looked to be Zeus and Hera. "This is incredible," she said quickly. "It talks about what all of this is!"

"Well, what is it?" Jeb asked anxiously.

She stared at him, a shocked look on her face. "It's the tomb of Hermes, Midas' brother."

"The one who overthrew him?"

"The one and the same," she said, before stopping for a moment. "I don't understand. This doesn't make any sense."

"Tell me about it."

"No. No, I mean… here, at the end, it... it says, *is mereor is ago pro totus infinito*. May he live forever."

"Yeah, so?"

"Well they were blood enemies, right? If Midas hated him so much, why would he want him to live forever?"

"Why would he build him a tomb in the first place? I don't get any of this," Jeb said as he looked around at the orgies and the golden dragons. "This whole fucking thing is insane. Where does it say what the next clue is?"

*"Hermes is the clue."*

"Hermes is the clue?" Jeb replied dryly. "What the hell does that mean."

"I don't know." Olivia shrugged. "I guess we'll just have to open it up."

"What? Why? So we can see a two thousand year old body? No thanks."

"Well what if it's in there!?"

"It's not in there!" Jeb said dismissively. "It's a riddle. Hermes is the clue."

"Well if it is a riddle, what does it mean?"

"I don't know, you're supposed to be the scientist here! *Ugh.* Where he was born, maybe? Maybe the next signpost is in Athens, you did say he was from Athens, right?"

"Well where in Athens, smartass?"

"I don't know!" Jeb threw up his hands.

Olivia shook her head. "No. No, the next clue has got to be here somewhere. There's got to be a map, or a set of instructions, or... *something.*"

"Maybe this is it. Damn it Olivia, just look at this place. The gold, the jewels. The treasure in here is worth a fortune!"

"It's not about the treasure, I told you that. This was my uncle's dream, Jeb, he died for it and I intend to see it through. Now this is not Midas. This is not the tomb. It's just a trail marker."

"Just a trail marker? Olivia, this stuff is worth millions!" He took her hand gently. "Look around you. I mean really look. We could take this and go away together. We could run away and never look back. Never worry about money, about the future, about anything."

"Stop it!" She pushed him away and pressed her hand against the gold sarcophagus at the center of the room. "We need to open this up. There could be something inside."

"Forget it," said Jeb. "Forget Midas, forget your uncle, forget everything. Olivia we can leave everything and everyone else behind and start off fresh in the Alps, or the Caribbean, or wherever. It doesn't matter to me where. We could have a hell of a time you and me, we could make things like they were before, we could--"

Jeb froze as the sound of clapping echoed from somewhere in the darkness. "Well, well, well, aren't you the little romantic." Virtrolli sneered as he emerged from the shadows, pistol in one hand, a cigar in the other. He aimed the gun at Jeb's chest and tensed his finger around the trigger.

"Son of a bitch." Jeb cursed as he stared down the Mafiosi. "Who let you in? Don't you know a private party when you see one?"

Virtrolli grinned, motioning with his gun for Jeb to move. "You heard the girl. Open it."

"Why should I?" said Jeb.

"Because you care, obviously," he said, shifting his aim from Jeb to Olivia. "Crank the box open now or the girl gets it, see?"

With a nervous twitch Jeb reached into his canvas backpack and retrieved a steel crowbar, its half rusted frame reflecting the dim light of the lanterns. A white flash reflected off of the bottom of it from some unknown source. "How the hell'd you even find us? I thought you were dead."

"You thought wrong," said Virtrolli.

"Unfortunately," said Olivia. "Though from where I'm standing it looks like you're all alone."

"Looks that way." Virtrolli smiled. "Spose yer curious what's become of your friends."

Jeb gritted his teeth.

"They're safe. For now," he said menacingly. "Whether they stay that way is entirely up to you."

Jeb turned the crowbar over in his hand.

"Now open it," The Mafiosi ordered, "open the damn box."

Jeb walked up to the sarcophagus and grunted, exerting every last ounce of his muscle as he pressed against the crowbar. "It's no use. This fucking thing is stuck."

"Push harder!" Virtrolli commanded. "We have to get it open, we-" He stopped as he began to cough wildly on the dust that hung in the air.

"Do you have any idea how much this weighs, you asshole? I mean its solid gold!"

"Just do it!" He walked over to Olivia and placed his arm around her neck. "Here, I'll help motivate you."

Jeb sneered as he grappled onto the lip of the sarcophagus, forcing the shimmering gold cover up with everything he had. Slowly but surely it began to budge.

"There! It's working!" Virtrolli cried out with excitement, and even Olivia's eyes couldn't help but light up with anticipation.

"Just gotta' keep pushing down!" Jeb said in a strained voice, as he shoved his broad shoulder against the golden cover, sliding it against the frame of the sarcophagus. As the cover slid off and clattered onto the ground, a rush of damp white fog poured out, swallowing up the room and traveling down the throats of the three as they hacked and coughed. There was a sudden sound of commotion in the fog, and when it cleared Olivia was holding the gun, having wrestled it away from Virtrolli who now lay splayed out on the stone floor.

"You God damned chump," she swore, as she cocked back the hammer. "You really don't know when to leave a girl alone."

Jeb looked at her with admiration.

"You bitch!" Virtolli cried as she kicked him in the gut.

"Watch your tongue, captain," Olivia said dryly. "I'm new to this whole gun thing. Might accidentally set it off."

Virtolli lay down in submission, his eyes gone milky white from the strange fog.

Olivia took her eyes off of Virtrolli and peered into the coffin. She gasped at what she saw. There it lay, a thin flea bitten veil covering what looked to be a man, the well worn cloth risen up in morbid rigor. A sickening odor of decay, like that of rotten, half digested meat rose up, sending Olivia rushing to cover her nose and mouth.

There was a grim look on Jeb's face as he saw the veil covered body. "You're not gonna take that off, are you?" he asked hesitantly.

Olivia looked over at him like she regretted it before she even said it. "Well.... yeah, I mean I guess I have to."

"Two thousand plus years of decomposition. It ain't gonna be a pretty sight."

She looked back into the coffin, closing her eyes as she pinched her nose shut. "How bad can it be compared to Virtrolli?"

"Why you bitch, I outghta--"

"She told you to shut your mouth!" Jeb shouted as he walked over to the gangster and kicked him. Olivia braced herself for whatever grisly, macabre sight awaited her, peeled back the veil and screamed. What she saw was more shocking then anything she'd imagined.

She ripped off the rest of the death shroud as she jerked back her hand, her face turning a stark shade of white, hands trembling at her side. *"Jeb,"* she said in a low, barely audible whisper, the blood retreating from her face, *"look."*

Against his better judgment, Jeb walked up to the sarcophagus, a slow, trembling hand lifting up the dim light of the lantern. There was a naked man with skin a pale shade of albino, a shaved face, and fingernails that had been plucked out. Across his perfectly preserved skin stretched a long, intricate tattoo of a map that reached down from his face to his feet. His limbs were chained down to the sarcophagus, and the poor bastard's muscles were emaciated beyond all reason, leaving his stomach a hollow, canyon of a thing. His skin was so pale and so white as to be nearly transparent, and Jeb could faintly make out a seemingly dead black heart under his ashen skin and brightly inked tattoos.

"What the fuck is this?" Jeb asked, as he turned towards Olivia, who was backing up quickly, past Virtrolli and towards the corner of the room, a shocked expression on her face.

*"I.......I don't........I don't...know,"* she whispered. She blinked as she clutched Jeb's chest and shoulders for support. "Jeb...." she said, clutching him as she brushed a strand of silken red hair from her still face. He looked down into her frightened blue eyes and nodded. She nodded back lightly, waiting for what seemed an eternity as Jeb retrieved the sketch pad from his bag and began to scrawl out a copy of the map. None of them spoke for sometime, not even Virtrolli, each silent moment passing with mounting dread. She groped out for an explanation when he asked for one, but she couldn't explain it to herself, let alone him. There had been people preserved in Italian catacombs in a way similar to this, but those were more recent. Within the last hundred years and in a Catholic church. This... this was something different. There was something evil to this. Something wicked. Two thousand years old. The man's face desolate. The tattoos so intricate and precise...

Jeb breathed a heavy sigh of relief as he finished up his drawing. His voice echoed off the walls as he walked towards her. "It's finished. Let's get out of here." He slid the sketchbook back into his bag and buttoned it up.

"I guess the only thing left to deal with is him," she said, motioning towards the cowering Virtrolli.

"You hurt me and you'll never see your friends alive again!" he shouted desperately. "I'm ya only ticket outa here."

Jeb shook his head, "you don't know how this game works, do you?"

Virtrolli eyed him warily.

Jeb gestured with his pistol. "Walk in front of us. Slowly."

Olivia walked up to Virtrolli, rested her hands on his injured shoulder, and whispered into his ear. "You can lead the way up. And, when we get there, if either Sam or Elizabeth have so much as a scratch on them, I'll end you just like you did my uncle."

Virtrolli eyed her nervously before nodding, and the three of them started to make their way towards the exit when a sudden low, hollow voice echoed out from behind, stopping them.

Olivia's lantern shattered as she dropped it to the ground, the oil fueled flame quickly flickering out. Jeb gripped her arm, motioning his head towards the sarcophagus. With tepid footsteps they approached it, Jeb raising his lantern high up above the pale man's head. Small black veins and wrinkles pulsating out from his barely visible heart, the man's eyes flickered open, revealing two shimmering black orbs. They were dark and whole and dense. Soulless, unforgiving eyes like a great white shark.

*"Carre Aspicio,"* the man said in a voice like death, his opened mouth like a window into the

netherworld.   The talking corpse smiled for a moment, its thin lips twisted into an awful grin.   *"Admiratio des la infinitio."*

"Behold," Olivia translated, "behold the wonder of eternal life."

# 29.
# THE TATTOOED MAN

Virtrolli watched as the corpse sat up in the coffin. He screamed and ran down the halls of the tomb, but both Jeb and Olivia were too transfixed with what lay before them to stop him.

*"Eternal life?"* Jeb whispered. "What in the name of God is this?"

The living corpse rattled the chains around his hands and feet as he seizured, his naked body flailing in the stench of the still crypt air. *"Cruciatus kalla,"* he said again, *"se dim diem sepetirna terra."*

"It says," Olivia said slowly, her eyes transfixed on the ancient creature, "see the torture of a never ending earth."

Jeb looked at her. "That can't mean what I think it means."

"He can't die," Olivia said in disbelief. "Trapped here in this hole in the ground, unable to reach heaven or hell."

"Who did this to him?" Jeb gulped.

*"Carnea avessa soutia?"* Olivia asked.

"Midas," the creature hissed unmistakably. Its throat seized for a moment as it regurgitated a small black marble, which it spat into Jeb's hand. Olivia leaned over and read the inscription on the marble aloud, her lips quivering as she spoke, *"Infinite life and ultimate power."*

"The story was true?" Jeb grabbed Olivia. "Midas is alive?!"

The words had gone out of her. Her mind was racing with possibilities she didn't dare speak. "I don't know. Maybe."

"Well then he found the fountain of youth after all."

"But that's impossible..."

"To live forever…" Jeb could barely comprehend the words. "To never grow old. But what does that mean, infinite life and ultimate power. What ultimate power?"

Suddenly there came a crash, and the sickening sound of scales sliding across the ground.

"What the hell is going on here?" Jeb shouted at the ancient creature chained forever to its coffin. "What's happening?"

The pale monster began to laugh, his black crevice of a mouth opening abnormally wide as he howled with delight. *"Lento creisie, minta!"*

"Beware the unholy one?" Olivia whispered as she turned towards him.

*"Lento creisie, minta! Lento creisie, minta!"* The once human creature continued shouting, his long black tongue flickering out snakelike.

"What was that?" Olivia screamed as a translucent white coil whipped out of one of the small tunnels in the wall, and across the floor.

"Where!" Jeb cried, as he waved his lantern around wildly and drew his revolver.

Olivia bolted towards the door. "Jeb let's get out of here, come on!"

"I'm right behind you!" he shouted as he ran after her.

A low hiss echoed in the room as the mass of inhuman flesh beat against the ground, two slitted yellow eyes staring back at Olivia from the darkness. As Jeb came closer the dim light of his lantern revealed the beast, a massive basilisk, and it's fanged mouth unhinged as it reared up on a limbless body. Olivia screamed as she tripped, stumbling backwards onto the gold tiles below.

Jeb took aim at the massive snake before him. The creature was thick, at least a foot across, its pale, sun deprived skin gone translucent, revealing a jagged, malformed spine covered in loosely hewn muscle tissue. Its head was a angular spade, an enormous jaw stretched out far past all reason, jaundiced yellow eyes gleaming: it was as if from Hell! **"POW!"** In a flash Jeb's gun roared out, the bullet tearing into the beast's open mouth and out through the back of its throat. The beast howled in pain, thick black oil streaming from its mouth as it sprang forwards, engulfing Jeb in its coils. Olivia screamed pure horror as Jeb dropped his gun and lamp, and they fell clattering to the floor below, the base of the giant snake now impugned in light amid the all consuming darkness of the tomb.

"Grab the -augh-" Jeb stuttered out, before being choked by the beast.

"Nooo! Jeb!" Olivia cried, watching helplessly as the creature wrapped Jeb in its coils, crushing his bones. She reached for the lantern and flung it at the snake, the creature screaming as the fire set him ablaze.

Jeb crashed to the ground, gasping for breath as the snake holocaust burned behind him. The creature writhed madly across the room, howling in agony.

"OUT, OUT, OUT!" Olivia cried as she lifted Jeb up and towards the exit. "Quickly!"

As they pounded down the tunnels for their lives, the basilisk snuffed out the fire, throwing everything back into black, all-encompassing darkness. They could hear the beast slithering behind them, could hear the sound of Hermes laughter, of his arms straining against his two thousand year old shackles as they ran down the tunnel, stumbling hands over feet over hands.

"FASTER!" Jeb screamed. "I can hear him! He's right behind us!"

"I'm going as fast as I can!" Olivia cried. Jeb howled in pain as the creature sunk its massive, half rotted yellow fangs down into his leg, tearing a wound through the tan canvas of his pants, poison burning the pink flesh of his body. With agonizing pain he dragged himself forwards, tearing his leg from the beast's mouth. Jeb reached down for his dagger, the snake's jaw dripping with his blood. With a furious motion he stabbed downward, plunging the dagger into the creature's scaly, spade shaped head. The snake recoiled down into the tunnel, black liquid draining onto the ground like a gushing pipe.

"We're almost there!" Olivia shouted as she ran. "Only a few more feet!"

The creature slithered somewhere nearby in the darkness, a thin beam of light coming down through the opening to the shaft as Olivia jumped up unto the gnarled and weathered rope, and began to pull herself up to freedom. Rain was pouring down the shaft now, carrying the dirt and mud with it, and the entire area around the opening had devolved into a slobbering wet cesspool.

The basilisk hissed and howled, diving wildly as it flailed in the mud. The rain water coming down from the monsoon outside was washing away the integrity of the shaft, and a massive chunk of mud and stone came hurtling down, knocking the monster on its head as Jeb struggled up the rope. The walls were growing more and more unstable now, clods of dirt and rock crashing down past his head.

His hand slipped against the mud as he strained to pull himself out, and with a defiant roar heaved his body up, and back onto the ground. As the cool rain ran down his face he looked up, his eyes still hazy, vision unsure. He blinked a few times, the fear returning to his face. "No... No! *Not you again!*"

"It's a pleasure ta' see you too," said a rain soaked Virtrolli as he loomed over Jeb with a slow burning cigar in his hand. He blew a smoke ring in Jeb's face and began to laugh maniacally. Jeb caught a glimpse of the massive airship that had been tailing them, now parked by the dead tree. Elizabeth was tied up, and Olivia was turning black and blue. Jeb let out a long, defeated howl before blacking out.

# 30.
# THE ZEPPELIN LANDED

"Wakey, wakey, Heir Chamberlain," the sniveling voice commanded, before slapping Jeb across the face.

"Auugh! Wuagh?" Jeb opened his eyes, his newly reddened cheek stinging, his mind an aching, groggy blur.

"You passed out, Heir Chamberlain. Come now, please. We have some... questions zat' need answering."

"What do you want with me?" Jeb groaned as he looked around. He was tied to a wooden chair in the center of a large tent. The German interrogator was standing over him, a mirthless smile on his thin, angular face. His pale blonde hair receded deep into a middle aged head, and he wore thick, coke bottle glasses. Virtrolli was standing in the shadows at the far end of the tent, along with a few other figures Jeb couldn't make out. There was a map strung up on the wall of the tent, and several small oil lamps illuminated the place in dim, sinister light. The fierce storm still poured outside.

"We already talked to ze' girl, Heir Chamberlain. We know zat you'll be just as helpful as she vas."

"Where is she?" Jeb shouted, fury in his eyes. "What have you done with her?"

"Ze' girl is safe." The German paused to push back his glasses. "For now."

"You bastard."

"As I said, misses Ostrum vas quite cooperative. As vas her sister, after a time. Zey simply needed the proper... *persuasion.*"

Jeb strained against the chair, screaming as Macky and another of the German officers appeared from the shadows to restrain him.

"Temper, temper," the commander said as he laughed, the insignia on his chest gleaming in the dim light. "Please, Heir Chamberlain, do try to control yourself. I'm a tolerant man, but even I have my limits."

"I'll piss down your grandmothers throat, you kraut bastard!" Jeb cursed, as he spit at him.

"I can see ve've gotten off onto the ze' wrong foot." He frowned. "Ah, how rude of me! Vhy, I haven't even introduced myself! My name is Hans. Hans Luthen." He put out his hand. "Vell that is quite rude. At least have the courtesy to shake *my* hand."

"Tell you what, *Hans*, you untie my hand, and I'll give you a handshake you'll never forget."

"Ah, tempting!" His eyes became obscured by the glare of his round glasses as he lifted his head up, and tapped Jeb on the chest. "Come now. Let's be friends, ja?"

"Ja," Jeb said through gritted teeth.

"Good, good, I'm glad you agree. You see, Heir Chamberlain, as my friend, I'd like you to do a little favor for me."

"Oh, anything for you, Hans."

He laughed softly. "Vhat I need is for you to tell me just vhat it is that keeps attacking my men down there."

"The snake?" asked Jeb.

"Der snake, ja. Every time I send someone down to go bring back ze' gold, poof, zey come back dead." He looked off into the distance. "Never have I seen anything take so many bullets and keep coming. How do I kill it?"

"Kill it?" Jeb looked surprised.

"Yes," said Hans.

Jeb began to laugh. "Kill it? You can't kill that thing."

"Of course I can! Of course I can kill it, you God damned lunatic. It's just an animal!"

Jeb shook his head softly. "Thanks to Virtrolli, you know about the tomb now, and you know about the gold. But there's something else down there. Something you know nothing about."

"And what," Hans asked, "would that be?"

"Maybe the secret to eternal life," said Jeb.

Hans laughed

"Think about it. That's why your men can't kill that snake. It's immortal."

For a moment the laughter stopped, as Hans looked into Jeb's eyes and considered what he'd been told. A crease pressed itself into his forehead as he broke out in hysterical laughter.

"What's so funny?" Jeb asked.

"Liar," Hans said, as he slapped Jeb across the face. He snapped his bony fingers, signaling to his soldiers, and they followed him out the tent.

"What are you doing with these people?" Jeb looked over to Virtrolli, who was sitting calmly in the shadowy gray corner. "I mean, krauts? Really? Even for you, that's gotta be a new low."

Virtrolli spoke slowly and deliberately. "I must say, Jeb, I'm surprised you've survived this long."

"Sorry to disappoint you."

"Yes. You will be. Trust me, you will be sorry you crossed me. I'll make sure of that." Virtrolli turned his gun over in hands as he walked towards Jeb, like a cat toying with its prey. "You really do disappoint me, kid. You do. A curious person like yourself, don't you even wanna know how we survived? How a couple a' boys from Brooklyn ended up on a God damned Zeppelin?"

"I'm sure it's a fascinating story."

"It is indeed. Suffice to say it took a little bribery on our part to get Komondor Luthen to see things our way but-"

"Down in the tomb, you never did tell me how it was you survived."

"Ya' ever hear of a life boat?" Macky charged forward, shouting. "We lost a lot a good men back there, thanks ta' you ya' son of a bitch!" Spittle sprayed out from his mouth as he slapped Jeb.

"I swear to God, if one more person slaps me..."

Virtrolli laughed. "That's nothing. You should a' seen what we did to little Olivia."

Jeb closed his eyes, anguish casting a shadow over his face. Virtrolli laughed as he pressed his pistol up against Jeb's forehead.

"You'd better pull that trigger now, Virtrolli, cuz when I get out a' here you're the first one I'm gonna kill."

The gangster leaned in close. "Big words for a man with a gun to his head."

"Bite me."

"I guess you got some fire in your belly after all. Even now. When you know ya' ain't got no hope left." Virtrolli sneered.

Jeb opened his eyes and stared Virtrolli in the face. "What's your first name, Virtrolli?"

"Why?"

"I wanna know, so that I can find your grave after I kill you, and piss on it."

A flash of hatred soared across Leonard Virtrolli's face as he pistol whipped Jeb.

"Let me shoot him, boss!" Macky cried out of the side of his mouth. "Don't let him talk to you like that. Kill him!"

Virtrolli lowered his pistol back into its holster. "All in good time." He smiled. "First though I want this palooka to watch what I do to his girl. Then we'll shoot 'em both."

Tyson Biggels laughed long and hard, his body doubled over.

"You know you're right about one thing." Virtrolli sneered. "About the fountain of youth, the eternal life. I saw that corpse wake up same as you did."

"You just better hope you manage to find it," Jeb said, vengeance clawing at the edges of his voice. "And you better hope an eternity here is better than in Hell."

Virtrolli smiled. "Let's go, Tyson. See if any a' the Komondor's men made it back wit' the gold. Macky you stay here and guard im'. Ya' can mess him up all you want, long as ya' leave him wit' at least one eye." Tyson followed Virtrolli out of the room, as Macky stood snickering.

"So what now?" Jeb asked dryly. "You gonna slap me around some more, you prick?"

"Something like that." Macky said with a twisted grin.

"Something like that."

# 31.

# BREAKING

*"Fanden wir den Schatz! Wir haben die gold, Komondor,"* the excited German voice rang out. *"Und wir das tier getotet!"*

Hans Luthen smiled as several of his men emerged from the muddy pit they had dynamited open, an enormous golden dragon hauled up by ropes behind them. *"Wunderbar."*

Several more of his soldiers rushed towards the statue, intent on helping to lift it up out of the muck. Their eyes drifted over the spires of gold glittering in the darkness of the sunken chamber room where Jeb and Olivia had found Hermes.

\* \* \* \* \* \* \* \*

The sisters were now tied back to back in the hull of the massive airship, their faces swollen from the harsh treatment of their captors. A lone guard watched over them with a blank, dutiful stare. With a poorly concealed look of desperation Elizabeth turned her head towards the guard. She knew they were planning to kill her. *"Hallo soldat. Haben sie einen namen?"*

The soldier turned towards her, a long wooden rifle in his hand. He too was wearing the dusty tan uniform of the German colonials. He was a young man, twenty two or twenty three at the most. *"Gute arbeit,"* he said as he arched his eyebrow. "You speak German well."

Elizabeth nodded. "And you speak English?"

He shrugged.

"It's good." She goaded him with a faint smile. "Is there anything I can do for you my friend? Any way I can help you? *Please you?* Why don't you untie us and I'll show you a real good time. Remind you of what you've been missing back home."

The soldier laughed, spiting on the ground as he turned away. "I'm not interested in your whore mouth." He held out his hand, indicating the wedding band around his finger.

Elizabeth tilted her head back and stared at the ceiling. *"Figures."*

* * * * * * * *

"What the fuck are you doing?" Jeb glared at Macky. The rain was still pouring outside.

"Just.... Getting ready," he sighed gleefully as he finished unbuttoning his shirt, and set his pistol down on the table next to him. He made his way over to Jeb carefully, a gleam in his eyes. He leaned over, pressing coddled lips up against Jeb's ear as he whispered with hot and bated breath., "hi there.."

A look of dread came over Jeb's face.

Macky smiled as he pulled off his shirt, revealing a slight, bony frame, pointed rib cage protruding through pale skin like rubber stretched out over a spike. He yanked the zipper down on the entrance to the tent before stepping back, a smile on his face. "Looks like we've got the place all to ourselves."

Jeb stared back silently.

"They're digging out more of that wonderful gold." He shrugged. "Not that I ever cared for the expensive things in life." He pulled a pair of pliers from his bag on the table. "I've always been a fan of the simple things, I guess." Jeb began to shout for help as Macky through his hand over his mouth, muffling his terrified screams. Macky grinned, retrieving a butterfly knife from his back pocket that he traced across Jeb's neck without drawing blood, moving his hand to the back of Jeb's head, gripping him by the hair. He yanked back hard, maneuvering the blade along the edge of Jeb's lips before sliding it inside. "I could cut you up so you'd never talk back again. I could make you beg me to kill you."

Jeb held his breath, trying not to shake as the knife nicked his tongue. "I..."

"Shhh." Macky quieted him, shaking his head. "Not now. The time for talking is over." He kept the knife in Jeb's mouth as he reached down and undid his captive's belt. "This is about action."

\* \* \* \* \* \* \*

"Lt. Veiken," Komondor Luthen said in a stern voice, as he made his way down the twirling metal staircase and into the airship's hold. *"Est ist das Ende fur Sie, meine Lieblinge."*

The soldier nodded. "On your feet," he shouted at Olivia and Elizabeth as two other soldiers untied them and led them out into the rain. Several more of the troops came in, along with Tyson Biggels, and began lowering the dragon down the metal ramp and into the cargo hold.

A clasp of thunder echoed out in the wet darkness as the dirigibles engines roared to life. Meandering across the muddy Savannah, Olivia watched out of the corner of her eye as one of the soldiers pounded bullets into the albino snake monster with a hand held machine gun, forcing it back into its undying crypt. Seconds later there was a scream as the basilisks head popped back up and dragged the soldier down into the pit.

The soldier leading them ignored his comrade's scream. There was a dark humor about him as he blindfolded the women and tied their hands behind their backs. "Line up," he commanded.

Olivia's breath quickened as she stepped into the darkness. She couldn't believe it, *how could Jeb be dead? How could Sam?* **"Click."** Olivia could hear the soldier raise his gun. Could feel the silence hanging in the air. *Could feel her death*. Knew that it must be imminent. She let out one last gasp, an alarmed feeling punching her in the gut as she realized the mistakes she'd made. She should have told him how she felt. How she longed for his touch every time she closed her eyes. And then she thought of the baby.

The gun ran out with a terrible blast and there was the thumping sound of a dead body hitting the ground.

Olivia cried as a firm hand untied her blind fold and turned her around. "SAM!" She threw her arms around him. "Where have you been?"

"He ran off when the dirigible landed," Elizabeth said coolly, as she undid her own blindfold, her blonde hair gone into frizzy wet strands, black mascara running down pale cheeks.

"You could have told me, I thought he was dead!" Olivia gasped. "Thank you thank you thank you, Sam! Oh my God, thank you!"

"Don't mention it." Sam nodded, face dripping, frame soaking wet. "Where's Jeb?"

The joy drained from Olivia's face. "I have no idea."

"He's probably dead," Elizabeth said, as she wiped the back of her palm underneath her eyes, smearing the wet mascara like war paint. "We'll mourn him later. It's only a matter of time before they realize something's wrong and--"

A scream echoed out from the Komondors tent.

"What was that?" Sam spun around.

"Come on!" Olivia said quickly, as she ran off ahead of the others, chasing the sound. "It's gotta be him!"

# 32.
# THE GREAT ESCAPE

"You don't have to do this. Please," Jeb begged as Macky pressed the blade against his thigh.

"Oh but I want to." Macky grinned as he brought the knife up to where he held Jeb's balls in his hand. "I *really* want to."

"Please…" Jeb pleaded. "Please…"

Macky shook his head. "Begging doesn't suit you. Begging is for women. Are you a woman?"

Jeb closed his eyes, trying not to shake.

"You're a weak little girl and there's nothing you can do. There's nothing at all." Macky squeezed tighter. "Tell me you love me, little girl. Tell me how much you want me."

"I don't… I don't…." Jeb gasped.

"Tell me you need this, little girl." Macky whispered. "Tell me you--"

There was a ripping sound as the tents zipper came down and Olivia bust in. "Oh my God, what the fuck?!" she shouted.

"Sweet Jesus, help me!" Jeb screamed.

"Put the knife down!" Olivia ordered Macky, as she raised the stolen German rifle towards the sailor's chest.

"Shoot him," Jeb begged, "Shoot him, Olivia!"

"Put the knife down," Olivia ordered. "I won't ask you again, you sick fuck."

Macky put his hands up and stepped towards her, dropping the knife to the ground. "Hey little girl," he whispered, "It's okay."

"Not one more step," said Olivia, "I'm warning you."

Macky took another step towards her. "I'm not gonna hurt you. Everything's cool. Everything's okay."

"Olivia, shoot him!" Jeb pleaded. "Do it, Olivia!"

Her finger tensed around the trigger. "I can't. I can't, I…"

"It's okay," Macky whispered, just a few inches from her now, "It's okay."

"Olivia!" Jeb screamed.

Macky grabbed for the gun as it went off and he slumped to ground, the blood gushing from his chest. Olivia collapsed, Sam and Elizabeth running in behind her. "Oh my God," said Sam.

Jeb stared at Olivia, meeting her unblinking gaze. "Thank you."

\* \* \* \* \* \* \* \*

The Zeppelin's engines were dangerously loud as they fired up on the untamed savanna grass. Tyson came up to Virtolli with a grin. "Did you get a look at all that gold they pulled out of the tomb?  We're rich, boss.  We're so fucking rich."

Virtrolli grinned.  "Only one thing left to do before I can enjoy it.  Let's toss Olivia's dead body in his face and kill Jeb."

\* \* \* \* \* \* \* \*

**"POW!"**  The bullet's impact echoed in the air as Elizabeth fired again into the back of the soldiers skull, and she and the rest of the group made their way up the gangplank and onto the airship.  Elizabeth hushed them as a second soldier came to investigate the blast, Olivia and Sam sinking into the shadows as Jeb jumped him, knocking him out.

"Come on," Elizabeth whispered, "the control room should be up this way."

Jeb nodded and raised his pistol.  After a few moments coming down the hallway, he rapped on the heavy steel door of the control room.

*"Was ist es?"* a voice called from inside.  *"Ist dass sie, Shneishenburger?"*  There was a creaking sound as the pilot turned the steering wheel on the door, and opened it up.  "Telegram," Jeb said, snapping the butt of his gun against the man's head, knocking him out cold.  "Get rid of him," he commanded. "Elizabeth, you still think you can pilot this thing?"

She crossed her arms.  "If I can fly a plane I can fly a balloon."

Jeb nodded. "First things first, we need a distraction. Something to get all these soldiers of the ship at once. Ya got anything?"

Elizabeth's brow furrowed as she headed over to the control panel. "Yeah," she said in a hushed voice, "I've got this."

Jeb looked over at Sam as Elizabeth found the intercom. "If we're all here, then what happened to Hunjii?"

Sam shook his head. "He never came back."

*"Achtung!"* Elizabeth bellowed into the intercom. *"Achtung! Es ist eine ernste Gaslek an Bord des Luftschiffes. Alle Gerate sofort evakuiren!"* Across the massive air ship the soldiers stopped whatever they were doing and fled, as the voice on the intercom alerted them to the presence of a dangerous hydrogen leak. Lt. Kreiner Veika waved them out, making sure everyone was evacuated. He froze as he looked out at the screaming figure of Leonard Virtrolli running through the rain towards him.

"They're on the ship! They're stealing the God damned Zeppelin, get back on there you fuckin' mook!" Virtrolli screamed like a maniac.

*"Ich nein sprechen Englisch,"* Veikan shouted back to him.

"LOOK!" Virtrolli screamed as he pointed up at the slow rising Zeppelin.

Veikan panicked. Quick as he could he gathered up his men and dashed back towards the ship, but it was too late, by the time they reached it the air ship was already more than a dozen feet off the ground, it's engines whirring like twisters. Virtrolli cursed as Jeb looked down at him from the ship's control room, a smirk on his face. Virtolli whipped out his pistol and began to fire, but it was no use, the Zeppelin was away.

"Damn you!" he cried out to the thundering heavens above, as his gold and his vengeance and his dreams drifted into the sky. "Damn you all to hell!" He wiped the pouring rain from his face, a pit of rage and hate forming in his stomach. Someday he'd catch up with them, someday he'd have his revenge, even if it killed him. He hid his face in shame as Tyson approached him.

"Those bastards have taken everything from me..." Virtrolli whispered, as he stared off into the distance and pulled down the brim of his gray fedora. "They fuckin' killed Macky."

Biggels frowned. "What are we gonna do?"

"Ain't nuthin left to do, it's over!" he shouted. "It's all gone to pieces! It's fuckin done, alright?!"

"Nah, Boss, we can come back from this," Biggels said softly.

"No. No, no, no..." Virtrolli watched as the rain came down over the brim of his hat. "There's nothin' left."

Biggels shook his head. "No. There's one thing left, boss. One thing left, and it's the only thing that matters."

"And what's that?" Virtrolli demanded. "What fucking matters now?"

"You know what," said Biggels.

Virtrolli returned to the tent where Macky's body lay. He knelt down, cradling the boy in his arms, trying to fight back tears. Macky's eyes were glazed over, the light gone out of them. Blood at his lips, the bullet wound in his chest still wet. His skin was so pale.

"I swear to you, my son," Virtrolli whispered, "I swear to God I'll make them pay."

\* \* \* \* \* \* \* \*

Of all the soldiers who had once served aboard the massive dirigible, SS Landa, only Hans Luthen now remained. As soon as the voice rang out over the intercom he knew what he had to do. All of his men had stormed out of the airship and into the raining African nightscape, but he alone had stayed. He alone had gone up to find the pilot and check the control room. Komondor Hans Luthen did not fear death as other men did. A gas leak? *"Ha!"* It would take more than phantom hydrogen to scare him off his own ship. And now he saw it. Now he saw their treachery. No gas leak. No real danger. Just four thieving English whores. Hans crept quietly as he inched around the corner, unseen, and peered into the room where the four of them were now laughing, celebrating their treachery. Hans cursed them, a horrible scowl upon his pale white face. He brushed back his hair with the gun gripped firm in his hand. It would all be over soon.

"I can't believe that actually worked!" Sam laughed.

"We got lucky, that's all," said Jeb.

Elizabeth smirked. "Luck had nothing to do with it, bunny." Their enemies now miles and miles behind them, the euphoria was contagious. Jeb stared out the window, and all his pain, all his regrets, they seemed like nothing. Nothing compared with what he'd just been through and the thought that he'd lost her. It all made sense now. Suddenly. Perfectly. It felt like the last missing piece of some arduous puzzle had finally fallen into place, and now he saw her and he loved her. Jeb smiled. "Come here."

Her mouth half open Olivia met his lips, her eyes fluttering as she drank him in. "I missed you kissing me," she whispered.

"I know," he said, "I missed kissing you. Olivia, when I thought you and I were lost down there, when I thought I'd lost you... *nothing* else seemed to matter anymore. Nothing made sense."

"Jeb come on. Get a grip on yourself," Sam said as he stepped towards them.

"Stay outta this, Sam," Jeb said as he put his hand up. "Please."

Elizabeth was standing in the corner of the room. Her arms crossed, face blanketed in shadow.

"We're not good for each other," Olivia whispered. "We burn each other up until there's nothing left except hurt. We've done it before and if we go down this route we'll do it again."

"I don't care.  I want you."

She shook her head.  "Sometimes that's not enough.  It's not enough for me."

"Tell me you still care about me," he said.

There were tears in her eyes now.  "You know I do."

"Tell me you want me."

"You know that too."

"Then be with me."

She began to cry as she turned away from him. "You know we're not safe for each other."

"Who wants to be safe?" asked Jeb.  "My brain is on fire most of the time.  Lit up and raging with all the things that I've done, and there's no rest, there's no calm.  Or at least there isn't without you.  You are my eye of the storm.  The calm center, and the fuel for a wild, heartbreaking wildfire that rips my world apart. When I'm with you the rest of the world goes quiet, and the universe whispers instead of shouting, and the fire grows warm and comforting instead of burning me alive, and-"

"Jeb, stop!"  She pressed her hand against his chest.

"You're right, Olivia, we're not safe for each other.  We're dangerous, we're unpredictable, we're not safety we're adventure.  And I wouldn't want it any other way."

Olivia tilted her head slowly, her lips coming closer to him.  She kissed him.  Hard.  "I do love you, Jeb."

His arms shook as he gripped her.

She growled, her mouth against his, lips pressed against lips as her hands ran down his body. "I fucking love you. I can't fucking stop loving you, you bastard."

He kissed her neck. "I know. I know."

"And that's what makes this so damned hard." She leaned in close to him, her voice barely a whisper. "Jeb, I'm pregnant. I realized it a few weeks after I boarded the ship. Colton and I had been trying, and--_"

The shot rang out like a freight train in the still, night air as Jeb collapsed to the ground, the bullet running through his back and bursting out his chest.

Olivia cried out as Hans Luthen stared from the shadows, pistol in hand, a sneer on his face.

Another shot, this time from Elizabeth, and Hans collapsed to the ground with a sickening thud. Olivia was screaming as she got down beside Jeb, the blood gushing from him like a fountain.

*"Sie sehen, in der Holle,"* the dying commander gasped as he dropped the stick grenadier down through the steel grated floor, and into the hold of the ship below.

Elizabeth screamed, diving for the miniature bomb, but it was too late. Time seemed to drip out in slow motion as the stick grenadier fell down through the still, hydrogen soaked air, the grenade making a horrible noise as it struck the hull some fifty feet below. Within seconds the entire airship was engulfed in flames, black, acrid smoke pouring out from the dirigible as its frame ruptured and shattered, its broken engine sending it crashing down. The ship tossed and turned as though a harpooned whale, and Jeb's body was sucked out the blown open window and sent hurtling down through the rushing rain. Olivia's scream was the last sound he heard, save for the thumping silence that swallowed him as the dirigible exploded, and a massive fireball containing everything he loved collapsed from the sky, hurtling down in a holocaust of flame.

White ash and smoke poured into the night sky, the last layers of the dirigible burning away like rice paper. A ringing lingered in Jeb's ears as he pushed off against the mud, struggling desperately to stand up, to chase after the scream. He roared, clutching his bloody chest, watching helplessly as ash fell like snowflakes in the rain.

She was gone.

# PART TWO
# (DEATH)

An End To Eternity

# 33.

# INTERLUDE III

## Summerset, New Hampshire, 1914

He'd grown up listening.

Listening to his mother and his father. Fighting and hitting, and... He'd listen. Sit at her side by the fire at night as she went on about her youth. About her dreams, about what she felt, how she felt, who she was. About why. Why did this, and why did that. And why did every damned thing in life have to hurt so much?

And now he was almost eighteen. His father gone four years and his mother still laying the blame at his feet. He still listening. She'd cry sometimes, convinced that he'd loved her. Berating Jeb for having pushed him over the edge. His disrespect having driven him away. At least that's how she'd chosen to see it, and Jeb knew he couldn't change how people saw the world around them.

Jeb sweat as he pulled up the weed roots. He heaved, straining against the brute pull of the thing. There was an uneasy feeling in his gut, a twisted, knotted up fear choking him like one of the weeds he pulled. There was something in the air. The corn wasn't growing right this season.

War had broken out in Europe. President Wilson had sworn to keep America's nose out of the old worlds new war, but none the less there was a definite fear that the US might get dragged in. Jeb hoped the pundits and editors in the paper were right. That it would indeed be a "little war." It wouldn't.

"Jeb?" A whiskey scratched voice called out from behind him. "That you?" Jeb turned around slowly to face the voice. "Come here." He smiled, the orange sun setting behind him.

"Why....? What are you doing here?"

"I'm back. I'm back and I ain't ever gonna leave you. Not ever again." He smiled a wide, toothless grin. His sun bleached clothes were torn and ragged, and the grizzled old man smelled of drink. "Come on," he said in a sterner voice.

"No," Jeb said. "No, you're gone. You left. You left us."

"I know I did, son. I know I did. It was the biggest mistake a' my life and I'm sorry. I'm so sorry."

Jeb stepped backwards, trying to hide his sun burned face.

"But I'm gonna make it up to you. I swear ta God I'm gonna make it up to you, boy. I promise. It ain't gonna be like before. It just ain't."

Jeb said nothing as he stared at the man.

"Jim! Is it really you?" Joan cried out as she ran from the house and towards her long gone husband. "Oh you're back! You're back!" She ran across the field, jumped and wrapped her arms around him.

"Things is gonna be good this time, baby," he said confidently. "I ain't leaving ya. Not this time."

She looked up at him and smiled.

\* \* \* \* \* \* \* \*

Jim and Joan were laughing at the old kitchen table as an oil lamp burned before them. Jeb stood stupefied in the doorway, impotent rage in his throat trying desperately to claw itself out.

"You left us," Jeb repeated. "You abandoned both of us, and now you just show up? You just come back and act like nothing's happened?"

"It's not like that, Jeb!" His mother cried desperately. "Don't be like that."

Jim grabbed her shoulder and nodded. "It's ok, darling. The boy just don't understand. Do you boy? You don't understand that's not what's happening here. I've come ta' make amends, to honor the vows I made your mother."

She smiled.

"I come back ta take care a' you."

"Well that's fucking great, but I -we- don't need you. We've been gettin along just fine on our own."

"Boy, watch your tongue!" Jim barked.

Jeb scowled.

Jim settled himself in his chair and cleared his throat. In a calmer voice he said, "Now, I know you're hurting. I know you are. And a part a that's my fault."

"You're a good man," said Joan. "Your fathers a good man, Jeb."

Jeb crossed his arms against his chest. "You're so stupid, you just believe anything he says, don't you?"

*"How dare you,"* said Joan.

Jeb stood up from his chair and stared down at her. "He could tell you the, the, the fucking moon was made a' cheese and you'd believe him! This guy beats us, and ruins us. Ruins the both of us, and you want him back! How could you ever want him back?"

"He's your father. He loves us very much."

"You're delusional! That man doesn't even know what love is!"

"Don't you talk that way to your mother, boy," Jim snapped.

Joan wasn't listening. "And you think you do? I am so sick of being insulted by you," she cried, staring at Jeb with wild eyes. "I'm sick of it, do you hear me?"

"Yeah that's right, that's right, you're sick of me and it's all my fault, mom. It's my fault you married the biggest bastard on the planet."

"Don't you talk about him like that!"

"It's my fault that you believe every crap thing he says. That he can't love you, or anyone else. You're like a big, stupid child, screaming when things don't go your way!" Jeb shouted.

"Get out of here! You leave, you get out!" Joan screamed.

Jeb picked up the vase from the table and chucked it at the wall where it exploded into a million shards. Joan tried to stop crying as she felt down at the stretch marks on her belly. She'd always felt ugly since the pregnancy.

Jeb rushed out into the cornfield. He ran, and ran and ran, the tall husks crashing into him like waves as he covered his tear soaked eyes. He knelt down in the middle of the yellow and green field, wiping at his cheeks with a heavy, dirt covered hand. He froze as he heard the low, familiar voice.

"Boy."

Jeb whipped around to face him. "What do you want?"

"Just wanna talk, boy. Just.... Just wanna try an' make up fer' what I done."

"Well it's too late for that now. I... I'm not afraid of you anymore. Not anymore."

"That's good." He smiled his grizzled, whiskey rich grin. "Man shouldn't carry fear around with him. It's bad for the soul."

Jeb sneered as Jim sat down beside him.

"Jeb I..." he said slowly. "Damn it, Jeb, I am sorry."

Jeb looked up, the tears glimmering in the low, evening sun. "I don't believe…"

"Yeah, I know." Jim nodded. "I know I done you wrong. Treatin' you and you're mother the way I did. Leaving you like that. But this time, well, this time it's gonna be different. I promise. I swear to God it is Jeb. Honest."

Jeb's voice cracked. "You don't really mean that."

Tears swelled up in his father's eyes as he lunged at him and hugged him tightly. "Yes I do. We're gonna be a real family again, you hear me? Just like we was always sposed' to be. We're gonna be a real family again, Jeb, I promise."

To see the man he only remembered as cruel. To see him crying... Had he been wrong? Had he willfully misremembered and let himself go cold like his mother said? He didn't wanna be there to find out.

Jeb left that night without telling anyone.

He never came back.

* * * * * * * *

### The Pacific Isles,    1916

Soft white clouds clung to the blue and pink sky as Cutlass muttered to himself, sweat dripping from his brow and onto the old, ochre colored map. "Almost there now," he said, digging the head of his shovel down into beach, grains of sand flying up and hitting against the brim of his hat before drifting down into his wild black beard. Gregor Cutlass' face was cracked and experienced and world weary as hell. His nose crooked and pock marked, his cheeks knotted. His shovel hit metal and he grinned madly, revealing stained lips and a mouthful of rot and gold filled teeth. With one tremendous heave he raised the chest up onto the white sand beach and knelt beside it.

"**POW!**"   The bullet erupted out from his flint lock pistol, blowing off the lock on the ornate chest. He laughed in a wild, devil may care way, his eye gleaming with hatred for Midas.   For what the ancient bastard had done.   "At last!"

He lifted the cover of the chest and reached down towards the folded piece of canvas at the center, ignoring the mountain of gold and gemstones beneath it.   He unfolded it carefully.

"....No...   No this cahn' be it!   This cahn' be all thar' is!" he screamed as he threw the piece of canvas down to the sand, and began to dig through the chest. "That's too far away, I can't wait that long!"

He emptied the rest of the treasure to the ground and collapsed.   "Fer' all the fuck in the world!"   He grabbed the piece of canvas, lifting it up to his face.   It was a set of instructions that said to be on a certain train, at a certain time, on a certain day, at a certain place.   They were instructions from Cutlass' god.

The pirate who had once been known and respected and feared across the seven seas let out a depressed sign.   "Seven years," he groaned.   "I can't believe I've got ta wait seven bloody years."

He'd started to stand up when he heard the piece of driftwood snap behind him.   "Who goes there?" he shouted as he whipped around.

"Captain   Cutlass,"   the   thin,   one   legged Englishman said with a smile.   He held a wooden cane in his right hand, a fearsome gun in his left.   "It's been a long time."

"Why if it isn't Edward St. John." Cutlass smiled. "Tell me, have ya yet gotten used to walkin' around on that peg?"

The man smiled back. "I'm glad to see you haven't lost your sense of humor."

"What are ya talkin' about? Ned me boy, that weren't no joke, it's a legitimate question."

"Spiteful to the last."

"If only."

"Oh this will be your last, Gregor Cutlass. I'll make sure of that."

"We'll see."

"You know for years I've been tracking you down, just waiting for this moment. My mind salivating over the thought of your death," said the one legged man.

"I know how ya' feel," the pirate replied.

"I dare say, I've practiced several thousand speeches. Dreamt of a thousand different ways of sending you back to hell, but... now that the moment has finally come? Now that we're both here? I find there's really nothing I want to say to you. No elaborate torture, or ironic death. No. No, at the end of it all, Captain, I just want to shoot you in the face.

\* \* \* \* \* \* \* \*

## New York City,   1917

"Come on trust me, you're gonna' love it," he said as he leaned down and kissed her on the white apartment bed. There was jazz playing in the fall air, the sounds of people hustling and moving down the crowded Brooklyn Streets. He'd been promising her big things for her first vaudeville show tonight, and she knew he wouldn't disappoint.

"I guess I'm just a little bit nervous, I don't know," said Olivia.

*"Shhh."* Jeb put his finger to her lips, and they were soft. She blushed. She liked the pressure of his finger. Thought of what else could cause that sensation. Time seemed to slow down, the grains of sand falling with not enough gravity through life's hour glass. There was a long pause as she grabbed his hand, and lost herself in his eyes. He looked like he could see right through her. Like he could tell. She pulled her long hair out its bun, and let it fall across her shoulders. "Is that good?"

Jeb froze. "Yeah."

"I feel like a whore." She smiled like someone with no idea what the word meant. The sheen of sweat gleaming on her skin. The trust in her lips as he kissed her again.

She liked the way he kissed her. Liked the feeling of his lips pressed against her, the strength of his arms as he pulled her against his chest and held her. Oh, the things he'd awoken in her! The rush that came with being taken, being made his. The rush that came with turning it all back around on him and making Jeb hers. That feeling, something like ownership, that knowledge that he belonged to her.

The little red theatre was packed that night. Fat men with cigars and coattails, slinky looking women with rouge red lips and sea blue eye shadow that made them look like very pretty drag queens. Smells and sights and sounds of the modern age, lights everywhere, everything all lit up a thousand different ways with electric bulbs. The show was a variety act because this was vaudeville, and so of course it was. An overstuffed woman in a Viking helmet opened the show, juggling oranges as she sang bad opera in made up Italian. Next a magician came out, The Great Zantini! Master of Majiks. He was a tall, eastern European gentleman with a great mustache, who opened his act with some sleight of hand before accidentally releasing a dove into the crowd. Next he sawed a tiny blonde women with heaving bosoms in half, and then for the big finale, disappeared.

Next up was the geek, who didn't disappoint the onlookers as he bit the head off of a live chicken and then left the headless bird to stumble aimlessly around the stage while he pulled out a harmonica and played turkey in the straw to thunderous applause. Ballet dancers followed in gray, worn out suits, and then a man with a trumpet was booed off the stage by the crowd. Olivia didn't know if he deserved to be booed or not, she was too busy making out with Jeb in the back of the dark theatre. She quivered as he ran his hand through her long hair, and kissed her breast. She liked the way he felt her up in the dark, it was dangerous and electric. She needed more danger.

They returned to their seats just in time for the finale: Miss Baudelaire Jones' Musical Orphans. They were a group of half a dozen girls, probably about twelve years old, and probably not orphans. They sang pageant style, as Miss Baudelaire Jones herself played piano. The girls wore simple white frock dresses, and their hair was all dyed an identical shade of peroxide. For their big finale song they each held a sparkler while signing the national anthem.

They laughed and laughed as they stumbled home drunk in the dark. They felt each other up in a dark alleyway, her panties yanked down beneath her dress. She squirmed in his hand, her back pressed against the brick wall, a gaslight glowing in the distance.

\* \* \* \* \* \* \* \*

### The Bed Chamber of King Midas,    1923

That night he had the dream again.

The layers of the universe folding in on themselves, all three dimensions become one, and dissipated across time. It was a good dream to have. His favorite dream. It was the only one left that hadn't become real or turned into a nightmare.

The endless stream of lights ran past him as his body melted into darkness and his eyes into fire. He opened them, waking up to the sound of his mistress snoring. She was a fat, golden calf, and he pushed her off of him. Gold bed posts rose up around him as he peeled the sheets from his boyish, sweat covered frame. The ceiling was painted with a fresco of angels, and they taunted him. The walls of the room were deep blood red. The floor gold tile.

He walked up to the mirror, touching his translucent face with boyish fingers, studying the reflection as he wondered how much longer he'd have to endure all this.

Not long.

He had felt the ghost last night. Felt it in his bones as a man named Jeb Chamberlain defiled his sacred tomb.

Sacred. Ha. Now there was a laugh.

For the first time in centuries he had hope. Hope that Jeb would find him. Find him and help him to unleash the infinite, long dormant power of the great Machine City that he had so long watched over.

He closed his eyes as he remembered the wonderful dream. The earth swallowed up, reality smashed on the floor. It was the only dream he had left.

# 34.
# THE MACHINE

He could feel himself falling as he watched the image of her eyes flicker by like film in a projector. The kitchen walls were cool green in the early morning light as water came trickling out from the faucet making a plop-plop sound. In the silence it sounded like a violation. Jeb sat up from the kitchen table and made his way over to the sink, the handle cool white porcelain in his hand as he twisted his fingers.

As the faucet halted, the rain outside began to pour. Gray clouds filling the sky as the pit-pat water slung itself against the tin roof. He listened. He'd always known how to listen.

There was a warmth coming from the living room and he followed it down the hall of the silent house till he found her with hair brushed back in a billowing mess and pale skin that hissed like steam as it brushed against his. He saw in her everything he had lost. In her eyes, promise. In her mouth, desire. A hungry feeling grew in his stomach, gnawing at his ribs, reaching its way up to his skull where it made his eyes itch and his brain go numb. The hunger broke open his mouth and the shadow climbed up into his throat and forced her way inside of him, pruning his insides like a rose garden as she made her way through. His wet feet slipped out from under him and he careened downwards for miles before breaking through the linoleum floor and crashing into the heart of some great machine.

He was a part of the machine, almost a power source. He could feel the gears whirring around him, hear the sound of pistons and circuits firing. Could see all of time and space laid out before him as he lay numb, and his tongue grew fat and stupid in his mouth, his eyes darting across the sinking, slipping core of the machine as a klaxon roared in the distance. As the world drifted away he could see her way up high, face cast in a million stars- a million stars free of the moon! And he, free to be with her. Free to live upon that great glowing surface, a fresh crater his and her only bed.

He awoke to the sound of nearby zebras, the sight of a pink midday sun hovering high in the air. It was hard for him to regain his balance, his atrophied legs were still so woozy. There was a ringing in his skull.

He looked up to find the sky dizzy, and unnatural. There was a body in the distance, and he approached it slowly. Coming closer he recognized the figure of his father. His filthy, squalid body lying bleached in the hot African sun next to a wooden door that led to nowhere, a wet yellow syringe only half filled in his right hand. He lifted his father up by his neck, kicked him through the empty door and killed him.

"Fire soldier, fire, fire!" Back in France he screamed above the mortars as he watched his captain fall dead into the mud. "Snap out of it! Snap out of it!" His voice grew desperate as the enemy approached. His friend was shell shocked. "Now, soldier! I need you right now!" He ducked just in time to dodge another volley of lead.

"Where have I been? No. Where am I?" He stumbled across the grassy knoll, his hands dizzy blurs in front of him, trying, trying, trying to find something to grab onto. His hands. His hands were not his hands, they were battered and scarred. His body. His mind. Oh God, his mind! "Where am I? Where have I been?" He felt cold. It was desperately hot out, but he felt cold. Layers, upon layers, upon layers, upon layers of wet, ice cold sheets clinging to his bones, snuffing out all warmth.

"Jeb?" a gaunt, sun ravaged man covered in rags and sweat, put his hand on Jeb's shoulders. "Can you hear me? Did you say something?"

"W-where am I?" Jeb whispered. "Where…" He looked around, finding himself amid a sea of hundreds of burned, starving men in the middle of the desert. "Sam?"

"My God," Sam whispered, his lips chapped and broken. "My God, you're back, you son of a bitch. You're back."

"B-back from where?" Jeb whispered, "How long have I been gone? How long have I been gone, Sam."

Sam shook his head, his eyes filled with hate and pain. *"Three months."*

# 35.

# AWAKE

The rail line was the only secure way up the continent, and after several days spent traveling in luxury the locomotive neared the land of the pharaoh's. Many of the passengers were sitting in the dining car when it happened, staring out the window, watching as the endless ocean of sand passed by. Ant like figures emerged from over the rim of one of the dunes, their bodies growing closer and closer as the train sped towards them. Closer. Closer. There were a dozen robed nomads riding atop camels outside the window, guns in each of their hands, and what looked to be a rusty artillery cannon beside them. There was a spark and plume of white smoke and then it happened. The conductor gripped tightly onto the locomotives controls. *"What the fu-"*

The artillery shell made a terrible sound as it crashed into the side of the train.

A second blast slammed the engine, and the train careened off the tracks and into the ground, a massive cloud of dust bellowing up, swallowing it whole. Two shifty looking outlanders in white and tan desert wear burst into the dining car, long rifles in each of their hands. *"Tania! Tania!"* the taller of the two cried out from behind the shawl that covered his mouth. He pulled a grenade from inside his robe and everyone on board screamed even louder than before.

The passengers raised their hands to block the blinding sunlight from their eyes as they stepped off the train and into the desert. White smoke brushed past them, blinding their vision, invading their nasal cavities as the throng of hundreds of refugee passengers bumped into each other.

Sam explained to Jeb that they were sand pirates, holding up camel merchants and luxury trains alike, robbing whoever they came across, taking prisoner any able bodied man to sell into slavery and any able bodied woman to take part of, and then ship off to some foreign harem.

The leader of the slavers was a man named Gourah Ahmed. He was a fat, glutinous beast with jowls that sagged down like brown breasts off his jewel encrusted face. In each ear he wore a fortune in gold and exotic emeralds, and in his nose a wide, circular silver plate. He had on a golden chest plate that Jeb recognized from Midas' tomb, and on his head he wore a billowing green turban. His flowing silk robes were green silk, nine gold ringed fingers poking out at the sleeves, his breast and belly exposed, revealing a carpet of black hair.

He was missing his tenth finger, the index on his left hand, and where it should have been there was a small burnt stump that he sucked on like a pacifier. *"Bu bulasik ne!"* he announced as he descended from his camel and slapped one his subordinates across the face. The subordinate cried out in pain, the leaders many rings like brass knuckles. The fat man started to make a proclamation to the assembled hostages, his voice cruel, his speech cut short by of the passengers.

"You listen to me, camel jockey!" One of the derailed train's former passengers shouted. "You can't do this to me, I'm an American!"

Gourah snapped his fingers. In an instant the slaver to his right raised up his rifle, blasting a hole through the man's skull. The blast rang out for miles as he fell into the blood stained sand.

* * * * * * * *

The new captives joined Jeb, Sam and the other veteran captives, and the group of hundreds was ordered to begin a death march to the north.

"You haven't talked, haven't said a single word in three months," Sam whispered. His face was gaunt and retched with sun burn, hints of raw flesh peeking out from behind peeled skin. He was naked save for some torn cloth wrapped around his torso and feet, chest an empty cavity, ribs poking out like the jaws of a shark.

"I don't understand," Jeb pleaded.

Sam looked furious. "NOT A WORD! You've been a silent, stupid zombie. I've had to force you to eat so that you didn't starve, had to beg for mercy so that they didn't kill you!"

"I was in a dream, I was-"

"You were catatonic!"

Jeb stuttered, his body a burned, aching red mess. "Olivia, Sam, where is she?   Where's Olivia?"

The last remaining light dimmed from Sam's already dead eyes.

"Tell me Sam!   Tell me, damn it, where is she?!"

Sam shook his head and turned away.   He didn't have to say it.   He didn't have to but he did anyways. "She's dead."

# 36.

# SLAVES OR WORSE!

*"Kasi!"* one of the slavers commanded as he whipped Jeb across the back. The leather snapped into his exposed flesh, leaving a skittering trail of blood dripping behind him. Gourah Ahmed, Sultan of the New Brotherhood, was carried across the sand in a glorious golden palanquin while his men rode atop camels, whipping any of the prisoners who fell behind as they marched in silent single file across the vast, dry emptiness of the desert.

Jeb couldn't speak to Sam. He didn't dare.

In the one hundred twenty degree heat of the desert a man can lose his mind, and it seemed to Jeb that everyone involved in the death march already had. One of the new prisoners, a man named Trevor, had made the mistake of talking back to his captors after they'd whipped him. Before the man could even finish his sentence his head was chopped off, leaving one final, horrible moment of terror frozen upon his face. After witnessing this, one of the other new prisoners made the further mistake of screaming. They cut out his tongue. The worst part of it all was the way the older prisoners, the ones who'd been marched across the desert for a month or a year or more, so easily accepted this barbarism. A horrified

Jeb had looked over at Sam for a moment, to find only a dull, desensitized expression on his friend's face. To him and the rest of the starving men, one less mouth to feed meant more food rations for the rest of them.

That night Jeb found himself freezing as he huddled around the ashy remnants of a bonfire, a broken shell of the man who had once been his best friend at his side. Neither of them were the men they had once been.

"What do you think my family thinks happened to me?" Sam whispered through cracked lips.

Jeb paused to think, his face a red welt. "I don't know... They probably think you're on vacation."

"They probably think I'm dead."

"Don't think like that," said Jeb.

Sam's eyes flashed hate as he turned towards him. "Don't you tell me how to think."

Jeb shrunk. "...sorry."

Sam sneered. "My mamma's heart must be broken. Worried sick. You see it ain't just me you hurt, it ain't just my life you broke, Jeb. Consequences. That's what you've got to understand. Life's got consequences for everything."

"I under-"

"No you don't! Not even..." A grim smile crossed his face. "I'm glad you're awake. Glad you're finally aware what's happening to you. Two weeks, old boy. Within two you'll be beggin' fer' death. Any luck, and it won't come for at least a few more months."

"You can hate me... That's fine, lord knows I deserve it," Jeb said in a hoarse voice as he raised the meager tin cup half filled with the rice they had given him for his daily rations. "But please, just tell me what happened to her. Please. I've got to know."

Sam nodded, his thin, bony neck hewn with the least possible bit of muscle. The smallness of it all made his head look huge. "Where should I begin?"

"How 'bout you start with the Zeppelin. You tell me how she died. You tell me how it is I'm even alive, and just how the fuck we ended up here...." His voice broke and he started to cough.

"That's the sand in yer' lungs. Ya never get used to it," said Sam.

*"Shhh!"* One of the other slaves shushed him as the guard gave a warning stare.

Jeb relaxed his shoulders and turned to Sam. There was something in his eyes that Jeb hadn't seen in years. Not since the war. And even then it wasn't quite like this.

"I don't know exactly how it happened," Sam said in a slow, carefully measured tone, "I just know it happened."

"What do you mean?" asked Jeb.

"Elizabeth she-"

Eyes wide as saucers. "Wait, is Elizabeth alive?"

Sam's face flattened. "God damn, do you wanna know what happened to Olivia, or not?"

Jeb nodded.

"Then shut the fuck up already, and let me finish."

There was a nastiness Jeb had never seen in Sam before. He was different now, more so, perhaps, even than Jeb. Sam brushed back a clump of mated black hair. He had a beard now, though it was thin, and splotchy. Jeb leaned out and touched his old friend's shoulder, a look of concern on his face.

Sam pulled back, his slight, bony arm seemingly in pain. "I'm fine," he wheezed.

"Sam I know you hate me. I know that."

Sam didn't say anything.

"I'm sorry. I'm so horribly sorry for the pain I've caused you. For this sickening mess I've gotten you into. I'm sorry, Sam. I really, truly am."

The same sullen and gaunt expression still dominated Sam's face.

"Sam. Please, say something. Anything."

"You came to me, Jeb. You came to me. Dragged me into all this."

"I know, Sam, I know. I'm sorry," Jeb gasped.

"Stop saying that," Sam said, as he fished through the clump of his beard with bony fingers. "I don't want your apologies. Or your pity."

Jeb looked down at his small cup of rice. "Take it." He lifted up the cup to him.

Sam looked down at the tin for a moment, his gaunt expression quickly turning to something darker. "I said no pity!"

Jeb looked into Sam's eyes, searching for some hint of his old friend. The Sam who had tended bars and grudgingly shoveled coal into the hull of a Trojan ship, the Sam who had laughed with him, who had fought next him in battle. That Sam was gone. That Sam was dead. Dead like Olivia. The soul starved right out of him.

Jeb eyes were watering up.

"Don't," Sam said quietly, "don't waste that water."

Jeb wiped it away quickly. Maybe this was all a dream too. He swore he could see two tiny angels and a gazelle circling atop Sam's head. Jeb blinked as snakes crawled out of his once friends eyes. He shook his head, trying desperately to regain his senses. "So... so, Olivia?"

"Elizabeth found her dead," Sam said without emotion. "Burnt to a crisp."

"No..."

"She didn't have ta' go like that. If you hadn't been distracting her with all your bullshit. Your obsession with her, or whatever it was-"

"Sam I loved her. I still love her."

"I guess you could call it that. Maybe some people would."

Jeb's chest heaved. "Not you though?"

"You think you were the only one? I loved her! Alright? I loved her too, she was my friend. Her husband loved her, her family loved her! And you've got the damn nerve to act like you're the only one?"

Jeb was quiet. He didn't say a word for a very long while. Finally, Sam broke the silence.

"These people. Not even people. Animals. Rats. It was the fire that drew them to us. I remember I woke up after the crash, beat up and bruised as hell, but not too much worse for wear. Elizabeth too, she survived just fine, aside from the burns."

"The burns?"

"Yeah," said Sam, "she ain't quite as pretty as she used to be." He gestured towards one of the slavers. "We thought they were there to help us at first, and we looked at them like rescuers. Boy were we ever wrong. They unloaded all the gold from the hull and took us prisoner, then started marching us across the plain. Wasn't more than a week before we stumbled across you, silent, alone, and inexplicably alive."

"HOW!" Jeb demanded.

"I don't know!" said Sam. "I don't know anything about where you were during that week, or what happened to you. For God sakes, I thought you'd be the one to tell me."

Jeb shook his head. "I don't have any idea. I don't' remember, just dreams, and nightmares, and…"

"They're slave traders, these people. Travel around buying and selling people. Gourah, he's their leader. He's the one Elizabeth's gotten so damn cozy with."

"So she's still alive?"

"Oh, she's alive alright. Whore's taken up with Gourah and become his concubine."

"That sounds like Elizabeth." Jeb smiled faintly.

Sam scowled. "Are we done now? Are we finished here?"

"Yeah, Sam. Yeah, I think we're finished."

Sam stood up like rickets and stumbled over to the pile of sand where he would sleep for the night. "I'm only gonna say this once, so listen up. Don't try and escape. If they see you running they'll shoot. If they don't, you'll dehydrate. No man can last more than a day in the desert without water."

"Sam…"

"And don't try and be the fucking hero either. Don't try and rebel. Don't fight it. They'll kill you, not that I really care. But if you kill one of them? If you really piss them off? They'll shoot ten of us. And one of those ten just might be me." He lowered his gaze away from Jeb's, trying to focus his hazy, death starved eyes as he walked away.

# 37.
# OCEANS OF SAND

The camel moaned as its rider leaned back and snapped the whip across Jeb's back. He winced in pain, biting down as hard as he could, careful not to scream. The Jeb that had existed before the Zeppelin crashed, before the dreams and the missing three months, the Jeb that didn't know that Olivia and everything else was lost or dead, that Jeb would have fought back. He would have strangled the bastard with that whip. But that Jeb was gone. Now he relented and put his hands over his head as another of the nomads slammed the butt of his gun into Jeb's ribs. The old Jeb wouldn't have stood for that. The old Jeb would have grabbed that gun and fucked him with it. But not this Jeb. For better or worse he simply took

For hours they marched on without rest before coming across a band of red clothed traders in the middle of the desert. Gourah signaled from his palanquin to halt, and his slaves lowered him down gently onto the sand. A tall African emerged from the group and came towards them. There was a long wooden staff in hand, and an orange kufi atop his head. *"Geshii!"* he called out in a deep voice. *"Mesh maka din dare?"*

Gourah nodded and stood.

The tall, red robed black man circled around the prisoners deliberately, his narrow eyes carefully trained in the business of picking slaves. After a few moments he smiled and handed over a few pieces of silver. Gourah gave a signal to his riders, and at once several of the slaves were unshackled and handed over to the red clothed men.

That night Jeb dreamed of Olivia. He almost always did. It was the thoughts of her that got him through those treacherous days. The memory of her face, the way she glowed, of how marvelous it had felt to hold her, to make love to her.

Salid was there too. Roasting on the cannibals spit. Burning. Dying.

Fire! It seemed such a constant in his nightmares and in his life. It seemed to Jeb that he could never outrun it, and of course there was no outrunning guilt. No escaping what he'd brought upon Sam and Salid. And then of course there was her face, reflected out across the oceans of sand. Every time he closed his eyes at night he saw her falling.

Where had he been during that week alone on the savannah? He had flashes of light, of needles, of religion, of something so dark no light could escape. By the third day after he woke up, Jeb was convinced he could see a flock of penguins waddling across the desert dunes. On the fourth day he saw rivers of gold and the great Machine City of his dreams. And then, on the fifth day, he saw Elizabeth.

"Jeb!" she whispered in the still night air as she crept towards him. "Jeb wake up!"

Jeb opened his eyes and saw that she was covered in jewels. "So it's true then, you're Gourah's concubine."

"You heard?" she said excitedly, pointing towards a elaborate tent, some fifty feet away. "It's not that bad really. Honestly it's..."

"I'm happy you're ok," he said.

She smiled. "I'm happy you're ok. Jesus, I can't believe that you're back, Jeb. I was afraid you'd never wake up, that you'd just walk around, silent and dead behind the eyes like that forever!" She brushed a strand of long, blonde hair from her face as she smiled. "Well how did you... how did you?" She looked off into the distance, recalling the grizzly details of that night. "You died. I saw it, Jeb. He shot you right through the chest!"

Jeb shook his head.

"And then getting sucked out that window!"

"I know, I know..."

"I don't understand," she whispered, "where have you been these months? How are you here?!"

Jeb took her hand, and placed it against his bare chest. "Look at it."

"What?" She asked again, eyes expectant as she felt his heart-beat.

"There's no scar. Nothing." He looked off into the distance.

"I know," she said softly. "Something happened to you after the crash. Don't you know what it was?"

"I don't know anything at all about these last three months... All I remember are these strange dreams, these dreams I can feel in my blood, dreams I can taste."

Elizabeth looked down at him, her mouth still and open, butterflies fluttering underneath the skin around her hair. "I'm sorry."

"Don't be." He took her hand and traced it up the length of his bare chest. "Wherever I was, whoever found me, they saved my life. I just wish I could say the same for her."

Elizabeth looked down, her eyes closed tightly. "I know."

"Why?" Jeb asked. "Why? She was so young."

Elizabeth nodded carefully.

"Sam he... he said you found her," said Jeb.

"I don't wanna talk about this."

"I need to know!" He grabbed her wrist, twisting it. "Please Elizabeth, I need answers. I need to know what happened to her!"

She let out a deep sigh. "I... I remember walking away from the Zeppelin after it crashed. Sam was nearby, but he was still passed out. I dragged him away from the fire. The whole place. I mean everywhere, the whole thing, Jeb, it was an inferno. My clothes, my arms, my face." She tilted her head to the side, pulling back her hair to reveal an unhealed burn running down the left side of her neck. "It was all burning. I made my way across the wreckage, cold rain drizzling down as I called out her name."

Elizabeth looked as though she were on the verge of tears. "And then I found her body, and it was cold, and that's it. That's all there was, Jeb." A tear slid down her cheek and she wiped it away. "The worst part of it all is that I never even got to say goodbye. She was already gone when I got there."

The cold hand of death reached down into his chest as he sunk back into the sand. The irony of it all. That face, those eyes he so loved. How could an ocean catch fire? Elizabeth wrapped her arms around him tightly. "Oh Jeb! Just hold me."

He shook his head. "I wanna be alone right now."

She studied him with cold gray eyes.

"Thank you." Jeb nodded as she let go of him, and he dropped back down to the ground. His tongue was heavy, dry like a rock. He longed for her touch, longed to see her again. But that was impossible. He realized that now. Any last doubt within him had been expelled. She was gone and there was nothing he could do about it. In his dreams that night he saw her face engulfed in flame. When he awoke the next morning she was sitting across from him, a knife in her hand and snakes in her hair. With a glossy smile and trembling hands she slit her wrists, the low, dusky light casting a glow about her as she drowned in her own red paint, her eyes stained by it. The hallucinations were getting worse.

Two more months went by. Two months living amongst the walking dead, sustained on dates and rice and bugs. Jeb's skin was burned off, hair matted, disgusting. Elizabeth came to him at night. She'd bring him table scraps of bread, oil to rub into his skin. It helped. They'd talk about Olivia. He'd tell her how he missed her, and she'd listen, put her hand on his shoulder, and share a passing glance. It was obvious there was something between them, but Jeb didn't like it even if she did.

"Sam still hates me. I... I don't know how to get through to him. I try, but..." Jeb said glumly. "You know he's the closest thing I've got to family. At least he was."

Elizabeth looked at Jeb with a pitying look.

Jeb shook his head. "He's different now, you know? This march we've been on. The starvation, the death. It's changed him."

Elizabeth frowned. "Jeb you can't blame yourself."

"The hell I can't!"

She sighed. "People suffer and people hurt, that's just the way it is. If he can't handle it that's his problem."

Jeb shook his head. "And how are you handling it?"

There was a dark smile lurking at the edge of her lips. She pulled a folded up piece of paper from the sash around her waist. "I've still got the map you drew up, you know, the copy of the tattooed man? I've still got it Jeb."

He looked surprised. "How'd you manage that?"

She averted his gaze. "You don't wanna know."

Dennis Badeau

"You're planning something, aren't you?" Jeb probed.

Elizabeth continued to look away. "You wanna get outta here or not?"

He reached out and took her shoulder, pulling her towards him. "I'm listening."

She bit her lower lip and smiled. "I've been planning it for months. Soon, I'm not sure when exactly, but soon we'll be close enough to Cairo to make a break for it."

Jeb nodded. "And not die from dehydration on the hike over."

"That's right," said Elizabeth.

Jeb stole a glance at the guard. "And what's your plan to get past them, you clever thing, you?"

"Ah!" She looked away again, this time trying hard to conceal a smile. "That's the fun part."

"You never realize how rotten it is to be hungry till you're starving," Jeb said through gritted teeth as he looked over at his new friend, the white hot sun beating down upon his naked shoulders.

Cutlass grinned. "Yer' far too young ter' be bitchin' like that, lad. You leave that to this old man."

Jeb laughed. That was a mistake. It felt like his insides were tearing themselves apart as soon as he took in air. He'd never been this hungry before or this tired. "Under the circumstances I'll bitch all I want to, old man."

Cutlass shook his head as the two of them continued their forced march onwards through the desert. He was a decent sort: A tall, stocky bohemian with rugged features and a patch over his left eye. He'd been on the derailed train before being captured. It might have just been him being tough, but it seemed to Jeb that the old man was the only one who had a sense of humor about the current situation. With rough hands he pulled a sand sled filled with supplies behind him, heaving it forwards with some unseen strength.

Each day trudged on in much the same way. Sticky, dizzy, miserable. What little urine there was came out in muddy streams. Flies and gnats buzzed around the unwashed masses, skin itching from burns and sand. Coming from the northeastern coast of the US Jeb wasn't used to the lack of humidity. Gone were the wet, sticky pools of sweat that would have formed under every crevice of his skin in a New England summer, here the sweat evaporated as soon as it hit the air, strong winds blowing sand in his eyes till they burned red and forced him to dig out the miniscule grains with sun scabbed fingers. At night the sky went black, and the temperature was near freezing. Dozens of the slaves died from exposure every week, and Jeb was surprised he wasn't among their number.

And then, in that cold, silent night there was her voice: *"You and I. Together, we can escape. We can still come out on top!"* There was a madness written upon her face now, her eyes wide, glistening like a cat ready to pounce. It was nearly midnight, the fire long gone out, and she'd snuck out from her tent to speak with him, just as she did most every night.

"We can't." Jeb frowned. "Not yet, not until Sam's ready."

"Forget him! Forget Olivia, forget everything." Elizabeth slipped her fingers inbetween his.

"What are you doing?"

"Don't you wanna forget about it all? Don't you? We can leave all this misery behind us, Jeb. Start again."

"We can't, Elizabeth, we can't just pretend it didn't happen. "He said the words with resignation. Something in her reminded him of Olivia.

"We've talked about this already, Jeb, you and me, the way it was meant to be. We can find the tomb together."

Jeb wanted to smack her. "What are you doing, Elizabeth, huh? It's too late for that, it's too-"

Slowly she leaned in, pressing her thick pink lips against him as she kissed the side of his face. "Forget her."

He shoved her off of him.

"She never loved you, Jeb. She was indecisive, she was cold, she was unhappy, she was never yours."

He looked away.

"But I... I'm not like her. I know what I want." Elizabeth pulled back, a look of something unknowable to Jeb in her eyes. "I want you. Jeb this is fate. Us being here together, it was meant to be."

"Elizabeth what are you talking about? We're slaves in the middle of the Sahara for Christ's sake, and you're coming onto me?"

"We won't be slaves forever, or at least I won't. Though you might be to her fucking ghost."

He lay down in the silver moonlit sand and closed his eyes. "You don't know what you're talking about."

She smacked him in the ribs, sending shivers through his empty stomach. "I'm making my break tomorrow tonight. I can't spend another god forsaken day here, and besides, we won't be this close again for months."

He looked back at her as he clutched his ribs, a pained look on his face.

"This is our chance!" she whispered.

"But Sam..." Jeb's hesitation lingered like the drag from a cigarette. He knew she was right, and that made it all the more terrible.

"He won't come, Jeb, he hates you. And even if he would come with us he's too weak, he'd only slow us down." Jeb thought about Sam. He knew the poor bastard would be dead soon. "You need to leave him in the past, and accept that things have changed."

"No." Jeb closed his eyes and prepared for sleep. "I'll try and convince him to escape with us tomorrow, but if he won't go, than neither will I."

"Damn it, Jeb!" Elizabeth scowled.

He lay there with his eyes closed. "I won't abandon him. His fate will be my own."

# 38.

## THE SPRAWL OF THE NIGHT

Jeb looked around nervously before one of the guards caught his gaze and winked at him. Adrenaline surged through him as he crawled towards Sam. "Sam!" Jeb whispered. "We're getting out of here!"

"Leave me the hell alone," Sam said as he awoke from deep sleep.

"Sam, you have to get up. Sam, we're making our move tonight," Jeb said through gritted teeth.

"No," said Sam, "I told you, I can't!"

"I'm getting you out of here!" Jeb cried.

"Stop saying that!"

"I have too."

"How?" Sam said in a voice just above a whisper. Jeb pointed at the guard who had winked at him. The man had left his post and begun to talk with the other slaver entrusted with guarding the prisoners. "There's our distraction!" Jeb hissed at Sam. "Now all we have to do is run and-"

The ground shook as the guard pulled the pin from his grenade and tossed it into the distance. He screamed "traitor" in Egyptian before retrieving his revolver and blasting the other guard keeping watch at point blank range.

"NOW!" Jeb cried, as he dragged the stumbling, half awake, half dead Sam through the sand, the great rush of fleeing prisoners passing by him, all seeing their chance at escape. Only a few of the most broken men stayed behind.

As Jeb and Sam stormed across the black, unlit desert, they could hear the screaming Gourah far behind them as he rounded up his men and animals. Jeb ducked as the sound of gun shot rang out inches from his skull, and for a moment he was transported back to France. One of the bullets tore through Sam's shoulder and he collapsed to the ground in a bloody mess.

Jeb sank to the ground with him, screaming as he cradled Sam's bloody frame in his arms. He shouted down at him. "Sam! SAM!"

Sam looked back with bloodshot eyes. His limp, broken body gushing blood. "Jeh- Jeb...." He coughed. "Don't leave me behind."

"Save your strength, don't say anything," Jeb cried. Suddenly he felt his friend's hand go cold, and it slept loose from his grip.

"Jeb!" Elizabeth shouted some twenty yards away. "Leave him, he's gone, Jeb, he's gone!"

He looked over at her with disbelieving eyes as another of the prisoners fell down next to him, a bullet in his brain. "No... no that's not true."

"Come on!" she screamed, a desperate look in her eyes. "Jeb we have to go now!"

Jeb shut his eyes, biting down on his lip so hard it split and began to bleed. Bullets tore past his head. "I'm sorry, Sam," he said as he lowered him to the ground.

"No...." Sam muttered as he began to cough up thick, coagulated blood. "No...."

"I'm sorry," Jeb said as he looked into his friends eyes. "But I don't have a choice."

Jeb caught a glimpse of Elizabeth running far up ahead, her body illuminated for a moment by the crescent moon before disappearing into the black horizon. "I don't have a choice." He cradled Sam's body in his arms, and his lungs felt like they were being stabbed. He thought back on how all this had come to pass, and he knew what he had to do.

\* \* \* \* \* \* \* \*

### Laconia, New Hampshire, 1921

He sat up and stretched. Tried to reclaim the pressure of her hand against him, but she was gone. His stomach was cold. His whole body was cold. Chills running down his skin, underneath his eyes. Chills like the ripple of her shadow.

He dressed and stepped outside. The grass was cool and wet beneath his bare feet. The sign outside read *Sunny Days Motel*, though the sky was anything but. He took a deep breath in the chilled air and scratched the back of his head. He was wearing a loose blue bathrobe with holes in the pockets. It'd been three months since he left Boston.

He sat down on a dew soaked wooden deck chair and began to taste the early morning air in lumps. There was a light fog rolling out from the woods that bordered the out of the way motel, birds chirping up in the trees. He rubbed the back of his neck and listened.

Back in the motel room wall there hung a picture of the nearby "Old Man of the Mountain," a local landmark he'd never bothered to visit. He pushed past the bathroom door, grasped for the handle of the shower, twisted it and sat down, letting the water soak his clothes. Sitting there on the brown mildew stained tiles of the shower, everything dripping wet, Jeb pulled the worn, black and white photograph from his pocket and examined it. He turned it over in his hand, studying the blue inked hand writing now washing away into smudges. "Coney Island. October 1st, 1919." There was a little heart she'd inked next to the date, with an arrow going through it.

He ripped the photograph into pieces, watching as they slipped down the drain.

* * * * * * *

It was morning now, the yellow sun shining high in the sky above. Jeb squinted as he looked past the desert before him and out towards the distant pyramids. Elizabeth and Cutlass were with him, as was Sam, who he'd carried to safety on his back. Most of the slaves had been shot or recaptured, leaving the three of them alone, sprawled out in the sand, the dark cityscape of Cairo so nearly within reach.

They got up and made their way towards the city, Elizabeth of course leading the way. It had taken months of planning and bribery, using gold and treasure stolen from Gourah's tent to pay for her escape.   The compromised guard had thrown the grenade only to kill the second guard so as to blame it on him later.

Once they reached the city Elizabeth pawned off the rest of the gold and jewels she'd smuggled from Gourah's tent, using the money to rent rooms at a local inn for herself, Jeb, Sam and Cutlass.   Jeb sat down in the cramped, yellow painted corner of his bedroom, a kind of sandwich in hands and a glass of water on the floor.   His hand trembled as he brought the bread up to his lips and stuffed the thing into his mouth.   He gagged trying to swallow the big cardboard chunks of it, dry heaving, unable to digest so much so fast. Spread out on all fours on the floor of the room, a sick, desperate wobbling in his gut, it all came up in a bubbling brown mess on the floor boards.   Elizabeth leaned over him, brushing back the oily hair from his face as he turned over, laying in his own mess, eyes sobbing red welts.

# 39.

# THE BAZAAR

## Cairo,   Two Weeks Later

Strange and fascinating people from across the world moved about the marketplace carrying baskets of fish, and tea leaves, and mangos on their heads. Jeb took in the heavy scent of spice wafting off of the roasted birds before buying two of them from the man behind the counter, who then proceeded to chop the birds up into quarters and stuff their misshapen pieces into hollowed out loaves of bread. Jeb turned around and smiled as Elizabeth walked up to him. "This is just like Harriramma!" she said happily, her new clothes looking gorgeous and clinging tightly to her. She was wearing a black pencil skirt with silk stockings and a white silk blouse, gold bangles around her wrists, and silver scarab shaped earrings. Her nails were painted blood red, and her hair was done up in wavy blonde pin up style.

"I know," Jeb agreed as he paid the man and took the two bread wrapped, heavily spiced birds into his hands.

"Looks good," she said, admiring the way he looked now that he wasn't in rags. He was wearing khakis and a tan safari jacket.

"Yes, it does doesn't it?"  Jeb said before biting down into the thing, careful not to stain his clothes. "Tastes even better."

"Mind if I?" she asked.

"Why do you think I got two?"  He handed her one of the bread wrapped chickens.  "You are the one who paid for it."

She laughed.  "Well, thank God for my sticky fingers, or we'd be as bad off as they are."  She gestured towards two children in rags, begging at the end of the street.

Jeb walked up to the children, giving them each a handful of coins before they ran off into the alleyways. "You can't do that," said Elizabeth.

Jeb shrugged.  "Why the hell not?"

"Because flashing money around like that gets people robbed."

"I'm not worried," Jeb said calmly, as he pulled a bowie knife from out of one of the pocket of his safari coat.  "Let um' try.  I could use a good fight."

"Is that right?"  She smiled, her eyes flashing like beacons.

"Come on, doll," he said as he took her hand, "let's go for a walk."

They made their way through the marketplace and up onto the balcony of a stone tower.  The tower cast long shadows across the row of colonial British mansions beneath it, cloaking them in darkness. Elizabeth's gray eyes shone as sunlight came through her bright blonde hair and off the corners of her clothes, covering her in equal parts light and shadow. She looked away, brushing the yellow hair from her face. "I know you miss her, Jeb.

"It's more than that," he said as he looked out at the city. "I always thought…"

A look of worry shot across Elizabeth's face. "Yeah?"

Jeb frowned. "I know it's stupid, but I really thought I'd locked her away in my past, that I'd moved on. And then the second I saw her again it was just like… I don't know what I'm supposed to feel at this point, you know?"

She turned away from him, hiding her face in the sun.

He took her shoulder and turned her to face him. "You do know what I mean, don't you."

"No, I don't," she said.

"Maybe we could've had a second chance, me and her," said Jeb, "maybe this was our do over."

"There was never any second chance," Elizabeth's smoky voice trailed off. "Jeb, she said that she couldn't be with you. Maybe she cared about you in her own way, but her husband was always going to come first. He was always the man in her heart."

Jeb sank back against the railing, his eyes glazed over.

"You need to move on and accept what's happened instead of being ashamed of it."

He shook his head. "I'm not ashamed."

Elizabeth smiled. "We're all ashamed of something. Something we did or didn't do, something we felt.  Someone we wanted that we knew we weren't supposed to want.  You're ashamed of yourself because she died.  You think it was your fault."

"It wasn't my fault."

"I don't believe that you believe that.  I think there's so much guilt wrapped around you, choking you, keeping the air out of your lungs, that you can't even think straight.  I think you want to hurt, Jeb.  I think you need it."

He crossed his arms.  "Are you done playing at Freud?"

"You don't know what you want.  You don't know who you want."

"Just shut your mouth."

She raised her eyebrow.  *"Make me."*

Jeb closed his eyes and thought about Olivia.  He thought of her as he pushed Elizabeth against the balcony's edge.  Thought of her as his rough, warm hands raced up to the back of Elizabeth's head, and he ran his fingers through her hair.  She moaned as he traced his fingertips past her lips, down the burn of her neck, under her shirt and across her belly, pausing only for the briefest of moments by her waistline.  She wrapped her arms around him, gray eyes searching his tired face, letting out a gasp as he kissed her.  *"You're so fucking guilty,"* she whispered.

They made their way down to a neighborhood of colonial British mansions, the neighborhood watch finding their whiteness reason enough to let them on their way unaccosted, broke the back window of the first empty one they found, and made their way inside. Elizabeth smiled wickedly as she pushed past him and entered into the great empty house. A too large couch lay at the end of the room beside a too small fireplace with a polished ivory mantle. A small golden figure lay atop the mantle, the fading sunset casting a dull gleam upon it as the light flooded in through the windows. Jeb watched as Elizabeth made her way across the red and orange tiled floor and pulled the blood red drapes together, suddenly casting the whole opulent room into dense and total blackness. *"We shouldn't be here,"* Elizabeth said quietly, *"we don't even know whose house this is."*

Jeb frowned. He couldn't see a thing in the dark mansion, but he could hear the sound of slow tapping footsteps as she made her way towards him, her newly purchased heels clicking across the tile like the letters of a typewriter. "You think we're living too dangerously now?" he asked.

"No, but I'm dangerous. I think that scares you," said Elizabeth.

He stifled a laugh as she lay her small, soft hands against his shoulder and began to speak. As her ruby red lips moved inches from his face, he could feel the heat of her breath. Taste the thickness of her strawberry perfume. It hung heavy in the stagnant air of the place. "Don't be afraid."

"I'm not afraid." He closed his eyes, and the room grew a little less dark.

"You sure?"

He shifted his head, moving his hands towards the base of her neck, choking her. She moaned as he held her within a hair of his flesh. "I'm sure." Even in the cloaked darkness, Jeb could make out the faint gleam of her eyes as she wrapped herself around him. He let go of her neck and she slid her invisible lips across his cheek and up to his ear, her tongue just barely in the cave of her mouth as she whispered, *"Good boy."* Jeb could feel the tug of her right hand as it slid down into his sports coat and gripped the handle of his knife. With a quick pull she slid it forwards, out of his pocket and up, just a kiss away from the flesh of his cheek.

*"Are you ashamed?"* she asked as she slid the cold steel of the blade across his cheek, cutting the top layer of his flesh, sending a slow trickle of blood dripping down. She shrieked as he grabbed her arm, twisting the blade away from her, sending it clattering down to the floor. She went to slap him with her left hand but he grabbed that too as she reached back with it. Silently he held her there in the darkness, her arms twisted high above her head. Deep breathing, their mouths only a few inches apart as she swung her hips and pushed up against him. For a moment Jeb loosened his grip and Elizabeth came closer, her tongue dancing as she flicked it out, dragging it slowly across his cheek as she took in the dark crimson of his blood. *"I like the taste of that,"* she moaned, *"I like it real good."*

Jeb searched the infinite blackness of the room for a moment, trying to find where her face should be, his own still stinging. "You're one strange bitch, you know that?"

She laughed wildly. "I told you I was dangerous."

He pushed her away, pulled a wooden matchbox from his pocket, and slid open its pale cover. With a quick flash he scraped the red tip of one of the matches across his thumb, the room once again glowing with dim light. He made his way to the wood stacked fire place and tossed in the match, quickly setting the dry palms ablaze. Jeb looked back towards Elizabeth, a wild look on her pale, yellow hair framed face. The fire started small at the base of the wood pile before growing larger, erupting as it licked up at the higher wood, quickly engulfing it in a red hot bonfire. Jeb felt at the cut on his cheek for a moment. It wasn't deep. He'd had worse.

Elizabeth stood still at the other side of the room, her usually calm gray eyes flickering with a new hint of uncertainty. Jeb laughed for a moment. "You really are crazy," he said as he undid the top button of his shirt.

She laughed. "Some men think so."

"Probably the ones that are still alive."

"That's rich."

"What really happened to Olivia?"

"She died."

"What really happened?"

"She died, Jeb."

He picked the table lamp up and through it across the room, where it smashed into pieces. "I don't believe that anymore."

Her heels clicked once again across the red and orange tile as she stepped towards him. "It's the truth."

"Liar!" he said as he put his hand around her neck.

This time she didn't moan. She paused, her cold eyes reflecting the shock of his sudden brutality. "Animal." He just stood there, looking at her as his grip grew tighter. The fire casting its own red pall over him. "Bastard," she whispered.

He tapped the edge of his blood stained cheek. "Now we're even."

"Not even close," she said as she leaned forwards, biting his lower lip before he pushed her away. She smiled. "It's in your eyes."

"What is?" he asked, the ever glowing roar of the fire shining across his emerald green eyes.

"Desire. Need. Guilt."

"Is that a fact?"

"I can see your soul." Her eyes lit up, and her smile faded into two thick red lips pursed together into a careful pout. "And I'll bet you weren't nearly this rough with my sister. Probably played the part of the gentle, proper lover, didn't you, Jeb? But that's not who you are." He released her once again and she stripped off her blouse, undoing each button carefully before letting the garment fall to the red and orange tiled floor.

"Who do you think I am?" Jeb asked.

"I think you're a fucking degenerate," said Elizabeth, her smooth, bare shoulders glistening in the light from the fire. She cupped her generous breasts over her bra, enjoying the weight of them in her hands. "I bet Olivia's husband was rough with her. I bet he made hard, angry love to her."

"What are you doing," he asked.

"I'll bet he fucked her raw and whispered terrible, degrading things into her ear. Names and rules and promises." She smiled. "How are we going to break the news about his wife to him, anyhow? I'm sure it won't be easy. After all he so loved fucking her in all the ways you never did."

"I'm sure," Jeb said, as he undid the last button of his shirt. More hallucinations: he could see her pale, ghostly visage staring at him from across the room, an arrow through her stomach. An ocean raging in her eyes.

"It always comes back to her though, doesn't it?" Elizabeth said quietly. "Every time you and I get to talking, it...." she sighed. "I suppose we'll just have to avoid talking next time." She lit a cigarette and took a long drag. "You're so scared. It's obvious." She blew out a puff of smoke. "I need you to stop doing that."

"You need a lot of things."

"You have no idea." The smoke rolled out like fog.

He walked up to her and undid her bra, leaving her topless before the fireplace. "I will not be gentle with you. I will not make you happy."

"Good," she purred, turning her back to him, pressing her ass against his crotch.

Jeb placed his hands at her waist and led her towards the couch in the corner of the stolen room. She pushed him down and crawled on top of him, whispering into his ear with heavy breath. "You can pretend I'm her if you want. You can even scream her name, hell, I could get off to that." She took another drag from her cigarette before she dropped it to the ground and snuffed it out.

"I don't want her ghost," Jeb said in an uneven voice, "I wanna feel good. So you better make me feel good." He grabbed her head and kissed her violently, flipping her over and throwing himself on top of her. "You better fucking make me feel so good, you piece of shit."

"Oh yes! Yes!" she moaned as he kissed her burned neck, tugging her black pencil skirt down below her knees. "Take me!" she cried. "Do it now!"

He pressed his lips against her swelling breasts, kissing them with hate. "I will never love you," he said through caustic breath.

"I don't want you to love me," she said as she pushed his head down, "I just want you inside of me!"

# 40.
# TREMORS

He shoved the long, snakelike metal key into the lock and turned it, listening carefully to the mechanical clicking noise it made, like a hobby horse bobbing up and down. "Where have you been?" Sam asked as Jeb and Elizabeth stepped in.

"Just seeing the city," Jeb replied. "What have you and Cutlass been up to?"

"The captain's asleep in the other room. No idea when he'll wake up," Sam said as he fanned out a deck of cards, laying them on the table before him.

"Solitaire? That's not a two player game, is it."

"It is not," said Sam.

Jeb motioned towards the door. "Elizabeth can you give us a minute?"

"Sure," she said as she left the room.

He looked back at Sam and smiled. "You look better."

Sam rubbed the bandaged over bullet wound. "I feel better. I think."

"You know I feel like we should talk. We haven't done much of it lately," said Jeb.

"Why you wanna talk?" Sam asked. "So you can remind me again that I owe you my life, eh old boy?"

"Forget about it, Sam. You know there was no way I coulda left you behind."

Sam rolled his eyes.

"The memories of what happened, those will fade. And.... and it 'ill get easier with time."

Sam stared at the bullet wound in his shoulder. "I'm gonna get a plane to Europe in a few days, and I can snag a boat back home from there. It's you the cops want, I can't imagine they still care about me."

"But what about the treasure?"

Sam glared. "Fuck the treasure."

Jeb looked genuinely surprised. "After all we've gone through?"

"After all we've gone through? Yes, Jeb, after all we've gone through! You of all people, I would have thought you'd learned something by now."

"Sam, there's a fortune in gold out there just waiting to be found."

"Yeah, yeah, and it can all be ours."

"That's right!" said Jeb.

Sam shook his head. "And at what cost? What about Olivia? What about the old man? Hunjii? What about everyone who's already died out here? Everyone we've killed. You think any of that was actually worth it? What about the hell I've just spent the last five months roasting in?" He closed his eyes and thought of Olivia. "Was it worth it?"

"I can't bring her back!" Jeb's shouted. "I don't...." He took a deep breath. "I'm not gonna fight you, I'm not gonna argue with you anymore. I think going after the tomb is what she would have wanted. Besides, I ain't goin' home empty handed."

"You greedy son of a bitch."

"Sticks and stones," Jeb snarled.

Sam threw up his hands. "Go Jeb! Go find your fortune and enjoy it. I mean that, enjoy the mansions and yachts and fine wine. Me? I'm just gonna salvage whatever remnants of self respect I've got left."

"I don't need to take this from you, you self righteous son of a bitch."

"Go on, Jeb. Go, enjoy it. Go feel good about yourself, and fuck Olivia's skank sister."

Jeb tried to look away.

"Oh you thought I didn't know? You think I can't see how close you two have been getting?"

"You can't say that to me... I've saved your life twice now."

Sam threw up his hands. "How did I know that was coming! But, yes, I suppose you did."

"And so what? Does that mean nothing to you?"

Sam turned away, refusing to look at Jeb.

"And you've saved mine too! Damnit, you were my best friend, Sam! What you and I have been through together, the bond of blood we share, that shit means something that you can't just throw away."

Sam stared at him. "I don't hate you, Jeb, honest. I wish I could because that would make it easier, but I can't. But that does not make you my friend."

Jeb frowned. "So that's how it is then?"

"I'm afraid so, old boy."

Jeb stormed off, opening the door to Elizabeth's room, and slamming it behind him. "What are you looking at?" he asked.

"Nothing," she replied.

"Really?" He shook his head. "That fucking asshole."

She came close to him, putting her hands around his. "We're so close."

He nodded, and she could see the look on his face. Knew exactly what it was he thinking about. Who he was thinking about. There was a flashing light in her eyes like a race horse jackpot, and a nymph dancing at the corner of her pupil, a glass of gin in its outstretched hand. Two tiny Zebras danced across her lips and up into her neon blonde hair as she threw herself forwards, wrapping herself around his shoulders. He kissed her once on the neck, and closed his eyes. Midas. He wondered where this would all lead. Would they really find an undead king? A titan with some strange, unending life? Jeb could feel her fingers dig into the flesh of his back as he pulled back from Elizabeth and asked where she expected the next clue to lead.

"Well not another giant snake, I'd hope," Elizabeth laughed as she fidgeted with the top of the black lace garter under her dress. "There's no way to know yet."

"Very reassuring," he said, as he looked down at his feet, and the fancy, black leather boots he'd stolen from the rich man's house. Elizabeth peered up into his eyes, "you and I, we're going to discover the secrets of this thing together."

"Yes," he said coldly.

"Never growing old, never dying." The light glinted in her eyes. "Together we'll discover the secret of Midas' power."

"MIDAS?" A scratchy voice boomed out from across the room, and Jeb whipped around to find Gregor Cutlass standing in the door way, his tangled black beard and rugged features peering out from the shadows. "What do you know about Midas?"

"Uh, excuse me?" Jeb said, trying to keep his voice calm.

"All that slammin' a doors woke me up from me' nap," Cutlass said as he moved towards them. "Couldn't help but overhear ya' makin' talk a' my most favorite topic of conversation."

Elizabeth took a step back. "I'm not quite sure what you're talking about, old man."

"I'm talkin' about Midas!" Cutlass shouted. "Tell me what you know, ya' scurvy dogs, lest I be forced ter' pry the information from ye' in most unpleasant a manner."

Jeb glanced towards Elizabeth for a moment before pulling the knife from his back pocket. "I think you need to relax."

"Just try me." Cutlass scowled. "Go ahead. It wouldn't be the first time sumon' ad' tried and regretted it."

Jeb lowered the weapon, admiring Cutlass' grit. "All we know about Midas is that he's got enough gold to last a lifetime. Maybe a lot longer."

"And so yer' tracking him down, is that right?" Cutlass asked, his black and yellow teeth shining out from behind a formative beard. "And here I thought I were the only one."

"You're looking for Midas' tomb as well?" Elizabeth asked.

"Aye, sweetheart." Cutlass nodded. "Have been for nearly two hundred and fifty years."

# 41.
# RELICS

He was bigger than he had any right to be. Dressed up in antiquated clothes and mannerisms, his beard a mass of tangled black thorns, the backs of his hands embroidered in intricate purple tattoos of an oriental design that swirled up past his elbows. He let out a deep, throaty cough as he sat down in a sun tanned antique of a chair that reminded him of himself.

"Let's get down to business," Jeb announced, as he walked back into the den of the hotel suite, the map in hand.

The old man drew his fingers down his monstrous nose and into the black thorns of his beard. There was an air of contemplation about him. Something that said he hadn't told this particular story in some time. "I serpose ya' have some questions, eh boy?" Cutlass asked.

"Plenty," said Jeb.

"Aye. And I'll be happy as a lamb on Good Friday ter answer all a' em'."

Jeb eyed him carefully. "Do you know where the tomb is? Do you know where the gold lies?"

"If I knew that I wouldn't be out here searching for it, would I?" said Cutlass.

Jeb shook his head. "No, but you didn't say you were looking for the tomb, you said you were looking for the man. Do you know him?"

"Aye, tis' me one great tragedy to have known him." His one eye winced painfully and he hunched over in the old, dusty leather chair and grinned at Elizabeth. "He says he just wants the treasure, but what of you, girlie? You just after the gold too, or do the prospect of life eternal make ye' quiver with desire?"

Elizabeth studied him. "I'm not sure."

Cutlass smiled. "Do you like what you see?"

"I like the idea of it," she said cautiously. "The idea of never aging has an obvious appeal."

Cutlass snarled. "Maybe it ain't all it's cracked up ter' be."

Jeb dragged his chair across the room until he was an arms-length from Cutlass, sat down, and stared. "And then there's the power."

Cutlass opened his mouth wide as he spoke, the small scar on his lower lip a faint reminder of what it meant to be human. "I'll tell you what I know, but be forewarned, 'tis a tale of woe and sorrow." He pulled a bottle of amber colored rum from his coat. "Well do ya' want sum' me lovelies?"

Jeb took the bottle, chugging down several shots worth before tossing it to Sam. "That's good stuff," he said.

Cutlass took the bottle from him, finishing off the last of it before he wiped the back of his hand across his mouth, the purple ink of his tattoos fading with age.

"It all began in the year of our lord, 1680. I was right near forty seven ah' the time, and Captain of the happy ship, Black Dawn. A good, sturdy ship she was, my friends, with as fine a crew as you'd ever meet. We were buccaneers. Men a' fortune. Pirates by any other name."

*"Pirates?"* Sam's mouth fell open.

"Aye lad, that we were, there'll be no denyin' it by me. Picture in your mind, if ye' will, the vast sweepin' blue of the ocean, a few bright clouds in the sky and the taste a' salt in the air. The kind a' fresh, real breeze that'll let a man know he's alive, that he's spit in his eye and fire in his heart. Why I swear amid the callin' out a' the crew and the roar of the waves I could hear the sound a' bleetin' trumpets cheerin' us on to victory on the high seas, that I could. My crew and I, we went where we wanted. We did as we pleased. We alone knew what ih' twas' ter me free men." Captain Cutlass grinned wildly, showing off his black and gold teeth. "Those were the days, laddy. Ya' never thought about tomorrow. Ya' never worried about anything atal'. Ya see knowin' that each day might well be yer' last, why that spurs a man on ter greatness. Knowin' that there be an end ta' things, and a quick one at that, it forces ya' ta make the tough choices and enjoy the consequences, whatever they may be." He reached out his old, weathered hand. "Be a dear and grab me another bottle, would ya, sweetheart?"

Elizabeth grabbed a jug of spiced rum from the suites liquor cabinet, along with several tumblers.

The captain smiled as she filled them, handing one of the hard drinks out to each. "Cheers," said Jeb.

The captain smiled as the four of them clinked their glasses, and he emptied his before speaking. "The waves were rollin' and crashin' and roarin', and the wind was screamin' like a leach wit' a rope round his neck. Even all these years later I stills remember it clear as if it were the back a' me hand. We'd been set sail some two months on a most prosperous voyage and our coffers were filled wit' enough gold and silver ter line a pleasure palace tenfold. Pirates in general being a sort of a greedy lot though, we were understandably charmed when we spied a lightly armed merchant galleon of ter' the port side. From where we stood she looked easy pickens."

"But..." Sam shrugged. "I still don't see what all this has to do with Midas."

"I'm gettin to it, boy! I'm gettin to it," he said dangerously. "I gathered up me crew and sez to them, 'Come one and everyman wit' me who's got a penchant in his heart fer' spillin' blood, and taken' treasure.' Then BAM! go the cannon fire as it blast into their hull!" Cutlass exclaimed, pounding his fist down on the table.

"I swung over the edge by me gatlin' rope, crashin' on ta' their deck wot wit' me sword and flint lock in hand, and ordered me men down inter' the belly a' the ship. I were about ter' follow um down meself when suddenly some black hearted bastard come at me from behind wit' a long, an' bloody sword, and forced me into a parry. We held at each other for a few minutes, each of us going blow for blow, until at last I had him on the ground wit' me sword to his chest. 'Pirates!' was all he said before I stabbed him in the heart. Twice, just fer' good measure."

"Suddenly, a scream rang out from below deck. I turned towards the stairwell. Suddenly another! And then another! I'd nay 'ave been so concerned were the cries not so numerous and so alarmingly familiar. I ran down ter aid' my men, only to find them all dead. It was then that I first saw the despicable figure of one *Salin Salid.*"

Jeb sprayed rum from his mouth. *"Who?"* He sat stunned. Speechless. He knew that it couldn't be the same man who had rescued him on the beach, who had died at the hands of bloodthirsty cannibals. It couldn't be.

"I fired me pistol at im," Cutlass said as he made an exploding motion with his fingers. "But he just pulled the bullet back out from his chest. He dropped the ball a' lead to the ground, and gestured for me to follow him. As I looked around at me' dead ship mates, I shrugged and did as he'd suggested. What else could I do?"

"I- I don't know." Jeb sputtered out.

"Well neither did I," Cutlass replied. "So I followed him down through the hull, and into the captain's quarters, and it was there that I first saw him."

Jeb leaned forward. "Who?"

Cutlass face was a grim mask, *"Midas,"* he said as he stood up from the couch, his legs shaky as he raised his hand up like Hamlet. "He emerged from the shadows, a small, leering figure, and for the longest time I couldn't see anything of him, save for the glinting reflections of gold and jewels against the light. He looked to be just a boy of ten or eleven and on his head a thorny golden crown. He had on a magnificent golden robe that moved like liquid rather an' silk. Golden rings and golden earrings. Two in each ear, and one like a bull through the septum of his nose. There were several men and women at his side, and one, Salin Salid, standing behind me back. He asked me who I was, and I told him."

"He looked like a boy?" Jeb asked.

"Aye, that he did," said Cutlass. "But I could see that behind his smooth, pale skin lay opaque black veins and his eyes had lost near all their color, leaving behind nothin' but unnaturally white on white orbs. He had a voice like a snake, and when he told me to sit down before him I could tell he were somebody used ter' gettin' his way with people, so I obliged him.

'He told me all 'bout his self, Midas did. I guess he was intrigued by me, for he introduced me to all his associates, from the slinking Salid, to the comely Virginia Dare."

Sam shook his head. "It's amazing to think of all he's seen, all he's been--"

"No, not amazing!" Cutlass shouted. "He's a mad man, he is. Driven to the brink by two millennia a' half life and too deep a' thinking'! A person can't go on forever without a destination."

"I understand," said Elizabeth.

"No, you don't. I don't even understand it, and I've been doing little else but thinkin' about it for the last two hundred fifty bloody years! That whole ship was filled with philosophers, poets and generals he'd collected over the centuries. Men and women he'd given the gift of life to in exchange for their freedom, and I doubt any a' them really understood it either."

"I don't believe you!" Jeb laughed. "This is bullshit, you've got no proof!"

"It's proof you want, eh?" Cutlass reached for his pistol, a scowl on his face. Jeb's eyes followed the pirate's hand, matching each minute movement as he drew his knife. "Are' ya' ready, lad?"

"Just try me," Jeb replied.

Cutlass laughed as he finished the last drop of liquor and dropped the glass to the floor. "This is gonna sting," he said, turning the gun towards his own chest.

"What are you-"

Sam screamed as the gun erupted, revealing a smiling Cutlass, and a bloody hole where his heart should have been. *"Here,"* he said, as he ripped open his now bloody shirt, revealing a patchwork of cuts and scars. His blood began to clot, and within seconds the grizzly wound had already begun to scab over, healing itself with as quick a pace as could be. Jeb leaned back in his chair, an astonished look upon his fright pale face. Pulling a small, peach colored rag from out his back pocket, Cutlass began to mop up the blood from his shirt.

"May I continue uninterrupted now?" Cutlass asked.

Jeb nodded timidly.

"Good," said Cutlass. "Midas had one of his servants bring me a long black box, had it lowered down in front of me, and told me to open it up."

"And did you?" Elizabeth asked.

Cutlass shrugged. "What choice did I have? I undid the clasps and threw open the cover only to find it filled wit' bones. He told me to dig through, and I did. Sticky, sinewy black residue sticking to me hands as I retrieved a golden flask from inside. He told me to drink from it and I did."

"And that was what made you immortal?" Elizabeth asked in an excited voice, leaning so far forwards in her chair that she nearly fell out.

The old pirate smiled. "I knew what it was as soon as it touched my lips, and as it ran down my throat I thought of the God I was to become. I pictured living forever without knowing fear or death. In the moment of it all, I'm sad ta' say that greed overtook temperance, and I took gulp after massive gulp until the flask was empty, and I dropped it to the ground with a cluttering sound. In me' mind there were no consequences. There were no mistakes. There was only the chance to be a god. My heart began to beat faster and faster, nearly bursting out a' me' chest. I gasped as me' vision grew hazy, my heart stopped beating, and in a moment of blinding white light I transcended mortality. The light faded, and for a singular moment I could hear the whisper of God, and then.... Nothing. Silence fell."

"Two of Midas' men came up on either side, grabbed me by me shoulders, and pinned me to the ground. I asked Midas what the meaning of all this was, and he says to me, he says in his petulant little boy voice, *You came here to take from me, didn't you, pirate?*

"There came a sudden realization of what was going to happen to me.

"He smiled an' told me he'd cut out me eyes and rip out me tongue. Chop the fingers from me hands piece by bloody piece, and the toes from me feet. He'd carve the muscles from me bones. Tie me up and throw me overboard, where the *fissshesss* could eat away at me flesh, bit by bit, until finally I washed ashore, a limbless, skeletal freak doomed to flop around in the sand, blind and speechless for all eternity.

"I screamed, straining against my captors with all my might, my mind barley comprehending the horror that surly awaited me. Midas smiled as Salid entered into the room from behind me, announcing that my ship had been sunk, and the rest of me crew slain. The scurvy bastard jammed a knife into my face, carving out me left eye and dropping it to the ground. A mad rush a' adrenaline shot through me, and I pulled away from Salid and butted him in the head, escaped up the stairs and onto the main deck a' the ship and threw myself overboard into the salty sea. Swimming down to the bottom of the ocean floor I walked due north fer weeks until I reached port. I remember walking up, soaking wet on to the beach, the knives hole healed, but me' eye forever gone. I can still feel it, ya know? All these years later the memory of it haunts me like a phantom," Cutlass shuddered. "From that day forwards I swore that I would have me revenge."

Elizabeth touched her hand to her throat. There was rapture in her eyes.

"For the next fifty years I sailed the seven seas, looting and plundering, and earning a reputation to be feared. Without any fear of death I could say anything. Do anything. It was amazing. *It is amazing.* But still, I longed for vengeance. Longed to exact penance for the eye and the crew and the afterlife he took from me."

"So what did you do?" asked Jeb.

"I studied him. Read through old books in musty libraries, consulted scholars and magicians and kings around the world, learning everything I could about him and his past. Eventually I found my first clue, a puzzle box that, when solved, became a map that led to a secret cavern beneath Easter Island: it was there that I found the second signpost. The clue I found there led me to a simple treasure chest buried in the south pacific, and in that chest a map which led me to Africa. And now fate has led us both here. Brought together by slavers in the Sahara. Never let it be said that the universe don't have a sense of humor."

"Fate?" Jeb asked.

Cutlass smiled. "What else would you call it?"

# 42.
# COMPROMISE 7:15

The next several days passed quickly, as Cutlass translated the map, letting them know that it led to a mountain peak in faraway Nepal. Elizabeth set to work arranging travel for all of them to Asia, and Sam, after hearing the illustrious tales of Captain Cutlass and still wanting nothing to do with the treasure hunt, much less eternal life, arranged travel abroad. As he walked out onto the flat, dusty Cairo city airfield, Jeb considered for a moment why he still hadn't told Cutlass of his own possible encounter with Salid. Perhaps it was out of the sense that he still owed him something.

"Good bye, Sam," Jeb said, black fedora pulled down low across his brow. A rich, black suit clung tightly to his thin frame in the stirring wind of the propellers.

"Goodbye, Jeb." Sam nodded, briefcase in hand, his own brown suit rippling in the heavy gust.

Jeb stared at his old friend. The roaring Howl Corp model B airplane was just a few feet away with the other passengers already on it, and Sam was ready to board. "You're sure you won't reconsider?" Sam yelled out over the mechanical scream of the propellers.

"Are you sure?" asked Jeb.

"Yeah," Sam sighed, "yeah, I'm sure."

"Well okay then," said Jeb, "I guess I am too."

"That's it then," Sam said with a frown. "Well, good bye."

"Good bye," Jeb said as he turned and began to walk away from the plane. The sky grew deeply overcast, filling with slate gray clouds, the airplane kicking up a tremendous amount of dust and sand. The guilt struck him even harder than before. "Wait!" Jeb shouted suddenly.

Sam turned slowly. "Yeah?"

"I'll say it one last time Sam, just in case I don't make it back. I'm sorry."

Sam snorted like a bull. "You put me through hell here, Jeb. You cost me my livelihood, my state a' mind, and nearly my life!"

"I know that."

"I've been shot at more times in the last seven months than I was over two fucking' years in the war!"

"I know that too," Jeb said.

"And.... and...." Sam stammered furiously, a look of death on his face, his fists clenching tightly.

Jeb grimaced, bracing himself for the worst.

"At least this will make for some great stories, I guess."

"What?" Jeb asked, slightly dumbfounded.

Sam couldn't help but grin. "I mean look at we've been through here? Secret mobsters, starving cannibals, psychotic English dames with a taste for magnums. We hijacked Jerry's airship for Christ's sakes!"

"That we did." Jeb grinned.

"Unraveled a secret that spans..... Generations. I mean even whole millennia, ya' know? Jesus, if it wasn't.... if it wasn't for Olivia, Jeb, I think I'd be able to smile back on the whole damned thing." He paused for a moment. "And I'm sorry for that, cause' I know how you cared about her."

Jeb looked down as he remembered the women he still loved, and her bluer than blue eyes. Her smile so familiar and out of reach. "Good luck out there."

"You too," Sam said as he climbed the stairs to the plane. "You can come with me, you know. It's not too late to stop this thing before it gets you killed."

Jeb shook his head. "It was always too late for me, Sam."

Sam nodded as though he understood. "Good luck out there, old boy."

\* \* \* \* \* \* \* \*

Jeb moved slowly the next morning. The soft cotton sheets clinging tightly to the sweat of his body as he stirred awake, he yawned and looked over at the clock on the wall to his left. 7:15. It was too early. He stroked his fingers through Elizabeth's soft, yellow hair. She sighed peacefully, her round mouth opening as she took a deep, sleeping breath. Jeb threw off the covers and looked down, a blank look on his face. He always seemed to wake up naked around her.

He pulled on the bathrobe hanging by the door and stepped towards the open, seventh story window. The sun was just beginning to rise over the bustling Arab metropolis, the spires and mosques towering above, mighty pyramids lying in the far off distance. Sounds of camels and vendors and soldiers filled the air, along with a thick, smoky haze like charred beef. Something was off. Something was wrong. He could feel it in his bones.

Elizabeth began to stir, her hands asleep, searching for the warmth of his body. She let out a heaving sigh before turning over in the clean white sheets, burying her head in the pillow. "Come back to bed," she said in a muffled voice.

He closed his eyes and the sick feeling returned. He blinked his eyes open quickly, only to find the visage of a hungry lion staring at him from across the room. "What do you want?" Jeb asked.

"I want you," Elizabeth purred, as she kissed his chest.

"Justice," the dark lion roared. His tight, beady yellow eyes glaring at Jeb with wholly malicious intent. "I want your soul," he moaned, throwing his head back, leaving the loose, knotted strands of his black and tarnished mane to sway in the breeze that poured in through the open window.

"Kiss me," Elizabeth sighed.

"You will die," the lion howled, his eyes leaking thick, viscous blood. "You will pay."

Jeb stared back at him, his gaze unsteady, lips trembling. "Damn you," he whispered, nearly inaudibly. "What'd you say?" Elizabeth whispered. "Nothing," Jeb said as he kissed her head. "Go back to sleep."

"You are nothing." The lion laughed, and his black pit of a mouth opened wide as he mocked Jeb. Great yellow fangs like daggers, full of intent.

"I've paid for my sins," Jeb whispered, his eyes fixed upon the mirage before him.

"In who's eyes?" The beast asked. "In yours? In Sam's?"

"He forgave me. I... I've atoned for what-"

"No. No, you haven't even begun. Because you don't even know what you've done."

"Fuck off."

The creature stared back with hate. Rage living in his yellow eyes, as he began to step towards Jeb. "Murderer."

"No."

"Murderer."

"Only ever in defense."

"Defense of what?" he laughed as his worn out, mud stained tail swished across the floor. "Your own sins?"

"I'm innocent."

"Innocent?" he roared with wicked fervor. "INNOCENT?"

"I am a decent man," Jeb whispered under his breath. "I am a decent man."

"You!" The lion roared, pressing his long, flea ridden snout up against Jeb's face. "Are already dead!"

"NO!" Jeb screamed as the horrible creature opened his mouth wide, revealing a whirring mechanical machine. A storm of locusts and flies blew out and into Jeb's face, swarming him. "NO! NOOOO!" Jeb batted away the bugs. "Jeb!" Elizabeth cried as she shot up out of bed and grabbed him. "Jeb what the hell is the matter with you?"

"I.....I...." He shook his head as the vision of the lion disappeared. "I had a nightmare."

"What? Jeb, you weren't even asleep."

"It was nothing I--" Jeb paused, struggling to regain his composure. "I'm fine now."

Elizabeth stared back at him with weary eyes. "Oh... okay."

"I'm sorry."

"It's okay," she whispered as she kissed his cheek. "It's okay. You're safe here. You're safe with me."

Jeb nodded, and forced a slight smile. Somehow he didn't believe her. He got up out of bed and dressed, pulling on his dark black coat and fedora. "I'm goin' out for a walk," he said.

She groaned, stretching out beneath the white covers. "Have.... fun..."

The streets were ancient and unkempt, filled with covered women and fez wearing men. Children ran through the densely packed alleys, while bitter, crippled outcasts and beggars cried on the corners. Jeb picked up a large, unwieldy map and a pair of binoculars before deciding to head for the practically named *'Egyptian Museum'* in Tahir square.

He caught a rickshaw, enjoying the ride through the teaming city before arriving at the massive, cherry colored structure of the museum. It was a gorgeous building, designed by the French in the later part of the last century, and he spent the entire afternoon perusing the exhibits and admiring the history of the Egyptian people, before arriving at the main attraction of the museum: The Royal Mummy Room.

The room was almost empty, at least with the living, with just two French tourists who stood off a dozen or so feet to Jeb's right, and an armed guard who watched over the proceedings. The placard read *Amenotep IV*, the mummy staring out into the air with empty sockets and black, putrid lips.

After a while the French couple left the room, followed by the guard. Jeb looked around, finding himself now completely alone with row after row of the royal cadavers. He gulped as an uneasy, sickening feeling began to form in the pool of his gut. He wanted to vomit.

*"Tavass naaaa....."* the cadaver hissed through the glass. Jeb leapt back, a panic stricken look etched upon his face. *"Murderer...."* the corpse seemed to whisper as its blackened, putrid face pressed up against the glass. *"Murderer....."*

"No!" Jeb strained under his breath. "No. Never."

*"Douri nass nouekii."* The mummy whispered as it raised its hand, and made the sign of the cross with boney, long buried fingers.

"This isn't happening... This isn't happening...." Jeb muttered to himself franticly. He closed his eyes, trying desperately to silence the collection of the dead, trying to will them away as they screamed and wailed.

They began to drag their long, pointed finger nails across the glass as Jeb stumbled backwards, each footstep heavier than the last, each movement as strained and painful as if knives were jutting out from the tendons in his thighs. Something grabbed him from behind and pulled him to the ground, a sick mixture of blood and saliva dripping from its black corpse lips and sewn shut eyes. Its patchwork shroud showing signs of wear, as hundreds of flies and maggots began to wriggle out from it onto the floor, casting the tile into shivering blackness, tricking Jeb's wide, frightened eyes into thinking that the ground itself was moving. A dozen more of the skeletal hands gripped him on all sides, pinning him to the ground as he screamed, the limp flesh of their mummified bodies hanging off like tattered clothes. "What do you want from me?" Jeb screamed as loud as he could. "What do you want, God? What do you want?!"

"No... God... here...." The corpse smiled, as it lowered its hand down into Jeb's throat, causing him to stutter and gag, as the hand reached down deeper and deeper into him. The screams and scrapes of the bodies grew louder and louder as they began to feast on him, nibbling at his hands and feet and gnawing on his ears. Amenotep laughed as he pulled out Jeb's still beating heart from his chest and thrust it high up into the air. Jeb looked up, screaming as his own beating heart began to rain with blood.   The mummy laughed as it stared down at Jeb.   "Why... are... you... here?"

"I don't know!   I don't know!" he cried.

"Why....   are...   you.... alive?"   The creature asked again.

"I don't remember!"

"Murderer."

"I didn't murder anyone!"   Jeb cried.

"You're doing it right now."

**"Thump!"**

"NO WAIT!"   Jeb screamed as two burly Egyptian guards threw him head first out the door, and onto the city streets.   "An' stay out you crazy English!"   The taller of the two shouted before heading back inside.

# 43.

# TRAGIC OCEAN

**New York City,    1920**

"I want you and I miss you.  I miss you, I miss you, I miss you so fucking much.  So fucking much," he said, pounding his fist against the table, making it shake.

She was crying; and the look in her eyes, the way she studied him, it wasn't what he remembered. Wasn't what he wanted.  "Jeb, we can't keep doing this.  It's over."

"It's not over!" he screamed.  "Not for me, I still love you!  You can't tell me you don't still love me too, you can't."

She shook her head, wiping away the tears from wet, red welt cheeks.

"Look, I wish I didn't.  I wish I didn't love you so fucking much, but I do.  Alright?  I do, I can't help it! What am I supposed to do with that?"

She shrugged through tears.  "I can't do this.  I can't do this anymore, Jeb."

He pounded the table again, grabbed the bottle of vodka from on top of it, and downed more than he should of in one tremendous gulp.  "I'm sorry I cheated, I'm sorry I'm a bootlegger, I'm sorry that I'm such a fucking piece of shit, but It's like having someone reach their hand up your ass and yank out your small intestine, and just spewing shit everywhere, everything stained by it, that's what it's like having you torn out of my life. And now, I! I have to sleep in the bed we shared, because you're the one who got to leave, and I had to stay. In that stupid apartment, in that stupid bed, with all these fucking memories of you haunting me like a ghost."

* * * * * * * *

## Alexandria, Egypt,    1923

Jeb hopped on the first bus he found without any idea where it was headed, visions of heaven and hell passing by the sand tinted windows as the bus left the city and wound its way across the desert. Hours passed before they reached Alexandria and Jeb stepped off the bus and made his way past a giant deer sipping on flowers, two small scorpions clinging to its lips.

Jeb walked the sprawling board walk for hours before stopping at a waterfront bar where he could drink his last bottle of wine and devour his last meal. He tipped the waiter and wiped the bread crumbs from his face. A soggy plate of *ful medames*, it was decent for a last supper. He jogged towards the orange sun lit pier, a long, creaking wooden structure stretching so far out towards the sea that from the viewpoint of the beach it seemed to disappear into the horizon. Black birds soared overhead like scratch marks as he stopped at the end of the pier and leaned out over the edge, watching the waves crash towards him, their thin white crests building higher and higher before sinking back into the depths of the ocean. Of course he thought of her. She was the only thing he could think of. Her eyes, her face, her hair, her hands, her smile. The way she turned, the curve of her mouth as she laughed, the dance of her fingers tips as she jotted down something in her notebook.

It was the way she talked, the soothing sound of her voice. It was the way she made him laugh, the way she grounded him in the present. She was infuriating and awful and wonderful and funny and brilliant. And she was gone.

Guilt. It was all he could feel as the wind pressed against his face, and a mammoth, ghostly visage of Olivia rose up from beneath and towered over the sea, row after row of skulls plugged into the empty holes where her eyes should have been. The vision loomed tall, stretching out long, ethereal hands towards Jeb. Her heart beating black and enormous, as the hands fell away and she sank back into the endless sea.

"No more of this," Jeb begged, "please God.... no more." He pulled off his clothes piece by piece until he stood naked, letting them fall upon the wooden slats of the pier.

He ran his once strong hands through wind tossed blonde hair, hating what he'd become, watching as the great orange sun faded beyond the blue horizon, casting out one last gleam, illuminating the sand and sea and sky before sinking, as it always did. The earth was for a moment cast in a swath of pale, robin's egg blue before falling into darkness, a full moon rising high over the other side of the ocean. "I'm sorry that I can't remember! I'm not the man I used to be, and I'm not the man I wanted to be either. I'm a fraud. A cheap, callous, horny son of a bitch, and for that, and for everything else, I am so, so sorry," he whispered, waiting for a reply that would never come. He tried to remember what had happened to him during that lost week on the savannah, but it was no use. The truth was so messy and obscured that it had become just as lost as she was.

A leviathan of a wave rose up over the edge of the pier and crashed across his naked body, dragging him into the sea. He struggled to swim to the surface, his lungs filling with salt water. He stroked his face with weathered hands as he crawled onto the beach, and the waves crashed around him.

The full moon rose higher over the ocean, casting its reflection across endless black waves. Dark gray clouds rolled across the black sky, a massive, roaring Sphinx stepping out from the greatest of them and hovering high, a half a mile above the sea. "JEB CHAMBERLAIN!" The creature's mouth opened and a powerful gust of wind knocked Jeb to the ground. "YOU ARE GUILTY!"

"Go away!" Jeb screamed. "You're not real, you don't even exist!"

"You see only the false prophets. You who are as damned as any man."

""Leave me alone!" Images of the war flashed across his stunned green eyes. Images of mutilated bodies. Women and children, nurses and doctors, soldiers and saints. He flashed back. Back towards the charge on Gunter Hill. Back to the roar of machine gun fire and the spray of mustard gas. Thousands dead, choking and gagging and ripped to shreds. Of Olivia, left behind in America. Waiting for a dead man to come back to her.

"MURDERER!" Again the sphinx roared, as Jeb remembered his field promotion to captain, his predecessor blown to smithereens before his eyes by a shrapnel exploding artillery shell. He remembered the deaths he had caused. Robert Sawyer, he was a good man. *"Go."* Jeb had ordered from behind their half sunken trench. "Go check if we're in the clear." Sawyer had nodded and followed orders. With a sickening thud he fell back, a bullet lodged between his eyes.

"MURDERER!" The sphinx roared again.

Jeb screamed as he remembered ordering the charge forwards, the hundreds of men falling and dying around him.

"MURDERER!" The cry sounded out even louder than before, as pictures of skulls and blood and death flashed before him in wicked succession like the spinning of a film reel. "My fault... My fault..."

"MURDERER!" The Sphinx cried aloud one last time, as Jeb remembered the night of September the 10th, 1918. The streaming of men out towards their mechanically mutilated deaths, smoke rising up from the fire like mist on the sea. Captain Jeb Chamberlain and all seventy or so surviving members of his squadron were held up behind the trench lines as General Counter and his lieutenants sat half a mile away in the safety of their bunker, planning the attack. Eight hundred American and French soldiers left all together, and nearly two thousand Germans waiting for them just a few hundred feet away. Jeb breathed in the smoke from his cigarette, savoring the familiarity of it, before passing it on to Garitty, a skinny Tennessee kid not cut out for the horrors of war. It was raining of course, and the blood soaked trenches were swamped with mud. Jeb turned towards Sam, who was still visibly shaken from their last failed charge against the enemy lines, where they'd lost over two thousand men, barely making a dent in the German defense lines in the process. Jeb watched the roaring bi-planes overhead as they began to dog fight, their crippling machine gun fire pouring out hundreds of feet up in the air.

With a booming, explosive crash, one of the planes burst across the sky, slamming into the ground a few dozen feet away.

"GET DOWN!" Jeb roared as he ducked to avoid the splintering shrapnel. Enemy machine gun fire began to empty out from the other side, tearing apart what little remained of the still burning plane, just in case the pilot had survived the crash. There was a clasp of thunder far off in the distance, and Jeb stood back up and peeked over the sand bag and barbed wire barrier. No man's land was still empty.

"Captain Chamberlain!" the small, hollow voice of a page rang out.

"Sir?" Jeb said after a brief salute.

"Orders from the General!" the small voice, which belonged to the General's envoy, Lieutenant Peterson, echoed out. "We are to make a second attempt to take the enemy's lines at once."

"What!?" Jeb cried. "With all due respect, sir, are you out of your fucking mind?"

"Captain, you're way out of line."

"I'm out of line? I'm out of line?! Damn it, sir, we don't have a chance. We couldn't do it with three thousand men, we certainly can't do it with what we have left. I'd say, what? Seven, eight hundred at the most?"

"The General thinks that we can, and that should be good enough for you."

"That callous son of a bitch can suck my bone."

"Cowardice is a crime in this time of need, Captain, and the General's had men hung for far less than that!" Peterson snapped as a sudden burst of artillery fire erupted from behind him and traveled out towards the enemy lines. "We attack in ten. Make sure your men are ready!" He turned in a huff before leaving to alert the other commanders.

"This is a suicide run!" Sam screamed as soon as Peterson had left.

"There ain't no way we're making this cap!" another of his men shouted.

Jeb felt a stiffness around his neck as he pictured what command would do to him if he disobeyed. "We don't have a choice. Gear up boys, you heard the Generals orders."

"But sir!" one of the ragged dough boys protested.

"You listen to me!" Jeb grunted as he grabbed the man by his tan colored collar. "You will fight and you will win! Do you read me, soldier?" The man nodded and Jeb released his grip and slid on his helmet. He wished he had something inspiring to say. Instead he just said, "between bullets and a noose? I'll take bullets." Which wasn't particularly inspiring.

The bugle sounded and the death run began. "GO! GO! GO!" Jeb screamed as he ordered his men forwards. The men charged, climbing up over the slippery, mud filled trenches, fat clops of the shit breaking off as they stepped up onto the long, wooden ladders and climbed out of the trench. Machine gun fire poured out from fox holes and pill boxes; monstrous bullets erupting out through soldiers backs in volcanic plumes of blood and flesh and death. Jeb dived down into the mud, dodging a storm of bullets as he watched his best men, his best friends, go down in heaps. Men fell by the dozens, American and French alike, as they stormed the German position. The tanks proved particularly useless in the mud, their sputtering treads sinking down deep into the pits formed by exploding mortar shells. "COME ON!" Jeb screamed as he signaled for his men to regroup behind one of the sunken tanks.

"Finally some fuckin' cover!" Sam yelled over the roar of death screams and bullet hail. Jeb looked around to find several other men joined with him behind the cover of the tank. A mortar shell ripped into the vehicle, causing it to burst into flames. Jeb looked back in terror, knowing the fuel would ignite at any moment. "GET OUT OF HERE!" he screamed as he led them backwards, the tank exploding behind them. One man flew up several feet in the air before crashing in a burnt heap, the rest of them charging forwards, beginning their climb over the barbed wire and into the German trenches.

Jeb waved his arm, signaling the men down into the trench, when a sudden eruption of fire threw him on his back. He looked on in terror as several gas masked flame throwers rounded the corner, their hollow glass eyes and long black breathing apparatus making them look like half man, half fly figments of some hellish imagination. Unreal, sinister figures spewing fire and death into the corpse world around them. Half a dozen soldiers ran out burning through the rain as the chemical fire ate away at their flesh and charred their bones. Jeb raised his rifle just as one of the flame throwers was about to ignite a swarm of twenty or so still climbing men. **"Click. BOOM!"** His gun roared as the bullet sailed out, piercing the krauts gas tank, exploding him in a fiery holocaust. The second flame thrower, horrified by his comrade's death, spun towards Jeb and readied his nozzle. **"Click. BOOM!"** Again Jeb fired, and the man flew up into the air like charred paper caught in the updraft of a bonfire. Jeb ran forwards, slipping in the slick, mud soaked trenches, as he caught himself against a wall. He wiped the soot from his face, looking around to find nearly all of his comrades dead or mutilated. Sam stood some ten feet away, firing blindly around the corner. He fired again and again as dozens of German soldiers charged forwards from both sides. Their faces were gaunt, dirty and angry, not so unlike his own, and they wore fat blue-gray coats and heavy steel helmets with pointed spikes.

"They're coming at us from behind! They're fuckin' boxing us in!" Sam cried before toppling down into the mud.

Jeb fired shot after shot, but they were hopelessly outnumbered, with dozens and dozens more enemy soldiers coming down each end of the corridor. "Retreat!" he screamed out to whatever survived of his men. "I'll hold them off, you get back to our lines, tell them to order a fall back to the general's position. Do it NOW!"

Several of the men stared at him with long, grave eyes.

"HURRY!" Jeb screamed, as he continued to fire. He dived out of the way as a stick grenade exploded nearby. "I'll follow you up."

**"Click. BOOM. Click. BOOM. Click. BOOM."** He fired until all his men had made the climb. "You want some a' this you sons a bitches?!" Jeb roared. "You want some? Come and fucking get it!" **"Click. ---- Click. ----"** Nothing. Fuck, he was out. The enemy had paused in their advance down the corridors for a moment, but they'd soon be back. Jeb jumped up the wall of the trench with everything he had, clawing madly onto the flesh shredding metal and twisting rivets of the barbed wire as he pulled himself up and out.

He dashed back across no man's land, dodging bullets and bayonets only to find the Allied lines in chaos, the Germans having already breached their defenses and overrun them. Realizing the battle was a lost cause, Jeb made his way down the winding, tunnel like corridors that led through the woods and towards the Allied fall back line a half mile away. Bleeding and out of breath, he made his way out, bursting through the tree line and out into a large, centuries old graveyard.

German bullets rattled out behind him, tearing into his leg and sending him stumbling down to the muddy ground. *"Hier Katzchen!"* One of the krauts shouted, as he slammed the butt of his gun across a fleeing allied soldier before shooting him twice in the face. *"Kommen sie heraus, wo sie sind!"* he shouted as he marched towards Jeb, a half a dozen more Germans emerging from the trees behind him. The pain in his leg was getting worse now. Jeb bit the bullet and crawled forwards, inching carefully from the cover of one gravestone to the next.

**"Rat-ta-tat-tat-rat-ta-tat-tat!"** The soldier's machine gun burst loudly, chipping away at the top of the gravestone, sending the tiny bits of granite across Jeb's face. Jeb roared as he turned, blindly firing off his pistol, the German laughing as Jeb missed completely. With no other choice he forced himself up onto his feet and began to sprint forwards, his head down as he zigzagged between the old stone markers and towering mausoleums. The krauts opened fire on him. Jeb could see the fall back position in the distance now, its gleaming guard towers raining down machine gun fire on the advancing forces below.

**"SPLAT!"** With a sickening spurt one of the bullets hit its target, scorching through Jeb's other leg, sending him spiraling face first into the mud, knocking his jaw on the corner of a gravestone as he fell. He could hear the hastened footsteps of the advancing soldiers as he dragged himself, mouth bleeding, behind one of the larger gravestones and used it as cover. "Rat-ta-tat-tat!" The gun sprayed into the back of the stone. The soldier crept forwards, his gun raised.

Jeb fired off his pistol, sending the soldier tumbling down to the rain soaked ground. **"POW-POW-POW!"** He popped up from behind the gravestone to let off a second series of shots, hitting another of the soldiers, sending them spiraling down. Jeb tried to remember how many were left now, but his mind was becoming fuzzy and faded as he continued to lose more and more blood. He was about to pop out again when he suddenly felt the cold steel tip of a gun against the back of his head. *"Zufrerien,"* a thin voice commanded, and Jeb dropped his gun to the ground, slowly raised his hands, and stood up. As he stood the muscle tendons in his legs began to tear and rip with hideous agony. He let out a low, tortured scream as he turned to face the man whose gun was at his head. He was tall and lanky, with a sickle shaped scar reaching from the tip of his forehead to the bottom of his chin. He kicked Jeb in his wounded leg, sending him spiraling down into the mud.

There were six other soldiers standing behind him, just as grim faced as Jeb's own men. The man stared down at him with ice blue eyes. He steadied his gun, and set ready to pull the trigger, his thin, blood red lips contorted into a reluctant grimace. Jeb thought back on his life. On all he had done. On all that he hadn't. He wondered if he'd go to Hell for all the people he'd killed. He wondered what Olivia would do when he didn't come home.

It started as a low, growling hum, but within seconds it had built up into a blistering roar. The soon to be dead German looked up, his gun still trained on Jeb. If it weren't for the sound he'd have already killed him. And then he saw it. Jeb still had his eyes closed, but the German, he saw it coming. It was at once beautiful and terrifying, like a great hand reaching down. His six comrades, who had all huddled up together in order to get a better view of Jeb's execution, now stared up towards the sky, perplexed at the sight of it. Bits and pieces of it shattered out in all directions as it hit the ground, the propeller breaking off and shooting into the back of the gun holding Germans skull. Had it not been for him standing there, acting as a human shield, Jeb would have been ripped apart by the bits of shrapnel as well.

Jeb opened his eyes slowly, gasping as he looked down at the man who had been prepared to kill him. The remnants of a propeller now embedded into the back of his head and coming out his mouth, a fiery plane crash not ten yards away. He remembered to breathe just before passing out into the thick mess of mud.

When he awoke several days later in an army hospital, the nurses let him know just how lucky he was that they were able to save both his legs. Of course, they didn't know the half of it. Jeb would spend the remainder of the War in that hospital, passing his time with sleep, crossword puzzles, games of mah-jongg, and letter writing back to Olivia. She wrote him all the time, saying how worried she was, of how she couldn't wait to get him back. But the boy who left her wasn't the same as the soldier who came home.

Jeb blinked back into the present, a well of tears built up in his deep green eyes, to find that the Sphinx had gone. He looked out towards the sea, the deep, ever present feelings of guilt now more powerful than ever. The shame had become such a part of him. Knowing that he wasn't special, hell, wasn't even good, it was a burden to carry around that kind of knowledge.

The beckoning of the Machine City led him further out towards the ocean, the sounds of it lost in the waves. The water was cold against his naked body and as it began to enshroud and envelop him he was struck with the strange sensation of shivering escape. He smiled as the water grew high and the waves began to crash over his neck and head, allowing him one last look at the full moon before he slipped down into the raging waters and began to drown. He opened his mouth wide, taking in as much of the churning water as he could, and sank to the bottom.

With his last breath of consciousness he could see, somewhere in the future, a bomb being dropped on Hiroshima, and a great, burning fire the likes of which he'd never imagined.   And the machine was weeping. And the sky was on fire.   And Olivia was burning.

Olivia; God, he missed her.

# 44.
# RIDDLES

"I wonder where he went?" Elizabeth said aloud, as she sat across from Captain Cutlass at the silk covered table of the Kuffi café and lounge. It was a rich, sweet smelling place, filled with tiny gilded replicas of the treasures of the Pharaohs: A long, black and gold oil painting of the pyramids hung high on the western wall, framed on all sides by a faux silver, painted wood frame, and hefty, crimson red drapes with little gold colored tassels at the ends. A tall, thin, very tanned waiter dressed in a black tuxedo and carrying a circular tray high above his head, strode across the large dining area towards the candle lit corner table of Elizabeth and Cutlass.

"Good evening," the waiter said, as he set down two wine glasses and a bottle of chardonnay. Elizabeth smiled curtly as she took a puff from her long, white cigarette. She was dressed to the nines in a tapered black dress, long blue silk stockings, and four inch heels. Her bright blonde hair had been done up into a steeply curving braid, and from her ears hung heavy, shimmering earrings crafted into the shape of ankhs. Cutlass smiled in his usual blue way. He had on black leather boots and a ruffled shirt that poked out from behind his suit collar and around his wrists.

Elizabeth made a motion with her eyes, seductively lowering her dark painted lids; curved, bee stung lips a cherry shade of red. She brushed her fingers lightly across the side of her cheek before bringing them to her bottom lip, her white French tips pinching it ever so slightly. The waiter poured each glass half full with the rich red wine before bowing and striding away. Neither of them paid any attention to him. "That Jeb's a lucky man," Cutlass said in his usual tone. "Course, I've had me' fair share a' maidens ter' be sure, but you: You've got somethin' special."

"I don't date older men," she said as she took another long drag of her cigarette.

Cutlass laughed.

"And you are old," she said, "living forever. I don't think you quite appreciate the gift you've been given."

Cutlass lit his own cigarette and took a long drag. "Ya' think so, huh?"

"To you, who will live another thousand, even a million years, my life must seem like a flower. Blooming for only a season before withering away."

"Maybe even less." Cutlass touched the rim of his glass. "It's true, I do share a different perspective on this world. I see a world where people never change. Oh sure, the technologies, the culture and vanities. I mean in my day, to be a man was to take. Nowadays, a man of the 20th century is nothing but anxious. Too afraid to take anything. Spose' that's why we got women like you."

She rolled her eyes.

"But the people. Deep down at the core, at the heart of what makes you all just human. That never changes. At least not since I been around."

Elizabeth took a long sip from her wine glass before bringing a silk napkin up to the red stain at her lips. "I like you, Captain. You're honest."

"Ha!" He laughed. "Hardly, but thank you."

She nodded.

"It's funny you should admire that in a man though, since you're so far from it yourself."

"I'm sorry?" she said with a flush of surprise.

"Don't kid me, lass. When you been around as long as I have ye' learn ter' read people. I know yer' hidin' somethin'. Somethin' big." He laughed. "It's as clear as the red a yer' lips."

Elizabeth looked away, considering what he had said. After a moment or so she took a second, larger sip from her glass. "You're right of course. We all have our dirty little secrets."

"Some dirtier than others," Cutlass said.

A pause.

"You want the truth, then?" she said quickly, her posture stiffening, growing noticeably uncomfortable. "Fine! I don't ever want to grow old, I want to drink from the water of life." She leaned forward. "I want to live forever."

Cutlass leaned back, bringing his hand to his chin. "True enough," he said after a moment of hesitation. "You do want to drink from that accursed fountain, I can see it in yer' eyes. But, what else are ya' hiding, little girl?"

"Ugh..."    She pulled back from him, a disgusted look on her pale face.   "Go to Hell."

"If only I could."   He smiled.   "Listen to me, lass, ya' don't want what I have, trust me.   Tis' a wonderful thing ta' live without fear of death, tis' true, but it's equally terrible ta live without its possibility. Understand, you don't know where you'll be in a million years, you might very well be in some other place, some other life.   But me?   I know where I'll be. I'll be stuck right here on this same damned rock. With these same greedy, back stabbing lot a' people."

"I don't believe in another life."

"So this is all there is?"

She shrugged carelessly.

"So your sister then, what about her?   Is she just gone?"

Elizabeth looked away for a moment, a guilty look flashing just below her eyes.

"Ahhh!"   Cutlass gasped.   "Well that confirms it!"

"What?" she scowled.   "Confirms what?"

*"Tsk, tsk, tsk."*   He smiled.   "Well now I understand why.   Yes.   You'd better hope you're right about that then."

She threw her drink at him, soiling his neat blue coat.   "Fuck you."

"Watch the language, lassie!" he laughed.   "Don't worry, I won't hold it against you.   If anything, I admire ya' for it."

"I don't know what you think you know, but you're wrong," she said dismissively, as she stood up and marched out across the pink tile floor.

"Is everything' alright miss?" The waiter asked as he stopped in front of her, his tray held high, filled with wine and bowls of green and yellow soup.

"Out of my way!" she commanded, knocking past him, sending his circular tray and its contents smashing to the ground. Cutlass leaned back, watching the scene unfold. "Hell of a women."

# 45.

# A THOUSAND REVELATIONS

He could feel himself falling. Falling and falling and falling away into raindrops, and stardust, and moonbeams. Some distant erotic laughter unraveled before him, and he sank down into the beauteous black caress of the dark. The dark was wonderful. The dark was infinite and gorgeous and oh-*c'est-la-vie*. The dark was spires of red and green and gold Christmas lights twirling around in a hazy fashion, almost as though they were trying to grab onto something: Something Jeb couldn't see, yet he knew it was there. *Come on*, he whispered, *come on and take me*. The laughter broke again. Shrill, wild, untamed. The laughter of the stars. They circled around him, bright as a fever, darting and whirring as they sank beneath his skin and out again, humming as they evaporated against his palms and became part of him.

The universe cradled him. The darkness swallowed him up and filled in all the empty spaces and all the unanswered questions. It poured out through his mouth like a glass hand and broke apart into stardust. Moonshine. Raindrops.

He had become something else, something he was not accustomed to. Still a man, yes, but more than a man. More than the whole of his parts and his body and his mind and his heart. More. More than anything he had ever dreamed. It was beyond the reach of words, beyond the conception of thought, it was magic in that most literal of ways, that most basic, unvarnished, unequivocal sort of way. Magic. And it was acceptance of what he was.

No more words now... only rest. Only the realm of love, the realm of angels. Jeb knew it now. Knew he would see her again, knew he would be with her again, knew he would look back into her eyes, and with that, the universe whole. My God she was beautiful. My God she was perfect! Down, down, down, he fell and fell and fell, living out every moment from his life, every inch of it in a flash. Childhood blooming again and again within him, he was a teenager, an adult, and so on and on and on. Painted streams like candy in his mouth, swimming down his throat, my God, where was she? My God, why can't I find her?

He straddled the line between heaven and hell, the chorus of blank eyed angels spinning around him, the universe folding in and out as it decided where he should go. In and Out.

In and Out.

The angles twisted around him like weeds, like thorns, embedding themselves into his flesh as he writhed about in the nexus of the beyond. He pulled away as hard as he could, his limbs tearing from his body as he rocketed upwards. Up! Up! Up! His eyes bleeding from terminal velocity, flesh tearing from his face, falling into the abyss of the darkness as his soul made its mad escape. As he saw the light below him, and the earth ahead, he knew what he was doing. His God pulled close and whispered into his ear as he fell.

And it was like he was being held by of all the universe in all its multi colored splendor. Blackness that stretched on infinitum. Splashes of light like hazy, multi colored lights rushing forwards and backwards, in and out of him. And it was like--

Jeb poured through the womb of life, his mind a swirling cosmology as he burst out into the world again, his lungs hacking up seawater and gasping for breath. Powerful hands grabbed his shoulders, dragging him out of the water and dropping him down onto the beach. He screamed as his insides tore him apart, his eyes looking around frantically for whoever had pulled him from the water, but there was no one there. No one at all. As he looked around, a cold, hollow sensation washed over him, and he could feel his muscles and bones shaking to life. The visions of his life and the revelations of what he really was faded from him as he lay on the beach, cheating death. Only one memory remained. The memory of what had really happened to him that week in the savannah:

He was lying in the mud, his body broken and bleeding, the wreck of the airship burning in the distance. Olivia stumbled towards him, blouse covered in blood and gun powder. With a gasp she collapsed to the ground, her hand stretched out inches from his shattered chest. "We're going to die out here," she whispered.

He stared at the gaping hole in her chest. "Yes. We are."

She shuddered as the soft rain came down, clearing away the blood and ash from her face.

But they didn't die. They'd been found by half crazed missionaries with fungus in their eyes. The missionaries had been drawn by the fire and carried the two of them across the savannah to the little ivory white church, the damned church, the place he now so desperately had to return to if his love was to be saved. Jeb remembered everything now. Remembered staying there with her, in that madhouse of illusion. She was still there, her mind still prisoner to the hallucinogenic mushrooms he had first tasted on the shores of the skeleton coast.

Jeb screamed, a naked savage on the shore of Alexandria. Madness in his eyes, vengeance in his heart! He remembered something else, too.

# 46.

# MEXICAN STANDOFF

### Cairo,    Three Days Later

Elizabeth winced as she slid past Cutlass, got out of bed, and pulled on a black lace bra.  She put on her war paint and brushed back long, blonde hair, a sudden, panicked feeling striking her as she considered if perhaps Jeb hadn't made his own copy of the map and went after it himself.  She wouldn't put it past him.

Elizabeth pulled the jungle wood cabinet open with a flick of her wrist, and picked up a small, neatly wrapped package containing two fat slices of *curukah* bread.  Elizabeth groaned.  She was getting tired of this shit Egyptian food.  Hadn't they ever heard of bagels?  The tea, a holdover from British rule, was good enough though and she made herself a cup of earl gray and stirred in some sugar.  She sipped the hot liquid carefully and sighed.

Elizabeth strode towards the door of the hotel suite and bent down, retrieving the darkly inked morning paper.  She spread it out over the table as she sat back down and took another sip of her earl gray.  *"December 5th, 1923,"* the Cairo Gazette read.  Its headline didn't surprise Elizabeth as she'd been expecting it for more than a year. "GERMAN MARK COLLAPSES!"

The thought of Germans brought up in her, of course, memories of the war, and more vividly, the events of the crash of the SS Landa. Elizabeth remembered how that idiot, Jeb, had professed some silly infatuation he had with her sister. How dare he! Was it Olivia he had made love to under the stars of Harriramma only the night before? Was it Olivia he'd taken? No. No, it was her. It was Elizabeth and she knew that she deserved him, that he was hers, not that bony little bitch of a sister. She was always taking things she didn't deserve, trying to take what wasn't right. *Dammit!* And he was hers. He was hers now, she'd made sure of that. No man would ever walk away from her. No man would ever dare scorn her again, especially Jeb. Running out on her like this? Disappearing without a word? Didn't he know he couldn't do that kind of thing? Didn't he know that wasn't allowed? Fuck him. She'd put a bullet in his heart the next time she saw him, just like she'd done to Olivia. She'd tell him what she'd done too, before she shot him. Then he'd know. Then he'd see what a fool he'd been to turn her away and choose Olivia. Then he'd see the error of his ways.

Elizabeth pushed through the veil of red glass beads that served as a makeshift door between the rooms, and stepped into the den. She glanced around, some vague paranoia left over from time spent with her father forcing her now to make sure she was alone. She was. Her naked heels made no sound, save for a soft shuffling as she strode across the well worn moss carpet and towards the liquor cabinet. She glanced at the clock. Only nine am. She picked up one of the finely etched wine glasses, loosely pouring vodka until it spilled over the sides. She giggled as she threw back her glass and swallowed it down. As she saw his reflection in the mirror she wiped at her mouth with the back of her hand and screamed; hurling the glass into the wall where it shattered with a tremendous clash. "What the fuck do you want now?" she slurred as she stared at him.

Cutlass lifted several strands of the red beaded tassels up over his shoulder and made his way into the room. "Little early, ain't it?"

She sneered and poured another glass.

Cutlass looked at the shattered glass. "You know, between the two of us we've blown through enough of those to open a bar."

Again she sneered, before gazing back towards the nearly empty brown cabinet. It had been full when they arrived the week before. "I've got three glasses left," she said as she took a sip from the third, "including this one."

Cutlass nodded, making his way over to her. He poured himself a half shot of whiskey but stopped before it reached his lips.

"What? Don't tell me you're not man enough, sweetheart?" She cocked her eyebrow.

He laughed without conviction as he tightened the cap on the whiskey and closed the cabinet doors. "It all feels a bit early, me lady."

She studied his ancient black beard. "Alright," she said with a sudden look of charm, as she brushed back long, blonde hair, and pouted her cherry red lips, "then dance with me."

"Dance with you?" He smiled as she pulled at the collar of his blue captains coat.

"Yeah babe." She sneered as she set down her still half full glass on the table by the liquor cabinet.

"Alright." He smiled hesitantly as he took her hand. "Let's dance then, me darlin."

*"Let's,"* she said as she tilted her head up.

*"Dum de dee de de dee dum, dee dee dum, do da dee doo doo,"* he hummed with as much gusto as he could manage as they twirled around the room, *"doo dee dee de dum, dee doo de da da da da da, tra la la la!"* He smiled as they waltzed from side to side and made another spin.

"Spin me again," Elizabeth muttered under the sound of his hum. Cutlass nodded with a smile and obliged. "Again," she commanded as she twirled into him, pressing up against his chest. "Again!" she shouted as he spun her a fourth time. "Again! Again! Again!"

"Relax me' beauty!" he said as he spun her, "take it easy."

A dizzy Elizabeth screamed as she pushed away from him, her face contorted into something nasty. "Relax?"

"Well I just-" he began, watching as she reached for her still half-filled glass.

"You suck at this!" she screamed as she hurled the glass at him, liquor spilling down the wall as he dodged the glass and watched it shatter.

"What the fuck was that for?" he roared.

She crossed her arms defiantly. "You suck at dancing. Where the fuck did you learn how to waltz, the polio ward at St. Mary's?"

"What the hell did I do?" He groaned as he wiped at the gin stain on the wallpaper.

"I just threw that at you! I'm treating you like shit, now what the fuck are you gonna do about it?" she screamed as she pressed up against him, her face not an inch away from his. "What are you gonna do?" she said in a whisper, as she raised up a delicate hand and wrapped it around his throat in an attempt to choke him. "What are you gonna do?" she screamed into his missing eye, as she grappled his neck with both hands and he began to choke.

"You -HEUNGH- you crazy bitch!" he roared as he threw her off of him and up against the wall. He raised his hand slowly.

She laughed harder. "Hit me! Hit me, you bad son of a bitch! Do it!" Cutlass froze before her, his hand raised high. "DO IT!" she screamed as she closed her eyes, and threw her head back, moaning in ecstasy. "OH, COME ON! DO IT! DO IT!"

Cutlass looked back at her in bewilderment, his hands at his side.

She stopped, calming her breathing as she opened her cold, gray eyes. "You fucking pussy." She pushed him away and made her way over to the coat closet. With careful, fashion trained eyes she looked back and forth between the dark green trench coat with the diamond pattered sleeves and breasts, and the thin, peach colored wool sweater she'd bought only two nights before.

Cutlass came up behind her. "Do you got everything packed up or not?"

"Yes." Elizabeth frowned as she pulled out a thin shade of burgundy lipstick from her purse and rolled it across her round, experienced lips. She smacked them together a few times as she returned the lipstick to her bag.

"You're worried about him?" Cutlass asked.

Elizabeth shook her head unconvincingly.

"Right," he said in a gruff voice. "We should look for him again before we leave. See if there's something we missed."

She shrugged.

"Something could have happened to him you know. He could have been robbed or kidnapped. This be a dangerous part of the world, after all."

"Jeb's a big boy, I'm sure wherever he is he can take care of himself. We can't bear to waste any more time here in this shithole city."

Cutlass sighed as he walked away. "I'll go get us a cab." He picked up two heavy suitcases made of green crocodile skin and headed towards the door. She nodded, still facing the long mirror as she lit a stiff white cigarette. "I'll be down in a minute," she called out. The smoke felt good as it traveled down her throat and into her lungs. She blew it out in a long, white stream, a thin smile crossing her wet, now burgundy colored lips. The smoke felt damn good.

A few minutes later there was a knock at the door. She wondered what Cutlass could want. Probably reminding her not to forget anything. "You know you really should-" she began to say as she opened the door.

"Hello there." Jeb said as he stepped towards her, the wooden floor creaking like an old ship.

"Jeb!" she cried. "Where the hell have you been?"

"Out to sea," he said, taking in the heady mix of perfume and whiskey in the air. Elizabeth grinned as she wrapped her arms around him. She went to kiss his lips but he shoved her away. "What the hell? Jeb that hurt!"

"Why'd you do it?" he asked. "Why'd you do it, Lizzy?"

"D-do what?" she stuttered. "Jeb, what are you talking about?"

"I just wanna know what the reason was. That's why I came back here, that's why I had to come back!" he screamed as he picked up a heavy wooden chair, lifting it high above his head before smashing it against the wall.

Elizabeth looked terrified. She screamed, "What the fuck is that supposed to mean!?"

"Please, now let's not play coy! I will find her you know- she is still alive."

"Find who?" she asked, trembling, as he circled her around the table.

"Who do you think? Why would you shoot your own sister anyway? Was it greed? Did you want the treasure all to yourself, is that what it was? I suppose that means you were planning on offing me next."

"I... I didn't kill anybody Jeb- I don't know what you're talking about!"

"You don't, huh?" he growled as he lunged towards her.

"No, I don't!" she cried, leaping back. "Where the fuck do you get off, accusing me of things like that anyway?"

"Don't you lie to me!" he roared as he lunged forwards again and pressed her against the wall with all his weight. "She was innocent! She never did a thing to hurt you!"

"Innocent?" Elizabeth's jaw dropped. "Oh honey, she was about as far from innocent as it gets!"

"So you admit it then?" Jeb said with wild eyed fervor, "you admit you shot her?"

She laughed in his face as he slammed her up against the wall. "Go piss up a flag pole."

Jeb gasped as he let go of her and spun around.

"Oh what's that, Jeb? You crazy shit! Huh? What, what, you feel guilty now, all of a sudden, is that it? Is that what this is meant to be? You feel guilty about pushing a girl?"

"Shut up."

"No you shut up, you self righteous son of a bitch! I don't know what the hell you think it is that I did, but you're wrong. You're dead wrong." Her chest heaved up and down with seething rage as she spat at him and cursed under dark breath. "After I took care of you? After I saved you? And you have the nerve to treat me like this?" She frowned as she reached into her purse.

He glared at her as he came to terms with it all, and the doubt faded away. "You tried to kill your own sister."

Elizabeth pulled a fat .45 magnum from her bag and pointed it right at his head. "You're damn right I did."

"You monster," Jeb said as he faced down the barrel of the gun, "you were jealous weren't you?"

Elizabeth erupted with derisive laughter as she turned her eyes down into black mascara lined slits.

"Yeah that's it, isn't it?" said Jeb. "You were jealous of what we had."

"What you had? Really?" She laughed again. "If anything *I had you*, you deluded moron."

"But I never loved you." Jeb sneered. "And that's the thing you couldn't stand, that I loved her over you."

"You conceited fucking cretin," she cursed as she stepped towards him, gun now lowered directly towards his groin. She pressed the gun up against his business, her finger on the trigger, body leaning against him as she whispered into his ear, "You really think I care what you think of me? Just try me, big boy."

Jeb gulped. "You wouldn't."

She flicked her tongue out, rolling it across the top of his ear. "Wouldn't I?" Jeb turned his head, looking her in the eyes as he smirked, "Not likely."

Elizabeth let out a gasp as she felt the boom! end of his pistol press against her chest. Jeb tilted his head over to her ear as he whispered, *"you want me to do it, little girl?"* Elizabeth froze, weighing her options. "How's this gonna end, sweetheart?" she asked.

"Hopefully with my testicles still intact," said Jeb.

"That's one possibility," she replied.

Jeb gulped.

"You lower your gun and I'll lower mine," she said in a cold voice.

"You first," said Jeb.

"No."

"Yes."

"No."

"Fine." Jeb acquiesced. "But move your gun first."

Elizabeth slid the gun from his groin and up to the temple of his skull. "Better?" She asked.

"Not really," he said. "Now... Both of us, on three."

"That wasn't the deal."

"Well that's what we're doing." Jeb's hand was shaking.

"Fine."

"Fine."

"One." Jeb counted.

"Two." said Elizabeth.

**"BAM!"** The door crashed open.

"What the?" Jeb's eyes darted to the door.

*"Gregor!"* Elizabeth shouted as the old pirate stepped into the room.

"How's it goin', buddy?" Jeb said, his finger tightening its grip on the trigger.

"Jeb?" he gasped. "What the hell is goin' on here, by God?"

"Tell her to drop the gun," he said.

"Shoot him!" Elizabeth shouted. "Do it now!"

Cutlass stood still for a moment before stepping forwards, drawing his pistol. "What's this about?" he asked.

"She shot Olivia," said Jeb.

"Christ kid, are you jus' figurin' that out now? I never even knew the lass, and even I guessed as much." He laughed as turned his pistol towards Jeb. "Now child, please, I'm gonna need ya' ter' drop yer' weapon an put your hands where I can see um."

Elizabeth laughed, punching Jeb in the gut as he dropped his pistol to the floor. She made her way over to the pirate with a smile and kissed him on the mouth. "Sorry mate," Cutlass said with a shrug, "but she's with me now."

*"Whuh..."* Jeb stammered, as he stared back at the pirate. "But she's psychotic."

Cutlass sighed. "Eh."

"No, I mean, seriously. That bitch is legitimately insane."

"Look, Elizabeth may be hell, but she's my kind a' hell, ya' know what I mean?" said Cutlass.

Elizabeth rolled her eyes. "Just kill him already, and get it over with."

"Oh, do we have to shoot im', me darlin?" Cutlass sighed. "He's harmless enough."

"Harmless?" she said. "Do you know what that son of a bitch called me? Do you know what he did to me? He needs to pay for what he's done!"

"Pay for what I've done? Are you kidding? You're the one who shot Olivia!"

She raised her gun and pointed it at his head. "Don't you dare judge me."

"Don't do this, Liz," Jeb begged. "Don't make the same mistake twice."

"Shut up!" she said as the muscles in her hand tightened around the tension of the trigger, her heels clicking against the knotted wooden floor of the living space as she stepped towards him.

"Click."

"Click."

"Click."

The sweat dripped down Jeb's face and into his eyes, blurring his vision.

"Click."

"Click."

"Click."

"You brought this on yourself, Jeb," she said as she closed in. "All you had to do was want me. That's all I ever asked of you... But what did you do instead? You toyed with me. You used me. Made me just another outlet to pleasure yourself, a syringe of heroin to ease your grief. You treated me like a plaything."

"You've got to let me save her, Elizabeth," he begged, "please, let me bring her back. It's the only way there can be any redemption now.    For either of us."

Elizabeth shook her head.    "Goodbye Jeb."

She smashed him over the head with the butt of her gun and he collapsed like a rag doll, passed out cold on the floor.

# 47.
# INTERLUDE IV

**New York City,   Eight Months Earlier**

Jeb smiled at her in that way he always did, and she melted. "Boy," she said, "you'll never understand."

She leaned in, unable to keep herself from him. They kissed and--

She woke up. Colton snored next to her and she reached out to touch him and reassure herself with his presence. She didn't feel much. Didn't feel like the whole universe was surging through her when she grabbed his hand and meshed her fingertips within his. He snored and she lay back down and waited for something.

\* \* \* \* \* \* \* \*

"I just have to, that's why!" she whined as she threw the dress into her suitcase and slammed the top shut.

Colton raised his eyebrow. "Just like that?"

She walked up and kissed his lips. "Baby if you want to come with me, you can come with me."

He sighed. "I've got a job, Olivia. Maybe you can just run off on a whim like a little girl, but I can't. I've got responsibilities."

"And you think I don't? You think this is easy for me?"

He pushed his glasses back. "Certainly seems that way."

"Colton, you're smothering me."

"How?"

"I don't know, you just are." she looked away. "Look I'm sorry, dear. I've got to do this. I just do."

"I just think it's incredibly selfish of you."

"To do what I love? To go on the adventure of a lifetime, and help my uncle, the man who raised me? That's selfish?"

"If that's what you wanna call it, yeah." He frowned. "Your place is here with me."

"What do you want me to do, Colton, just stay home all day and pump out babies for you? Should I make you a sandwich too while I'm at it?"

He threw up his hands. "Jesus Christ, can you just act like an adult for once in your life, instead of a spoiled little girl who can't get everything she wants."

She looked hurt. "You do not get to talk to me like that."

"You're right. I'm sorry." He leaned over and kissed her.

She said, "I know this is difficult for you."

He nodded.

"Colton I love you!" said Olivia. "Take a risk with me! If you really want to, then just say fuck the world and hop on that boat with me. If you really love me, Colton, then you don't need anything else."

"No, you're the one who shouldn't need anything else! If you loved me you'd stay here at home, if you loved me you wouldn't be able to bear leaving like this."

She didn't dare say it out loud, but maybe he was right. Oh God, how could she think like that? Colton wiped at the tears that streaked down his cheeks, turned and walked away into the next room. She didn't call after him.

# 48.
# THE SEARCHER

Jeb screamed as he awoke naked in the middle of the hotel room. He patted himself across his chest and face. There was blood everywhere. Jeb rushed over to the bathroom, slipping on blood as he put his hand up to the mirror and gasped. He was alive, but there was a word written in lipstick across his chest. Jeb squinted as he wiped away blood from his body, trying to make out the words. He shuddered. "WHORE."

Jeb pulled together his clothes, put them on as quick as he could, dashed out of the hotel and made his way to the airfield. By the time he got there Cutlass and Elizabeth were already well on their way to Nepal, not that it mattered. He made his way over to a tall, tanned British pilot and charted a plane, the engine roaring to life, propellers spinning as the small two seater headed up the runway and took off.

Many hours and two refueling stops later, the biplane landed outside of the small, rural village of Gesthethamene. Jeb had studied numerous maps and the freshly untwisted fabric of his own memories as he tried to piece together where the Zeppelin had been when it crashed, and what distance that site was from the ivory colored church where the missionaries had taken them. Mapping out where they'd flown over after leaving the tomb and working back from there, Jeb pegged the best starting point for his search to be here in Gesthethamene, some two hundred miles outside of Johannesburg. The village itself was a strange, beautiful little thing, bustling with a people and traditions that would soon be lost to the march of the modern age. A cross made of sun scorched black thorns marked the entrance to the place, a throng of women and children meeting them as they came in. Jeb tried to explain to them that he was only looking for a room to spend the night, a place to buy supplies and a horse or a camel, but it was useless as hardly anyone there had ever even seen a white man, let alone understood English. Luckily the pilot spoke enough of the native tongue to get him a room for the night and supplies for his journey.

Jeb set out the next morning with two bags worth of food, a compass, lantern, oil, paper, and other basic supplies, as well as a sturdy, caramel colored horse. Jeb had never ridden a horse before, but with a little improvised training from the ranch hands he quickly got the hang of it and set off into the sunrise, his map and revolver in hand.

The temperature that first day out on the African savannah was 114° and rising. Jeb rode out fast and hard on pounding hooves, past acacia trees and elephant herds. For lunch he stopped by a group of giraffes and enjoyed a sun roasted pita bread, rabbit and celery sandwich.   As night fell he pitched a steep, gray canvas tent and tied his horse up at the top of a brilliant black stone ridge.   Jeb sat outside, stoking a crackling red fire, a pot of water ready to boil as the great pink sunset rose up over the ridge.   He was almost happy. Almost at peace for the first time in ages, knowing that he'd see her face again.

He felt like some strange jungle cowboy as he rode out across the rolling green plains the second day, like the outlaw Jesse James heading towards some great train robbery or a showdown at the OK corral.   He came across a small village, the whole place in a wild tizzy, the locals rallying around a bullfight.   Hungry eyes spotlight focused on the battle, sticks high in hand, raised, chanting.   A circumciser moved stealthily through the crowd, his hair done up like a rooster, face painted in wild circles and semi circles.   Blood would pour everywhere as he snuck up on a target and cut and cut and cut-

Frantic singing, boys going into frenzies as the circumciser continued to cut and cut and cut- a dozen boys in a hour, who had, by the festivals end, earned the right to stand among the men.

On the third day he was chased by lions.   The big cats leapt at him, tearing at his horses hind quarters as he snapped the reigns, hooves pounding across the grassy field like the pneumatic heaving of pistons, Jeb screaming as the lions grew closer and closer with each passing second.

Their lean, sinewy bodies arched back and forth like springs as they ran.   They were born for this chase, this running down of a gazelle or a zebra or Jeb on a horse, their thick, powerful jaws built for ripping apart raw flesh and bone. They were beautifully single minded, and they were getting closer.

"Giddy-up!" Jeb commanded, as he cheered the galloping stallion onwards. "Ya! Ya!"

There was a long, lonely crevice up ahead. A deep crack in the earth, at least half a mile long, six hundred feet deep, and a hundred feet wide at its longest point. But at its shortest point? From the edge of the small, dusty tip that jutted like a misplaced diving board, only twenty five feet.

The lioness roared as she overcame the weary horse and jumped up onto Jeb's back. Jeb waved about wildly, digging his feet deep into the spurs of the saddle as he threw the beast off his back and onto the ground. There was no time now. They were catching up. They were too fast, they were--

Jeb gasped as he looked down at the ravine, hundreds of feet straight below. Two of the lionesses sailed through the air, screaming as they made their too short jumps and toppled into the ravine below. The other two skidded to a halt at the edge of the rocky outcropping. They hissed, bristling with rage as they stared Jeb down from across the gap.

# 49.
# COMPLICATED GAME

The air was damp and humid, and his body, hours after the lion attack, was still shaking. Jeb knew that Elizabeth and Cutlass must have reached Nepal by now. He didn't care if they found the treasure, not really, not anymore. He'd trade all the gold in the world if it meant finding her.

Up ahead, some thousand or so feet, he could see the frame of the Zeppelin reaching up towards the sky like the black jaws and cracked tusks of a dead mastodon half buried in the ashen earth. He charged the horse towards the dark portent, swiftly dismounting as he reached it.

Such memories.

Such nightmares.

Jeb stepped over the half melted metal beams and burnt canvas heaps like dead buffalo as he headed through the cage like support structure, and over to the seared remains of the hull. He could still make out a part of the faint, red lettered title, *SS LANDA*. Jeb fought back the flashes of death as he found the ruptured, bomb twisted remains of where he'd been sucked out. *"Olivia,"* Jeb whispered to himself, "she was here." He gauged the direction the Zeppelin had been headed when it crashed, which was not an easy task, and settled on which way to head out, in the hope that he might stumble upon his own crash site, and take the next step from there.

It took two days to back track to where Olivia had found him and where they'd collapsed into the mud. Two more to figure out where they had stumbled and bled as the missionaries led them to the empty village, and the small, ivory colored church at the center of it all.

Jeb rode over the hill towards it, the flood of memories coming back to him as he looked around.

He dismounted and hitched the horse to a slim wooden post that jutted out from the wet soil of the cemetery. Jeb pushed past stone crucifixes and ancient tombstones, glancing back every few steps towards the pale red buildings. Houses and stores and even a school. All of them empty. All of them dead with silence. All except the white church.

Even before he entered Jeb could taste the hallucinogenic, uneasy hue of the air. He could see the strange, pollen secreting mushrooms that covered the white planks of the church, and the tips of the gravestones. The structure itself was quite large. Not quite a cathedral, but no chapel either. It was something inbetween. A fat, blue lettered sign sat in front of him, next to the entrance of the church. He wondered if it was a warning.

As soon as he stepped through the doorway he was engulfed by a green fog and the madness overcame him with a whirlwind of sounds and images. Jeb could feel the influence of the drugs wafting up from the thousands of mushrooms that sprouted in the church. Every wall, every ceiling, every floor, every pew. The thick, fat, green and brown mushrooms had imbedded themselves in foundation of the building, and the whole place had the feel of crawling into some enormous mouth. Wet fungus and yellow puss oozed out from the plants, all of it combining together into a big, messy soup that scabbed and crusted over everything from the stained glass windows to the altar and the gold leafed bible. Strange, gangly throngs of parishioners and nuns walked about the church, lighting candles and kneeling down to pray at the altar of affixation.

Jeb dipped his hand into warm, green algae holy water and made the sign of the cross as a bony hand grabbed his shoulder. He turned around to find that the bony hand belonged to an elderly priest. "He stole my memories," he said.

"I... I'm sorry..." Jeb muttered, as he began to back away.

"I'm not." The priest smiled. "You won't be either."

Jeb nodded uneasily as he made his way up the aisle, searching desperately through the green haze for any sign of Olivia. Two enormously fat, grease covered rats scurried past his feet as he stepped through the crusted over bile and bilge that covered the path. Jeb stopped as he stared up at a huge fresco of Jesus weeping, its corners eaten away by mold and bile. His vision was growing hazier, he could feel it all slipping away as he turned and made his way into the nunnery and meeting rooms that lay behind the altar.

It was a long, dark hall, dimly lit by the moss and mushroom covered windows, but then, so was everything else in there. Jeb thought back to the angels, back to the vision of clarity he'd known in heaven and on the beach, back to the love he'd known in the ocean of her eyes. He turned the corner past two lonely, hallucinogenic souls who sat naked, plucking out each other eye lashes. He wished he could save them. Hhheee wished he could save all of them. A very tall woman i n an abbot strode towards him, her eyes blurry and unfocused. S h e h e l d in her arms a crying, green skinned baby, with long, black tar covered fingers t h a t glimmered in the green light. The women dropped the baby to the floor and began to laugh. Jeb looked down, horrified, and grabbed the child. The baby felt rough. Scratchy. Just a shape. Jeb rubbed at his eyes with his free hand and began to blink, dropping the shape as he realized it was a pollen covered burlap sack. Jeb ran from her as s h e l a u g h e d, trying to cover his nose and mouth. He knew he didn't have much time left. Where wwaass sshhee?

There was a flight of steps at the end end end o f t he se con d fl o o r hallway, a nd h e made hi s way u P. the stairs and into the attic where aaa dark colored fig ure sat depressed and alone on a red velvet stool in t he mid dle of the room, staring into her reflection in a dark mirror. There was on ly o ne window in the attic room and it w a s covered by a heavy burgundy red curtain, that str e tched down to the fl o or, of the the black tiled floorand red, and green stripe wall wall wallpapered walls.

"OLIVIA!" Jeb ga sped as he saw his beloved and dashed towards her. Jeb grabbed her, wrapping his arms around her now thin, delicate frame. He held her in his arms, not believing it was h e r, not believing that s h e w a s alive! Broken, silent, but alive! Her hair hung below her shoulders, thick and curled and twisted into a dark red mess that was beautiful like a birds nest or a storm cloud. She wore a slinky blue dress covered in rips and tears, paired with l o n g, drooping strands of glass rosaries around her neck and arms and wrists. "Olivia! Olivia it's me! It's me! God, it's me, it's Jeb!" The wetness of his tears wiped off onto her still pale face, as she stared back at him with hollow eyes that were at once more gray than blue. Jeb winced at the w r e c k she h a d bec ome.

"Come on," he whis pered as he grabbed the cold, almost gray flesh of her arms. "Come on", he said as she touched him with damp fingertips and smiled. "Jeh- Jeb," she whispered in soft, cho k ed tones as he ran his hand through her wild red hair. "Jeb?"

"That's right baby, I'm here. I'm here, I'm back for you, I came back!" Jeb whispered as he picked her up in his arms and carried her out of the room and down the stairs.

# 50.
# ONCE UPON A TIME

"Olivia?  Olivia can you hear me?"  Jeb asked yet again, as he touched her chalk pale cheek.  She moaned, turning against the blanket Jeb had laid out for her on the soft ground under the tent.  She'd been passed out for hours now.  Jeb stepped out to tend the smoldering fire outside, tossing another twisted branch into the campfire before stirring the mush of canned beans he'd laid out on the frying pan.  The horse whinnied, the approaching darkness making him as uneasy as it always did.  There was a new scent in the air, and a new sound coming from inside the tent.

"Olivia?" he said as he stepped through the dark canvas flaps and made his way in.  She was sitting bolt upright, her dim gaze focused somewhere far away.  She spoke softly as Jeb grew closer.  "I know where I am."

"You do?"  Jeb asked, an air of hope in his voice.

"Yes."  She nodded.  "I watch here, on this sweet smelling chair, on this sweet smelling beach, watching the tide go out.  Watching the breezes collide and collapse in on each other.  I..."

"Oh, Olivia."

"I can see things you couldn't imagine. I can everything there is except for that which was taken from me, that which I'll never know."

"I just wanna help you."

"You can't, you don't even exist. You're just a figment of someone else's imagination. Someone else created you in their warped mind, just to work out something inside themselves. There's no freedom in any of this."

Jeb grabbed her shoulders and stared deep into her smoky, less than sane eyes. "It's alright, Olivia, everything is going to be alright. It's me, it's Jeb. I'm back. Do you hear me? I came back for you, and I'm never gonna leave you again. Never again."

She smiled faintly, as though in a trance, before passing out against his chest. He wrapped his hands around her, hugging her tight as he pressed his cheek up against her shoulder. He wrapped the blanket around her still cold, still wet frame, and lay her down gently at the edge of the tent. He listened to the sounds of the jungle around him that night. The distant roars and chirps, the howl of the wind blowing out across the tall green leaves of grass, and the deep rustling of a faraway stream. Most importantly of all, he could hear her. For the first time in years she lay beside him. He could hear every heartbeat, every breath that escaped her soft parted lips. As he lay there that night, in the pitch black darkness of the savannah, he learned, for the first time in his life to really listen.

The days passed slowly and miserably, as though in a haze. Jeb had hoped that Olivia would regain some sense of reality, some sense of truth, but things only seemed to be getting worse. As they rode out on horseback towards civilization, Olivia would call out with thick lips that a monster was attacking, that she could see the great unnothing, taste the smallest leaflets of imagination. Again, and again, and again, some unseen force would wrap its tentacles around the fabric of her mind and bellow out with kerosene lips, *"we are you, and you are us, and we are all together,"* the strange mantra of the lost church. Every morning she would wake up screaming with the vestigial nightmares of a thousand guilty thoughts gripping and clawing at the corners of her darkest imagination. At noon she would whisper, with swollen lips, of the tastes she had known and the sounds she'd imagined. By sunset she'd begin to recite Shakespeare and make up stories and false truths. She would grip him tightly as they rode out on horseback, and smile and say how much she loved to be with him because he understood, he understood why she had had to have done it. And every night, after he'd made her dinner and lay her down to sleep, she would beg him to kill himself. Beg him to understand what she had learned while she slept within the great white whale. That the only truth is there is none.

And she was insane.

Jeb knew it. He didn't accept it, but he knew it. His own period of silence and madness had lasted for three months and he'd only been in the clutches of the church for a week or so. Olivia had spent more than six months living in that nightmare, and he had to wonder if she'd ever recover, or if her mind wasn't irrevocably broken. It had been nearly two weeks now, and as they sat alone at the top of the thin, blue ridge overlooking Paraxhaus City he began to lose hope. He couldn't even bring her into town, not as she stood, still as a statue screaming at the top of her lungs, as she had been for the last two hours. Jeb kept his fingers in his ringing ears, hoping she'd stop eventually.

She did, after a while, her voice gone hoarse and numb. She looked over at him with dim, darkened eyes as she began to pull at her fingernails. Jeb rushed over and pulled her arms back to keep her from ripping them out. She screamed and tried to bite him.

"Ow!" he cried, as she sank her teeth into his hand and hissed like a wild animal.

"Get your hands off of me, you whore!" she said.

Jeb remembered the words Elizabeth had written on his chest and sat back down. It was all so hopeless. Is this what he had cheated death for?

He wondered if salt water was the cure for her madness. It seemed to have been what cured him of the hallucinations, but then, he also wondered, if he had drowned in that ocean why he was still alive now? And Olivia too, shot in the chest and burned in a crashing zeppelin, and yet she didn't have a mark on her. He decided that it must have been that the same moss that caused the hallucinations also had some kind of miraculous healing properties. It was the only explanation he could think of.

"I miss you, Jeb." Her voice was like an echo as she crawled closer to him, a flame burning in her like some far off star. She touched his hand and kissed his cheek with suddenly warm lips.

Jeb inched closer, his hand wrapped within hers as they lay on the ground. "Come back to me," he whispered, "come back to me."

She closed her eyes. "I'm trying. I'm trying so hard."

\* \* \* \* \* \* \* \*

Jeb rode down to the city below the ridge, tied the horse to one of the posts by the edge of the market, and helped Olivia down. Arm in arm they made their way through the bustling city, as Olivia drifted back and forth, in and out of semi consciousness. He booked a room at an inn and settled Olivia in the room before heading out to get the horse.

As he made his way down the dusky alleyways that led to the stable he almost felt as though he were being watched. His body tensed up, hair standing on end as he moved faster and faster through the shadows. Something was following him. Something familiar, something he thought he'd left in the past.

He felt a dull slap at the back of his skull and everything went black.

# 51.

# DANCE WITH THE DEVIL

Jeb awoke bound to the back of a chair, his face bloody and bruised, the room pitch black. "I trust you're comfortable," an unseen voice said with a laugh. "I want you to be comfortable."

Jeb struggled against the gag in his mouth, unable to reply.

"So quiet. So still," said the voice in the darkness, "you don't know my name, but I know who you are. Oh, yes, Mr. Chamberlain, we all know who you are." A yellow light flicked on, revealing a half dozen skeletal men and women crowded around him in a small, sparsely furnished room. A light bulb dangling from the ceiling provided the only light.

Bound and gagged, Jeb struggled without effect. One of the men in the group, a bluish-white skeleton with flowers in his ribs and hollow eyes, ran his finger down Jeb's cheek. "So tender, so soft, so young."

"Typical," a green, skeletal framed woman whispered. "Young and handsome, that's original."

"Well of course he looks young and handsome," said the bluish-white skeleton whose fingertips rested still upon Jeb's cheek, "how else would he look?"

The green woman shrugged. "Personally I was just hoping for more diversity. I mean does he have to be a white male?"

One of the other figures, a coal black skeleton with red eyes, moved across the room towards a gold phonograph. She fiddled with several dials on the machine until a strange, thumping beat began to play. The music was like nothing Jeb had ever heard before; thumping beats, dark rhythms, unnatural sounds. The woman at the phonograph bobbed her head in sequence to the music, her red eyes flashing like spotlights.

"I love this album," the skeleton said, turning to face the woman. "Dial up the bass."

Jeb searched the faces of the men and woman before him, trying desperately to make sense of what he was looking at. He couldn't. Most of them were pastel colored zombies with elongated, unnatural bodies, pale eyes and shaved heads, or walking, living skeletons. One of the skeletons, a tall, bone white creature who seemed to be in charge, pulled a purple vile from his pocket, beads of light gleaming from it as he waved it in front of Jeb's face. *Lysergia Noreemex.* In small quantities it acts as a powerful hallucinogen. Mixed properly with certain algae's, it becomes a fast spreading fungus and even more powerful hallucinogen."

He slipped the vile back into his pocket and smiled. "It wasn't hard for Midas to infect that whole town with it. Once he knew the formula, and once he knew where, exactly, that airship of yours was going to crash. All part of the plan, see?"

"You've been a patsy." One of the other skeletons hissed. "Another cog in the machine."

*"The* cog in the machine!" The blue zombie frowned. "The most important one." She took Jeb's chin in her sinewy hand, lifting his face to meet her gaze. "There is a great, ancient machine, built by Midas and his minions over thousands of years. In that machine rests the key to the *ultimate* power," she said as she ripped the gag away from Jeb's mouth.

"What is the ultimate power?" Jeb asked.

"We can't tell you that," the bone white skeleton interrupted.

"Why not?" Jeb asked.

The skeleton shoved the gag back in Jeb's mouth. "We thought we were Gods when we built The Machine. Praying at the altar of our own egos, worshiping our own footprints. We had become like the blind prophet who runs through the sand as he listens to the roaring of the ocean waves, and declares God to be dead, and the noise to be king! So hungry for what we could not see, and what we could not perceive. Even now I look hopelessly at this existence before me, not because it is never ending, but because it is never changing! I am an evolutionary dead end, a road that leads to an unfinished bridge. I can go no further, do you understand? I can see only what is, only what lies before me. I cannot peer beyond the fog and the mist and the haze. I can stand at the furthest peak, the highest pinnacle, at the edge of the ocean, but I am unable to see the other side. The other world, across the ocean. Even with the keenest eyes, and the most powerful telescope, for the earth is round.

"And so is he. God, aka, the bastard who created the universe. We wanted to be like him, wanted to rise up and become something greater than this mortal flesh allows us to be. Wanted to feel the light that dances off a cloud, and see the blackest reaches of an impossible star. Taste, and sense, and dream, and be... Everything. Everything intangible, and everything unthinkable and..... Ahhh! I still scream! I curse the heavens because I! I who am so cursed! I am the one! I am the thing, the being, the creature who will never know. Who cannot even hope to imagine the limitless possibilities of what lies beyond this coarse human life. I who will never know what it is to sing as a bird, or exist as fraction of a neuron on some small, far off particle in outer space. You drink whiskey and enjoy its taste, but I! Oh, I drink whiskey and I long to be the drink! I long to exist as something more, or something less, or something... Anything! Anything other than this flawed human caricature of the senses.

"Taste and smell and sight and sound and touch are not enough! After sixteen centuries; after one thousand, two thousand years, you cannot help but want for more. That is human nature. To always be in need of more. That's what fuels progress. You understand? Do you understand? I understand! I understand that everything is nothing! That nothingness is filled with such ethereal, unknowable joys that I will never know! That I can never be! I tell you my friend, I tell you with all my heart, that I would give everything for one look into that other plane of existence that God holds so selfishly to himself."

Jeb looked away, trying not to breathe too quickly.

The skeleton shrugged. "The first three hundred years or so are great. You are invincible, you are indestructible, you are immune from death. It's incredibly empowering. And of course, even after a thousand years, not everyone is quite so deep thinking as I. Many are content to eat, play and fuck through the centuries, devouring all the pleasures of the flesh as though a whale in the ocean. But for those of us who think. Those of us for whom the thought of an eternity of this is unbearable. Oh, eventually everyone sees the same problem. And two ways of solving it."

He popped a boil on his face, bringing the puss coated fingers to his bony lips. "Midas and his ilk became obsessed with death, and the six of us with life. Midas is suicidal, he wants to use The Machine to put an end to it all. We have other ideas though…. *and other plans for you.*"

\* \* \* \* \* \* \* \*

Olivia lay still between fitted blue sheets on the mattress. Helpless. There was a creaking noise as the lock was picked and the tall, thin stranger entered the room. He searched the place with quick yellow eyes, his red robe flowing as he closed the door behind him. Silently he mouthed some ancient incantation to himself and removed the purple vile from his purse.

The willowy creature held it up to the light of the window for a moment as its solution gleamed.

With careful hands he brought the vial up to Olivia's trembling lips and poured it down her throat, the viscous fluid going down like cough syrup, sending Olivia's chest into convulsions. The stranger touched Olivia's cold forehead and mouthed a second silent prayer as he watched her breathing grow faint. He didn't have time to stick around, there were other, more important places to be. His task complete he climbed out the open window and jumped to the street down below.

* * * * * * * *

"You're going to kill me, aren't you?" Jeb asked. The room was dim and lonely, the cavalcade of skeletal freaks staring him down with hollow eyes. His hands were growing itchy and numb, chest drenched with sweat, mouth sore and dry. "You're going to kill me because somehow I pose a threat to you."

The skeleton beside shook his head sadly. "No Jeb. Killing you is the last thing we want. You're much too valuable to throw away like that."

"Why? Why am I valuable?" he demanded.

The skeleton shook his head again. "All in good time."

The coal black woman made a gesture towards one of the others, and a long, iridescent green syringe emerged ready for use.

"What is that?" Jeb stared. "What are you gonna do with that thing?"

The skeleton shushed him as he brought the needle closer. "It will only hurt for a moment, then everything will be gone. You won't remember any of it, not even your own name."

Jeb struggled against his bindings as the creature drew closer, his feet moving silently against the wooden floor. Closer. Closer. The needle was at his neck when the door burst in and the gun went off. The skeleton let out a blood curdling scream as the machinegun blast from the shadowy figures gun went off, sending the entire group of creatures to the ground in rapid succession, their bodies blown apart. The shadowy figure stepped through the low, smoky light, reaching down with a blood soaked hand to undo Jeb's bindings.

*"Are you aright?"* the long gone voice asked.

"Well I'll be damned," Jeb gasped, as he stared into the familiar face. "How did you know? How did you know to come here, Sam?"

He looked back at him and spoke, as though slightly embarrassed. "It's a long story."

Jeb grinned, the breath stolen from him for the moment, before directing his gaze towards the mutilated remains of the immortals. The eyes locked in the remaining top portion of one of the zombie heads blinked and darted wild retinas around the room in desperate fashion. Sam sneered, lifting his gun high up into the air. "Rest in pieces," he said as he butted the gun down into the still living head again and again and again, until all that remained was a grotesque mush of goo.

Somehow though, Jeb could feel that the creature was still alive.

# 52.
# LA FIN DU MONDE

There was a silence hanging in the room as Jeb pushed open the door and stepped inside. Scarce light escaped through the windows, everything dark and yellow and hazy. Her body seemed so still as he made his way over to the coat rack and hung his blazer. Seemed so pale and fragile as he pulled the gun from its holster and lay it on the table. Sam made his way into the room, his eyes trained on her body. "She ok?"

The thud of Sam's voice broke the silence so suddenly and so violently that Jeb nearly jumped. Silently he stepped towards her body, kneeling down to lay his head against her chest. He waited.

Silence.

Stillness.

Panic shook him as he called out her name.

"Olivia?" he said. "Olivia?"

Her chest lay motionless.

"OLIVIA!" Jeb cried as he took her face in his hand, cold air stabbing at his lungs.

Her lips pale and frozen, Olivia gasped a sudden deep, desperate breath and her great blue eyes shot open wide.

She gagged, chest heaving violently as the grayness began to fade, and color seeped back in through her pours, re-illuminating her face. She shook violently, her muscles tightening and rippling around her. "Olivia!" His voice seemed far away as the light exploded out across her retinas, as though spreading itself out through her whole body. Her breathing slowed to something almost normal as her body calmed itself, taut muscles relaxing. The dim grayish hue that had embedded itself like water condensed into silt faded away, and in a moment the blue came flooding back and the ocean returned to her eyes. He brought his hand down across her chest and neck, bringing the light touch of his fingertips up towards her trembling lips.

*"Jeb?"* she whispered.

"It's me," he said as his face grew closer and closer to hers, "I'm here."

*"I feel..."* she struggled, hiccupping the words as the dimness left her. *"I feel like I've just stepped out of a fog."*

He helped her up as she arched her back against the headboards of the bed and brushed the tussled red hair from her face. "Talk to me, where are you right now?"

"I'm here. I'm right here," she said, and the melancholy filled her voice.

"Are you ok?" he asked, "can you see me?"

She nodded. "I'm ok." There were tears in her eyes. Tears like he hadn't seen in years. Tears he'd last seen on the bathroom floor. Both of them drunk, and wet, and full of confessions.

"I'm ok," she said again, as if trying to reassure herself. "What happened? The last thing I remember is the crash, and then there's all this blur, and nightmare, and…."

He grinned. Couldn't help it. "You're back. You're really back."

She brought her hand down to her belly. "The last thing I remember I… Jeb how long? Where am I, how long ago was…"

"It's been months, Olivia. Months since-"

"Elizabeth." Her lips trembled. "She shot me. That bitch, she shot me."

He took her hands in his. *"After the crash you and I wound up in this weird, lost village out in the jungle. I got out somehow, came to my senses and thought you were dead, but-"*

She stared down at her belly as the realization set in.

*"-but when I found out you were alive, when I knew you were still back there I came for you, I came as fast as I could-"*

There was a pain in her chest as she pulled away from him and stroked flat, taut stomach muscles. Ghosts hovered at the edge of her vision.

*"-Sam, Elizabeth and I, we wound up in Egypt, escaped from slavers-"*

She could barely breathe, the thing was so black, so inescapable. No getting around it, no cheating, no way out.

*"-and then just a minute ago I was kidnapped. Taken by this group of immortals who want to use me.*

367

*Make me a part of some massive machine. I know it sounds insane, but there's so much more going on here than we thought, so much more than we-"*

He kept talking but she couldn't hear him, couldn't hear anything but the blood pounding in her ears. She wanted to scream. Wanted to tear apart her insides until blood sprayed on the walls and dripped off her hands onto puddles on the floor. The whole world was going black. Was going black and red and cruel. The one thing, the one perfect thing she'd ever made had been taken from her, and the whole world was going black. In the back of her mind the hints of madness were still there, clawing at her, trying to escape and run rampant across everything. Swirls of paint and dreams of machines the size of cities, and a baby that wasn't there. That wasn't there, that wasn't there, that wasn't--

He grabbed her hand, enmeshed his fingers with hers. "Look at me."

She shook her head.

"Olivia, please," he said. "Nothing else matters, none of it. I'm just glad you're here. I'm just glad you're back."

"My child, Jeb," she said, her eyes welling up with tears, "where is my child?"

"We shouldn't-"

"Where is my baby?" Her voice grew sterner.

"Olivia now isn't the right time to-"

"Where is my baby, Jeb? Where is my baby?!" Her voice was building louder and louder, tears running down her cheeks, eyes defiant,

He shook his head. "I'm sorry."

"No." She stroked her belly, trying desperately to fight back the rush of tears. "No, no, no, it's not true. It's not true. Fuck you, it's not true. I don't believe it, fuck I don't, I don't!"

He shut his eyes as tight as he could, throwing his arms around her, pulling her close to his chest.

She felt the cold rush into her chest and lungs as she dug her nails into him and held him as close as she could. Fuck, it hurt so bad. So fucking bad, the way everything seemed to just pour out of her onto the floor. Like they were back on the bathroom floor of their apartment. Drunk and crying and filled with confessions. "Fuck! Fuck it's not fair!"

"I know."

"Fuck! No. No!" Her voice was a defiant shriek, like they were back on the bathroom floor the night before he was set to leave for the war. And she knew how much she'd miss him, and his smile was like whisky and terrified her with all the places it might lead. "Don't let me go." She said, nails digging deep into his flesh as she reached up to the back of his head and felt his body warm against hers. "Don't ever let me go."

He squeezed her against him, tears going down red cheeks, his voice barely a whisper. *"Never."*

# PART THREE
# (CREATION)

# 53.
# FULL FORCE

## Three Days Later,

## Nepal,   March, 1924

Two shadows crept along the glistening white mountain ledge on their way to the summit, the frozen wind clashing against the scraping of metal picks into ice and sliding, desperate boots. A gasp escaped as the first shadow slipped on the vertical sheet of ice. The second shadow shot out its arm, gripping the fallen shadow's hand. A quick, uneven smile, and it lifted the hand up so that it might find some grip on the cliff face and avoid death eight hundred feet below.

The first shadow laughed. "That was a close one!"

"What?" the second shadow called back in a muffled voice over the roar of the wind.

"I said that was a close one!" the shadow said again, this time louder.

The second shadow shook its head and tightened its grip on the rope.

The first shadow ripped off its face mask and roared. "THAT WAS CL-"

"What?"

The shadow's face froze as he looked up at the hulking mountain of cracking snow before him.

"AVALANCHE!" he screamed, and that was the last straw. With a thunderous crash an ocean of snow and ice gave way, pummeling down upon the two shadowy climbers, sending them hurtling into the jagged chasm below.

*"Look at that!"* Cutlass said, peering out from the charter plane's port window. "The whole side of that mountain just collapsed!"

"Yeah, that'll happen in these parts," Elizabeth replied as she rolled the plane out over one of the higher mountain peaks, and back down through the flurry of falling snow towards the mountainside landing strip at Fort Wylde. The propeller stuttered around and around as the engine snarled and gasped, trying to keep from freezing. "Hang on to your butt!" Elizabeth shouted as she pulled up on the landing gear. Three tiny rubber wheels popped out as the plane dove, and began to skid and scratch its way down the runway. Elizabeth yanked on the lever for the emergency brake and the long piece of metal scraped deep into the ice, nearly tearing the plane in half as it buckled and twisted before coming to a smoking halt. *"Holy shit!"* Cutlass roared, letting out a heaving gasp. "That was bleedin' intense!"

"Don't get to used to the view," Elizabeth said as she pumped open the door and stepped out into the whiteout snow storm. "This isn't gonna be a long trip."

Cutlass breathed a sigh of relief as he planted his old feet back down onto solid ground. Here they were at the top of Mount Kangu, and he could hardly believe it. "Alright, Elizabeth," he said with foggy, cold choked breath, "now what?"

"Now we pay this temple of ours a visit," she said as she pulled up the heavy hood of her coat and slid on a pair of black goggles. She tugged at the scarf around her face and motioned towards something in the distance. Cutlass looked over at where she was pointing and shuddered, not from the cold, but from the sight of the towering stone temple looming over the makeshift city of tents and pillbox ice shelters. A burly looking man emerged from behind one of the tents, bounding towards them with a smile. "Welcome to Fort Wylde!"

Cutlass nodded.

"Honest to shit, I sure never thought you'd stick that landing! Shit, don't ya'll know ya'll ain't 'sposed ta fly round in a snow storm? That just ain't right," the stranger said with a thick southern drawl.

"The flight weren't so bad," said Cutlass.

"Yeah, sure it weren't pal." He laughed. "Names Kyle by the way. Roman Kyle."

Cutlass stuck out a hand that was leathery even without the glove. "Cutlass be the name."

"Alright," Kyle nodded, "and how 'bout you, mister?"

She pulled up the heavy black glass goggles and smiled with slate gray eyes that shone colder than the ice. "I prefer madam, actually."

Kyle blushed, though you would hardly know it underneath his wild blonde beard. "Well I'll be damned. Shit then, alright, you two must be freezing! You come with me, I'll get you all set up with Peschovich, he's the one in charge here. I'm from Georgia, 'case you couldn't tell, but uh, pretty much most of everyone else here is Russian. Shit, they're just better with cold then the rest of us I guess." Again he smiled.

Elizabeth nodded curtly, sliding the thick black goggles back on as she and Cutlass followed Kyle across the snow and towards the headquarters of the mountaintop mine, a long, metal building, shaped like a tube half sunk into the ground. A loose tent blew past Elizabeth, nearly knocking her to the ground, and she watched it waft up and down in the fierce arctic winds before crashing into a miner down below, as he hauled ore out from the cavernous mine which opened out from the side of Mt. Kangu like an artificial mouth. Cutlass ignored all this as he stared at the lithium thermometer on the side of the horizontal silo. It was Fahrenheit -60° below zero.

Kyle strained hard against the frozen metal cogwheel door before it finally budged and entered into its auto mechanical opening. Once the ratchets and gears had ceased their turning and clicking, Kyle pushed up against the door and it swung open, revealing a warm, sparsely decorated interior. Elizabeth pushed past Kyle and made her way in, brushing the snow from her coat.

*"Da'?"* came a Russian voice. It was like one long hallway once you got inside. One big room, with a door at one end and a desk at the other. There were

triple decker cots lining each side, and a warm oil burning furnace at the center. There were two book shelves, five brutally oversized stacks of gear and equipment, dozens of lamps in various states of illumination, a bright orange cat, a radio, three clocks, two oxygen tanks, and one very angry, very tall Russian, who was now striding towards them.

"Ev'nin, sir," Kyle said as he waved at him, "uh, these are the two surveyors who radioed us, the ones commin' up from Jumlikhalanga. They just landed out on the ice strip boss! Right in this damned snow storm, can you believe that? That's damned impressive, I'd say."

The Russian nodded grimly. "Certainly. Though I vonder vut vould bring two 'surveyors' all zhe' vay up here in zhe' middle of winter. In zhe middle of avalanche season, no less. In fact I wonder vhy ve vould get anyone here, at a spot on zhe map zat isn't even supposed to exist."

"We just wanna visit the temple," Elizabeth said carefully. "We're not here to bother with your mining operation, or any other illegal business you've got going."

"I don't know vut you're talking about," he growled.

"Like hell you don't. Not that I care. It's like I said, jack, we're just here to check out the temple. It's just about a mile west of this place, da? We saw it on the way in."

"Give or take," he growled again. "My men stay away from that place. Is too dangerous. Cursed."

"I like dangerous," she said.

"Well I don't," the Russian said as he pulled a Nagant M1895 from his coat pocket and held it in his hand. "I don't like visitors here either."

"I can see that. Your manners are terrible," she said.

"I no like your attitude, it make me nervous." He turned the gun over before pointing it at Elizabeth. "And I'm not particularly pleasant ven I get nervous."

"Put a sock in it, comrade," she said sharply. "I told you we're just here to visit the temple, understand?"

"Fuck you!" he said as he spat at her.

"I'm warnin' you, matey," Cutlass growled, as he reached into his pocket.

*"Na kahleni, suka!"* Peschovich shouted, whipping his gun towards Cutlass and blasting him twice in the face.

Cutlass shouted as the blast of the gun knocked him down to the floor.

Peschovich laughed as he turned the gun back towards Elizabeth and ordered her up against the wall. She sighed as he pushed her face first up against the rounded aluminum shelter wall and pressed his 7.62mm against the back of her head. *"Now,"* he hissed, "you'll tell me vhy you're really here. Who sent you? Zhe Government? Hong Kong Chang?"

"Actually we're here on account a' Midas," said Cutlass. The stunned Russian whipped his face around just in time to make contact with the pirate's fist, knocking him to the floor. Elizabeth grabbed the

378

gun as Cutlass let out a low, painful sigh, and pulled one of the bullets out from the center of his good eye. Peschovich screamed as the bloody gap in the eye suddenly regenerated, healing itself completely in a matter of seconds, along with the large tear in his cheek. His face and eye restored, Cutlass swished something around in his mouth. *"Pffft."* He spit the bullet onto the floor, where it clattered about with a life of its own. He tapped at the corner of his freshly healed eye.

*"Chyort, vashim! Sobay'chta!"* Peschovich whimpered from the ground.

"Listen up, Ruskie, just see that you don't get in our way, that's all. We're going out to check on that temple, just like I said before, see? Then we'll be out of your hair, no problems, no questions asked," Elizabeth said. "That is, as you play ball and stay out of our way. We want food, a guide and enough hospitality to damn the Thames, *comprende?"*

*"Com- What?"*

"Do you understand?"

"Of.... of course." the Russian nodded.

*"Good."* Elizabeth smiled. "And no funny business with our plane either, or I swear to whatever fucking higher power you believe in there'll be hell to pay!"

\* \* \* \* \* \* \* \*

"Yer playin' with fire, me dearie," Cutlass said as they stepped back outside

"Fuck you." Elizabeth scowled. "You don't even know what that means."

Cutlass chuckled.

"Don't laugh at me," Elizabeth snarled. "You tell me I'm playing with fire, or any other lame assed, condescending bullshite again, an' I'll burn your face off. You catch my drift, sunshine?"

*"Catch your drift?"* Cutlass asked. "Aye girlie, cuz that were' real subtle like."

There was a loud clanking sound coming from behind them that echoed out over the Nepalese mountainscape. Kyle stepped out from the metal ice shelter, smiling a shit eating grin. "Shit, so what happened back there?" he said cheerfully.

"What's the deal, kid?" Cutlass groaned, already tired of the incessant smiling.

"Ah... Mr. Peschovich has reversed his decision on you two, uh, he told me to help you in any way possible."

"How generous of him," said Cutlass.

"Yes, such a lovely man." Elizabeth scowled.

*"Yes.... um..."* Kyle seemed to struggle in finding the right words. "Can I offer you anything to eat?"

"Just lead us to the God damned temple," said Elizabeth. "And be quick about it."

"Certainly!" Kyle smiled, and led them up swiftly through the waist deep snow, towards the ancient temple. The storm was still raging, and it was growing harder and harder for Elizabeth to see through the sea of white.

Dennis Badeau

The temple rose up out of the snow like a hand looming large and dark over everything else; its stone spires like wiry fingernails clawing at the raised sun and the empty moon in equal measure.  It was a huge building, especially for something constructed at the peak of a mountaintop some ten thousand feet in the air.  Cutlass knocked on the massive wooden door with black onyx dragon handles.

They waited a moment.  No reply.

"You didn't really expect anyone to be home, did you?" asked Elizabeth.  "It's weird enough already that it's above ground."

"Indeed it is," Cutlass agreed.  "But this is where the map leads, so…"  Cutlass knocked again, this time harder, and the doors swung open.

# 54.

## WILD SYMPHONIES IN SHATTERED GLASS

"Why's it so humid in here?" Elizabeth whispered to Kyle as she set foot inside the temple.

"Shit, I dunno," he whispered back nervously.

Cutlass sniffed the air, closing his eyes for a moment. "There's steam in the air," he said as he turned towards Elizabeth. "My best guess is this place is built over a volcanic vent."

"Swell," she said in a hushed voice, as she pulled off the heavy hood and ran long, ungloved white finger tips through her sleek blonde hair.

"Obviously we're not alone," she said, gesturing towards the hundreds of lit candles that lined the long, dark red tunnel they now walked. The hall came to an end, and they entered into a large room with towering cathedral ceilings and a mile high skylight. The room was filled with giant ivory sculptures, gardens, and exotic birds. "Gardens. Fresh fruit." Kyle salivated under his breath. *"Shit."*

Elizabeth glanced around nervously at the place. "Where do we look?"

"Let's check the stairs," said Cutlass.

"What stairs?" Elizabeth asked.

The pirate walked over to the far end of the room and pulled a small glass lever that stuck out from the wall in hidden clarity. With a clanking sound of hidden gears and machinery, a polished staircase made entirely of glass lowered down from the unseen pulleys of the white ceiling and onto the white floor below. It clunked down and Elizabeth traced its steps up to a hidden, white washed door above. "How the fuck did you know to do that?" Elizabeth asked.

"Lucky guess." The pirate shrugged as he made his way up the stairs. "You two commin' or not?"

Elizabeth gave the huge white room full of gardens a last once over and followed Cutlass and Kyle up the polished glass stairs. They opened the hatch at the top of the steps into a second hallway, this one also made, like the staircase, of shimmering, infinitely reflective glass. Elizabeth led the way, moving cautiously into a mammoth, oval glass chamber. There was a man knelt in reflective prayer at the center of the glass room, his hands held aloft.

*"Robert Yoon?"* Elizabeth gasped, dropping her gloves to the floor.

The man bolted upright, his brown eyes opening wide with fear.

"Robert Yoon?!" she smiled, this time pouting her fat, red glossed lips as she said the words. "My my, I certainly didn't expect this of all things."

*"You?"* he mumbled under his breath. *"What are you doing here?"*

"I have a long list of people who I don't like, Robert, and you're near the top of it."

"Don't come any closer. I... I'm warning you!" Yoon said defiantly.

"This is a helluva nice place you got here, Robbie. It really is," she said as she stepped closer, "the glass rooms, the exotic locale and the weirdo decorations. It's got some real kinky touches, and I'm sweet on that."

"Who is this?" asked Cutlass.

"My gardener when I was a kid. Haven't seen him in years. Not since he hung himself."

Kyle gasped.

She shook her head. "You're not real, are you?"

Yoon crossed his arms. "I'm as real as you remember me. As real as any memory."

"I knew this was leading somewhere trippy, but I have to admit I never imagined *this.*" Elizabeth scowled. "It's a test right? Midas has conjured up something wicked from my past. Some ghost for me to confront, is that it?"

Yoon smiled.

"So tell me," she said as she pulled back her goggles, unaware of the dim red ring they left pressed around her eyes. "Where is it? The next clue."

He frowned. "That's not the right question, and you know it, you fucking monster!"

"My, my, my, Robbie. Why I've never seen you so damned angry! Hell, I didn't even know you could get like this."

"Do you know what this women is?" Yoon said, turning towards the men. "Do you know what you're dealing with here?"

Elizabeth glared, long black eyelashes framing cool gray eyes, her mouth twisted into a scowl. "This is funny, meeting some ghostly apparition of you half way across the world.   A real laugh and a half."

Yoon's brows twitched nervously.   "Tell them what you did.   Tell them what you did to me!"

"Tell me where the next tomb is!" she commanded as she shed her heavy coat in the humid air, revealing a turquoise wool turtleneck that clung tightly to her full chest.

"You think I'm some kind of pervert.   Some kind of monster, I'm sure!" he said pleadingly, as he looked up at Cutlass and Kyle.

"I don't know anything."   Cutlass shifted uncomfortably.   "Just know that the sooner you tell her what she wants ter' know, the better things are gonna be fer' you."

"She didn't tell you why she said I did that to her. Why she had me chased out like a wild animal!"

"Shut up," Elizabeth said again, this time more forcefully.

"No!"   Yoon cried.   "I'd been working at her father's estate.   She was just a little girl then, maybe ten or twelve.   Just a kid playing out in the garden by the pond.   And that's where I saw it.   That's where I found her-- I found her killing the cat.   Stabbing it with the kitchen knife, and that's why she did it.   The little fucking sociopath!   I saw her!   She didn't know anyone was looking, but I saw her!   She turned, and she caught the reflection of my eyes in the--"

"That's a filthy lie!"   Elizabeth snarled as she pulled the gun from her waist and pointed it at his head. Cutlass turned away from her, trying to hide the look on his face. "It's a lie!" she screamed again. "The little bastard's out to make me look bad!" She cocked the hammer back on the gun.

"I went to tell her father, just like she knew I would after she saw me there. I went to tell him, but she'd already beaten me to it. I found her crying in that big board room. Big crocodile tears. She said I'd molested her out in the garden. Said I'd felt her up and called it her special place and told her never to say a thing. Of course he believed her. Why wouldn't he? Why wouldn't my wife? My kids? I lost everything because of you."

"Maybe if you'd just kept your prick in your pants!" she hissed, the gun trembling in her hand.

"It never ends with you, does it?" Yoon said as he stared down the gun. "There's nothing else you can take from me."

The glass floor shattered out into a million broken rings as the bullets passed through his chest like he was made of fog and collided with the floor. His smile grew long and sinister as he stepped towards her, and in her mind she was a child again. In her mind she was in the garden playing with the cat's lifeless body like a rag doll. And his hands were on her. Sweaty and cold. His hands traced down her chest and found themselves somewhere they weren't meant to be. And the cat was so cold. So, so cold. She lay down in the garden and then--

Elizabeth stared at her adult self, so tall, tanned, beautiful, so rich and smart and charming, anything she wanted in her grasp. The cold gray eyes looked back at her as she strangled herself, hands wrapped around her neck until the life went out of her eyes and she collapsed. Elizabeth let the doppelgangers corpse fade away as she motioned towards Kyle, who was inching his way towards the stairs.

"Hey brother, come on!" Kyle stuttered out desperately. "I ain't such a bad guy! I ain't never hurt nobody man, come on!"

"Do me a favor, Kyle," Cutlass said as he raised his heavy, Volcanic pistol. "Show me that big ole' smile just one last time."

Kyle looked at him with sad eyes, and forced a wide, beaming white smile.

"That's better."

*"Shit."* Kyle gasped through clenched teeth as the bullet burst through his skull, and down into the cracked glass floor below.

"Well we've certainly made quite a mess of things," Cutlass conceded, as he looked about the roomful of death.

"Certainly," she said in a low tone as she kicked aside bits of glass with the toe of her boot, and made her way to him. She grabbed the collars of his fur coat and pressed her mouth up against him-- her lips raw from the cold, buried under layers of red lip stick. As she pressed their mouths together she trained her eyes up and around to all the levels of the mirror glass room around them. She pushed him back against one of the hazy, moisture fogged walls and smiled at the millions of overlapping reflections in the wild glass room. Cutlass gripped the back of her head with a strong hand, bringing her deceptively beautiful face up to his. "What is all this?" he asked as he kissed her hard on the mouth.

"Take off your pants," she commanded as she dragged a wet tongue across the top of her over done lip.

"Why would I do that?" he asked.

"Because," she said, as she traced her fingers across the flesh of his never beating chest. "I'm gonna fuck you right here, and you're gonna like it."

They wrestled down on the shattered glass floor, their naked bodies strobing out in ten thousand reflections of death and sex, like a broken mirror ball. She came with a scream as she rolled around in the mess of blood on the floor, her nails digging deep into the flesh of Kyle's chest as Cutlass took her from behind.

# 55.
# SHOGUN SHOWDOWN

Cutlass and Elizabeth stepped slowly down the long glass staircase. She popped the collar of her rich fur coat as her foot pressed off of the sleek glass stairs and back down onto the white tile floor. "What the hell is this?" she muttered under her breath as she looked around the room, finding the place filled with human forms covered with long golden cloaks.

Cutlass descended from the last step, his boots making a loud thud as they hit the ground. Everything in the room was eerily calm. Eerily still. There was no sound but for the labored breaths of the two murderers, and the only smell in all the air was the breathy moisture that seemed to hang all about the place. A tall Asian man in flowing white robes came from the door they had first entered through and made his way towards them, his feet barely touching the ground. He had a magnificent white beard and a long mustache that sank down past his chin. With bony fingers he snapped, and in an instant two red silk robed monks emerged through the door behind him, long silvery katanas in each of their hands. The monk stroked his beard as the gold cloaked shapes around the room began to chant, *"Midas. Midas. Midas."*

Elizabeth recoiled, her eyes searching wildly around the room. *"What is this?"*

"I speak to you in your language," the old man said.

*"Midas. Midas. Midas. Midas,"* the chanting continued solemnly.

"Welcome to the Kangu Mountain sanctuary."

"Pleasure ter' be here," said Cutlass.

"We are the guardians of this ancient place." The old man smiled, his thin oak colored eyes lit up from afar. "We, of course, know why you have come."

"Is that so?" Cutlass asked.

"Of course," he said in a harsh tone. "We have, after all, been expecting you for some time."

*"Midas. Midas. Midas. Midas."*

The old man continued to stroke his long white mustache. "We guard this place so that only the worthy may leave and proceed towards the final test. You are not worthy."

"You don't say?" Cutlass snarled. "Personally I find that rather insulting."

The monk released his flowing white beard, gripping the hilt of his blade with both hands. "You will not leave this temple alive!"

"One can only hope," Cutlass growled as he cracked his knuckles. The monk roared as he pulled back his katana and ran forwards. With a trained hand he brought the blade screaming towards Cutlass' throat, but the pirate was too quick. With weathered hands he clasped the blade between his palms and twisted it from the old man's wrist. The katana sank through the air for a moment before the pirate caught its hilt, bringing its tip up to the pale monk's neck in a flash of ancient reflex. "Is that all you've got, bilge rat?" he said with salt in his one good eye.

The monk trembled as he laughed. "You fool! Just because you can beat me, you think you have won?" The ring of gold clothed figures suddenly tossed off their disguises, and the monk roared, "Now, let us see how you fare against my deadly ninjas!"

The black robed, black masked ninjas sprung forwards as their golden shrouds fell gently through the air, each one of them drawing some terrible weapon from behind his or her back. The bearded old man howled with laughter. "Show them no mercy!"

"Well, well, well." Cutlass sneered, as he beheaded the old man with the grace of a master. "Ain't we got fun."

She pulled down the thick goggles to hide her eyes, but the pale twist of her mouth betrayed Elizabeth's fear.

"You know this might be it for us, kid. Or at least for you," Cutlass said as the ninjas circled around them with spinning weapons and a taste for blood. The two red robed monks closed their eyes as they disappeared back into the throaty shadows of the hallway.

"They can't kill you though, right? I mean you can protect me, can't you?!" Elizabeth choked.

"Dunno," said Cutlass. "Can they kill me? No. But if they chop off my head or cut me in half and I can't reattach, I'd call that a fate far worse. Ain't no way I wanna live forever like that."

*"Shit."* Elizabeth frowned as she pulled out her pistol. The assassins were growing closer now, their black booted heels dancing across the all white tiles in the all white room. The thinly hewn fiber of Elizabeth's muscles tightened against the trigger of her gun as she trained it on one of the black masked attackers. They had formed a circle around them now, with Elizabeth, Cutlass and the glass staircase right in the middle. Her breath grew still as she waited for the inevitable. And then it happened.

One of the ninjas roared as he leapt up high into the air, drawing his katana above his head.

The pirate sliced his blade out across the ninja's chest, sending his bloody, severed torso crashing to the ground, a look of terror hidden behind his red stained mask.

The spiked end of a mace came flying towards the pirate next and he ducked seconds before it hit him. With a shogun's battle cry he palmed the thorny metal ball in his immortal hand, and reamed it up into the ninja's now shattered skull.

Elizabeth blasted one of them in the face and chest as he dove towards her. "Damn!" she cried, as her gun jammed, and she tossed it aside. With quick feet she grabbed one of the fallen ninja's blades and dashed towards the glass staircase. She danced up each step with fevered grace, remembering her fencing while slicing off the arms and legs of one of one of her attackers as he leapt up behind her. Cutlass was still on the ground, locked in a whirling sword fight, matching his opponents hit for hit. He bent backwards, dodging a fevered blow before swinging back, goring the ninja in his chest. With wild eyed fury he swung, and bit, and clawed at the bastards, leaving no hearts still beating. With a heavy, blood covered palm he ripped a pair of nun chucks from his opponent's hands and strangled him with it. The black cloaked man gagged before tumbling to the ground. Elizabeth breathed a heavy sigh of relief from atop the polished glass staircase as she looked about the grizzly, white and red room. "Is that all of them?" she asked.

"Looks like it," Cutlass heaved, as the bloody gashes in his palm and chest healed over into bright half scabs. With a trembling finger he counted the silent bodies strewn across the room. "one.... two...."

"I think that's all of them," Elizabeth called down.

"four... five..." he mouthed silently. "six. I think we're missing one."

"What?"

"I said I think we..." A look of horror came across his face. *"Tip... Tip..."* He could hear the clicking breath behind him.

"LOOK OUT!" Elizabeth screamed as the seventh deadly ninja leapt up from behind, his blade drawn high above his head. Cutlass whirled around but it was too late- With a thunderous crash the villain's blade came down atop the pirate's head. It dragged down raggedly, ripping through his chest and down his guts, bisecting him in two. Elizabeth let out a blood curdling scream as Cutlass fell split to the ground in a stuttering, lobotomized heap. The ninja turned towards her with cold, gleaming eyes, and dashed forwards. Elizabeth knew what was coming, and her reflexes were just quick enough. The blood pounded through the muscles of her legs as she leapt off of the glass staircase and into the air, the ninja's red blade shattering through its base, bringing the whole enormous thing tearing downwards to the ground in a wild cataclysm of shattered glass.

Elizabeth screamed as she landed catlike on the white tiles, thin glass splinters raining down around her. She hurled the blade across the clear monsoon where it plunged straight, deep down into the jugular of the assassin. He coughed up blood, clutching at his neck, gasping wildly as his blade clattered to the tile floor and he collapsed in a messy heap. Elizabeth moved silently towards the ninja's body, a look of white, hot, hell in her gray eyes. "This is for Cutlass," she said, and the ninja gasped as the sword tore sideways across his throat and his head fell screaming to the floor.

# 56.
# OUT OF AFRICA

Sam said he wanted to visit Athens.

Jeb turned as they crept out from the shadows of the station platform and onto the roaring yellow and black train that would take them to Cape Town. Olivia smiled hesitantly as he met her gaze. She was so beautiful. So perceptive. There was a bright flash in her eyes as the steam from the engine reflected across them. Jeb took her hand and they stepped aboard.

"C1."

"C2."

"C3." They sat down side by side at the booth near the front of the long coach. There was a rectangular wooden table in the middle of the two booths, like at a sit down diner, only with thinner, more uncomfortable seats. Sam pushed past an old man with a mustache as he made his way over and sat across from them. "Were we followed?" Jeb asked, turning his head to look from one end of the coach to the other.

Olivia shook her head. "I don't think so."

"Good," he said, smiling cautiously, "good."

Sam took a small paper bag of sunflower seeds out from his pocket, pulling several of them up to his mouth. "You want some?" he asked inbetween chews.

Olivia shook her head.

"No thanks," said Jeb.

Sam shrugged, continuing to eat with nervous energy. The police had been all over them as they made their escape from Paraxhaus. They'd ridden off on horseback and arrived here in "Mbhazima Mashitile" after two days of dangerous riding.

Olivia smiled at him and Sam began to blush. She closed her eyes as Jeb ran his fingers through the tips of her mousy red hair. She pressed her head up against his chest, where he held her.

"There's one thing I still don't understand," said Jeb.

"What's that?" asked Sam.

"How you found us."

Sam seemed to fumble for the words. "Uh, like I said, I went looking for the Zeppelins wreckage and followed your tracks here."

"But how'd you know to look for me?"

"I had a dream. A dream that I was supposed to find you. I know it sounds stupid."

"I suppose stranger things have happened," Jeb said, unsure.

Sam waved him off. "Forget it. I don't know why, or how I knew how to come here, but... As far as I'm concerned, you should just be happy that I did."

"I am, Sam! Believe me I am!"

He nodded. "Well ok then."

Some time passed onboard the train, and after a while the wheels began to lurch forwards. Their coach was about two thirds full, and it was a democratic audience. White and black, fat and skinny, rich and poor. *"Billet?"* a tall, blue clothed man with mutton chops asked quickly.

"Uh, yes," Jeb said as he groped at his breast pocket. "Here you are."

The blue suited man studied the tickets for a moment before punching them. *"Merci,"* he said in a loud voice, before continuing down the train.

The three travelers had much to discuss, and spent the next several hours doing so. Sam explained more of the strange dream that had led him to them, and Jeb told of his meetings with Salid, Cutlass, Elizabeth, and the supposed creator of the universe. He didn't tell Olivia just what had happened with Elizabeth though, and that made him feel guilty, but how could he ever confess to her that he'd slept with the women who'd killed her unborn child?

Sometimes Olivia still smiled, but…. she was cold. She was quiet. *Oh God.* When she looked inwards there was only emptiness.

"Are we still chasing Midas, then?" asked Sam.

Jeb shook his head. "I thought that you were the one who didn't want to?"

Sam looked nervous. "Well. But all that gold. *The power.*"

Jeb stared at Sam quizzically. "Since when do you care about any of that?"

Sam shifted in his seat. "You said the next tomb is in Nepal, right?"

Jeb laughed. "Jesus, I don't even remember telling you that, these last few days have been so hectic. My mind is just a blur."

"Those people who tried to kill you, Jeb. Aren't you worried?" Sam asked.

"Of course I am. Jesus Christ, that was the most fucked up shit I've ever... I don't even know anymore." Jeb looked away.

"It's all so crazy, isn't it?" Olivia shook her head. "We should just get away from it all and take a vacation."

"With what money?" asked Jeb. "I don't even know how we'll get back home."

Sam bit his lip. "I've got some money. I... Found it."

"What?" said Jeb.

"I mean, Elizabeth gave it to me before I left."

"I didn't know that," said Jeb, "how much?"

"Plenty." Sam smiled in a way Jeb had never seen him smile before. "I've got fake passports too. How does a holiday to Greece sound?"

\* \* \* \* \* \* \* \*

All was quiet in the broken, blood gorged white room.

Elizabeth stood trembling over the lobotomized remains of Gregor Cutlass. With careful hands she grasped his broken, bloody body, desperately pulling the two shivering halves of it together. Suddenly the flesh began to melt together like a pot of pinkish mucus forming atop his skin and all along his innards. It was a ghastly black and red equation of gore as the two halves of the ancient pirate were rejoined, and his eyes opened wide, mouth splitting open in a terrified gasp. He blanked out the words with mournful glass lips and tongue. "Bastards."

Elizabeth let out a desperate, happy gasp. "You're alive!"

"Of c-c-c-c-course." Cutlass stuttered through choked, black blood and mucus gurgled breaths. "Of course... I... am."

She smiled as the quaking pink puss settled down into his skin, and his light scabs and scars began to fade away. Deep within his mind the two halves of his brain were reconciling themselves back into one cursed individual. His organs and tissues and blood vessels joined back together in a few instants, as Elizabeth wiped away at the viscous puss and blood that covered his face.

"Thank...... Yeagh...." Cutlass groaned with the broken lisps of an invalid. "Thank..... Yea- yea- yea- you."

"You're welcome." Elizabeth smiled at the abomination before her. The inhuman creature grinned back at her with missing teeth. "Now. Leh- leh- let's find ou- out deh ma- ma- meahning of thhhis."

"Let's." She said, with a crack of her knuckles.

Down the throaty red hallway and out towards the door they went. Elizabeth leading the way, the pirate, with gun in hand, stumbling, still healing, behind her.

Out of the blackness she caught a glimpse of two thin white eyes lurching towards her. **BANG!** The blast of the gun rocketed out and the half obliterated monk fell dead to the floor, sword still in hand.

"D-d-d-don't d-d-d-do that." Cutlass gasped. "W-w-we n-need to know, w-why they t-t-t-t-tried to k-kill us, and w-w-w-w-where the next c-c-clue is."

"I didn't have a choice." Elizabeth scowled.

"Only wa-wa-one llleeehft," he said through slurred and tattered breath, the language centers of his brain still reuniting.

Elizabeth took a deep gulp of the humid air and stepped forwards carefully. Silently.

Step.

Step.

Step.

She pulled the long katana sword from the monk's dead fingertips and clutched it in her right hand, her left still firmly pointing Cutlass' revolver far out ahead, like a roman war eagle. Her cheeks felt flushed from the tension and the heat, her eyes dilated wide in the darkness. A sound? **BANG!** She fired off the pistol, but it made no mark but for the heavy red walls. Elizabeth froze, pulling back on the hammer a third time. Waiting, carefully, for the faintest sound.

Step.

There it was again! She fired, the bright gun blast illuminating some diving shadow, but again she only hit the wall.

"Be c-c-c-careful!" Cutlass shouted.

*"Shhhh!"* She hushed him as the tension grew around her. She could hear the bastard's breath. She could taste his presence. Her sighs came out like cold smoke in the humidity as she steadied her aim. One shot; one well placed bullet, that was all it would take to survive this nightmare. Tension.

Tension.

*"There!"* her mind screamed as the shadow dove towards her. There were no footsteps. There was no breath. Only heart beats. Hers and his. She swung the sword up and fired the gun. The dense, humid air illuminated for the briefest of seconds, allowing her eyes to find their mark in the strobing light.

**"AHHHHHHHH!"**

The monk screamed as the blade sliced across his liver, shredding his gut.

Elizabeth dived after him as he tumbled to the ground, gripping his neck with one hand, wrestling his sword away with the other. "This is what happens to people who try to fuck with me!" she hissed.

The monk screamed out in Mandarin as Cutlass came up behind them both. Cutlass pulled a match from his back pocket and scraped it across the wall. The ancient pirate knelt down, calm fire in hand as he held the flame up to the monks face and whispered, *"Bow hai cho xiong li?"*

Elizabeth turned towards him in the dim orange and yellow light. "Since when do you speak Chinese?"

He shushed her. The monk quivered as Cutlass brought the match closer to his face. *"Wu zhaing chie!"*

"Yes!" the monk cried out, as his intestines slipped out through his fingers. "I'll tell you! Please. Please, just don't let me die!"

Elizabeth glared in the murky light. "Confess."

The monk whispered, "I'm mortal. We all are. He promised us eternal life if we guarded his temple."

"Who p-promised you that?" Cutlass asked.

"Midas." The monk hacked up blood. He wasn't much longer for this world.

Elizabeth grabbed him. "Why did you say we weren't worthy?"

"I... I..." The monk struggled against her, his body becoming a thrashing, bloody mess. "Don't let me die! Don't let me die!"

She slapped him. "Where's the next clue, damn it?"

"It... it... it's in Athens," he gagged.

"Where?" she asked.

"B-buried. Or at least it was. Someone dug it up a few years ago, but they didn't know w-w-what it was. It's hidden in a statue in the Athens Museum. Big statue of Thanatos, about six feet tall, you can't miss it."

Elizabeth looked at Cutlass and nodded.

"Please, p-p-please don't let me die here. Midas promised me I wouldn't have to die!"

"He lied," Cutlass said, and finally the match burned out, the white smoke twisting its way around the pirate's fingers like a lizards tongue. With a shrill gasp the monk expired on the floor.

# 57.
# EVERLASTING PULL

**The Mediterranean,    Two Weeks Later**

*If it had been a girl, she would have named her Violet.*

Jeb looked at her and frowned. She was draped over a faded sun chair, her arms dangling limply at her side. Her eyes like a grave, her mouth sad and jealous. Even though her skin was deeply browned and tanned, it still felt pale somehow. Thin and wet and shiny, like some kind of plastic. Her dark painted eyes squinted slightly, studying him. Her off white, silvery bikini like tainted sex.

She touched him and it was like a rapture of misery smeared across her marble hands. Her mouth twisted itself into something that was like a smile, but not quite. As much as she tried, she just couldn't fake it. She couldn't pretend that anything about the world felt right anymore.

Jeb looked desperate to regain some sense of normalcy. He tried to understand, but he couldn't. Not in her eyes, and the bright ever blue of the Mediterranean sea and sky. Not in the lazy touch of her fingertips. There were no answers there. It was

like some unseen force were pulling at his soul,
clawing away at his reasoning, his purpose, and
everything he once thought he'd known. Everything.
Everything he'd ever felt was thrown into question
now. There was a scar that he couldn't see.

\* \* \* \* \* \* \* \*

Jeb and Olivia were sitting in the smallish, wooden
planked cabin. There was a small, round window
looking out at the blue Mediterranean, and a bulky
wooden night stand. Olivia was sitting on the bed, her
body clothed in a purple sun dress that felt like a lilac
petal more than anything else. Her lips were frail,
brown and chapped in the hazy electric gas light of the
room, her eyes red and exhausted. Jeb was no better.
He was haggard and torn and washed out, and all that
nasty business depressed people don't talk about. His
hands felt wrinkled. They smelled like old linen, and
sheets that needed to be washed. His fingertips had
the taste of straw and molasses. Curious taste that
was.

With exhausted eyes they looked at each other.
She patted the bed, motioning for him to come hither,
and he undid the laces of his shoes and lay down beside
her. He took her hand, hungry mouths lying empty as
they faced each other, their heads each turned towards
the other as they lay on the fluffy, sun and sweat yellow
sheets of the bed. They played with each others hair,
and groped aimlessly at each other. They sighed and
sobbed, and cried out in that kind of mad silence that

drives people insane. He hugged her. She kissed the back of his head. His hair, rough, sexual, like a blonde mane. "I miss the way things used to be," she said.

"I know," he said, "I know."

They cried without tears. Cried without catharsis. Just cried. Painfully, and silently, and secretly.

Gone was such mad hope! Such mad dreams of winters gone, and summers eternal! Wrecked like ships on the shore of things they couldn't take back.

\* \* \* \* \* \* \* \*

Later they came back up on deck. There was supposed to be a buffet, and everyone from Sam to Jeb to Olivia to the cabin boy were there. Jeb held tightly to Olivia's hand. There was a hollow smile on her face, a smile that came from the idea of having her stomach full once again. Bitter blasphemy, yes she knew, and all that.

The food was good, at least by Mediterranean steam ship standards, and Jeb and Sam and Olivia grabbed a nearby table, right at the bow of the ship, and sat down. Jeb munched hungrily at his food before gulping it down with a tall glass of red wine.

His arm draped around Olivia, they gazed out together at the setting sun. The grand, marmalade colored orb dipped down beneath the horizon of the ocean, casting the infinite blue waves in infinite golden light. Orange crested wave tips brimmed with white sea foam as they billowed and rolled endlessly. There was something soft about it all, something soft and mellow and peaceful.  She kissed the side of his face.

*If it had been a boy she would have named him Jeb.*

# 58.

# KISS THE GREAT BLUE SKY

Olivia woke up early the next day. She pulled herself up out of the musty yellow bed and threw on some clothes. Down the hallway and up the stairs to the deck of the Greek steam ship Zorbana. The mist rose up from the waves and wafted around her, the fine sea salt licking her face. Her heart felt whole in the depths of the sea. Her heart felt full in its madness and its mysteries. She imagined for a moment what it would feel like to sink into the sea. To breath in all the raging density of the water, and swim around in it. Free and open and alive, like some short lived fish waiting to be caught or swallowed up by a whale. The seaweed and coral would dance around her heels like sunlight filtered through the currents. And maybe it would be better to die full of sea water, then live empty of everything. She leaned forwards against the rails, her chest heaving over it. She closed her eyes and took a deep breath. Better to be full of something. Better. Better to be anything. Her heels pushed off, and a strong, sudden hand grabbed her from behind, pulling her back. She turned towards him and leapt into his chest. He held her tightly, his head rested on her shoulder as she began to cry. "Please… not again," Jeb whispered, "I can't lose you again."

\* \* \* \* \* \* \* \*

After breakfast there was a short period of restlessness among the ships passengers as they waited to make landfall at the port of Saint Maltese. It was a small Mediterranean isle just a hundred or so miles off the coast of Greece. Everyone on deck *oohed*, and *awed* as the lush green and white island came into view. Its pristine white sand beaches flanked by towering cliffs of gray and mossy stone. A fat, breast shaped mountain rose up from somewhere in the middle of the island, a thin haze of fog enshrouding it's nipple like a veil.

The captain of the ship had said the isle was sparsely inhabited with only the population of a few vineyards and fishing villages. They would dock there for only a few hours, to take on supplies for the final stretch towards the port of Athens, but as the wind currents grew sweet and warm, everyone on board knew that a few hours would never be enough.

There was the great howl of a foghorn as the steam ship pulled into the dock. Sam, Jeb, Olivia and most all of the other passengers made their way down the weathered gangplank, the crew reminding them all the way that if they did not make it back to the ship by the time they cast off, they'd be left behind. A white pebble and brown dirt pathway led up from the dock, over a field of sea green grass and rolling hills. Sea birds cawed high overhead, their wings flapping and stiffening in equal measure as they rose and dove and soared. Jeb knelt down by the side of the path, where he plucked a small red flower. Olivia smiled as he slid it over her ear.

The tourists and travelers came up to the end of the path that led into town: a bed and breakfast, a fish shop, and a general store. A massive, rusted anchor stood sentinel near the centre of the town, it's hulking, moss covered black chain snaked around in coils at its base. There were sun bleached apartments and market buildings, a dozen little houses peaking up from the grassy island hills. White clouds dotted the sky like finger paints, the azure sea in the not too far distance. Jeb took a heavy, heaving breath of the Grecian air. It felt wonderful.

Jeb and Olivia split off from the group and ran barefoot through a field of wild flowers. They ran and ran until Olivia caught sight of a vineyard in the distance and climbed the high wooden fence, her thigh exposed as her dress rode up along the wooden pickets. Her toes sank deeper and deeper into the rich soil of the earth as she walked towards the grape vines. "It isn't fair."

"No it's not," he said as he vaulted the fence and walked up behind her. "It's not fair at all."

Her lips dipped into a frown. Her face was full of sadness, body slumped. "This isn't what it's supposed to be. This isn't what I wanted my life to be. What I planned."

"I know," he said.

"I didn't... I didn't want all *this,*" she said as she threw her hands in the air and knelt in the vineyard, her white dress spread out across the grass. "I was happy where I was. I mean, maybe not happy, but I was secure. At least back then I knew where I stood. At least then I knew what to believe." The sun came across her back, and she lit up like gold. "There's something ugly inside me now, Jeb. And I feel so numb and confused and wanting."

"I know the feeling. It's how I felt when I came home from Europe. Like I never knew what to say, or how to feel."

"I feel guilty." Her chest heaved as she took a deep, melancholy breath, and lay back. She spread her arms out on the grass, like wings, green weeds twisting up between her fingertips. "I should have protected... it. I should have done something different. My responsibility."

"It's not your fault," Jeb said as he came close and knelt beside her. He put his hand over hers. "None of this is your fault."

"All of this is my fault!" she shouted, shaking him off. "None of this would have happened if it hadn't been for me. None of us would be here if I hadn't gone on my uncle's stupid expedition. I should have talked him out of it, I should have told him not to go, I should have-"

*"Olivia."*

"I shouldn't have left my husband behind," she whispered. "I shouldn't have let you back into my life."

"I don't know what you want me to say to that," said Jeb, "I don't know what I can say."

She shook her head. "You slept with my sister, Jeb. Didn't you?"

"What?"

"I know you. I know the way you are," she said. "Tell me the truth."

"Olivia…" he began.

"Did you sleep with her? When I was gone, when you thought I was dead. I wanna know."

He looked down. "I… I did, yeah. And I'm not proud of it, it was a mistake and I'm sorry, and…"

She stared at him without saying anything.

"I'm sorry," he whispered. He went to touch her but she stood up and walked away. He got up and followed her through the hedgerow maze of vines. "I'm sorry!" he shouted. "I'm sorry, alright? I don't know what else to say."

She pulled off her shoes and started to run as fast as she could, her white dress trailing behind her in the breeze.

"Olivia!" he shouted as he began to chase after her. "Olivia, wait!"

She didn't say a word as she ran and ran and ran through the maze, refusing to look behind her, refusing to hear what he said. She ran and ran for what felt like forever, until she was out of the vineyard and she could see the stony gray cliff before her.

"OLIVIA!" he shouted.

She ran, the ground beneath her feet turning from grass to rock as she came closer to the edge, ready to throw herself into the ocean. She screamed as he grabbed her legs and tackled her to the ground, tears streaming down her cheeks as he held her down. "Let me go, let me go, let me go!"

"Olivia! You can't do this," he begged her, "you can't do this!"

"Get away from me!" she screamed, hitting him with her hands as she slipped away and dove for the edge of the cliff, him catching her foot and pulling her back, kicking and screaming to the soft grass of the vineyard. "Let me go, please just let me go," she cried, her face soaked red with tears. "I can't do this anymore."

"Olivia…" he whispered, tears in his eyes. "Please."

"I hate you," she said. "I hate you so much."

"I know," he said quietly.

She ran her hands up to his face, sobbing. "I hate you so much. I hate that I care about you."

"I know."

"You don't deserve it," she said as she ran her hand up his cheek, pressing her fingertips against his lips. "You don't deserve anything. I hate you so much."

Jeb shook his head. "I swear I didn't know what she did to you. What Elizabeth did, I didn't know."

She dug her fingernails into his chest, the tears in her eyes blurring her vision. "You should have."

"You're right," he whispered, his face coming closer to hers, "I'm sorry for everything."

"Shut up," she said as she beat on his chest with her fists. "I don't want your sorry's, I don't want your fucking pity. I don't want anything from you, Jeb.

Not anymore. I don't want anything from anyone. Not ever again."

There was an ugly feeling in his in his chest as he grabbed her wrists, holding them in the air as she struggled against him. He fought against the urge to say it. The urge to scream it. "...I need you."

She shook her head as she pulled her hands back from him. "Too bad. I'm gone. You can't have me, or us, or the way things used to be." She brought her hands to his chest and began to undo the buttons of his shirt, exposing muscled flesh. "Things are too fucked up."

"What are you doing?" he asked.

She lay back in the grass and pulled him on top of her, putting her hands on his bare chest, the weight of his body pressing her into the grass. "You can't have me, Jeb. We can't do this."

He stared into her eyes, admiring the character of her face, the way her red hair came spread out in waves on the grass, the way her poets lips parted just slightly. Her chest heaved, her hands racing up to his face, searching the contours of him nervously.

"There's this ugly, poisonous monster in me and it's waiting to escape, waiting to get out into the world."

He winced as her finger nails dug into his hips, and she unbuttoned his pants.

"I don't want you around when it gets out. I don't want you to get hurt by it," she said.

"I'm not afraid of monsters," he whispered.

She shook her head. "You should be."

She let out a gasp as he moved his head down, kissing her neck. His lips lingered in the air, just above her mouth. She tried to kiss him, but he moved back and held her down. "I need you."

*"I know,"* she whispered, pulling her dress up, hiking the hemline as high as she could. She kissed him as he pulled down his pants, pushing her panties to the side as she bucked her hips against him in the grass, her moans echoing out hot and heavy, drenched in sweat. She screamed rapture as he took her, clenched finger nails clawing at his flesh. "You know I love you, God damn it,"

He kissed her hard on the mouth. *"I know."*

# 59.
# RECTIFIER

**Athens, Greece,    Two Days Later**

The belly of the aluminum plane screeched across the tarmac like a castrated cat, its wheels bouncing up and down, tiny flecks of blue and white paint shaved off like sawdust as the plane collided with the runway. Elizabeth stepped out and threw back her head, her wild blonde mane flapping like a flag in the wind.   She turned and kicked the rusted, smoking bucket that had just barely made the trip over from Nepal, and it groaned like a hangover.   Cutlass stepped out, dressed in a heavy brown bomber jacket, and took a deep breath.   "It's nice here.   My bones appreciate the warmth."

Elizabeth spun towards him, a smile fixed on her face.   She gripped the handle of the pistol underneath her coat, enjoying the comfort of it.   Two Greek flight officials working the air field rushed towards them. She nodded to Cutlass as they drew closer, pulled the pistol from her coat and gunned them down.

And they were off!   The two of them hotwired an old red and brown *1917 Mercer Raceabout*, and sped off down the long, winding streets of Athens.   It was a beautiful place lush with culture and history. Thousands of buildings of every century and style, rising up over a landscape painted in garish colors. A million bird flock cawed above the ruins of the Parthenon before disappearing like black mist into the shadow of Mt. Hymettus. There was a roughness to it all- like an old, time worn stone you'd find along the edge of some grainy yellow beach. There was a smell like dough splashed with wine. A sound that was loud and busy and boisterous and growing louder and louder.

\* \* \* \* \* \* \* \*

They sat in golden hued deck chairs, their faces half shadowed by pink and red umbrellas with faded wooden poles. Sometimes a wave would crash up higher than usual and wash across the deck, soaking anyone caught in its path. Sometimes a seagull, or two, or even a whole flock, sometimes they'd buzz around those pink and red umbrellas and perch atop the crow's nest, or the slanted metal and wood rails. Thick nets were cast off the side to trap fish and sea urchin. The crew would drag them back up, bit by strenuous bit, and smile at the feast ahead. Jeb leaned over the edge of the rail, smiling as he caught sight of land. "We're here."

Here in Athens, at the port of Piraeus. The Zorbana's massive steam engines roared as they took their last gasping steps towards the shore. The gang plank lowered, and Sam, Jeb and Olivia stepped off into the tawdry orange and blue day. It was noonish. The three of them headed towards customs, presented their fake passports, and filled out whatever paper work needed filling out. A tall man in a bluish-black bowler hat nodded as they passed through a slanted white metal gate and onto the wild, maniac streets of the Mediterranean city. It was gorgeous, all of it. Slim yellow apartments and robust brick and mortar bakeries. Blue domed churches that rose up into spiraling minarets towards the sun. Dark, dusky alleyways and forgotten corridors full of secrets.

The three travelers came upon a shy, almost empty cobblestone street. A man played trumpet, poorly, for pennies- some old, half-forgotten tune. There was a sign post inscribed in red painted Greek. A green finch hovered overhead, picking at the berries of a treetop. Jeb saw it and recognized his own hunger. "Let's stop in here for a sec," he said, gesturing at a café built along a row of tall, skinny shops.

There was a black and gold painted sign hanging up above the door as they walked *in "The Icarus,"* a warm, dark little hole in the wall. There were fuzz covered booths of velvety green, and a handful of family portraits and black and white shots of fish and fisherman lined the walls. A waiter with a cleft lip lit two candles, and the three of them sat down.

The drinks came first, some good strong stuff Olivia had picked out, followed by a basket of bread sticks, and then the main course, *pork souvlaki.* The food tasted good, rich with an authentic, homemade kind of touch. They were halfway finished when the waiter sat a couple down somewhere ahead of them. Jeb couldn't see them too clearly through the dark, dusky room. A woman's eyes, cool and gray, flashed against candlelight for a moment, before the figures all but disappeared behind a high backed booth. There was a short grunt as one of the figures waved the waiter away. Jeb strained closer as the two started to talk. He thought he recognized the woman's voice.

"Oh yes," she said in a wispy British accent that rang all too familiar.

*Could it be?* Jeb thought to himself slowly, opening up his mind to the remote possibility that it was her. Sam said something and he shushed him. Another laugh. Another crisply inflected phrase. Something. Was it her?

Olivia touched his arm, saw the concern reflected in his eyes. The panic at his lips. What was it he saw? No. He lowered his eyes and shook his head. No. The passing headlights of a car strobed in through the corners of the shades, illuminating the women's face. It wasn't her. Of course it wasn't her.

\*\*\*\*\*\*\*\*

He frowned as he said it: "You're tired. Tired and small and miserable, and I'm sick of it."

Then came the laugh.

"I'm serious," he said with an air of bitterness. "All of this way, all of this good fortune, and all you can do is complain, you ungrateful sod. I can't stand you sometimes. And just so we're clear, this isn't going to be easy."

"That's for sure," she said, her breasts heaving. "We'll need help. And if anyone can help, it's Jack Finn."

Cutlass nodded as they turned the corner onto *Mosan Veiku*, and walked up towards the blinking sign. She stopped, frozen in front of some dusky hole in the wall kitchen. A couple and a group of three were sitting inside the dark little place, a scratchy Greek phonograph leaking out through the half open door. "Let's stop here," she said, her eyes drawn forwards. She was transfixed by it, as though some otherworldly force were holding her there, compelling her to step inside. Her feet began to move independent of herself, her mind awash in mystery and riddled words. Her mouth fell open but she hardly even noticed. There was something. Someone. She could feel it like a ghost, like a memory half faded or veiled, something was drawing her into that restaurant. Her hand pressed up to the wooden door, trembling at the threshold of discovery. She pushed lightly at first. Slowly. The light streamed past her, illuminating the inky blackness within. Someone, a man, looked up at her, his eyes wide.

Slack jaw.

Trembling fingertips.

Her body felt numb. Everything felt numb. She raised her leg almost unconsciously to step inside, when the hand grabbed her from behind.

She gasped as she spun around, the door falling back as she let go of it.

"What are you doing?" Cutlass asked. "Come on, the hotels right up here."

"I just.... I think I just wanted something to eat."

"Well later maybe, I don't know." He looked up and down the cafe. "Whatever, just not at this dump, alright?"

She looked back at him, her mind wandering, wondering what it was about this place that had seemed so important just a moment ago. She shrugged and followed him. Whatever it was, it was gone now.


"Did you see something?" Olivia asked, as she stared at a mystified Jeb.

"What?" he asked.

"I said, did you see something?"

"I... No. No, I guess not."

"You sure?"

He blinked, trying to shake off the strange feeling. "No. I'm sure it was nothing."

She put her hands down on the table and stood up. "Alright, well you and Sam take care of the bill. I've got this sudden urge to go out for a walk."

# 60.

## SHE SANG REVELATION/SHE SCREAMED DEATH

The air was hot and oppressive like a stranger's breath. There was a great armada of birds, hundreds of black shadows up against the sky, flying south towards the ocean. They weren't in any formation. Random. Wild. It was like black hun cavalry charging through the sky. Elizabeth watched silently as they moved past the top of the hotel and out of her view. "There it is," she said, motioning towards the tall, tan art deco building. It was new, and it felt it. A big, glaring sign read *"Thessalonopis Plaza Hotel"* in cursive letters. Elizabeth tilted her head. "You go on up to the room. I'll just be a minute."

"And where, might I ask, will you be?" Cutlass asked.

Her voice was somewhere far off. "Darling, I'm going for a walk."

"Don't take too long. I ain't gonna wait fer' yer' pretty ass all day."

She rolled her eyes. "Gregor, you're absolutely beastly."

\* \* \* \* \* \* \* \*

*Step. Step. Step. Step. Step.* Olivia whistled to herself as she walked alone down the Athens street. It was an old tune. Something from a musical? John

Hodges maybe?  Perhaps.  Or perhaps not.  It didn't really matter.  The song was already stuck in her head. One two three, one two three, one two three, step, step, step.  And one two, and one two, and step, step, step, step.  It was a simple song.  Something about girls and the moonlight.  *"Buffalo gals won't you come out tonight, come out tonight.  Buffalo gals won't you come out tonight.  Come out tonight."*  Something like that.  Something.  Elizabeth could feel it too. That force.  Something compelling her to snake down this street or that one.  She hummed to herself as she walked.  Something.  Some old half remembered tune she'd learned back when she was a child.  Back before her mother died.  *"Won't you come out tonight, won't you come out tonight.  And dance by the light of the moooon."*  She hummed it aloud, feeling out the rhythms of it.  It was simple, really.  Why couldn't she remember it better?  In a thousand years, if all her plans went right and she was still alive, would she even remember any of this?  Any of who she was now? How long.  How long would her memories even last?

*Step.  Step.  Step.  Step.  Step.*  Turn, and one, and two, and *step, step, step.*  *"Won't you come out tonight, won't you come out tonight.  And dance by the light of the moooon."*  There was a humming sound calling her forwards.  Drawing her further and further along the path, further and further into the darkness. Her legs broke into a sprint as she went farther and farther into the twisting back alley street.  *Step.  Step. Step.*

Elizabeth whipped around to face the humming sound. The sound was haunting. Familiar somehow. It was like that damned song. It was- yes- she knew it completely, but then at the same time she didn't know it at all. It was maddening. *Step.* Yes. *Step.* *Step.* *Step.* Yes. *Step.* Like at the restaurant. That feeling was back. That feeling of, oh, something. She followed the strange sound. It was a drumming wasn't it? Something like that.

Around a dark blue corner and six little Greek flags. Into an alleyway. That feeling. That sound, it was there. It was something undeniable, something familiar. The same haunting deja'vu she'd get when she saw a stranger on the street and something about them, something, reminded her of an old lover, or friend, and then, for one brief moment she'd be back with them.

*She saw her first.*

She gasped.

*Unbelievable. Her muscles tightened, her pupils constricted. It couldn't be. It just couldn't be. Could it?*

Elizabeth yes. Yes, it was her. The yellow hair, the gun metal eyes. Her teeth bit down hard, barely stifling a scream. *"Buffalo gals won't you come out tonight,"* she hummed the broken tune out loud.

*"Ghost,"* Elizabeth whispered.

Her blue eyes flashed furiously, her fists tightening. In her gut she could feel her empty womb. Elizabeth, it was all her fault. Murderer. Killer. Impossible that she should be here. That she should find her here. Impossible. Olivia wanted to kill her right there. Stab her in the neck and the heart and the face and anywhere else she could sink a blade. *Blood blood blood, there would be blood everywhere!* Vengeance erupted in sweet release. *Blood. Blood.* Her eyes widened, the ocean engorged with hate as she ran down the long, black and gray ally. Shadows danced across her sleeveless dress as she tackled Elizabeth and punched her across the face. There was something new in Elizabeth's cold, hollow eyes, something Olivia had never seen before. *Fear.*

"You can't be alive," Elizabeth said breathlessly, as her phantom sister wrapped her hands around her neck. "I shot you! I watched you die!" Elizabeth's voice grew desperate.

"You took everything from me!" Olivia shouted, her face twisted with hate.

"I'm not afraid of you," Elizabeth gasped, as she punched back at her sister, wresting Olivia's hands from her throat. "You're nothing more than a bad memory. A wave of mist wafting off the black cliffs that stand as a monument to my life of flesh eternal... You were unafraid to die, well I'm unafraid to live."

"You betrayed me!" Olivia screamed, slugging her sister in the gut.

Elizabeth recovered and hit back, knocking Olivia to the ground. "I proved you wrong! I took what was yours and made it mine. A few months of loneliness, and a sway of the hips and Jeb was all over me like a dog in heat. You really think he cared about you?

You think he ever gave a fuck about you? You think anyone ever did?"

"He loves me." Olivia's arms trembled as she pushed herself off the ground.

Elizabeth sneered, dodging a blow and knocking Olivia back. "Who could ever love you? All he ever loved was that soft spot between your legs."

"You're wrong!" Olivia shouted.

"You are nothing, phantom! Little more than an undigested bit of beef. Less grave than gravy." Elizabeth laughed as she pulled back her hand and slapped her sister hard across the face. Olivia stumbled backwards, her back thumping against the stone and vine wall. "Get away from me, Elizabeth."

"Or what? Bad digestion or vengeful spirit, either way you hold no sway here. Go back to the land of the shadows. Go back where you belong." Her words slid into each other, her mouth frothing with hate for the twin who'd always thought she was so much better. *Well who was better now?* Who amongst them would live forever more, and who was already dead? Fountain of youth, elixir of life. No spirits there. "You may well haunt me forever, spirit. But it will be *forever*. For tonight I will take the final piece. I will go to the Athens Museum and retrieve the final clue. Encased inside the belly of Thanatos lies the last piece of the puzzle, the last portent. And tonight it's all mine."

Blood ran from Olivia's nose, dripping past her lips and onto the ground.

"Lie there and bleed, spirit! Go back to the netherworld from whence you came and watch, bleeding and powerless as I claim the golden throne of the universe. As I conquer death the world will know my name, spirit. Even your God will tremble when I speak, once I unravel all the mysteries of life. The secrets of the universe mine alone to control!"

Olivia slumped against the wall, her stomach a sick, churning maze. "There's something you need to know. When you shot me I was pregnant. Did you know that? You killed my baby. How does that make you feel, knowing what you've done?" Her voice trembled. "How can you live with yourself for even a second, let alone an eternity, knowing that?"

"Oh God, you're quaint." Elizabeth laughed, her body moving closer, lips slithering about at the edges of a smile. She spoke in low, mocking tones as she placed her hand on Olivia's shoulder and smiled. "You thought I didn't know?"

Olivia collapsed to the ground, her mind a whir of images and light, of twisted sounds and echoed self reflections. *"Buffalo gals won't you come out tonight. Won't you."* Elizabeth walked away, leaving her sister a bleeding shuddering mess crouched down in the middle of the alley. There was an echo in her mind as she heard the humming noise again. *"And dance by the light of the moooooon."*

# 61.

# PRELUDE TO A FUNERAL

**Five Days Earlier**

"I'm impressed," said Cutlass, "really, I am."

"It's not *that* impressive," Elizabeth said coolly, "have you forgotten who my father is? Even in death, his name holds sway. At least in these parts."

"Any reason in particular for that?"

"Yes, as a matter of fact, there is."

There was a pause as Cutlass waited for her to finish. "Yeah, and?"

"And what?"

"What's the reason?"

She smiled as she stepped over the curb and crossed the street. "That's a story for another time."

Cutlass swung open the great, green painted doors to the pink townhouse. "And these friends, they're up for this kind a' thing? Even on such short notice?"

Elizabeth turned to him, her eyes catching the seedy gas light glow of the room. "What thief can resist a fortune?"

They were a motley bunch, all seated in the kitchen around a large oak table bathed in smoke. A tall, thin man with leathery skin and a gaunt face stood up and shook Elizabeth's hand. Cutlass took a hard look at the man. He had long, oval shaped eyes that creased into burgundy slits as he smiled.  A thinish brown mustache framing thinish blue lips, that lined a mouth filled with tiny, corn yellow teeth that would have looked more at home in the mouth of child then a grown man.  His nose was long and angular, hands rigid and sprouting with blue veins.  He wore a dark green suit that was just a tad too small, pink tie, silver embossed snake pin and crocodile hide shoes.  Cutlass could tell this was his house.  As he said *"hello"* his voice came out in a dull cough sounding, not-quite-Irish brogue.  "Elizabeth my dear!  And who," he went on in his hack of a voice, "Is your lovely friend?"

"The names Cutlass," said the pirate.

"Meet Jack Fin," Elizabeth said with a smirk, "the meanest bastard in Greece."

"You're too kind," croaked the gaunt shadow man.

"A pleasure."  Cutlass took his hand hesitantly.

"And this, of course, is my crew," Jack Fin said, gesturing towards the six or so figures hunched over the oak table.  "Please, sit, sit.  We.... have much to discuss I think, eh, *heh heh.*"

Elizabeth nodded as she and Cutlass took their seats.  They were thick velvet backed chairs and they were itchy.  The room around them was, in a word, grey.  Grey tile floor, grey painted walls accented with faux silver frames, ebony cabinets, and a real silver sink.  A transvestite in a grey tuxedo, blonde wig and heels, stood hidden in the shadows of the hallway, a rifle in his hands, and the ceiling was masked by bluish grey smoke.  Almost everyone at the table had a cigarette or cigar.  Jack Fin was quick with the pleasantries as he poured them each a round glass of red wine. He smiled and took a puff from a long black cigar banded in the middle with cheap gold foil.

Things started off with small talk. Catching up, and coming down, and *"oh, so sorry to hear about your father,"* and *"oh, the son of a bitch is better off dead."* Back and forth between Elizabeth and Jack. Cutlass would mutter some smart assed comment from time to time but for the most part he kept quiet. The gaunt man's crew, for their part, sat in almost total silence. One of them, a women with red, cold sore welted lips, blew Cutlass a kiss before disappearing into the smoky mist of the room. "They call me Mean Jack Fin," said the man, his slit like eyes red and burning from the smoke, "just don't ask me why." Elizabeth laughed wildly as he said this, but Cutlass stayed quiet. If that had been a joke, he didn't get it. Finally, over a green leafy salad sogging in translucent brown dressing, they got down to business with a, *"so you wanna rob the museum?"*

"That's right." Elizabeth smirked.

"Awful short notice, init' it? I mean for a job like this. A job a' this size."

"Well if anybody can do it, it's-"

"Flattery will get you nowhere, dearie. And why does it have to be done so soon? Why not wait? Take time to better plan it out," said Fin.

"I'm giving you almost a week," she said.

"That's still a rush job," said Jack.

"Well here's the thing," she began, "I'm just not the kind of girl who likes to be kept waiting."

He paused for a moment and took a drag.   "I see."

"And this item we're going after.   I'm... *We're* just so excited to finally get a hold of it, if you understand.   It's like a present, lying there under the tree before Christmas.   You just can't wait to open it."

"I wouldn't know about Christmases."

She laughed nervously.   "Well it's just that-"

"Stop.   There's no need to explain, girlie.   I don't know why you want to break open this statue, and I don't care.   As long as I get paid."

"Oh you will."

"I know."   He smiled placidly.   "Because I know you.   And I know that you know what I do to people who fuck me over."

# 62.

## THE GREAT MUSEUM ROBBERY

The guard crumpled to the ground as Elizabeth beat him over the head with a rusty lead pipe. She grabbed the keys as two of Mean Jacks men beat the other main entrance guards to death.

**"Click!"**

With a quick, metallic sound the lock turned, and the mighty oak door pushed open. There was a quick gasp from one of the guards, a man who'd managed to stay hidden up until now. Slim Sovoronopolis, one of Jacks hired guns, leapt into action, clubbing the guard before he could scream, bashing his head in like a mid-November pumpkin. He signaled to Elizabeth with a thumbs up-- the coast was clear and they were in. Somewhere, miles away, Mean Jack Fin was sipping a cup of tea. If he could've seen the efficiency of what had just happened he'd of been proud of his team. Slim whispered out a long *"Shhhh...."* and he, Karl and Elizabeth (Team One.) stepped inside (Teams Two and Three were, at that same exact moment, entering through the back and side entrances.).

"Four bodies!" Slim said in a Greek accent. "Aight, Elizabeth, hep me move zem inside."

\* \* \* \* \* \* \*

In order to understand the structure of the robbery and its execution, it was important to examine the structure of the National Archaeological Museum of Athens, and the many exhibits contained within. To begin with, the shape of it, at least when seen from a bird's eye view, started off looking like a broad pair of shoulders. This area was huge, roughly as large as two football fields, and contained most of the main exhibits.

It was like this:

Picture a large square head sticking out from the middle of this shoulder like structure. This square, which was composed of massive outlying columns and a great marble ceiling painted in frescos, served as the main entrance to the museum. Next the arm sections, which jutted out in the same direction as the head, but from the end of both the right and left shoulder side of the museum. It is in these auxiliary halls that the special exhibits were held, as well as most of the pottery collections.

But simply knowing the layout fails to convey the grand majesty of the place. It was a monstrously huge museum, containing thousands of artifacts and ancient treasures. It's outside lined in Grecian columns like some modern day Parthenon, its halls pure marble, reflective of pure, classic elegance.

The bandits came through the massive white washed doors and into the great halls which glowed by day with electric light, and now, by night, were swallowed up in darkness, the only light a few moon beams that danced about like rippling waves in a bath.

Slim Sovoronopolis, who was in charge of team one, shot an angry glance at Elizabeth, who had just dropped down one of the guards bodies with a too loud thud, before flicking on the switch to his torchlight.

Slim's voice was low, just above a whisper. "Stay frosty."

* * * * * * * *

Jeb watched it all with bated breath. He felt like a bastard hiding there, crouched in the bushes as those men were slaughtered. But what could he do? They had guns and numbers on him, and what did he have? Sam had called the police, only to be laughed at, and so now they waited alone for the imminent invasion, Olivia at the west side arm which overlooked a short, flowery hill, and Sam at the back. (The east side entrance faced a street, and so it was assumed that the bandits would not break in from there.) The plan, as it had been hastily made after Olivia ran to them and told tale of her fateful encounter with her sister and the plot to steal the final clue, was simply to watch and wait. It was hoped that Cutlass and Elizabeth would break in alone after dark, overpower the guards at one of the main entrances and break in. From there, whoever it was that spied them would just follow them in, wait for them to get the missing clue, wherever it was in the museum, shoot and kill Elizabeth, incapacitate Cutlass as best as they could, and take the last key to Midas' Tomb for themselves. That was the plan anyhow. It wasn't very good of course, and there were more than a few thousand places where it could potentially go wrong, but hell, it was the best they could rig up with just a few hours notice. Once the door had slammed shut, Jeb stepped tepidly out from the bushes. He brushed back his hair with his left hand and took a deep breath, his right shaking as it gripped the handle of his gun. Slowly, he made his way up the white marble steps and opened the door.

\* \* \* \* \* \* \* \*

Elizabeth and Slim continued down the moon lit hallways, past masks of gold and plates of silver. Magnificent statues of Zeus, Hera, Heracles and Aphrodite. Untold riches of art and knowledge and gold, but none of it mattered. It was all but dust compared to what she was after. A long oil mural of the underworld, painted in glossy blacks and reds, Hades gazing forwards at the fiery kingdom before him, Persephone's eyes wet, her skin graying, feet covered in ash.

Footsteps echoed out. Hushed voices mingled in the air. The smashed floor tiles came together into a mosaic: Kronos eating his children.

An exhibit on Egypt: a mummy, an obelisk, a sand blasted Osiris. Two green eyes hidden in-between moonbeams, peering out across a chest of scarabs; two sphinx etched into the wall nearby.

More history. More treasure. They were getting closer now.

One of Mean Jacks men made a grunting sound, oily black hair cascading over his shoulders. A laugh. That's what that grunting sound was, or at least, that's what it was supposed to be. He smiled a graveyard smile at Elizabeth, though she failed to return the favor. *"What?"* she whispered, *"what's so funny?"*

He shrugged, ruffling his ill-fitting, sun-wrinkled suit. "Nothing." A cold, eastern European pause. "It's just, like, you know, all dis stuff. All deez things we cou' steal, ahn we're going after some stu'id statue? I on't get it."

"You don't need to *get it*, Frankenstein, you just need to do what you're told."

He looked hurt, the lines on his weirdo, almost inhuman face turning down towards his mouth as he spoke. "I always do."

More treasure. More footsteps. More gold.

And there it was! Elizabeth sprinted towards the statue of Thanatos, her mind racing almost as fast as her legs. Cutlass and several of Jacks henchmen were standing beside it, and there was a mighty grin already plastered across the pirates face. "What took you so long?"

"Shove it," she said, her eyes tilting up towards the top of the statue.

"Where's June?" Slim asked. "Dmitri, Stacy, all a' team three?"

Cutlass turned his gun over in his hands. "Beats me."

Once again Slim groaned. He didn't like this job. Didn't like it one bit. There was a shambling, stumbling ruckus of a sound coming down from the right hall. Slim whipped his head to face it, his hand reaching for his gun. *"Fuck!"* It was the portly and beautiful June Finn, daughter of Mean Jack Finn, and plenty mean herself. She was wearing a tight, white leather body suit covered in blood, and holding a sledge hammer that was plenty gore covered itself. "They jumped us! Bastards jumped us!" Her voice was horse, wild, out of breath. "Fucking pigs shot up Dmitri, and put a knife in Stacy's back. Fuck!"

Zlim was trying to stay calm. "An' you?"

She swung the sledge handle up, and gripped the mallet in her left hand. "Me? I'm ten shades of fuckin splendiferous pal, what do you think?"

*"Swell,"* said Slim. "So how much time we got?"

"Dunno. Maybe two maybe ten, or anywhere else in-between. You wanna bet whether or not we can get this peanut out of its shell by then?"

"Give me that!" Elizabeth sneered, snatching the hammer away from her. "Idiot. How in the hell did they get the jump on you, huh? What are you, some kind a mongoloid?"

June looked plenty taken aback by this. "Why I oughta-"

"Yeah, yeah, yeah, you oughta. You oughta a' not got yourself caught." Sharp, crumbling chunks of marble blew out as she slammed the sledge across the chest of Thanatos, the force of it all making a sound like dynamite. Cutlass stepped forwards, his eyes wide and expectant with more than a century of waiting. Elizabeth knelt down and picked at the rubble until she found it. She took it in her hand, appreciated the craftsmanship of it, the solid, expensive weightiness, the intricate details carved in gold. She smiled, her eyes wild, teeth biting at the right side of her bottom lip. There were two delicate levers at the top of the metal device, and with careful hands she pressed down on them. A sudden mechanical whir, and the top of the device opened up with a parade of gears, and a whoosh of steam, and there it was! At last. At long, long last. She removed a rice paper scroll from inside and brought it up to her face. She smiled wildly, feeling happier than she had in much too long. At last, there it was. The map not to any clues, or portents, or temples, or riddles, or lies, but the map to Midas himself. To his golden tomb!

June Finn looked down at the pirate and the whore, who were both huddled down in the mist of marble dust, studying the map. "That it?" she asked.

"Aye," Cutlass gulped.

"Good. Now can we get the hell outta here?"

Elizabeth stood up slowly, the map clasped tightly to her chest. She nodded and was about to say yes when she was interrupted by the sudden sound of more than a dozen footsteps charging down the hall towards them.

June frowned, her eyes sharpening. "Fuck. Time to go."

So they ran. The bullets started flying, the Greek cops started shouting, and Mean Jacks hired guns started to fall.

If the cops cared at all about being careful not to hit any of the artifacts they certainly weren't showing it. June dived to the ground as a stone carved bust of Aristotle exploded behind her. Her glossy painted nails scratched across the pink tiled floor as her plump body slid around a sharp corner into the east wing, where she looked around for Elizabeth and Cutlass. Her men were dropping like flies, and the ones that had gotten them into this whole mess were nowhere to be found. June glared as she watched them disappear into the shadows far up ahead. "Fuck."

\* \* \* \* \* \* \* \*

"Come on!" Cutlass dragged her arm through the long black halls with only torchlight's and moonbeams to light the way. *"Ooof!"* he cried out as he tripped over a shadow hidden bench and stumbled to the floor. "Help me up!" he cried, the mammoth face of a stone carved Zeus towering above him.

Suddenly a voice came from out of the shadows. "Not so fast."

"Who the fuck?" Cutlass muttered. **"POW!"** The bullet tore through the pirates shoulder and embedded itself into the floor. He screamed, as did Elizabeth, as she toppled down to the ground from the shock of it. "Show yourself you coward!" Cutlass roared, as his wound went into a kind of cold numbness before beginning to scab over.

There came only silence from the darkness.

Cutlass fumbled for his torch and stood up. "I said show yourself!"

Jeb stepped out into the streaks of moonlight, his eyes dark emerald slits, right arm raised, hand gripping a pistol. "No..... no!" Cutlass stuttered, "That's impossible!"

"Shut up!" Jeb shouted and fired again, this time into the pirates face. He was in no mood for mercy.

"You!" Elizabeth hissed. "I should have chopped your fucking head off when I had the chance."

He stepped towards her and kicked away the gun that lay near her wrist. "Yeah. You should've. Now gimme' the map."

"How do you know about--"

"I said give it to me."

She glared at him. "Cutlass, do something!"

**"BOOM!"** Jeb fired off another shot, and the pirate dropped his gun and slumped back onto the floor, his skull a caved in mess. "The map. Now."

"You're not messing around this time, are you Jeb?"

"Nope."

"I really should have killed you." Then came a short, angry pause. "How did--"

He snatched the map away from her. "I think I'll be going now." He began to turn. "Oh."

"What?" She sneered, frothing at the mouth with hate

He turned back towards her. "Just one more thing."

Her face had gone mad with fear.

Jeb pulled back the hammer and aimed his pistol at her. "This is for Olivia. And her baby."

**"RUN!"** Came an unknown voice. Jeb turned to face the six dark figures running towards him, the wail of bullets suddenly growing louder. One of the figures, a tall, rubenesque vixen in knee high alligator skin boots and a white leather body suit splattered with blood, raised up a rifle and fired it off. Jeb's eyes followed the bullet as it zoomed into the chest of a guard coming from the opposite end of the hallway.

"Who the hell are you?" she shouted, turning her rifle on Jeb.

"I was about to ask you the same question," said Jeb.

*"Kill him,"* cried Elizabeth.

*"We're boxed in!"* Slim wailed.

"I SAID, WHO ARE YOU?" June's voice was a wild, high pitched scream, wrapped up in fear.

"Just a tourist in a museum."

A hail of bullets grazed past Junes head. "Fuck!"

"Whah' du we du a' June?" Slim cried, as two more guards came down from each end of the long hallway.

"I'll deal with you in a second," said June, glaring at Jeb. She made a sudden motion of her hand and one of the bandits dove at Jeb, wrestling the gun from his hand before trapping him in a headlock. She turned towards Slim. "Your pack, give it to me."

The Greek nodded, pulled it off, and tossed it to her. June rummaged around inside for a second before retrieving a rather long, rather red, rather frightening stick of dynamite. She tossed it to Elizabeth.

"What do I do with this?" Elizabeth asked.

June rolled her eyes and reached back into the pack, retrieving several more sticks of dynamite. She unraveled and attached a short, five ended fuse, struck a match against her arm, and flung the lit cluster of dynamite at the wall. Her pretty green eyes traced the sparkling white and blue fuse through the darkness, her lids slamming shut as the fire reached its destination, and the dynamite slammed up against the eastern wall of the Athens History museum.

**Boom.**

SISTER ACT

# 63.
# SISTER ACT

The explosion rang out with a cacophony of sound like a locomotive running off the tracks, slamming into the pulpified crowds of Grand Central station. The bright white mason walls exploded out. June pulled her arm from her face and began to cough.

"Whadu we do wit this guy, huh?" Slim shouted, his voice a dim ring in June's shell shocked ears. A long pause. "Well?"

She whirled around, the smoke groping at the edges of her white leather body suit, blood and ash sprayed generously over her shoulders like sea mist.

"Give me that pipe"

"Wait--" Jeb gasped. "We can work this out! I don't know who you are, but I'm telling you--"

June pulled back her arm and let him have it, slamming the thick metal bar against his head. "Drag him, carry him, whatever- just bring him with us."

"What?" Elizabeth cried as she chased after June through the enormous dynamite blown hole in the wall, the edges of which were still crumbling.

"I'm taking him alive," said June.

"You can't!"

"Oh yes I can. That son of a bitch, whoever he is, wanted you dead. Wanted whatever that scroll is that you've got, and I wanna know why. I wanna know what it is that's so damned important I just lost half my crew over it."

Elizabeth stared at her, the red flames reflected in her eyes growing smaller and smaller as she continued forwards across the grass. Everything was chaos at that moment. Everything. She pulled the scroll from Jeb's pocket, knowing what she had to do.

She had to run.

Away from June, away from the cops, away from everything. Out into the darkness. Out towards destiny. There wasn't any choice. What if they listened to Jeb? What if they took his side, and cut her out, and went after all of the gold and power and eternity for themselves? She couldn't risk it.

So she ran.

June shouted out behind her and raised her gun, but it was too late. Within seconds Elizabeth was gone, dissolved into the darkness like chalk in the rain. Her feet pounded across the ground, heart racing, breath uneven and afraid. She ran and she ran and she ran, never looking back. She ran. She ran right into her.

*"Y tu, Gemeni?"*

She was wearing a long black dress that grew wispy and lacy around the edges. There was a fat, turquoise cloth wrapped around her waist, and she had on matte silver boots. In her bluer than blue eyes the moonbeams all but disappeared, swallowed up in their opacity like far off tides fading into the sea's horizon.

"Ghost?" Elizabeth asked, as she came up over the top of the hill and stared into her past.

Olivia frowned as she stepped towards her sister. "No."

Elizabeth gagged as her sister plunged the dagger into her chest. Olivia glowered, twisting the blade with her wrist, sawing at her sister's heart. Elizabeth's fingers went up, shaking weakly around the hilt of the blade. "You- *You-*"

"ME." Olivia's voice was steady. The monster in her had escaped. She spit on Elizabeth as she crumpled to the ground. "Know this as you take your last breaths, as you taste your last sour regrets: I win. For all your treachery, for all your lies. I win."

"You--" Elizabeth gasped, her speech breathy, uneven. "You win- nuth-ing."

"I get to live. That's winning enough."

Elizabeth screamed. "It hurts!"

"Good. That's for my child."

"Oh fuck! It really fucking hurts!"

Olivia shook her head, dropping the bloody knife to the ground. "How could you do it, sister? How could you do what you did to me?"

"It was… easy," she choked. "I just… thought about how much I hated you."

"Why?"

"Because you got everything, and I got nothing!" Elizabeth lunged forwards, collapsing back into the dirt, her fingers tearing at the soil. "I grew up with a father who beat me and s-servants for friends. I… was raped. D-do you know that? By a fuckin' gardener! I remember just lying on my back, saying prayers...."

"That's not an excuse."

There was a manic look in her eyes. "It is an excuse! I only ever did what I had to survive."

"You're a vindictive, manipulative bitch. You're evil."

*"Oww! Aaaahh-- Aaaaahhh!"* She screamed as she clutched at her wound, the blood spouting out into the smoke and ash drunk air. "I got a barren womb and got a baby you didn't even deserve. So yeah, I wanted your life. I wanted to be loved. Was that wrong? Is that what makes me evil?"

"No." Slowly, Olivia unwrapped the turquoise scarf around her waist, revealing a bare midriff here the bullet had gone through like shattered glass. "That does."

Sweat streaking down her face, Elizabeth began to tremble and laugh, her hand reaching behind her back. *"A ha, ha ha ha ha ha."* It was the desperate, sick kind of laughter reserved for the halls of asylums. Olivia froze as her sister pulled a match from her back pocket. "I'll see you in Hell," Elizabeth said with a smile, blood coming out through the cracks between her teeth. She pulled out the dynamite and struck the match on its side.

*"Nooo!"* Olivia threw herself backwards.

Elizabeth clutched her chest as she blew apart and burst into flame, her silk and lace-bodiced shirt catching the fire, spreading it like gasoline. She let out one last, terrible scream, her arms bloody stumps, before collapsing face down on the ground. Olivia pulled back, the flames snapping at her. She knew what she had to do. She had to- *"Oww!"* The fire singed her as she pulled the map from Elizabeth's severed, holocaust hand. She tossed the rice paper scroll to the ground, the edges burning away like waking dreams.

# 64.

## NOBODY FUCKS WITH MEAN JACK FIN

"…….what do you mean you don't know? Unacceptable. Do you understand, that's unacceptable!" Mean Jack roared, spittle spraying out from between his blue lips. He was wearing a dark green suit and a pink tie. Pinned to his chest was a glossy, turquoise snake pin. His thin, tanish fingers were clad in rings of silver. He was thin and ugly, as was his mustache; and his breath, more than anything, smelled like road kill.

Jeb, on the other hand, was bleeding, and tied up to a high backed wooden chair in the middle of a humid, pink wallpapered room. Jack stood above him now, grinning as he stroked the hissing python around his shoulders. "Here," he hissed as he lifted the slithering creature, thick with reticulated muscle, up off of his shoulders and placed it around Jeb's. Jeb coughed and gagged as the snake tightened its coils around his neck.

"Pl- Pleh!"

Mean Jack sneered. "Perhaps that will teach you to answer when you are spoken to." The old man leered before pulling out a small, dead rat from the left breasted pocket of his green suit. *"Chh-Chh-Chh-Chh-Chh."* He made little clicking noises between his tongue and his teeth, and the snake lifted its green, spade shaped head, it's slitted eyes flickering at the mouse. "Here." He smiled again, tossing the rat to the floor, and the snake unwrapped itself with a terrible slowness and slithered down to it. "Sir, that was a warning from one gentleman to another. Nobody fucks with Mean Jack Finn."

A veneer of sweat rolled off Jeb as he gasped, fighting to catch his breath. "You- You son of a-"

"I ask you for the last time, sir. Where is Elizabeth Shaw?"

"I told you I DON'T KNOW!"

Here there was a pause. The whole room eerily silent, save for the muted hissing of the serpent. "Sir, you disappoint me. Very well then."

Jeb screamed as the old man shoved his chair backwards, knocking him onto the floor from where he could only look up as Jack pulled a gun from behind his back and cocked back the hammer.

\* \* \* \* \* \* \* \*

Olivia moved down the empty streets, her mind a foggy mess of confusion. She knew that Elizabeth deserved it, and she knew she'd do it again if she had to, but-

Still.

There was a word for what she'd done: sororicide. It seemed like there was a word for every type of killing. Patricide was killing your father, avunculicide was killing your uncle, omnicide was killing everyone. But having a word for it didn't make it feel any easier. Or any less terrible.

There was a terrible dragging in her stomach, like the pit of a peach still undigested and brown, a nausea all consuming. It felt like she was standing in the middle of a dark field, her hands reaching up, feeling at egg sized lumps in her throat. The lumps were choking her, making her mouth dry. Making her feel like she couldn't breathe.

She gasped for air, trying to hold back the nausea, trying not to puke in the alleyway. The dragging sensation wretched upward, consuming her, threatening her sanity, throwing everything into darkness as the image of her sister's mangled body flashed before her eyes.

\* \* \* \* \* \* \* \*

"I'll be back," Fin said as he lowered his gun and left the room, slamming the door behind him. "So whadu we know fer sure?" he asked in his sneering, not-quite-Irish brogue, a cigar clinging to his bottom lip.

"Not enough." June said, looking up from the kitchen table as her father walked in.

"Well that Cutlass fella must know something, mustn't he?" Slim asked.

"Aye," the green suited, pink tied Jack Finn agreed with a puff of smoke. "Darling."

"Yes?" said June.

"Find out what he knows."

June stood up, nodded, and walked out of the kitchen. Slim eyed the other men nervously. Karl, Dmitri, Tammy: they were all dead. Someone needed to take the fall, and soon. The old man was steaming. Hadn't been this mad since June got knocked up back in the spring of '13, and even then... Hell, half the crew was dead now. "I wanna know everything. Everything that happened," Mean Jack growled.

"But sir we already--" Slim began.

"I wanna go over it again!" Jack snarled. Slim kept his eyes down as he retold the story for a fifth time, his voice shaking with each word

\* \* \* \* \* \* \* \*

Cutlass looked up as she entered the room.
"Hello June."
"Hello."
Her plump frame was squeezed into the same tight leather body suit from before, though at least she'd wiped some of the blood and ash off of it. She ran her fingers through her wild red hair and pouted. "Cutlass?"
"Aye?"
"What are we gonna do here?"
He looked her up and down. "Does that thing come with a zipper?"
"Stop it."
Cutlass laughed. "What do you want? I already bloody told you all I know. Son of a bitch is named Jeb Chamberlain. Kid from the states, been trailin'

Elizabeth and me since Egypt. Been after the map, same as us."

"You still haven't said where it is that map leads."

Cutlass smiled. "When Elizabeth came to you, you said that didn't matter. Said you'd do it all as a favor in memory of Elizabeth's daddy dearest. Said as long as you got you're sixty thousand--"

"Well that's the thing, isn't it? We don't have our sixty thousand, and Elizabeth's gone. And, I'm afraid, that means you're the only collateral we've got."

He laughed. "I'm sorry?"

"This operation has been a disaster for us. We need that money."

"Well I don't know what to tell you. Like I said, I don't know where she is. Have you talked to Jeb, maybe he knows."

Her expression went sour. "Of course we've talked to him! What kind of fools do you take us for?"

Cutlass shrugged.

"You'll be sorry if we don't get our money soon. Trust me, friend, you will be." She bent over, her pear shaped ass raised up high in the air as she pulled a long knife from inside the heel of her alligator skin boot, and pointed it at his neck. "And don't try anything stupid."

Cutlass grinned. "Ye' really don't know who it is you're dealing with here, do ya' lassy?"

\* \* \* \* \* \* \* \*

Jeb was lying on the floor, still as he could, face dripping in cold sweat as the python slithered along his chest. He was useless to these people and he knew it. It was only a matter of time before they killed him.

He just wished they'd get it over with.

There was a scream!

Jeb whipped his head to the right.

Another scream. This time closer. Who was it? Had they found Elizabeth?

-Sam!-

A heavy force bashed the door open and Jeb looked up. No, not Sam--

Cutlass.

He looked down at Jeb, a knife sticking out of his empty eye socket and a rifle in his hand. Behind him was a scene of carnage, blood and cut up limbs strewn about the kitchen, every last member of Jacks crew dead. (Well, almost everyone. Cutlass didn't realize it but Mean Jack and his daughter June were still alive. Neither did Cutlass realize how much Mean Jack hated him.) The pirate tossed his gun to the floor and bent down, undoing Jeb's ropes. "What are you gonna do to me?" Jeb gasped, as the pirate picked up the python and tossed it across the room.

"I'm gonna smash in yer' kneecaps, break yer' nose off, and cut yer' tongue out with a dull knife before feeding what's left a' you to that big ass snake."

Jeb's blood ran cold.

"Nah, I'm just kiddin'," the Pirate said with a laugh. "But I really am gonna kill ye' if ye' can't give me what I want."

Jeb groped for words. "The map, Cutlass. I-I-I saw it. I know where it leads."

The pirate shook his head. "And how the hell did you translate it?"

"I didn't have to," Jeb sputtered. "I recognized the drawing on it. Midas' temple, it's built inside of Cannon Mountain."

"Inside what now?"

"It's in New Hampshire. There's a rock formation, they call it the Old Man of the Mountain. I recognized it and I can take you there, but you gotta let me live."

Cutlass stared at him. "Thanks for the info kid, but now that I know where the tomb is, why I do need your help to get there?"

"You'll need help confronting Midas when you get there. With Elizabeth gone to God knows where, I can be that help." The sweat dropped down Jeb's face as he waited for Cutlass answer, his heat pounding faster and faster and faster.

The pirate turned away from him, hands behind his back as he made his way towards the wall.

"So...?" Jeb said to him. "What are you gonna do?"

Cutlass looked at Jeb, one eyebrow arched, a smile at the edges of his lips. "I suppose I could use the company."

# 65.

# HOME

### Three Weeks Later

Ellis Island, World Series baseball, skyscrapers, radio, flappers, the movies, Greta Garbo, Billy Sunday, taxi cabs, pole sitting, beauty contests: This was home. This was *America.*

The ships horn blared, gulls cawing overhead, the sounds of NYC drifting over the water towards them. The sky, big and endless and orange-pink, every cloud a cotton robin egg, every thudding wave a slap from a hand. Jeb kissed her, her mouth dry velvet, lips soaked in smoke and tequila. A kiss, hard, and salty, and almost a crust. She had on too much mascara and too little rouge, and her cheeks were a blank white canvas for the little black drops that came down into freckles from her sea mist wet lashes. She'd been drinking too much lately.

He squeezed her hand before crossing the deck and shaking Cutlass' hand. "Good luck."

The pirate frowned. "You sure about this?"

Jeb looked at Olivia, and then back to Cutlass. "She needs time, she needs peace, she needs..."

"What?"

"What she needs, all the gold and all the revenge in the world can't give her."

"It's a bad idea for you to come back to New York."

"You're right," said Jeb. "But it's where she belongs, and I have to bring her home, I have to do this one last thing for her before.... before it's all over."

"It ain't all over yet," Cutlass said as he shook his head. "You have three days to take care of your business here. Then we leave for the tomb, and you keep your end of the bargain."

Jeb pulled the map Olivia saved from the fire out of his back pocket and nodded. "My bargain. Not Olivia's and not Sam's."

"Do they know that yet?" The pirate asked.

Jeb shook his head. "I'll handle it, don't worry"

"I wasn't," said Cutlass.

Jeb watched as the anchor dropped, splashing into the grimy harbor water. "Mind if I ask how you're gonna spend the next three days, pirate?"

Cutlass grinned. "Drunk and in bed with cheap hookers. You?"

\* \* \* \* \* \* \* \*

It was a foggy morning, ground wet with dew, air full of hesitance. Customs was quick enough, the fake passports Sam had provided all the way back in Africa being of substantial quality, and all three of them were eager to get their feet back on solid ground. By this point Chief Macalister had been in the ground for nearly a year, and his murder all but forgotten. *Still*. Jeb was more than cautious, and he knew he had more on his plate then he could handle.

Example A) He still had a warrant out for his arrest. If they caught him, he'd get the chair for sure.

Example B) Olivia's husband. He was living here in New York, and Olivia was determined to close things out between the two of them. Confronting another man about the fact that he was sleeping with said man's wife-- Talk about *déjà vu*.

Example C) *Midas*. He'd already sent a group of assassins to kill or capture him once. Jeb was sure he'd try again.

They crossed Canal street, making their way into the heart of the Big Apple. The streets were misty, almost dreamlike, with sky scrapers and brownstones stretching as far as the eye could see before disappearing like half reflections in steamed up glass. A preponderance of electric streetcars and taxis sped along, dodging flappers pushing little wooden carriages, and men in fedoras who walked with hollowed out canes filled to the brim with whiskey. Jeb took Olivia's hand as they stepped into a dress shop where a pair of oxford bags sold her a gorgeous pea green number that stopped just above the knees. Pizza and a jazz bar on Fifth avenue, and then onto a show. *"Abie's Irish Rose,"* the longest running and most reviled show on Broadway. Afterwards they got drunk and went down to where the "Owls Trumpet" used to be. It was a furniture store now.

\* \* \* \* \* \* \* \*

"We got a lead on Jeb Chamberlain."

"What? Who?" Chief O'Reilly scratched his head as he looked across the table at the young lieutenant. "What the fuck are you talking about?"

Jones looked shocked. "Yer' kidding right? The louse who killed Macalister. You do remember him? Guy who had the job before you?"

"Don't get smart with me, lieutenant!" O'Reilly barked. "I remember." He leaned back in his chair, and pulled a cigar to his lips. Jones waited impatiently as the chief took a long, indulgent drag. *"Pheeeeew...."* He blew out the smoke from his lungs with a kind of contempt for the lieutenant. "So where is he?"

"Here in New York."

"He really that stupid ta' come back? What, is he trying to get caught?"

Jones shrugged. "I just hope the lead is solid. Got a call from down at the docks from someone who saw him an recognized him from the wanted poster. If it was him, won't be long before we close in."

Chief O'Reilly nodded. It would look good, this, catching his predecessors killer. Very good indeed. Just what he needed to get internal affairs off his ass about all the cops on the take. He took another long, patient drag. Cops sellin' out witnesses and suspects, not ta' mention takin' bribes. Hell, even he took home more money each week in a blank envelope than he did in a month's paycheck. One more drag. One more patient stare. "Let me know the second you've got him pinched."

Jones nodded. "Of course, sir."

O'Reilly scratched his neck. "Lieutenant, you're dismissed."

\* \* \* \* \* \* \* \*

They took a taxi cab up to the west end of Manhattan the following day. It was a warm June day, and everything was beautiful outside. Her hair was long again, gorgeous and red, wispy and soft and dangerously beautiful. She was wearing tight white pants that clung to every curve in just the right way, and a slinky red blouse that screamed ravishments. It was cruel to her husband, the way she was dressed. Maybe that's the way she wanted it. Jeb was dressed in a white collared shirt, a gray pin striped vest with a flower in the left breast pocket, and matching pants. He squeezed her hand and she dropped the cigarette she'd been dangling between her fingers. "You're sure you want to do this?" he asked.

She nodded. "It's ugly. But it has to be done."

"I suppose you're right," he said in agreement. A kind of choking silence carried through for a moment, and then…. "Shall we?" Her voice was clear. Conviction, that's what she had. They made their way up to her house. Up to the door: She rang the bell. Nothing. They waited. Then she rang it again. Still nothing.

"We should go," Jeb said quickly. "We can come back another time or we can-"

The door opened slowly.

"Olivia?"

"Colton."

He gasped, throwing his arms around his wife. "I thought you were dead!"

"I'm sorry," she whispered.

"Goodness." His lips quivered as he tried to formulate words. "H-H-How."

"That's not important, Colton."

"Where have you been?"

She looked up at him. "I'm sorry I couldn't reach you. But, it's complicated."

"…..Complicated?" He looked back and forth, between Jeb and Olivia. "Who… who is this?"

Olivia pulled away from him. "This is Jeb."

Jeb stood silent. A statue.

"Oh hi…" Colton Ostrum scratched his head. "I… Tell me this isn't. Oh Goodness, Olivia, don't tell me it's what I'm thinking it is…"

"It is," she said. She looked back at Jeb, and took his hand. "I'm sorry."

Colton just stood there. Didn't say a word. He brought down a few personal belongings, lovingly preserved in a jewelry box. "I'm really sorry," she said as she took the box in her hands and stepped out the front door and onto the scratchy brown welcome mat. Colton stood there in the doorway. He was a quiet man. He didn't scream or curse or call her a whore. He didn't fight Jeb or try to kill him. He just stood there. And when they left he went back into the kitchen and hugged his fiancé'.

"Who was that?" she asked.

Colton shrugged. "Nobody."

\* \* \* \* \* \* \* \*

### Hell's Kitchen

Pis Pin hovered over the furnace in the back corner of the filth glazed room, half a scrambled egg stuck to his beard. A knock at the door.

He turned towards the sound, a curious look on his face. He motioned towards Gaby Gahrgh, a five hundred and eight pound pimp with a penchant for bondage, and she thundered over to the door. "What you want?" The big black girl muttered through the metal slit in the door.

"Pis!" a craggy, not-quite-Irish voice shouted. "Is Pis here? Open the fucking door."

Pis Pin was a tall, scrawny man with a beard like a bee hive, and glasses thicker than most bottles. He wore white slacks with black polka dots like a Dalmatian, a yellow t-shirt ripe with grease stains, and a gray ascot. He ran his hand through oily hair and took a few steps forwards. "Who is it?"

"God damn, Pis, it's me, let me in!"

"Who are you?" Gaby said in a growl of a voice.

"The name, Madame, is Jack."

"Mean Jack?" Pis' voice was trembling.

"Yes, Mean-bloody-Jack! Now let me the fuck in!"

Pis looked suddenly scared, and hurried Gaby to unlatch the door.

"Finally!" Jack groaned. "Fuckin' colder out there than a witches' cunt."

"Er... Ok." Pis Pin muttered.

"Ugh, forget it, ya fag." He looked up and down Gaby, shuddered, and sat down on a nasty looking plaid easy chair. "Light," he said, snapping his fingers, and Pis fumbled in his coat for a blunt and a match, both of which he tossed to him. "Thank you kindly." Jack took a long, deep drag and leaned back. "That's the stuff fer stayin' cool on a hot day, ye' can keep yer' fuckin ice cream."

"A ha ha," Pis Pin laughed nervously. Very nervously.

Gaby looked over at him, a 'what the fuck is this?' look on her face. Pis made a wave of his hand. Silent for another few moments as the smoke poured out Mean Jack's mouth. "So," Pis asked finally. "What brings you back here... Uh... Jack."

Jack sucked on the tip of his blunt for a moment, wetting his lips with it before taking another inhale. "Reefer?"

"Uh. Yes, that's what that is."

"I know that! Reefer."

"Reefer?"

"Do you push it, dumbass."

"Oh!" Pis gasped. "Uh, yeah, yeah a' course." Jack nodded.

"Is that why you came here? You want in?"

"No, that's just curiosity." He took another drag. "I don't want in on your piss-poor lemonade stand of an operation, you dumb fuck, I'm here for revenge."

"Revenge?"

"That's right, sunshine, now you're gettin' it. Came all the way back here from Greece fer' the bastards, after I heard this is where they were headed."

A rush of warm air came in as another figure burst through the door. "Ooh, baby I could have you turnin more tricks than a damn magician." Gaby said to the girl as she entered the room.

"That's my daughter, you dumb whore!" Jack barked.

Gaby glared at him, her chubby hands ready to strangle him, crack his trachea like a biscotti.

"Easy now, Gaby." Pis stepped in. "Easy now."

"My daughter. June," said Jack.

"Lovely girl." Pis wheezed nervously, as he took in the chubby vision before him.

"About these men. I know you're gonna help me find um', Pis."

"Oh, of course, of course! Why Jack, you know I would do anything for you!"

"I know you will, Pis. I know you will."

Pis nodded quickly and bit his nail.

"Because you respect me, and because you owe me."

"I-I-I-I-I, uh, yeah that- that I do."

"After I made that whole mother situation a' yer's disappear."

"You did Jack, you did. You're a very good man. An upstanding citizen, I always said."

Mean Jack nodded. "That's right."

"So. Does- does he have a name, er, they have names?"

"Cutlass and Chamberlain."

"Did you just say what I think you said?" a rusty voice called out from the shadows. "*Jeb* Chamberlain?"

"That's right." Mean Jack called out to the figure in the unlit corner of the room. "Who the hell are you?"

Pis Pin spoke, as a tall, haggard figure in a cheap blue suit came out from the dark corner of the room, baring gruesome yellow teeth. "His name's Virtrolli. He used to work for that big shot, Cools McCreary, but he's all washed up now, so he come work fer' me."

"Jeb Chamberlain ruined my life," Virtrolli snarled. "If he's here- in my city. God, he is gonna pay!"

"So you hate him almost as much as I do?" Mean Jack smiled.

"Hate him? No. No, I don't hate him. I loathe him. I despise him. Jeb Chamberlain is the most miserable, God-forsaken pariah that I ever came across in my life. When I find him I'm gonna strangle him with his own intestines, and pull the scrotum up over his head. What I feel for him is far, far beyond hate. What I feel is so all encompassing that it's almost love."

Jack smiled. "I like the enthusiasm!"

# 66.

# DREAMLAND

### Dreamland Park, Coney Island, NY

They could have taken the train or drove there in a car, but most of them came by ferry. It was more romantic that way. That's how Jeb and Olivia came anyhow.

They said that it should have burned down twelve years ago, back in the spring of 1911□. They all knew the story of the fire. Workers had spilled hot tar inside of Hell Gate and of course it caught fire. For God's sakes, the ride was called Hell Gate, what did they expect, tempting fate like that? Somehow though they'd put it out before it spread any further. Somehow. The rumors that had become an urban legend. That a yellow eyed man, probably one of the side show freaks, had been the one to put the fire out and save the park. Rumors, and just that.

They said a lot of things. They said that it was the greatest fun park in the world. That its thrills were unmatched, that its pleasures were of a breed extinct in the outside world. Only here, they said, in Dreamland, could you still revel in the kind of fun that could kill you. Dangerous and exotic, but not too much so. Just enough they said, just enough danger so that it was thrilling without being too thrilling. That's what they thought.

Up the bowery along Surf Ave, past hot dog vendors, fortune tellers, phrenologists, head shrinkers, and milk bottle games. Cheap carnival prizes and side show grift, popcorn and hot corn and apples and pop. A big "Test Your Strength" game with a rubber mallet and a meter that went from '*Skinny Weakling*' to '*Hercules, Look Out!*' Smells of fried food feasts and unwashed masses. Fire swallowers, mechanical oddities, and sideshow freaks galore: The Lizard Lady of Anawassa, 'BIG' Tom Thunder, and 'tiny' Tom Thumb. The Headless Lady, the Invisible Man, the Harem Women of the East! Unholy delights for a curious people.

*Your mind won't believe what your eyes tell you is real!*

~A one of a kind, **EDUCATIONAL** spectacle, **NOT TO BE MISSED** by anyone from six to ninety six!~

*SPLENDORS* and *WONDERS* on loan from the *oriental* empire of *SIAM!*

# IT WILL KICK YOU.
# WITH EXCITEMENT!

**_Scientifically produced to delight all 5 modern senses_**!

*THE THRILL OF A LIFETIME!*

Do you dare to **SEE!** the strange and terrifying **DOG BOY** of Kuala Lumpor? **WATCH!** as **ZAZALON THE GREAT** performs death defying feats of sword swallowing to astound and bewilder the imagination? *Never before seen! All new!* Technicolor posters, barking barkers, wild women, and maniac midgets. Tents, wagons, stages and cages. **THE WORLDS -NEW- FATTEST WOMAN**: a moving mountain of flesh, and bone! *THRILL AS SHE DEVOURS AN ENTIRE WEDDING CAKE, BEFORE YOUR VERY EYES!*

Speaking of enormous women:

Gaby Gahrgh was standing near the back of the brown and purple warehouse, huffing reefer and looking not at all pleased. She was wearing a big chinchilla coat and six inch heals that chaffed her butter ball ankles. Pis was pointing to something in a crate, Mean Jack smiling at whatever it was. Virtrolli was there too, getting a blow job from one of the working girls while he cleaned his gun. Tyson Biggles appeared suddenly, casting a long shadow as he walked in through the rusty metal door. He looked at Virtrolli and flashed a grin.

"This is good." Jack smiled. "This is *real* good."

Pis made a little bowing gesture. "Only the best fer' you, pal."

Virtrolli let out a low moan of satisfaction, and the working girl wiped her mouth. Gaby looked over at him and rolled her eyes before taking another drag of reefer. There was a loud clattering noise as Jack pulled out a Thompson machine gun and tossed it to the midget. "Catch."

*"Ooof!"* Tyson wobbled a bit, struggling with the gun half his size. Jack laughed in a cruel way, and looked back inside the wooden crate.

"What's in there?" Virtrolli called out, as he pulled up his pants.

"Why don't you come over and see fer' yerself?" Mean Jack barked as he slid his hand through greasy hair. Gaby followed Virtrolli across the cement floor, gasping when she saw what was inside the crate.

\* \* \* \* \* \* \* \*

*"One, two, one two three four."* A band struck up a tune near the entrance to Dreamland Park. An old waltz played up like a jazz ditty. Sam had a big smile on his face, like a telegram, as he pushed past the gates below giant Beacon Tower, with its hundred thousand electric lights. The park was surrounded by massive white walls, like an old Roman city or a funhouse Harriramma. Water fountains, and fruit trees, and flowerbeds as far as the eye could see; mechanical swings and whirling inverters, and a magnificent dance hall as big as a football field. Jeb took her hand and they ran around the place like school kids. They rode the massive Shoot the Chutes over the sea wall and right into the ocean. He kissed her there on that little wooden boat, floating on the waves as a man with a pole pulled them up to the dock and hooked the boat

back onto the conveyor belt up the ramp. They rode the Whirl-and-Twirl, the Pirate ship, the Witching Waves. Jeb bought a bag of popped corn and he and Olivia sat at a bench under an apple tree to eat it while two great Dragon statues with electric light bulb teeth stared at them from the other side of the path.

Dreamland was the biggest, the most elaborate, the most wonderful and ingenious park in the world. In the last few years a number of improvements and new attractions had been added. There were the elaborate Hell Gate and Creation, obscenely complex creations, more magic shows than rides, that gave visitors a simulated tour through paradise or the inferno. There were the incubator babies, Midget City, and a new African village recreated with imported natives and authentic wild animals.

The best of all the new attractions was sprawling and full of splinters: The Queen Anne's Revenge was the biggest rollercoaster in the world. Built for the 1921 season to compete with Luna Parks Comet, Queen Anne was longer, faster, and meaner than any trick railway that had ever come before. The line stretched around for hours in the summertime, when kids would come in from the slums to escape life for a few thrilling moments. It creaked, and bellowed like the jungle animals in the recreated Congo below, duel trains careening up, down, and around over banked turns, and an oversized loop where last summer Carla Summers had fallen out onto the tracks. It wasn't the twenty foot fall that broke her neck, it was the train crashing into her. After that the ride was twice as popular.

Olivia screamed as they flipped upside down and then came back right side up, screamed again as they soared down the hundred-twenty-five foot drop that ran along the edge of the sea wall, looking out towards the ocean. They walked away shakily and headed for the Big Wheel, an unimaginatively named Ferris wheel brought across the Atlantic from the World's Fair Paris, twenty years earlier. Thousands of unlit electric lights clung to its metal frame, like dew in the mid-afternoon light. Beautiful topiaries lined the path up to it, filled with lilacs and daisies and tulips and red, red roses with thorns as thick as nails. Jeb and Olivia went up the elevator car and walked along the sea wall, looking out through penny telescopes at the view. They were more than a hundred feet up, only the massive beacon tower and the tip top of the Queen Anne soaring above them. Even the birds glided down below, picking at French fries and pretzel scraps on the boardwalk.

She leaned over coyly, whispering in his ear; the sea salt mist rising up around them, casting everything in a cool blue tranquility. "I'm happy. Right now, with you. I'm happy, Jeb."

"Me too," he said.

"Not feeling guilty today?" she asked.

"Nope."

"Then let's just forget about it all, you know? We'll just let it be me and you right here, right now. And we'll let ourselves be happy."

They kissed.

\* \* \* \* \* \* \* \*

Jones ran down the halls of the police station, bursting through the doors to the chief's office without knocking. "We got him!" he shouted with a big, stupid grin on his face, like he'd just won a pissing contest with the Sheik.

"Where?"

"Coney Island."

O'Reilly glanced at the cigar he held in hand. He tossed it into the ash tray. "Let's go."

\* \* \* \* \* \* \* \*

He took a deep breath as they made the gentle corner around the Canals of Venice, a tunnel of love that moralists had called debaucherous and sinful when it opened. A vulgarity emblematic of the 20th century.

Making out in the faux canals of faux Europe was all well and good, but what Jeb wanted was excitement. Something dangerous. As they left the ride she took his arm and they strolled along the path. "Wonder what Sam's doing?" she asked, and he shrugged. Captain Bonavita, the famous one armed lion tamer, was sharing the stage before them with Mabel Stark, sex goddess of the circus and a damned fine tiger trainer to boot. Jeb's mind flashed African memories as he heard the roar of the big cats clawing at air. The crack of whips, and the howling of beasts. Jeb looked over at one of Mabel's performing tigers up on stage and the big Bengal caught his gaze, uttering a low, guttural growl. A warning. That's what it was.

They turned the corner and Jeb looked up, his eyes not quite believing the massive structure of the Big Wheel, its supports on the ground a veritable Atlas. Jeb and Olivia got loaded into one of the squeaking blue and white metal cars and soared up and around the wheel, laughing and teasing each other as the ride paused at the top, offering an unparalleled view, not just of Coney, but the Big Apple in the distance, and the glittering blue sea before them. It was quiet and calm, the sun still up, about three in the afternoon. Children and tigers and barkers and waves called out far below. Romantic. That's what that was. *"Embrasse-moi, vous tromper,"* she said as she kissed him.

"What's that?"

"French."

"Ha!" he laughed. "Well ooh-la-la, how do ya' like that. And that's real French is it?"

*"Oui.* And don't you dare try any of your old tricks on me."

"Well I'll be damned." He put his arm around her shoulder and they looked out towards the sea, taking in the whole vastness of it.

"Jeb?"

"Yeah?"

She shifted in her seat as another couple loaded into one of the carriages down below and they started moving again. "You remember once you asked me what I would do with all the money in the world?"

*"Mmm-hmm."*

"And then you said, well are you gonna ask me, and I said, well, I will eventually, when you have something more than a snaky remark on the tip of your tongue and that way you'll have time to really think about it."

"I remember."

*"Well?"*

"Well what?"

"All the money in the world, Jeb. What would you do with it?"

Jeb looked at her, his gaze steady. "You know I've been thinking about this for a long time."

She smiled and kissed the edge of his lips. "Tell me what you want."

"Well I used to have a really wild, elaborate answer about speedboats and white wine and wild Parisian parties,' he said with a smile. "It was really great, trust me. It was clever and funny, and it had all sorts of exotic details and outlandish expenditures. I had this whole scenario worked up about renting a riverboat in the Louisiana bayou and throwing extravagant Mardi Gras parties that would make you blush. But the honest answer, Olivia.... the honest answer isn't funny, it isn't clever, and it isn't expensive. The honest answer is that at this point, after all the shit we've been through, after all the wild, death defying situations and danger and close calls, after all the pain, and all the fuck ups, and all the things I've messed up, I just wanna go to the beach and lay in the sand with you and eat curly fries. I wanna relax, and I wanna listen to the ocean, and I don't wanna feel guilty about anything anymore." He took her hand. "I love you, Olivia, and I want you to trust me again."

"I do trust you, Jeb," she whispered.

"I just want some cool adventures with a jazzy, brilliant English girl who likes to wrestle in the sand, and make out in exotic locales. Can I buy that?"

"You can try," she said.

He smiled, and in his eyes was that wild, devil may care look he had the very first time he lay eyes on her. Olivia stared at him for the longest time as the wheel turned down, and the operators opened their car at the bottom to let them out. She smiled. "We should get married."

# 67.

# DESCENT

The half dozen police cruisers pulled up silently onto Surf Ave: They didn't wanna scare off their prey. Chief O'Reilly stepped out onto the bowery, a short Cuban cigar clinging to his bottom lip. He looked over at Jones with a look of contempt. "Is the guy who tipped you off, this 'Sam Ammatto', as good as his word?"

*"He better be."* Jones muttered, as he squinted into the distance and pulled out a cigarette.

Across the street five gangsters were stepping out of a long black sedan. Pis looked over at the fuzz, whispered something like, 'fuck', and handed June the cello case with the Tommy gun in it. Mean Jack Fin stared at the cops as he talked to Pis. "I thought your informant at the station said we'd have a half hour jump on the pigs?"

"….I don't know." Piss said uneasily. "…I don't know-"

"Stop saying that!"

"Things must have moved along quicker than he anticipated."

"Son of a bitch."

"Well you're not still going through with it, are you?"

"Of course I am!" he growled. "Nobody fucks with mean Jack. *Capish?* Nobody. And I'll be damned if ima' let the pigs get this guy before I do. I need him to tell me where Gregor Cutlass is hiding."

"And I need him to pay for the death of my crew," Virtrolli snarled, as he stepped out of the back of the car, black clam shell cello case in hand.

"Good luck," Pis said warily, his eyes darting between the squad of blue trench coated police and the entrance to Dreamland.

"Hey!"

Pis gasped, his eyes flying to the hand on his shoulder.

June Finn stared down her nose at him. "Keep her warm fer' me."

Pis nodded shakily, and sat back down in the Sedan.

* * * * * * * *

*"Sooo,"* he said playfully, as they marched down the terrace towards Creation and Hell Gate. "Now that we're getting married, does this mean we have to give each other silly pet names?"

"Oh God, I hope not!" she laughed.

"He kissed her again. "Are we insufferably cute?"

"Right now? Probably. Why, is that what the world is saying about us?"

Dennis Badeau

"I'm afraid so," he said.

"Well you know what?" she said.

"What dear?" he asked.

"Fuck the world."

"My feelings exactly."

They kissed, his hand reaching up, holding the side of her face, caressing her cheek. *"Fuck all of 'um,"* she whispered.

"Oh, I like the way you just said that," said Jeb.

"The word like is so tepid."

"I love the way you said that."

*"Fuck?"* she asked.

"Fuck," he replied.

*"Mmm...* has a nice ring to it I suppose. It's a bit dirty. A bit risqué."

"There you go with that French talk again. That's supposed to be my shtick."

She smiled coyly and looked up and down his face. He met her gaze and lifted up her chin, angling his head down slowly. Their lips a breath away, someone called out his name.

"JEB?"

"Huh?"

"Oh my God, Jeb, old boy, it's really you!" Sam came running towards them, his arms outstretched.

"Who else would it be?" Jeb asked.

Sam was beaming as he came closer. Suddenly he froze. "Olivia?"

"Uh, Sam?"

His expression was shattered. "...you're alive?"

She looked taken aback. "What the hell, Sam?"

He hugged her, squeezing her tightly. "You're alive! You're alive!"

"You look different, did you change your clothes?" Jeb asked.

"Oh my God!" Sam let go of her, big sobbing tears running down his cheeks.

"Sam where have you been?" Olivia asked.

"Where have I been? Where have you been!? God Jeb, I felt so bad, you don't know how many times I regretted leaving you there on that runway after everything we'd been through together. Tell me, where's Cutlass? Where's Elizabeth?"

"Elizabeth?" Olivia's face went violent red. *"What the hell, Sam?"*

"What?" Sam looked confused, like he'd been sucker punched. He was about to speak when Jeb gasped at something behind him. *"No way."* Olivia looked at the impossible sight. It was Sam. Not the Sam standing in front of them, but a second, duplicate Sam, standing out in the middle of the crowd. It was him. They were both him. The Sam that was closer looked back and forth between Jeb, Olivia, and his double. The other Sam stopped and walked over to them. "That's me," he said.

"Who are you?" Sam asked.

"I'm me."

"No you're not, I'm me."

"Then who am I?" asked Sam.

"That's the question."

Jeb looked between the two of them. "You don't have a twin, do you?"

"No." They both answered at the exact same time. "You look just like... me."

"Right..." Jeb muttered. Taking a step back, he pulled Olivia towards him.

"My name is Sam." They both said at exactly the same moment. "I don't know who this is- but-" It was the most surreal thing, like looking into a mirror and not recognizing yourself. A small crowd gathering around them now, perplexed looks on the strangers faces.

"Who are you?" The first Sam whispered to the second. He reached out and touched his own hand, and yet it wasn't his own hand.

The second leaned in closer, grabbed the hand. "I'm Sam Ammatto."

He pulled back. "No you're not, I'm Sam Ammatto!"

One of the Sams grinned.

"How did we get here today?" asked Jeb. "You-you seem different. You don't seem to know what's going on."

"We took the ferry."

"I took the train."

"We were all staying up at the Nora Jane Hotel," said one of the Sam's.

"No we weren't. *We* haven't seen each other, Jeb and I, since Egypt," said the other. "I didn't even know Olivia was alive! What are you?"

"I'm me."

"No, I'm me. What does that make you?"

Sam smiled, leaned over to the other Sam, whispered into his ear, "things are about to get very ugly for us now. You'll see."

He pulled back, stared at himself. "What are you talking about?"

"You'll see." He grinned. "You'll see."

Olivia clung to Jeb. "Jeb I'm scared."

"Yeah." He nodded. "That makes two of us."

"The police know you're here, Jeb," said one of the Sams.

"What?"

"Look for yourself."

"Oh my God." Jeb could see more than a dozen cops, armed to the teeth, marching towards him. Their eyes met, his, and O'Reilly's. It was on. "We have to run. Now," Jeb whispered. He looked back and forth between the two identical Sam's one more time. "Is this really happening?"

One of the Sam's closed his eyes. He grinned, his lips curling up like a politician.

"What are you smiling at?" Jeb asked.

About a dozen feet away was a group of four cello players. No. Not cello players. Virtrolli cracked open his black clamshell, dropped it, and hoisted up the machine gun.

**"BRRRAT-A-TAT-A-TAT-TAT!"**

The bullets hit one of the Sam's and he burst into flames, his eyes pouring out smoke as they turned a hideous shade of yellow. He began to laugh, stumbling backwards he fell onto the carousel, setting it ablaze, the dry wooden structure going up in seconds.

His curved lips whispered, *"Welcome to Hell,"* as his face morphed from Sam to Jeb to Cutlass and then to something unrecognizable, his yellow eyes the only constant.

Virtrolli froze, stunned at the human inferno. "Why are there two of them?"

"Who gives a fuck?" Mean Jack sneered. "I need Jeb alive. Kill the rest."

The whole crowd of the park was screaming bloody murder, rampaging wildly. The cops ran forwards, pulling out their own guns, but the fire was spreading and the crowd was mad and Dreamland was done for.

# 68.
# THE LAST INFERNO

The fire consumed everything.

Jeb dove out of the way of a falling beam from the 'Air Ships' ride, the burnt carcass horses of the apocalypse spinning slowly around the carrousel, a warped version of "Maple Leaf Ragtime" still playing on the organ. Sam was nearby. The other Sam, not the one who had burst into flame and whose face had shifted from being one person to being several others.

There was a massive explosion as one of the gas generators caught fire and went up in smoke. The cops and the gangsters were battling it out as Jeb grabbed Sam, ringing his neck. "Who are you? What are you?"

"I'm just me! I'm me!"

"Well then who was that thing? That other Sam, who combusted when the bullets hit him?"

"I don't know!" he said as he struggled against Jeb's grip.

Jeb dropped him. "Fine. But which one are you?"

Sam rubbed his neck. "What do you mean?"

"Are you the Sam who saved me and Olivia from those skeletons, or are you the Sam who left me at Cairo and never came back."

"That one. The one who didn't come back."

"Well then who the fuck did? Who was that, if he wasn't you?"

Sam shook his head.

"We don't have time." Olivia grabbed Jeb. "I don't know if that's Sam standing there or not, but we have to get out of here." A bullet whizzed by her head. "NOW!"

They bolted past the flames, Jeb turning back only for a moment to shout at Sam, "You coming?"

Sam just stood there, trying to unravel all that was happening. An impossible task. "Right behind you."

Red at the edges, then orange and bright gleaming white at the center. Yellow streaks poking through, crackling like sun beams. It was the battlefields of France, it was the furnace in the hold of the She Wolf, it was the air ship SS Landa hurtling through the air and crashing into the ground. It was the last inferno before Hell. It was the day that Dreamland died.

June pulled a grenade from her belt and lobbed it at the cops, sending a clump of them flying up into the air like dirt. O'Reilly and his men shot back, blowing out Mean Jack's head like a smashed coconut.

Virtrolli was right behind them now. He'd pushed past the main firefight and was closing in. "JEB!? JEB CHAMBERLAIN!?" The fire gleamed in his vengeful, lunatic eyes as he ran. Red, and orange shadows crossing his face as he ducked falling beams from the crumbling 'Air Ships' ride, and fired into the air. "WHERE ARE YOU?"

Jeb grabbed a pistol from one of the downed cops, leaned out from behind the supports of the Queen Anne's Revenge, and fired at Virtrolli.

"IS THAT ALL YOU'VE GOT?" The gangster sneered, firing back with his Thompson. The burning wood supports of the roller coaster splintered into ash as the bullets hit them, the mighty wooden leviathan, Queen Anne, groaning and straining like a dying beast of burden as it began to crumble. One of the trains still on the track ran screaming down and flew off the melted rails, soaring through the air like an avenging angel before it tumbled down head first, smashing into Virtrolli on the ground. His hand fell limply to his side, body flattened out like a pancake under the burning, six hundred pound weight of it.

The fire was as wild and untamed as a typhoon, if not more so, as it spread across the park, engulfing Dreamland in grainy plumes of smoke and ash. Lions with manes of fire charged out screaming, Mabel rushing to Bonavita's side as a stray bullet hit him whilst he was trying to save his cats. Jeb gripped Olivia's hand as tight as he could and pulled her through the smoking row of collapsed amusement rides and charred bodies. A bullet grazed his arm, and he turned, firing off blindly until his clip was empty.

**"POW! POW! POW!"**

"Fuck!" he screamed, and threw the gun into the fire. There was a great lurching sound, and suddenly everything that was left of the world's biggest rollercoaster collapsed, rocking the earth like an earthquake as it hit. The smoke blew out, black, blinding Jeb, filling his lungs. He coughed, choked, stumbled, hitting his head on a fallen support beam, his shirt catching fire, he screamed and tore it off, threw it aside.

"There's no way out! There's no way out!" Sam shouted from somewhere in the black haze.

There was a magnificent crash as the giant Beacon Tower, crown jewel of Coney, went up in flame and collapsed to the ground, its hundred thousand electric glass light bulbs bursting like kernels. The sound of bullets had stopped now. The screaming hadn't.

Jeb stared into Olivia's terrified eyes. "Are you Ok?" She shook her head no. The edges of her white and blue lace dress were singed, turned black and yellow-brown. Her cheeks ash gray, mouth bleeding as she hacked up smoke. "I'm not gonna lose you again," he said, "I won't let that happen." Jeb turned back and ran into the fire, his hands burning as he tore a hole in the black wood wall of collapsed coaster that surrounded them. "COME ON!" he shouted, his hands blistering as the three of them crawled through and made their escape to the other side. They could see it now; The Wings of Eros were burning, the Chutes were burning, the Waves were burning, all Creation was burning.

Black and red demon Lucifer, the figure that sat atop the entrance to Hell Gate, broke off, his vast, reptilian wings shattering into a thousand bits of broken plaster, his thorny red skull bursting into flame, glass eyes melting into goo. Hell Gate was burning. The

Devil was burning. His pitchfork toppled, cutting Sam and Olivia off from Jeb.

"Jeb!" Sam called. "Are you ok?"

"I'll manage!" he groaned from somewhere in the black ash haze. "Is Olivia safe?"

"I'm fine," she called out. "We can see the exit from here!"

"Go. Go on ahead. I'll meet-" Jeb began to cough violently. "I'll meet you at the exit."

"No, Jeb, no!" Olivia cried. "We can't split up!"

"Make her go with you," Jeb coughed as he ordered Sam, "make sure she's safe."

The face of the forty foot white Aphrodite statue guarding the gardens and boat rides of Creation had now become a bonfire. Her hands into torches, breasts become holocausts, the gardens at her feet now blooming black, greasy smoke. Jeb climbed over the collapsed pitchfork, trying to make his way towards the exit. The dragons crumbled, the Spinning Gears stopped, the House of Unimagined Ecstasy and it's collection of a thousand wonders was made an incinerator. Fire alarms were ringing, drowning out the panicked screams. The white walls of the park went up like a forest, the fire spreading out onto the boardwalk, out to the Freak Shows and vendors and try your luck games galore. The tattooed man and the bearded lady indivisible as they clutched each other, burning, melting inside their show cages, which no one had bothered to unlock. Like the Siamese twins, like the human cannonball stuck inside his cannon.

He was close to the exit now, close enough to taste bits of sea breeze within the particles of smoke. And then it happened. Jack. Mean Jack. He stepped out in front of the exit like a troll, like a gate keeper, like a bastard-- which is what he was. His face was gleaming with sweat and ash, black suit burned, torn up like an old rag. He pulled the trigger on the gun but nothing happened. Out of bullets, he sneered, tossed the Tommy aside, and pulled out a pistol. Raised it, pointed it at Jeb as Jeb ran towards him and tackled him to the ground. They struggled for the gun, each one with madness in his eyes, desperation written across his face--

**POP!**

Mean Jack flopped backwards into the fire, his mouth agape, bleeding, as the bullet blew straight through the back of his neck, just missing his spine. Jeb stood there, watching him as he writhed around in the flame, his flesh going black, boiling and bubbling up like the worst nightmare he'd ever had. He was burning up like Salid, like Elizabeth, like Dreamland.

The flames hadn't stopped. They were growing closer. Jeb turned away from burning Jack and towards escape. The ocean was glistening behind him, smoke casting a pall across it. He didn't see that Mean Jack was still twitching on the ground. That he was still breathing. Jeb opened his eyes and drank in the ocean.

*And then it happened.*

Jeb gasped as Mean Jack shambled up from the ground behind him, plunging a knife through Jeb's back. Jeb gagged as the knife came out through his chest. Spun around to find Jack standing there laughing. *Laughing!* Jeb looked down at his chest and the red blood covering his hand like paint as he sank to the ground.

Jeb tried to raise his head but it felt too heavy. Tried to stand up on trembling legs but they felt too weak. He thought back to earlier that day. Up on the Ferris Wheel, when he'd made his confession, and she'd said, *"Let's get married,"* and everything felt right. And everything.... The sunlight in her hair, soft and red, golden yellow light, the prettiest laugh, the prettiest girl. He was getting cold now.

NO! He pounded his fist on the ground. Screamed up at God or whoever would hear him. Screamed! Dragged his hands across the dirt like claws, ripping out the earth. Teeth bared, eyes squeezed shut. Memories. A million memories dripping in his gut like stones. He couldn't let it end like this. Not when he was so close! "I'm gonna rip your guts out, and shove um' down your throat like stuffing," Jeb said, as he forced himself to stand.

Jack snickered.

"You think that's funny? Huh? You laughing at me, you sick bastard? Laugh at this, do ya' hear me, Jack? I'm gonna make the last moments of your short fucking life as miserable as humanly fucking possible, *Ok?!* I'm gonna make you beg for death, and when it comes you'll wish you hadn't!"

He shrugged. "But I'm not Mean Jack." Suddenly his face began to whir and melt, dissolving into something else. Now he was Sam. "Look familiar?"

"Who are you?"

"I'm Sam," he said with a smile, and again his face melted into something different. "I'm Cutlass."

"What are you?"

"Maybe I'm your father." His face turned into that of Jim Chamberlain. More melting, more twisting and whirring. The features of his face dissolving, reshaping themselves like clay, tiny bumps, tiny invisible fingerprints molding him, painting his skin a new color, his body changing too, his voice. And now- "I could even be her." His face and body changed, and now the shape shifter looked just like Olivia.

*"You bastard."*

"What's the matter, Jeb?" it said in a voice exactly like hers. "Don't you love me anymore?"

Jeb's body was cold and shaking. "What are you?"

The face morphed again. This time it was a pale, ancient man with yellow eyes. "You already know exactly who and what I am."

"That face isn't ringing any bells," said Jeb, the knife wound in his back bleeding profusely.

The shapeshifter let out a shrill, riotous laugh. "It was I who saved you from those skeletal traitors in Paraxous before they could use you to their own end. I'm the one who delivered the antidote to Olivia and freed her mind, the one who pulled you out of the ocean when you tried to kill yourself, and released you from the fog of the mushroom church in the first place." His face and body molded itself like clay and he became Salid. "I was the one who found you on the beach, Jeb. That was me. It's always been me. You should respect me for what I've done for you, Jeb. You should love me."

*"Love you?"*

"As one loves a God," he said, as the fires raged around him, the exit almost completely cut off by flame now, the air greasy, impenetrable.

Jeb squinted his eyes, barely making out the dim, wicked figure in the smoke before him. "Salid? Is it really you?"

He smiled. "One and the same."

"Cutlass talked about you."

He laughed. "I'm sure he did."

"I'm gonna hurt you," said Jeb.

Salid smiled. "You will try."

Jeb ran at Salid, his fist failing to connect as the shapeshifter dodged his blow and knocked him to the ground. He beat and kicked Jeb until he couldn't breathe, then turned and ran towards the fire.

Jeb pushed up against the ground, desperately trying to stand. "Get back here!"

\* \* \* \* \* \* \* \*

"What in the God damned hell happened back there?" said O'Reilly, his face red, sweaty and terrified.

Jones looked down.  He could hear the fire engines coming now.  Bells going crazy, sirens wailing.  "I don't know.  I don't know."

"You don't know?!"  O'Reilly grabbed him by his collar and shook him.  "I just lost five cops! Dreamland up in smoke!"

"I-I-I don't know!" he gulped.

"This is a God damned disaster!"  He dropped Jones to the ground and turned, walking away from the fire, one hand wiping the sweat from his face, the other up to his mouth, where he bit his nails.  Chewed on the edges of them till they got rough and broke off. "They'll have my head for this.  They'll have my head."

\* \* \* \* \* \* \* \*

Feet pounded across the bubbling pavement, fire licking at his heels as he pushed through the burning maze of gardens, away from the exit and back into the heart of the park.  Every inch of his body was numb. Every bit of him like cold plastic, like it didn't feel real, like he wasn't even there, like it wasn't really happening.  Felt like one of those dreams where everything goes tingling and numb and you can't move, but there's a car coming, and you know if you don't move it's gonna hit you.  But this was no dream.

"You'll never catch me!"  Salid laughed from somewhere up ahead in the black fog.  "You'll never catch me!"

Jeb leapt over the remains of a collapsed chairlift, madly chasing after the voice. There it was. The Big Wheel, not far up ahead. It had stopped spinning, but it creaked and bellowed all the same. At least a dozen passengers were still trapped on it, three hundred feet up in the air. Somebody jumped, the smoke and the noise too much for them. Jeb screamed as they splattered onto the ground beside him. The bolts snapped, the fire melting them at the seems. The shadowy figure of Salin Salid leapt up onto the Wheel, grabbing the spokes like a ladder as he pulled himself up and began to climb his way to the top. "Just come and get me, Jeb, if you think you're man enough!"

Jeb looked up. With a groan he climbed up onto the operators booth, and from there leapt onto the Wheel.

The steel was so hot it felt like pressing his palms onto a frying pan. He climbed, steam coming off of him as he chased after the yellow eyed assassin.

Another scream as someone else jumped off the ride. A dull thud as they hit the ground.

Jeb scurried up the spokes. Closer. Madness in his heart. Closer. Closer. Numb, dense, high-pressurized madness. He was nearing the top of the Big Wheel now, his hand slipping off the spokes, flailing out in the air as he tried to regain his balance.

"It's over!" Salid sneered, appearing out of nowhere as he pressed the heel of her boot down onto Jeb's other hand. "Time to go to Hell."

Jeb screamed as his feet slipped, struggling to get a grip on the melting steel carnival ride. The knife again! Salid swung, splitting open Jeb's free hand. He twisted his heel, smiling as he listened to the cracking of the bones in Jeb's hand. The blood poured out. It was slippery. It ran down his arm and blew into his face as Salid twisted his foot down again.

Jeb screamed as his crushed hand slipped out from under Salid's heel, and he toppled down to earth. One last scream before the whole Ferris Wheel broke apart and shattered to the ground, throwing up a mound of smoke and dust that could be seen from miles away. And he fell. And he fell.

# 69.

# THE BLACK ORB

The black orb at the center of it was its rulers dark heart: Colder than ice and so black that it swallowed up the light around it, it lay in the middle of a frozen lake with the body of a fallen angel, feeding on the spent sins of mortal souls and casting them into the despair of nothingness for all time.

Jeb fell. He fell into the mouth of it, into the pit of Hell. Fire and brimstone and more horror than rational minds could hope to conceive. The denizens of Hell hissed at him. They had hairless red skin, wrinkled faces with eyes sewn shut and lipless mouths whose teeth collapsed into each. They were kings and ministers and thieves and murderers. Rapists whose scrotums had been hollowed out and filled with sawdust, their skin made into a kind of green paste that slopped off and fell to the ground in puddles of puss. Fanatics and heathens and faux holy men. Murderers whose bodies had become prisons, whose flesh had become twisted into tiny sculptures of the heads and bodies of their victims. Victims on their arms and on their eye balls, screaming, reliving their deaths over and over and over again for all time. Their pain, and the pain of those who lost them, burrowing itself deep into the murderer's ghoulish flesh. Thieves for whom everything was given and then taken away. Misers forced to live alone for all eternity in tiny rooms filled only with vapid, material things. There were the gluttons, the traitors, the heresiers, the robber barons. Everything and everyone burning forever without a sun or a moon or seasons to give rest.

Demonic white creatures with horns made of bone and faces carved out of teeth walked around on all fours with their genitals hanging out of their shoulder blades. They cried and bemoaned their wretched existence as they fed on the flesh of the wicked and the damned. They had teeth covered in caramel yellow veneers, eyes made of dust, hands knotted up into bulbous balls of flesh, and skeletal wings that jutted from their backs.

And there was ZanaZaleem, the lieutenant of Hell. His face a mutilated sex organ, he paraded around the fiery underworld in a headdress of dead children, whipping the sinners with his chain of despair. His feet were the opposite of human feet, just as Hell was the opposite of Heaven. Instead of that ethereal feeling of peace, here there was only agony. Only twisted nightmares that tore at the minds of the sinners like tiny wasps crawling around their brains, eating their minds alive- bugs burrowing into the synapses and turning all but one decent memory into sawdust, so that they were left only with the horrors and their crimes. They let them keep one good memory, always just out of reach, so that they could remember what it felt like. So that they could appreciate just how far they'd fallen.

Lucifer laughed as they chained Jeb up and led him down into the frozen lake at the ninth circle of Hell. Down where the heads of Judas, Omari, and Vlad were forever devoured, each one conscious in one of the mouths of the three headed beast.

"I don't belong here!" Jeb cried. "I have seen Heaven!"

"And now," the beast smiled, "you have seen Hell." The lake of fire flew at him and he found himself lying on the ground, the hulking metal wreck of the Big Wheel next to him. He coughed, the fire spreading up his leg. He screamed and snuffed it out, screamed as he saw the long black burn. There were men running towards him. Men he didn't know. But at least he was alive.

*Alive.*

He felt at his chest and realized it was healed. The words seemed impossible even as they took shape in his mouth. "Still alive."

Dennis Badeau

# 70.
# LOCKED UP

**One Month Later**

Sam was sitting in a bent, uncomfortable folding chair in the middle of his one room apartment. There was a pull out bed in the wall and a communal sink and toilet down the hall. Sam's eyes were closed but his ears were open to every sound.

The squeak of a mouse skittering across the floor. A bag being dropped down the hall. Two people fucking in the apartment three floors up. The walls were like paper. Outside, in the ghetto of Harlem, he could hear jazz.

"Doppelganger," he whispered to himself.

There was only one light in the dim Harlem room, a single bulb that dangled from the ceiling. On the floor there was a brown suitcase filled with clothes, and a half dozen or so empty glass bottles. Sam stood up and made his way to the corner of the small room where a broken mirror with a long, thin crack across it showed his split reflection as he pulled a cigarette out from his back pocket, and struck a match against the wall. Deep, breathy intake. *"....Pheeew..."*

He turned, suddenly, as he heard a knock at the door.

497

\* \* \* \* \* \* \* \*

The cell opened up and the lawyer stepped inside. He wore a slick brown suit, and his hair was gray and curled like a wave like a man much younger than himself might have. His nose was crooked, eyes glittering black pearls that betrayed a cool intelligence. He raised a thin finger to the side of his cheek in a way that suggested meticulousness and calculation. Every twitch of his lip or turn of his head seemed labored somehow.

"Tomorrow's the big day," said Jeb.

"We just need to go over a few final things," said Sol.

"What kind of things?" Jeb asked.

"Well... I've been going over our defense, trying to build up you're character, make you likeable, that sort of thing. Unfortunately your past's not making it easy."

"Oh?" said Jeb.

"The great state of New York frowns on bootlegging."

"It was exciting work and it paid well. Hell, everyone was gonna drink one way or another, I figured I might as well run the stuff."

"Yes, why not? What is the law anyhow, to a man like you? For God's sake, you've already got a record. Is there any way we can sell it as a sob story? Say you needed money for a sick mother or orphans or something?"

Jeb shook his head. "Afraid not. Haven't seen the old lady in years."

Sol sighed. "You say you didn't start the fire at Dreamland, fine. But you did kill the chief of police. You can't deny that."

"Yeah, that's right, that's right I killed him. But it was in self-defense! The whole thing was an accident, I swear!"

"Sure it was. And it was an accident you were banging his wife like letters on a typewriter."

"That was a mistake. I admit that. Say, whos side are you on, anyhow?"

Sol shrugged. "Considering the circumstances, I still say you should just confess and plead insanity. Throw yourself on the mercy of the court."

Jeb shook his head.

"Damn it, you don't have a choice!" Sol snapped. "They want blood, Jeb, and you're expendable. The fire at Dreamland has been a disaster. Somebody has to go down for this."

"Somebody being me."

"Plead guilty, avoid the circus of a trial, and they might give you life. With that and a little luck and good behavior you just might see the sun again before you turn eighty. Look, I got other clients and time is money. When you come to your senses, and you're ready to deal, let me know. Anything else, sit on it."

"You have got to be the worst lawyer I've ever seen."

"Please kid, no jokes, I've heard um all."

Jeb sighed. "Fine. Fine, I'll do it."

\* \* \* \* \* \* \* \*

## 11th District City Court, New York City

"Order, order!"   There was a great shuffling noise in the court, the judge's gavel pounding wildly, press, jury, and ruberneckers straining for a better look at the defendant.   "I said, order!"   Judge Chesterfield bellowed, and for a moment all fell silent.   Then it started up again.   Chesterfield, dressed in dark black robes with white cotton trim and an orange walrus mustache, banged the gavel again as someone snapped a picture, the bulb exploding like a firecracker. "Bailiff, get him out of here!"   He ruffled his feathers indignantly.   "I said no pictures!"

Jeb was standing in the defendant's box of the wild, kangaroo court.   His lawyer, the slender Sol Atkins stood next to him, a sneer written across his face.   He poked Jeb's side and leaned over to whisper in his ear.   "Welcome to the zoo, kid."

Jeb gulped, nodding solemnly.   "Are we staring out of the cages, or looking in?"

Chesterfield's gavel pounded out in rapid succession like a rat-ta-tat machine gun.   His voice was growing hoarse as he screamed, "Shut up, you clowns!"

Again, silence fell over the court.   This time it lasted.

"Bout' time," he grumbled.   "Jeb Chamberlain, you are charged with arson and murder in the 1st degree, how do you plead?"

Every eye in the court zoomed over and parked itself on Jeb. He took a deep breath, thinking about what his lawyer had said. He thought about the craziness around him, the circus of newspapermen and radio gonzos. Betty was sitting near the back of the room, ready to testify against him. He wanted to talk to her, tell her how sorry he was for getting her into this mess. He caught her gaze and she turned away sheepishly: Poor kid. Jeb's lawyer nudged him, the judge glaring down from behind the pulpit. Jeb stood and cleared his throat. "Guilty. Guilty, your honor."

A flurry of gasps rose up from the crowd, the sudden click-clack of the stenographer's machine filling the air. "Order! Order!" Chesterfield pounded his gavel. Jeb looked over at Atkins. The thin lawyer winked at him. "Good job," he whispered, and then, leaning over to speak into the microphone: "Your honor, my client throws himself upon the mercy of the court. His crimes were the product of a disturbed mind. The wild fever dreams of a madman. But that is not the man you see here before you today, your honor. Before you today is a new man; a man who is deeply regretful of his crimes, who is repentant, and remorseful, and ready to pay his debt to society. Your honor, with all due respect, we ask that you sentence my client immediately and give him the chance to repay the kindness and forgiveness of the people of New York. Your honor, as a man of faith and an American citizen, I implore you to listen to the better angels of your nature and spare this man's life. Allow him to serve out the fullest sentence of the law in a place where they can help him with his afflictions. Help him to someday, in fifty or sixty years, rejoin society a better and more productive citizen of this great state. Give him that chance, your honor. If not for him, then for we the people. Use him to prove to just what depths of compassion the great people of this state and this republic are capable of."

"Are you finished, Mr. Atkins?"

"Ahem. Indeed I- Yes. Yes, the defense rests, your honor."

Judge Chesterfield groaned, his eyes tightening. "Finally, you blustering, bloviating, liberal windbag! Listening to you talk is like putting my ear up to a nun's backside, and letting her rip a wet fart. And only half as entertaining."

"Your honor?"

"I'm not finished. Furthermore, your client, Mr. Jeb Chamberlain, is one of the most blatantly heinous and unremorseful defendants I have ever seen in my long and illustrious thirty years on the bench. Thirty years of murderers, drunkards and thieves, and not once- not ONCE, before have I ever suffered the feeling in the pit of my stomach of knotting illness and sick churning, that I feel looking at you. Yes, you, Jeb Chamberlain, if that is your real name. Because I mean, *really*. Jeb? That can't be a real name, that just can't be. Jeb sounds like the air whooshing out of my ass when I take a ferocious shit. Are you sure that's your real name? Are you sure it's not Jebediah, or Jebezekial, or some other middle-of-nowhere bible thumping bullshit? Honest to God, Mr. Chamberlain,

Mr. *Jeb* Chamberlain, you make me sick. How dare you come here and plead guilty, and expect mercy from this court. How dare you. Where do you get the nerve to come into my courtroom and admit to killing a beloved police chief, burning down our cherished Coney Island in an inferno that has claimed almost two dozen lives and cost millions of dollars in damages. I loved Dreamland. I used to take my son there on Sundays and go swimming out in the sea. Well now it's gone. You've gone and broke it. How dare you come here with that blood on your hands and expect a handout, you sniveling piece of garbage.

"You have blood on your hands, Mr. Chamberlain, cold, messy, crimson blood. And for that you will pay." He leaned back and straightened his starched white collar. "It is the ruling of this court that you shall be executed. Capital punishment shall be carried out as expeditiously as possible, and preferably in whatever way which shall cause the most severe amount of bodily pain. Since hanging has a certain kind of romantic, Wild West flair, and execution by firing squad is out of style, I eagerly suggest that you be given the chair, especially when one considers that an electric funeral should elicit the greatest possible scream."

Jeb stood gaping at the blustery, red faced judge. His lips tried to form words but nothing worth hearing came out. The judge leaned over the pulpit and smiled. "Buh-Bye."

Suddenly the air came rushing up his windpipe. He realized at last the severity of what was happening. "NO! NO!"

"Take him away!" Judge Chesterfield roared. The press in the room became wild apes, storming the front of the court as two burly, anchor armed cops in blue came up and grabbed Jeb from behind. He struggled to fight them off as they twisted his arms and slapped on the cuffs. "Come on, move!" The one on the left grunted, as they shoved Jeb through the throng of gawkers and newspapermen. Bright yellow light streamed like a spotlight as they burst open the great wooden doors and stepped out onto the marble steps of the court. Jeb was trying to tear away from them, fight the pigs off, but they were too strong. He screamed, "fuck you!" as he saw the paddy wagon parked at the bottom of the steps, that would take him to the state prison. "NO! FUCK YOU, NO!"

*"Jeb! Jeb! Over here! -Jeb! What's it feel like to know you're gonna get the chair? -Do you feel you had a fair trial? -How does it feel to be the most hated man in America? - Give us a headline for the kids, Jeb, give us a quote for your obituary!"* The reporters clamored all at once, poking him in the rips with microphones and big, blocky camera's with exploding bulbs that shattered, spraying little bits of glass and phosphorous into his eyes. "OUTA' THE WAY!" The cops yelled as they pushed past them, and somebody pulled open the back door of the paddy wagon. "No! No!" Jeb could see the dark belly of it now. Could see his life flashing before his eyes.

Could see Olivia in his mind's eye. Was she watching all this right now?

**Kaboom.**

The police wagon flew up into the air like a cardboard box as the pipe bomb exploded underneath it. The fire blew back Jeb and the two cops, knocking all three on their asses, though luckily there was no one inside. The newspapermen screamed as the big, red fist of a fireball spun up, carrying the paddy wagon skyward for a moment, before dropping it back to the ground with a thunderous crash.

A burly, purple tattooed hand slammed across the first cops jaw. Another punch and the second was down on the ground. Cutlass grabbed Jeb's neck and pulled him through the smoking confusion of the exploded truck. "This makes it twice I've had to save your sorry ass."

Jeb panted as they plowed down the street and jumped into the back seat of a white Studebaker, Olivia crying as she threw her arms around him. "Oh, God, I was worried."

He kissed her. "You sure you still wanna marry me now that I'm a convicted felon, you brilliant, gorgeous, wonderful--"

"Oh, save it for the honey moon!" Sam groaned as the engine shit out lightening and the car peeled out, sparks shooting off the tires as they scraped across the pavement.

Jeb gasped. "I guess I owe you one too."

Sam peered back from the driver's seat, a big, shit eating grin on his face. "I guess you do, old boy."

# 71.

# THE GREAT STONE FACE

**Franconia, New Hampshire,    One Week Later**

*"Men hang out their signs indicative of their respective trades; shoe makers hang out a gigantic shoe; jewelers a monster watch, and the dentist hangs out a gold tooth; but up in the Mountains of New Hampshire, God Almighty has hung out a sign to show that there He makes men."*

*-Daniel Webster.*

Up at Cannon Mountain they followed the rice scroll map along an old dirt road through ancient Pemigewasset, Indian country, passing by twisted oaks and grazing cows as they went. It was a strange day. A furiously, oppressively, sweat everywhere hot day.

Baby yellow birds feet with petals delicate like silk. Sand blue chicory, and brilliantly red Indian blankets with petals that spread out and fainted at the edges. Calendulas dark and red as pulsing blood. The sun, midday, orange, a thousand miles high. The clouds empty; gone from the blank, shale-canvas sky.

Jeb's feet kicked up smoke gray pebbles and bits of dust as he walked, his shadow a long scraggly sliver. A gust of wind came across him, bringing with it a moment of cool respite from the heat.

It rose up out of the earth like any other rock face, a mass of granite interspersed with brown, black and white minerals. Mossy fingertips crept upwards like a blight of green ink spots, and then a face that jutted out in way that shouldn't have been. Pointed and rugged and powerful and it didn't fit. It wasn't natural. The face of a man, the old man of the mountain, as proud as the Indian chiefs that once reigned there. Neck slanted up and back, jaw and chin bent into a disillusioned frown, eyes heavy and ancient.

"We don't have to do this you know," said Olivia. "We could run away and never look back."

Jeb shook his head. "He'd find us. One way or another, this will never be over until we confront him. Figure out a way to use his own machine against him, and destroy the immortals once and for all."

"And the gold's a nice bonus." Sam grinned. "Now let's kick this bastard's ass."

Jeb looked at Cutlass. The pirate had been waiting for this moment for a long time, and it would've happened weeks earlier if the news of the Dreamland fire hadn't reached him. The fire was a deadly reminder of Midas' power and reach.

Yes him, *Midas*. This was his hidden tomb. This was his home. They'd followed the map to a hidden trail behind the mountain, through an underground cavern, and now to a massive stone lion head that stared back at them with emerald eyes. Jeb could feel his hand moving independently to the sculpture, could feel his palm pressing against it, his fingers wrapping around cool granite, cupping it in his hand. He gulped. His heart stopped. A loud thud. A deep resonance. His heart started up again. It was done. Cutlass pulled the gun from his waist as a bright light emanated out from around the lion and the whole mountain began to glow. A door appeared from nowhere, beckoning them to come inside. Sam gulped. "Let's do this."

They made their way through the door and down a rocky tunnel, bending their heads as they entered a room covered in a fungus that crawled across the walls like spiders. There was a slurping sound, and a smell like sulfur and eggs gone bad. Jeb's jaw clenched. His chest was covered in sweat and he could barely breathe. He could barely.... There was a light coming from somewhere nearby. It was closer, brighter now. A black figure stepped into iridescent light.

He was tall. Naked. Covered in tattoos from head to toe. Face baring a strikingly stupid expression. Dim white eyes, jaw slacked and open at a right angle, his nose crooked and bent upwards like an erect phallus. He smiled, revealing grayish teeth broken at the tip. His were lips curdled and his beard was black and wiry. He blinked one eye, paused, and then the other. His laughter was a kind of a low gurgle, an imitation of human laughter, and it filled the chamber in hollow spurts. He lifted a wrinkled rainbow inked limb. "Welcome home. We have been expecting you, Jeb Chamberlain."

"How do you....?" Jeb shuddered, and didn't bother to finish asking his question. He could see now two other figures further back in the darkness. The first a gluttonous, naked bag of flesh. Cheeks like hams stuffed into glossy plastic bags, eyes tiny black buttons. The second figure was a short woman with wicked Cleopatra eyes. Her lips thinner than razor blades, and twice as red as the blood they cut into. Nose thin and fake looking. Skinny frame with enormous breasts. Naked as well and frighteningly pale, with a tattoo of a twelve legged spider that crawled down her neck and spun a web tattoo that reached all the way to a nail pierced through her clitoris. Her ankles and feet were covered in dried blood and her hair was long, black and split into two halves, each one sewn into the plates of her back, black string interwoven through white-pink flesh. She sneered and took a drag from a cigarette. White smoke. Her thin lips forming a hypnotic 'O' shape. She reached her hand down her throat, like a snake swallowing a mouse, and retrieved a long metal sword.

"Who the fuck are you?" Cutlass sneered.

"We friends. Friends of God king. Here to escort you to an audience wist im." The pale woman's tattoos glistened in the underground light as she talked. She snapped her fingers and one of the other freaks pulled a lever. There was a great mechanical whirring noise as a golden elevator rose up from the ground. On its brightly polished dais stood a cluster of well armed immortals, all painted gold. Eyes moist and dull, liquid gold leaking out from their noses and mouths. The woman smiled as she looked towards the lift. "Midas needs Jeb and Olivia in one piece. As for the other two.... no mercy."

# 72.

# BATTLE ROYALE

Tendrils of silvery fog reached out from the elevator like scribbles, fast running chains cranking and spinning as dozens of golden men and women stepped off the dais. The massive series of gears and pulleys that covered the walls commenced to grinding and spinning about with a slow moan, their mechanizations opening up holes in the ground from which a series of glowing plastic neon statues rose up, bathing the room in iridescent pink and green light. The statues strobed, their mechanical bodies coming to life as they began to gyrate and dance, their plastic frames spun about by clockwork gears and exposed battery circuits. The golden freaks crept around the dancing statues as a sound of African drums began to pound from somewhere far below.

Jeb watched as the immortals drew closer, their bodies casting shadow against the gyrating plastic statues. *"Tell them to back off,"* he shouted.

Cutlass stepped forwards, pushing Jeb and Olivia behind him. "Let me handle this one," he said as he pulled two long broadswords from behind his back, scraping them across each other like shivering beasts. The immortals, gold paint flaking off their naked bodies like picked apart sunburns, eyed him curiously.

They were men and women. They had bodies both perfectly sculpted and hideously deformed. Some wore elongated helmets and rubber gloves, others had their frames embedded with spikes. All of their eyes were dimmer than darkness. All of their weapons were raised and spinning above their heads.

Cutlass closed his eyes and took in a deep, low breath in the darkness as they ran at him. Muscles still. Motionless. *Step. Step. Step.* They ran towards him. *Step. Step. Step.*

Gladiators and Janissaries met his blade and toppled to the ground, a handful of Seljuk Turks screaming as their figures clashed against the pink and green light, casting them as snarling black smears, more dogs then men. Cutlass wheeled duel swords through the air, blood spraying out as his blades peeled into the chests of the golden men, dropping them like flies. He marched ahead, tossing the limp, cut-up bodies of his enemies over his shoulder like sopping rags. A fat lipped Frenchman screamed as Cutlass disemboweled him, leaving him to grope at his organs with bloody hands, desperately trying to stuff them back in as they slithered onto the floor. It wasn't working.

The pirate laughed like this was the most fun he'd had in years. The men still attached to their heads scarred up quickly and got back on their feet, one of them, an ancient gladiator, whipped a mace into Cutlass' skull. The pirate screamed and stumbled back as he ripped the weapon from his shattered cheekbone, his arm swinging blindly. With a

Dennis Badeau

satisfying splitting sound, he knew his sword had found its mark.

Olivia and Sam fired pistols into the stampeding army, as Jeb flailed about with a stolen sword. "I didn't know there'd be this many!" Olivia cried.

"Me neither," Jeb gasped, as his sword broke like a wave across the chest of a golden Janissary. "If I did I would have brought a tank!"

"Cutlass, my friend." the familiar voice rang out.

"Who is that?" The pirate sneered, his vision hazy yellow and red blocks of smear as his eye regenerated. "Who goes there?"

"Don't tell me you don't remember," said the man.

Cutlass gasped as the shadow grew closer, and someone knocked the swords from his hands. He could feel a man's fingers on his face and a knife at his neck.

"You've never looked better," he said as he smiled into the bloody pit of his face.

"Salid!?" Cutlass strained at the knife against his neck, his eye still weak.

"Miss my face?"

"Like the plague." Cutlass said as his eyesight returned and he pulled the knife from his throat. Salid shrieked as Cutlass knocked him back and picked up an ancient katana blade from the floor.

"I'm gonna' kick your ass, Gregor!" Salid glared, his eyes coming down into slits as he pulled a long rapier from its sheath.

Cutlass scraped the sword across the stone ground, sending up bright white sparks. "We will see about that."

They lunged at each other, their swords clashing thunder in the darkness. Their faces were scribbled with pink strips of gaseous light, muscles rippling in wiry fetish-green as they plunged their weapons forward. Salid turned, angling his body sideways to dodge the maniac pirates fevered blows. Cutlass screamed as Salid brought down the rapier on his shoulder blade, severing his left arm. He leapt back, sneering in the darkness as the blood sprayed like a fountain out from his wound. "God damn you, Salid," Cutlass said as he bent over and picked up his arm, groaning as he plunged it back into its socket, and the tendons re-wrapped themselves, scabbed, and healed.

Salid scraped his sword against the ground. "I'm just getting started."

They charged at Olivia, the gladiators, the Janissaries, the lepers, and the massively tall masochist Friedheim Gustat, a man bound in leather, nails, buckles and razor blades. Friedhaeim's eyes had been carved out centuries ago and replaced by glass balls covered in human skin. His lips sewn shut. His dick a whale, restrained by fishhooks and nylon string. Grubby, meat eating hands stretched out, groping for flesh, as he saw the world through the twisted prism of vibration and all-consuming hunger.

Jeb's feet pounded across the ground like a runaway tomahawk drum as he ran towards her.

"OLIVIA!" he screamed, shoving her out of the way as the masochist brought down his axe. A slender giraffe woman with the India ink hair emerged from the shadows behind them, a net in her hands. She knocked Sam out of the way and threw the net around Olivia, tossing her over her shoulder and carrying her away. Jeb dived at the women, trying to wrestle Olivia away but before he could do anything the masochist grabbed him from behind and slammed him down across his knee, snapping Jeb's back. Jeb stumbled across the ground, as far away from Friedheim's grasp as he could get until his back hit against the solid plastic weight of one of the dancing statues. The masochist's feet came down like stampeding elephants as he made his final charge. *Elephants*; Jeb remembered the elephant's foot. Remembered blowing Macalister out that window. He swung his sword across the giant's neck, watching as the fucker's head went flying through the air like a football and spilled onto the ground. Another tall giraffe woman lunged at him and Jeb slashed his sword, lopping off her arms. She flailed about like a broken wind-up toy, the blood spraying out from her stubs.

Jeb went to turn back when someone grabbed him from behind.

"Eaugh!" Salid gagged as Cutlass lunged forwards and grabbed him by the neck, shattering his trachea with his powerful grip. *"Eugh! Eugh!"* Salid struggled against him, his fingers itching desperately at the leather pouch hanging from his waist. "Fuck you!" Salid laughed as he pulled up a vile of green acid and smashed it across the pirate's face. Cutlass screamed as the acid gushed across his jaw, burning away his flesh as he collapsed to the ground. Salid rubbed his broken neck, cracked it back into place, and smiled.

"Have mercy!" the pirate pleaded, his face a blind, bubbling mess, his skull exposed.

Salid laughed. "Not on your life."

Jeb flipped himself around to see whose hand it was at his back. "Sam!" You ok?"

Sam nodded and they ran forwards through the dark cavern until they came out by the entrance to the tomb. Sam threw the door open and stepped outside, gasping as he reached freedom. "Come on! Let's go."

Jeb's face went slack. He shook his head. "No Sam. They have Olivia. I can't leave her behind."

"But you'll be killed! Jeb look at these freaks! You're not gonna beat them, you're not, you won't survive this!"

Jeb nodded. "You're probably right. But... I don't have a choice."

"Yes, you do!"

"Fine Sam, you're right, I do have a choice. And I'm making it." He placed his hands on his friends shoulder. "But you can't come with me. Not this time."

Sam looked back at him. "What do you mean?"

"They'll kill you, Sam."

"And they won't kill you? Look Jeb, if your fool ass is staying, then mine is too. I won't abandon you again."

"You never abandoned me, Sam. You're the best friend I ever had." Jeb put his arms around Sam, pulling him towards his chest. "But this is something I have to do on my own."

Sam looked at Jeb like he'd gone mad. "I'm not gonna leave your side, old boy."

"I'm sorry, but this might hurt." Jeb slammed the butt of his pistol against Sam's head, knocking him out. He dragged him down the entrance tunnel, slamming the tomb door shut behind him, where it glowed for a moment before disappearing back into stone.

As he made his way back into the chamber, it didn't take him long to notice the stillness in the air. Someone had shut off the strobing neon statue lights, and there was only the sound of the jungle drums and the voice in his head that told him to run. The voice was screaming at him now. Run, damn you! Run while you still can! Then there came a dry, hungry moan. The footsteps grew louder. Run damn you! The woman with the alabaster skin grew closer. Closer. Closer.

And there she was.

Body teetering on the impossible, flesh chemically manipulated into something wholly pliable, bones shattered, mended, and reshattered a thousand times over until they became something like firm dust, the pale, black ink haired giraffe woman with the hungry lips lurched towards him, a net drooping from in-between her hands. She let out a shrill gasp of laughter as she cast the net over his head, tied him up, and tossed him over her ten foot high shoulder. There was no way out.

# 73.
# NO WAY OUT

Jeb's head drooped, shaking from side to side as the elevator lowered into the ground with a whirring of ancient machinery. Deeper and deeper they traveled, miles into the core of the earth, until at last the shaft came to an end and the doors of the elevator opened up. Jeb stared in awe at what he saw. It was the place from his dreams, the place of grinding and whirring and pumping. Everything was in motion like some small piece of a greater whole. The walls were not walls, the floor was not a floor, the men and women were not men and women. It was a whole, massive underground machine the size and shape of a city, the fruit of two thousand years of labor and knowledge, and it was designed with only one purpose in mind, and one man capable of operating it.

Jeb struggled against the giraffe woman's net as she carried him through the great machine city of his dreams. Factories were part of the engine, smokestacks were pistons, roadways were circuit boards. The freakish immortals toiled in the grease of the underground city machine, slaves to labor and intellect and sex, thousands of black soot miners and mutated cattlemen moving in single file lines towards the production goal, where they emptied the raw material of the earth's core into the great furnace.

The color gold, the shine of it, permeated everything. The giraffe woman boarded a black tram car that carried Jeb for miles and miles, past underground gardens and skyscrapers all lit up in electric light. The upper class bourgeois with their sewn on lips and synthetic bodies of flesh and glass looked down with dim fascination as the tram passed by and sped along into Midas' palace. The tram came to a stop and the giraffe woman carried Jeb past the golden artificial sun, and into the inner chamber of the tomb.

*And there he was.* Buried miles and miles underground, his golden temple surrounded on all sides by the water of life; he sat on a great golden throne at the center of the Machine City, surrounded by his immortal court. Vast, ancient tapestries hung from impossibly high golden ceilings and archways. Gold waterfalls fell upside down as musicians and dancers played out strange rhythms never heard in any other place but down here, miles underground in the heart of the machine. Lips upon lips, upon thrust upon thrust, as hundreds of men and women rolled on the floor in an orgy, laughing and playing with the intimate bits of each other in games they knew would never be enough to sustain them. Depressed orgasms in young, ancient girls, faces that seemed to peel like kids at the beach, the gold flaking off into puddles of mineral ash on the floor.

And Midas, standing at the center of it all and watching… Midas was a child! Pale and ancient, and looking all of ten years old. He stuffed his hand up one of the immortal orgy goer's twats, sending her head reeling back as she moaned in wet, golden ecstasy and began to piss on him. The God King laughed, liquid gold washing over his hand like communion.

Jeb looked around himself, incredulous, finding only a group of bored, under worked elites who fancied themselves intellectuals and connoisseurs. Men and women who had tasted all there was to taste, who had felt all there was to feel.

Midas raised his hand as he saw Jeb at last and a hush fell over the room. The eyes of the immortals studied him, searching his face for answers. The tall woman dropped the sack, knocking Jeb's jaw against the ground where it began to bleed. Two slack faced gladiators pulled him up by his shoulders and brought him towards the boyish king.

"I thought you'd look older," Jeb spat, as the blood dripped from his mouth.

"We have ways here of manipulating appearance," said Midas. "I find this form suits me just as your form suits you. You know the funny thing about the forms we choose is how our inner sense of self grows to fit the outer. He wears a mask and his face grows to fit it."

"Can it with the philosophy," said Jeb. "Honestly you son of a bitch, just cut the shit and tell me what is it you want with me."

"Straight to the point. I like that!" said Midas.

"If you like it so much then answer the fucking question."

"The question of what I want with you?!" Midas laughed. "I want everything from you, Jeb! I need you. You realize that, don't you? I need you, that's why I brought you here." Midas smiled in a hungry way. "Because you are the one who can bring an end to all this. Who *will* bring an end. That's why you're so necessary to me, don't you see?"

Jeb looked curious. "And here I thought you wanted me dead."

Midas laughed. "Gods no! Jeb, believe me I didn't want you killed, I needed you here alive! That's why I sent Salid to protect you and guide you in the right direction. It's why Salid saved you from those traitors in Paraxhouse who'd have killed you and spoiled my plan, and it's why the key glowed in your hands when you reached the Devils arch, why when you touched the mountain it opened for you. You're the protagonist, Jeb. You're the key."

"The key to what?" he asked, his hands trembling at his side.

"To this!" Midas raised his arms. "This whole city is one massive mechanical machine built with one purpose." He gestured with his finger. "One."

"The ultimate power," said Jeb.

"That's right." Midas smiled. "The power of creation."

"Creation of what?" Jeb asked. "Your new universe?"

"You understand." He paused. "You've seen them both, Heaven and Hell. Now all you need to do is reach out with the machine and bring them together on earth."

Jeb shook his head. "And why would I do that?"

Midas sat up from his throne and stepped towards Jeb. The little boy was dressed in a golden tuxedo with pink flowers in the lapel. Big cherubic eyes that masked thousands of years of bilious hate. "We have the power to see into the future," he said, "we have the power to sculpt flesh, to manipulate fate, to reshape the world in whatever way we see fit, we have the power to be Gods! But even with that power, even with the world in our hands, we still find ourselves so fucking BORED! So fucking tired, even with all these wonderful toys." He gestured towards the golden whores lying at his feet. "I want more, damnit! More! I want to exist as other things, other people, other ways of being." He traced his fingers across some part of the great machine. "This is our escape valve. This is our way out from these tired flesh prisons and onwards onto something new."

The ancient child reiterated what the machine did. Explained that it allowed the user to strap himself in and reach out into a different reality, into Heaven above or Hell below, and bring it back with them, smashing the two together and begetting something radically new.

"So why don't you use it then?" asked Jeb. "Why don't you use this enormous machine of yours, use it and get it over with."

Midas snapped his fingers and one of the immortals, this one a living, walking skeleton, came up behind Jeb and grabbed him, holding him in place.

Midas walked towards him. "I'm afraid only you can do that."

Jeb shook his head. "Me? Why... Why me?"

"You've already done it twice, don't you remember? The first time when you drowned in the ocean, the second when I burned down Dreamland and you fell off the Big Wheel. Do you see? Do you understand? At the brink of death, and the height of emotion, you are capable of transcending these human coils and seeing into another world. Now, I need you to use that power, and turn on the god damned machine!"

"I won't do it!" Jeb shouted, defiantly.

"You will!" Midas roared. "You will because you fell out of an airship and lived, because you were shot and maimed and starved, and you lived. You'll do it, Jeb. You'll do it because you too are immortal, because you have been from the moment you opened Herme's sarcophagus and breathed in the mist of the water of life. You'll do it because you're the only one who can, because you're the protagonist and this is your story, and if you don't then we'll all be trapped here, unwritten and stuck within the pages of this book forever."

"....This book?" Jeb stopped, unable to think.

"Do you know how terrible it is to become aware of the fact that you exist only as a supporting character in someone else's story. Do you know, Jeb, how shitty that feels? We had to find a way out somehow. We had to."

"What are you talking about?" Jeb took a deep breath.

"We were only created to exist as villains in your stupid adventure story. Normally you'd know you were just a character in a story, Jeb, but we've been stuck in this one for two thousand years. Two thousand years of waiting around, two thousand years of being ancillary. It was maddening."

"W-what was?" Jeb stuttered.

"OUR EXISTENCE!" Midas roared. "It was pointless. Eventually we found the outline to the plot, and saw that we lost in the end. We didn't like that Jeb. We didn't like that at all, see, 'cause we were tired of having the 'bad guy' lose. 'Cause we were tired of being characters in a second rate book.

"So we changed things. We went to key moments in your story and fucked things up. We made it so that instead of meeting up with Sam and Olivia on the shores of the Skeleton Coast you ran into Salid. We wanted your mind expanded for use in the machine so we created a whole hallucinogenic village for you to wind up in after the crash. When you tried to drown yourself we saved you, and when you went off course we had Sam redirect you back to Athens so that you could find the final clue and arrive here. We manipulated you, Jeb, just like the writer of the book did. We saw what we didn't like and we changed it to suit our own needs."

And at that moment I realized that I wasn't writing their story anymore. I realized that the immortals were acting on their own now, speaking for themselves, building for themselves, and I shuddered at the idea of what their machine could do if Jeb managed to make it work.

So I had him get inside of it and come talk to me.

"Just let yourself go in there. Let your mind float away, and then, once you reach heaven, grab it and bring it down here to me!" Midas said to Jeb as he was hoisted up by a great crane and fitted into the heart of the Machine City, and a long white cord was inserted into the back of his head, straight into his brain stem. Jeb could feel himself falling. Falling down into the abyss. Midas screamed like a banshee, "DO IT NOW!", and the entire Machine City came to life in an instant, lights powering on everywhere, mechanical joints erupting as they pulled and strained against all of everything.

"Do it, Jeb. Do it and free us from our prison, free us from this book!"

# 74.

# APOTHEOSIS BY FIRE

He could feel himself falling. Falling. And suddenly he understood… everything.

As the machine city lit up the immortals realized that at long last it was time. One by one they took their opiates and swallowed, allowing themselves to spend their last moments drifting into ecstasy as they passed out on the ground and awaited the end of the book and their new creation's arrival.

He could do it. He realized that now, now that he was in the machine. The whole universe like clay ready to be reshaped and reformed with a few strokes of the keyboard. I talked to him. Talked to him about how long I'd been writing his story, and about how long the immortals had been stuck between paragraphs, and about what they'd done to escape once they realized how horrible their fate really was. We talked about divergent plot lines and rewritten characters. Talked about things he might have done, or had done in past versions of the story. I told Jeb what it was like to build up his whole world and apologized for all the holes and shortcomings of it. I told him I was sorry for the shitty things I'd put him through.

He said he understood.

He said that it was strange to meet the person who was writing his story.  I agreed and told him I would find it very strange too, if I were to meet whoever was writing mine.  He said that he was glad I was a human being.  I told him that I was glad he was too and I hoped the same of whoever was writing me.

Then I reminded him of an important plot point.  I reminded him who else had been down there in that very first tomb when he'd cracked open the sarcophagus and let flow the mist of the water of life that had made him immortal, and Jeb remembered and climbed down out of the machine.

A bullet blasted Midas in the back of the head, exploding his skull into a million directions, where it landed in puddles of blood on the golden bodies of the other passed out immortals.

"Hello, Virtrolli."  Jeb frowned.

"Hello, Jeb," he said, as he lowered the smoking gun, and shoved Olivia to the ground.  "I followed you here after that rollercoaster landed on top me and I realized that something was terribly, terribly wrong.  I followed you after your big jail break, picked up your trail on your way through Massachusetts, and tailed you all the way here.  I found your gal locked up in the other room and thought I'd do you a favor and let her out of her cage."

Olivia rubbed her head and stood up.  She looked over at Jeb.  "This whole time?"

Jeb nodded.

Olivia shook her head. "So what's your plan, Virtrolli, huh? Now that you can't kill us. What will you do with your revenge?"

"I don't know. I don't really…" Virtrolli shook his head. "I mean I'm kind of overwhelmed here."

Jeb looked about the place with uncertain eyes. "I know what you mean."

Olivia stepped past one of the sleeping immortals on the ground. "Look, you're gonna need help getting out of here once they start waking up, Virtrolli. Why don't we just call a peace and work together. There's more than enough gold to split between the three of us."

Virtrolli licked his lips. "And why would I ever trust your ass?"

Olivia sighed. "Look, so you killed my uncle. You tried to rape me and you tried to have both Jeb and me killed. You betrayed us and lied to us and frankly I have every reason in the world to hate you. Just like you do me."

Virtrolli's eyes grew wary as he raised his gun at her.

"But what the hell." Olivia shrugged. "We're immortal now, we should be bigger than all that. We should…. grow up. And forgive."

Virtrolli frowned. The golden bastards probably would wake up soon. And when they did… damnit she was right, he'd need help to get out a decent sized amount of the treasure without taking too long. A smile began to creep at the edges of his lips. "Alright, maybe you got a deal, girlie."

Olivia nodded. "Good. Let's shake on it."

Virtrolli dropped his pistol to his side and walked up to her, a look of hope on his face. In his mind he thought about all the wonderful things that were to come. Thought about all the wonderful things he'd be able to do now that he had such complete and total freedom from fear. He felt like a new man. Felt, in a way, like giving in to forgiveness and moving on into someone and something better. He gasped as Olivia picked up a sword from the ground off one of the sleeping gladiators and lopped his head off.

"My uncle's dead because of you!" she screamed as the gangsters severed head plopped to the ground. She walked up to what was left of Virtolli and brought the blade down once again, splitting his skull in two halves, lobotomizing his brain. "And today, I am the right fucking hand of vengeance."

"Jesus, Olivia," Jeb said breathlessly.

She panted, dropping the sword to the floor. "I told you there was a monster inside me."

"Y-y-yes you did."

She shrugged and took a deep breath. "How long do we have before these golden bastards wake up?"

Jeb looked stunned. "I don't know... I really have no idea."

She crossed her arms. "Well you're not really gonna give Midas what he wants, are you?"

Jeb shook his head. "I have a better idea. Follow me."

Olivia walked with him up to the control panel of the machine, and the chair where he had sat with his brain plugged in. "So what's your plan?"

"Well, when I was in the machine, I could see the future, the whole spectrum of humanity laid out before me. Look I've got some bad news, honey."

"What?" she asked, with a look of worry.

Jeb sighed. "We're not really immortal. I mean we are, but not really. Not like Gods, or anything."

"What do you mean?"

"Well it's just that, from what I saw when I was in there, there's one thing that can kill us. The same way that Cutlass' eye couldn't grow back once it was gone. Matter can't come from nothing."

"Okay..." she said, looking confused. "So how does this help us?"

Jeb sat down in the chair, plugged himself in and fell back into the trance of the machine. The lights came back on, power surging throughout the underground city. Suddenly he opened his eyes, and a massive, torpedo shaped metal thing materialized inside the chamber.

"What is that thing?" Olivia gasped, staring at the alien object.

"In Hiroshima they call it an atomic bomb. I found it in the future and brought it back here. When it explodes it'll atomize every living thing in this city. The flesh won't be able to heal anymore, 'cause there won't be anything left."

"But Jeb..." she said slowly. "I don't wanna die."

He nodded. "Yeah, me neither. There's still too many places I wanna go with you."

"I wanna go everywhere with you," she whispered.

He reached out to her. "Take my hand."

"Do you really want to die holding hands?" she asked.

He grinned. "That thing goes off in thirty seconds. When it does-"

"Everything here dies," she said.

"Come on, take my hand and get in the machine with me. I'm gonna' take us somewhere far away from here."

She stared at him, unsure what to do. There were so many wonders before her, so many questions, and mysteries, and--

"Trust me," he said, "one more time."

Olivia smiled as her fingers enmeshed with his and they fell backwards into the great whirring energy of the machine. She could feel herself falling.

# 75.

# INFINITUS

And in that instant she could see all of the infinite possibilities before her. All of the infinite actions and reactions and consequences that could arise from a single touch and last for centuries. A million different ways to raise a hand, and a million different universes created for each one. Each one a bubble, flowering in one brief, beautiful instant before wilting into ash as another choice was made and another world created.

Space and time rushed past her in infinite neon streams like tears from God, her memories slipping between the cracks in her head. She was riding a carousel built out of time and it was running out, the horses and lions leaping off and running into the stars. She could hear distant songs being sung, strange music the likes of which she had never heard before. Airplanes flying into space and mingling with the stars, machines as big as countries, that housed the minds of men. A new kind of immortality, artificial intelligence, brains built out of magnetic ink and strips of lead. A tunnel. A bridge. A paradise built in space. A bomb that would destroy everything. So many mysteries. So many unspeakable truths. Lies without liars, death without death. Olivia could see it all, just as Jeb had when he entered the machine, could see the knowledge of the centuries reaching out into distant worlds and ideas, because she was really the protagonist of the story too.

\* \* \* \* \* \* \* \*

With the fission of an atom the bomb went off and everything in the underground complex, immortal or not, was disintegrated. All into ash and dust. To the outside world it was little more than a tremor. Only Sam, alive and laying alone on the hill above, knew what had happened. He could feel it in his gut as the roar rose up like an earthquake and the old man of the mountain toppled to the ground. A cold wave washed over Sam as he realized all of the immortals were gone now. His eyes opened wide and he screamed. "JEB!"

\* \* \* \* \* \* \* \*

Atoms scattered into dust, drifting up through irradiated air forever and ever as starlight streamed by. Page after page, centuries passing like seconds, millennia less than minutes. Their consciousness floated up like the last air bubble gasped by a drowning man. They went up into stardust as the earth bloomed and wilted, watching as Man burnt it down in nuclear holocaust. Rebuilt. Destroyed again. Rebuilt and set out for the stars, leaving behind a dead world. Millennia passed. The radiation faded away. New men now. Green again. Cycles begun again. Fire. Wheel. Alphabet. Society begun all over again.

New creatures. A new world. The old men, from the old earth, revisit their ancestral home. Man builds himself up again. Nuclear war. Dead. Reborn. Dead. Reborn. The cycle was always the same. Again, and again, and again, out from the ashes and then, inevitably, back into them.

Finally, the cycle could no longer sustain itself. The earth's core cracked, shattered. It sent their minds flying out into space as time sped by faster and faster and faster. The sun supernova, obliterated everything in its path. They were drifting through the darkness. There was emptiness.

Total Emptiness.

Stars sinking into each other, whole galaxies collapsing, as billions upon billions of years became trillions, as time rushed by his eyes like film reels, as the universe collapsed in on itself. Their minds had become something else now, had become one with the universe. They were stardust, they were light struggling against the pull of a black hole, they were the black hole.

Jeb and Olivia trembled at the edge of the universe, peering into the darkness. Their creator emerged from out of it, like a face submerged in oil. Lips rising out of it. Eyes blank, murky fog. He was old. He was tired. He was me. Now everything was at an end.

As the Universe collapsed into less than dust, a new supernova rang out and all creation began.

She lay on a soft cotton blanket spread under an oak tree, letting the sun warm her face now that she was back home on earth, in 1924 again, and I was writing her a happy ending.

"So what happens next?" she asked, holding her baby in her arms. "I mean, what do we do?"

He shrugged, and his mind felt at ease for the first time in years. "Everything's infinite now. Every possibility laid out and open for us."

"Yeah, but that doesn't answer my question," she said. "What do we do now?"

He kissed her, long and hard and lingering. "First thing we do is go see Sam, let him know we're not dead, 'cause I'm sure he's worried sick."

She laughed. It was a beautiful laughter. "Then what?"

"Anything we want. Dive to the bottom of the ocean or picnic on the moon. We can go back to Africa or build a rocket ship and set sail for far beyond the stars. He's done writing the book now, he won't be there anymore to tell us what to say or do, he won't be there to write our destinies for us. We get to make our own path now."

He was right.

Again she smiled because she couldn't wait to kiss his lips again. "So we can do anything we want?"

He grinned devilishly as he looked at her with that look, that look of a madman, that look she'd first fallen for: "*Anything.*"

Dennis Badeau

Dennis Badeau

# ACKNOWLEDGMENTS

This book has been a labor of love and frustration for nearly five years now, and I couldn't be happier or prouder to at last have it out in the world. Such a feat would not be possible without the love, support and inspiration of a number of wonderful people, many of whom I'm about to forget to thank. First and foremost I must thank my parents, Ann and Dennis, without whom I'm reasonably sure I wouldn't exist and to whom I owe everything, and my sisters, Emily and Lilly. They are talented, wonderful girls who are both much smarter than I, and whom I can't imagine life without.

I'd also like to thank Sara Key and Melanie Lohrer for their friendship and Mariah St. Armand, who is as beautiful as she is brilliant, for being exactly who she is.

Finally I'd like to thank John Marcoullier, who is the closest thing I could ever have to a brother, and Ray Harryhausen, whose artistry and imagination have always inspired me beyond words.

You are all kind people in a too often cruel world, and for that I am eternally grateful.

www.ingramcontent.com/pod-product-compliance
Lightning Source LLC
Chambersburg PA
CBHW061521050726
47503CB00015B/2246